THE STORY OF THE MOVIES IN COMICS

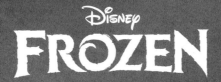

DISNEY FROZEN

ALESSANDRO FERRARI
MANUSCRIPT ADAPTATION

MASSIMILIANO NARCISO
ART

KAWAII CREATIVE STUDIO
PAINTS

LITO MILANO S.R.L., ABSINK
DESIGN & LETTERING

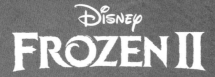

DISNEY FROZEN II

ALESSANDRO FERRARI
MANUSCRIPT ADAPTATION

MANNY MEDEROS
LAYOUTS & INKS

GIULIO RINCIONE
PAINTS

CHRIS DICKEY
DESIGN & LETTERING

MANNY MEDEROS
ART & DESIGN DIRECTOR

GIULIO RINCIONE
COVER ART

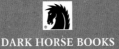

DARK HORSE BOOKS

DARK HORSE BOOKS

PRESIDENT AND PUBLISHER
MIKE RICHARDSON

COLLECTION EDITOR
FREDDYE MILLER

COLLECTION DESIGNER
SARAH TERRY

COLLECTION ASSISTANT EDITOR
JUDY KHUU

COLLECTION DIGITAL ART TECHNICIAN
SAMANTHA HUMMER

Neil Hankerson Executive Vice President • Tom Weddle Chief Financial Officer • Randy Stradley Vice President of Publishing • Nick McWhorter Chief Business Development Officer • Dale LaFountain Chief Information Officer • Matt Parkinson Vice President of Marketing • Vanessa Todd-Holmes Vice President of Production and Scheduling • Mark Bernardi Vice President of Book Trade and Digital Sales • Ken Lizzi General Counsel • Dave Marshall Editor in Chief • Davey Estrada Editorial Director • Chris Warner Senior Books Editor • Cary Grazzini Director of Specialty Projects • Lia Ribacchi Art Director • Matt Dryer Director of Digital Art and Prepress • Michael Gombos Senior Director of Licensed Publications • Kari Yadro Director of Custom Programs • Kari Torson Director of International Licensing • Sean Brice Director of Trade Sales

DISNEY PUBLISHING WORLDWIDE GLOBAL MAGAZINES, COMICS AND PARTWORKS

PUBLISHER Lynn Waggoner • EDITORIAL TEAM Bianca Coletti (Director, Magazines), Guido Frazzini (Director, Comics), Carlotta Quattrocolo (Executive Editor), Stefano Ambrosio (Executive Editor, New IP), Camilla Vedove (Senior Manager, Editorial Development), Behnoosh Khalili (Senior Editor), Julie Dorris (Senior Editor), Mina Riazi (Assistant Editor), Gabriela Capasso (Assistant Editor) • DESIGN Enrico Soave (Senior Designer) • ART Ken Shue (VP, Global Art), Manny Mederos (Senior Illustration Manager, Comics and Magazines), Roberto Santillo (Creative Director), Marco Ghiglione (Creative Manager), Stefano Attardi (Illustration Manager) • PORTFOLIO MANAGEMENT Olivia Ciancarelli (Director) • BUSINESS & MARKETING Mariantonietta Galla (Senior Manager, Franchise), Virpi Korhonen (Editorial Manager) • CONTRIBUTORS Valentina Cambi, Carlo Resca, Izel Tamayo (Illustration Manager Comics and Magazines), Marina Crouse (Editorial Assistant)

Special Thanks to
Peter Del Vecho, Michael Giaimo, Jessica Julius, Jasmine Gonzalez, Renato Lattanzi, Laura Hitchcock, Heather Blodget, Stephanie Lopez Morfin, Nick Ellingsworth, Alison Giordano, Andrew Elmers, Ken Shue, Teri Avanian, Arianna Marchione

Disney Frozen and Frozen 2: The Story of the Movies in Comics

Published by Dark Horse Books
A division of Dark Horse Comics LLC
10956 SE Main Street
Milwaukie, OR 97222

DarkHorse.com

To find a comics shop in your area, visit comicshoplocator.com

First edition: May 2020
ISBN 978-1-50671-738-8
Digital ISBN 978-1-50671-747-0

1 3 5 7 9 10 8 6 4 2
Printed in Korea

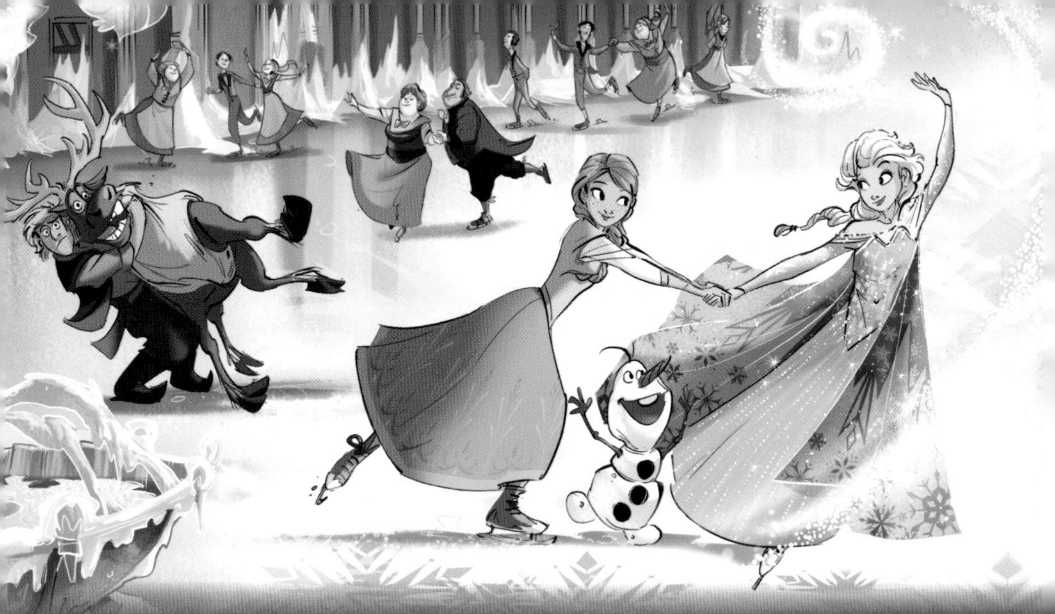

TABLE OF CONTENTS

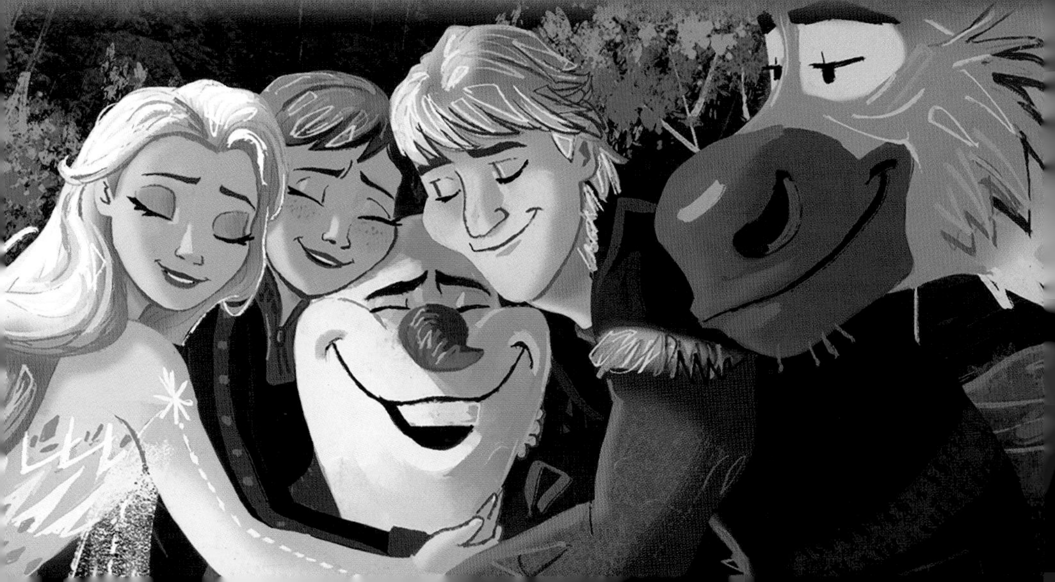

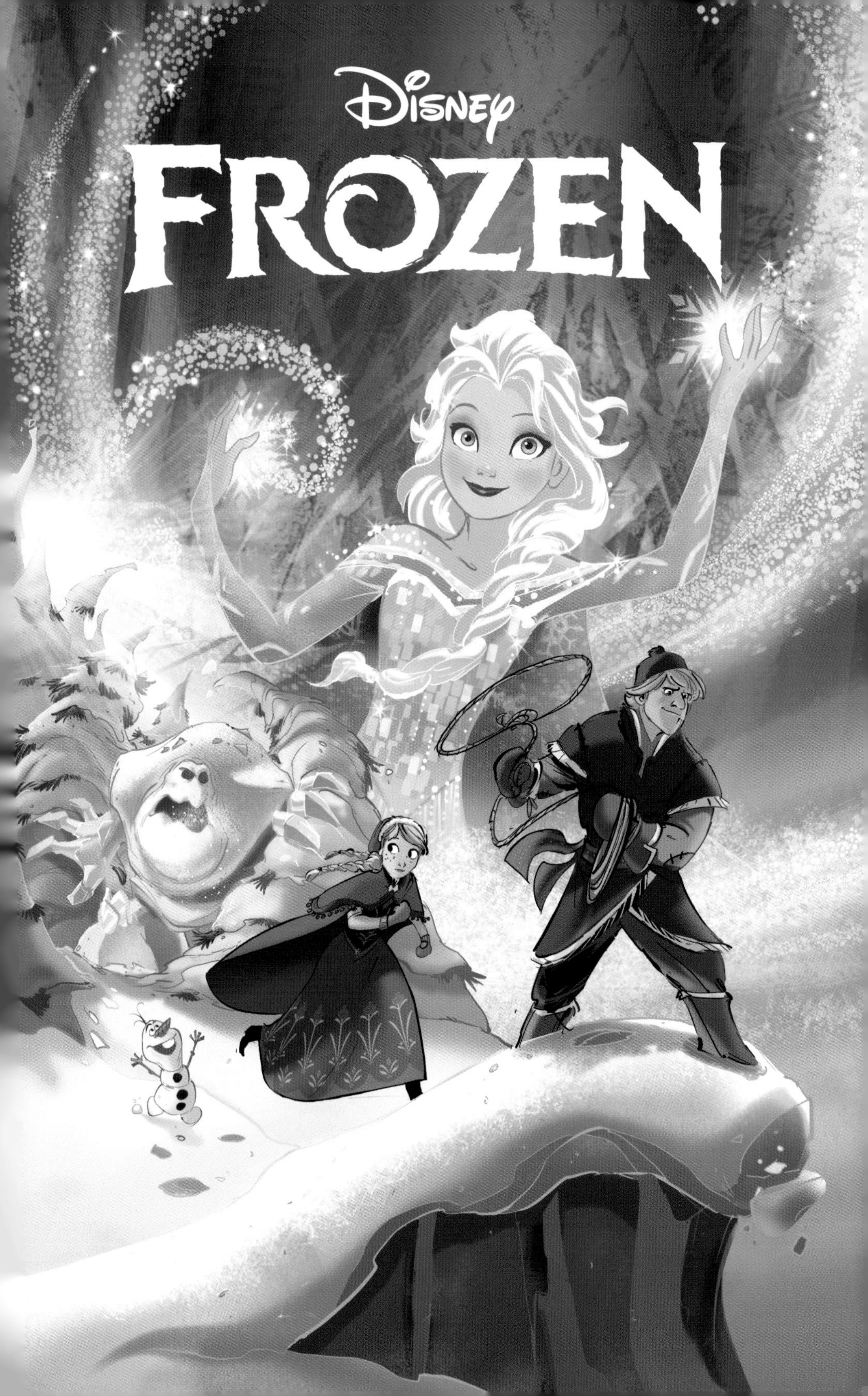
Disney
FROZEN

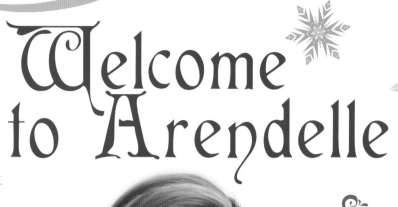

Welcome to Arendelle

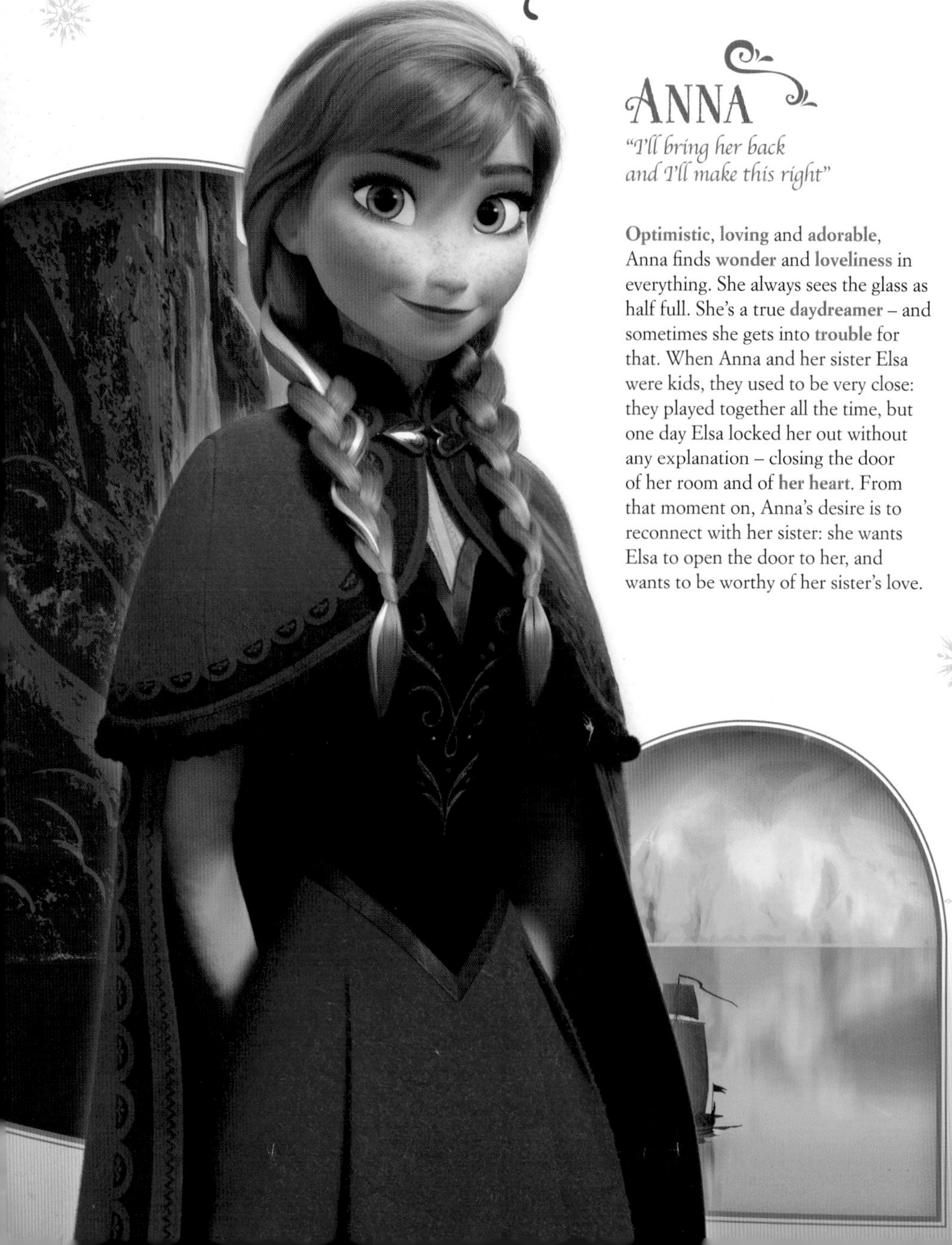

ANNA

"I'll bring her back and I'll make this right"

Optimistic, **loving** and **adorable**, Anna finds **wonder** and **loveliness** in everything. She always sees the glass as half full. She's a true **daydreamer** – and sometimes she gets into **trouble** for that. When Anna and her sister Elsa were kids, they used to be very close: they played together all the time, but one day Elsa locked her out without any explanation – closing the door of her room and of **her heart**. From that moment on, Anna's desire is to reconnect with her sister: she wants Elsa to open the door to her, and wants to be worthy of her sister's love.

Elsa

"I never knew what I was capable of"

Elsa is the heir to the throne of Arendelle. She's a **natural leader**, she's **controlled**, **regal** and **graceful**: everybody in the kingdom loves her. But she has a **dark secret**, a secret she hides even from her sister Anna. Elsa has the **power** to **create ice** and **snow** with her hands, but she's not able to control it at all times. She needs to wear **gloves** most of the time, otherwise she'd **freeze anything she touches**. That's why she shut Anna out – to protect Anna from her powers. She'll soon learn, though, how important it is to open your heart and let the ones that love you in.

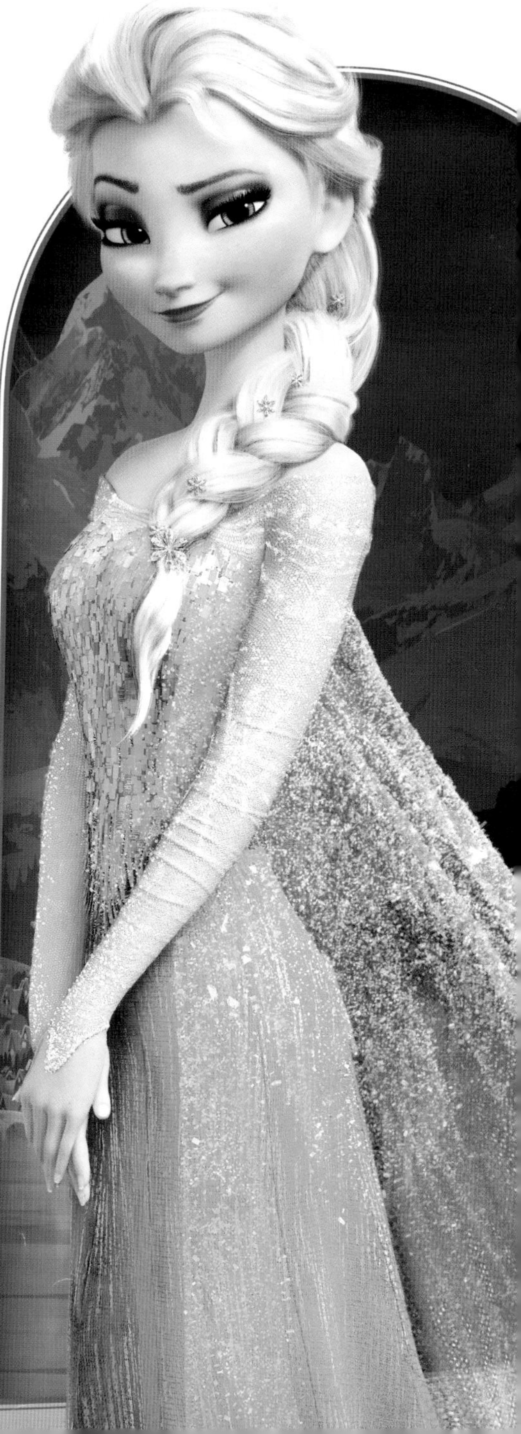

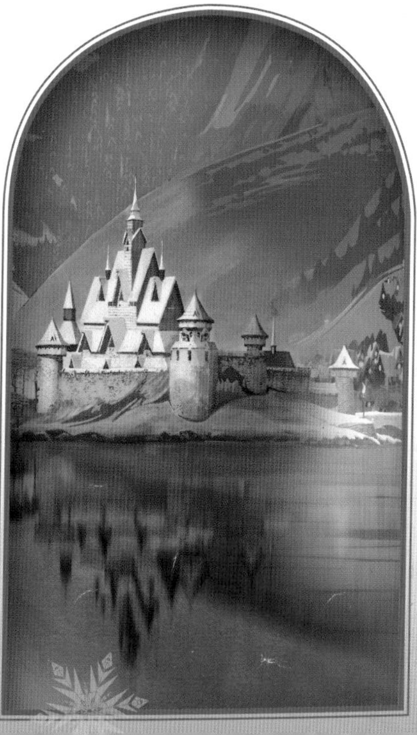

KRISTOFF
"Doesn't sound like true love"

Together with his reindeer – and **best friend** – Sven,
Kristoff gets blocks of ice from the **North Mountain**
and takes them to Arendelle on his sledge to sell. He
spends a lot of time outside and he enjoys his work.
Kristoff deeply believes that sooner or later **people
always end up hurting you**, so he avoids getting
close to anyone – even to the love of his life. Anna
asks his help to meet up with her sister Elsa. Two
people in the whole kingdom
could not be more different . . .

SVEN

Sven and Kristoff have been
inseparable life companions since
they were little. This friendly
reindeer is crazy for carrots, and
would do anything for his human
friend. Although he cannot speak,
Kristoff speaks for the two of them,
often putting words from his own
conscience into the animal's mouth.

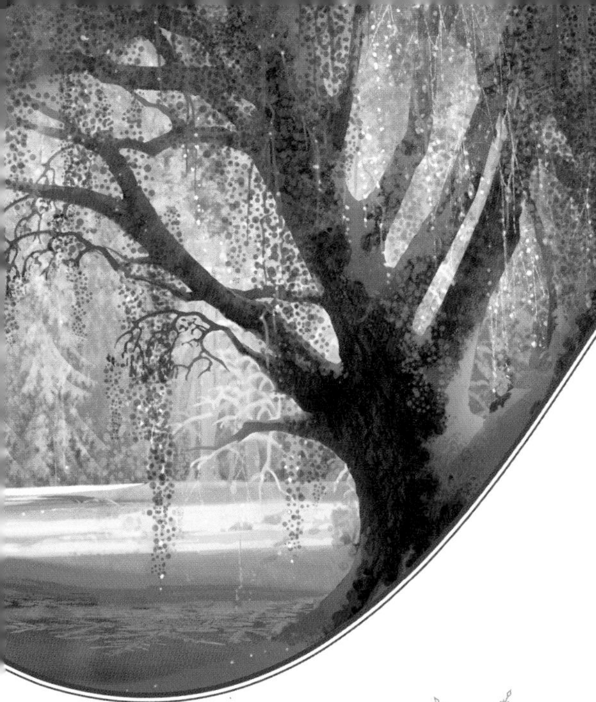

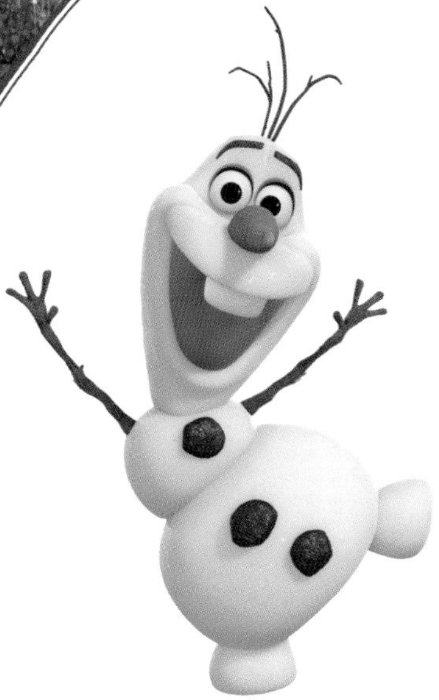

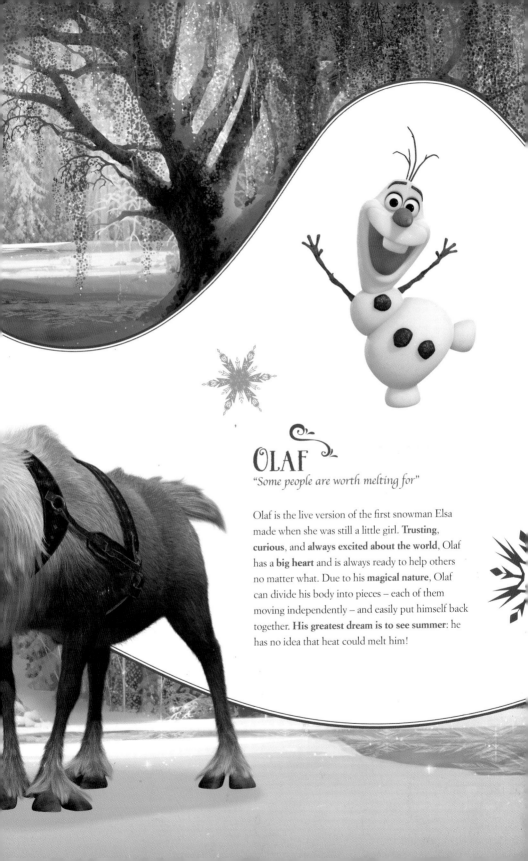

OLAF

"Some people are worth melting for"

Olaf is the live version of the first snowman Elsa made when she was still a little girl. **Trusting, curious**, and **always excited about the world**, Olaf has a **big heart** and is always ready to help others no matter what. Due to his **magical nature**, Olaf can divide his body into pieces – each of them moving independently – and easily put himself back together. **His greatest dream is to see summer**: he has no idea that heat could melt him!

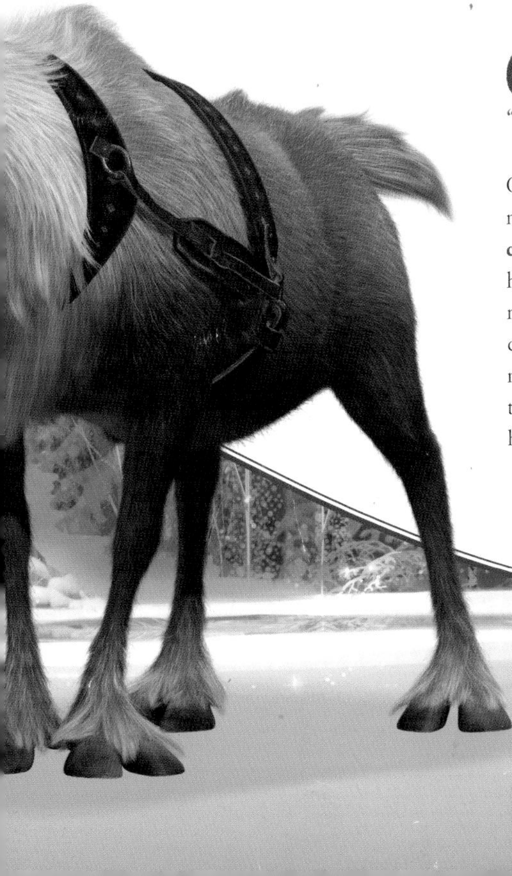

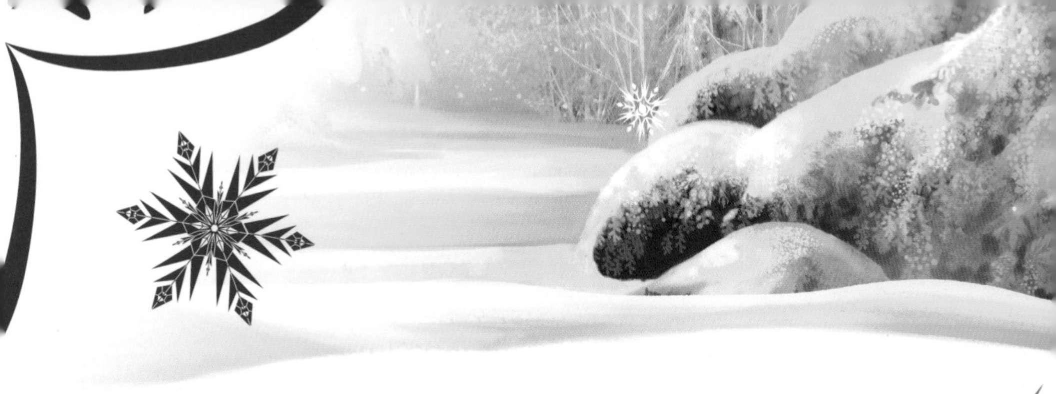

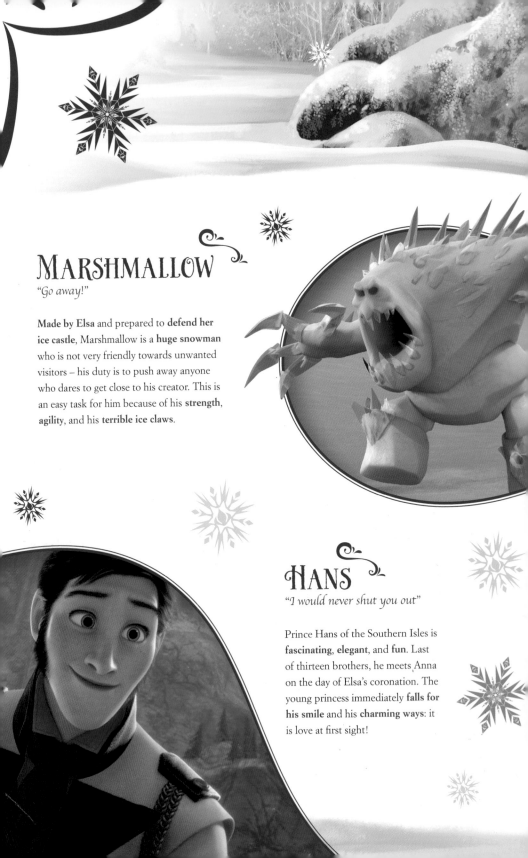

MARSHMALLOW

"Go away!"

Made by Elsa and prepared to **defend her ice castle**, Marshmallow is a **huge snowman** who is not very friendly towards unwanted visitors – his duty is to push away anyone who dares to get close to his creator. This is an easy task for him because of his **strength**, **agility**, and his **terrible ice claws**.

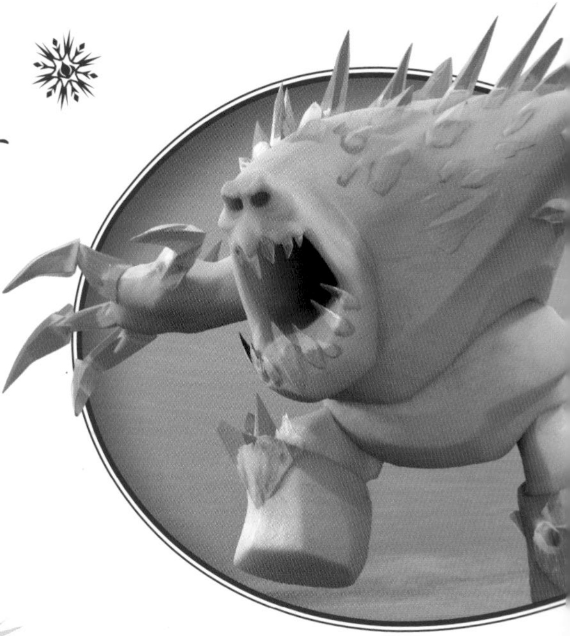

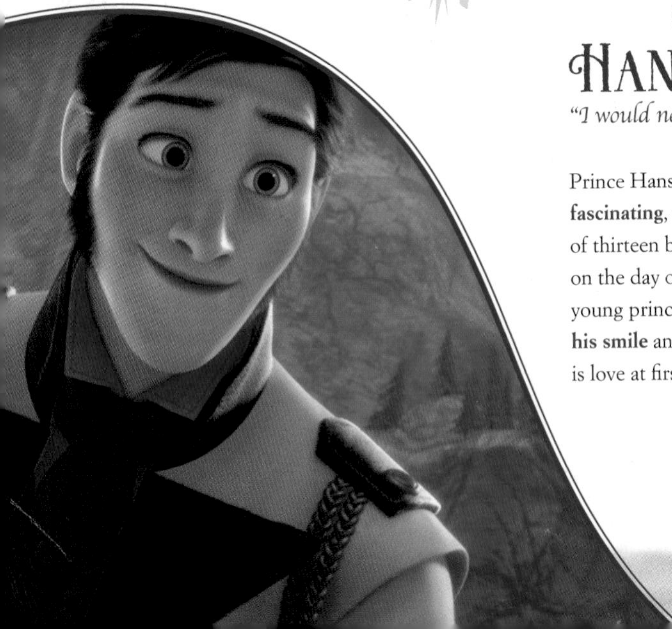

HANS

"I would never shut you out"

Prince Hans of the Southern Isles is **fascinating**, **elegant**, and **fun**. Last of thirteen brothers, he meets Anna on the day of Elsa's coronation. The young princess immediately **falls for his smile** and his **charming ways**: it is love at first sight!

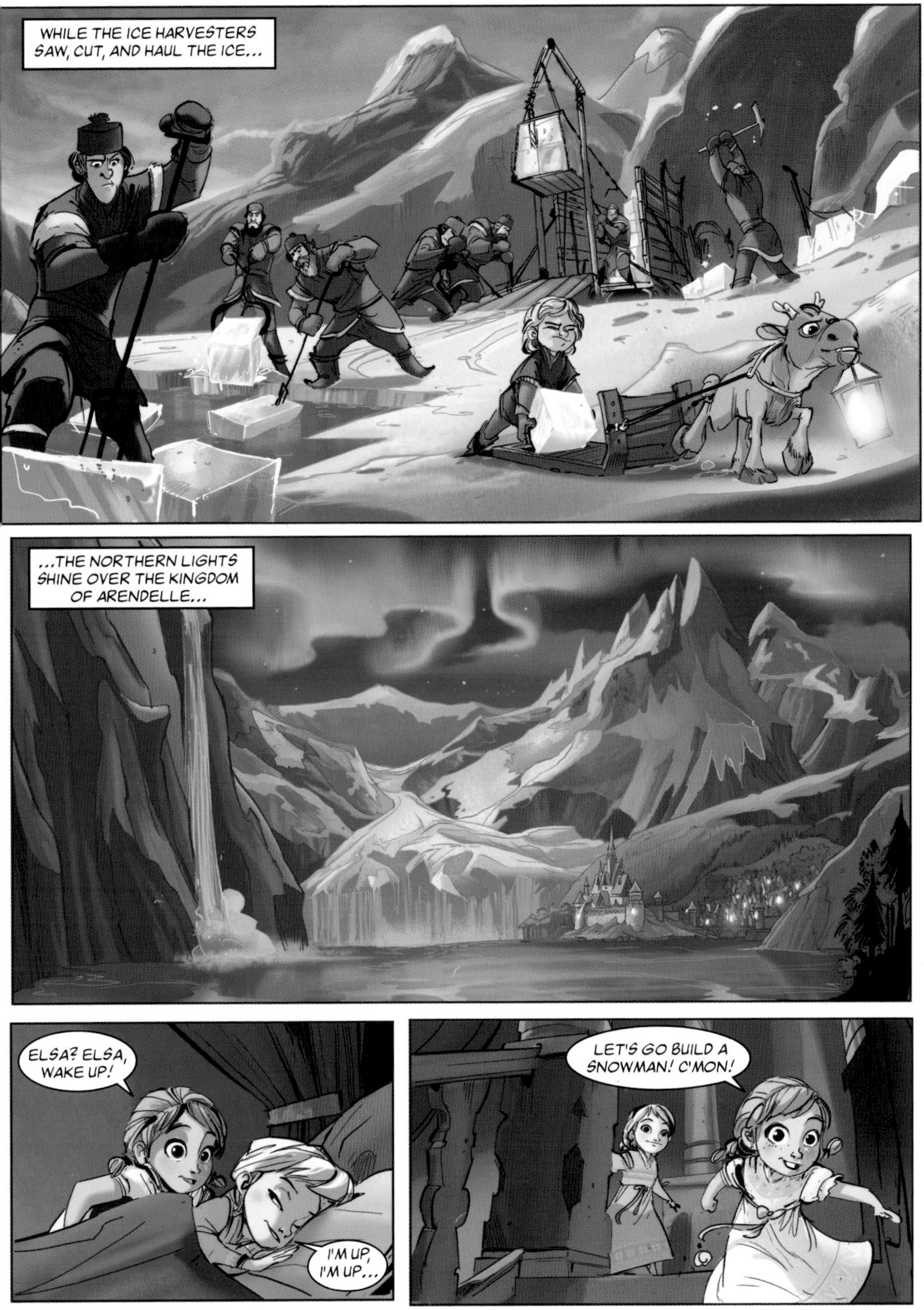
WHILE THE ICE HARVESTERS SAW, CUT, AND HAUL THE ICE...
...THE NORTHERN LIGHTS SHINE OVER THE KINGDOM OF ARENDELLE...
ELSA? ELSA, WAKE UP!
I'M UP, I'M UP...
LET'S GO BUILD A SNOWMAN! C'MON!

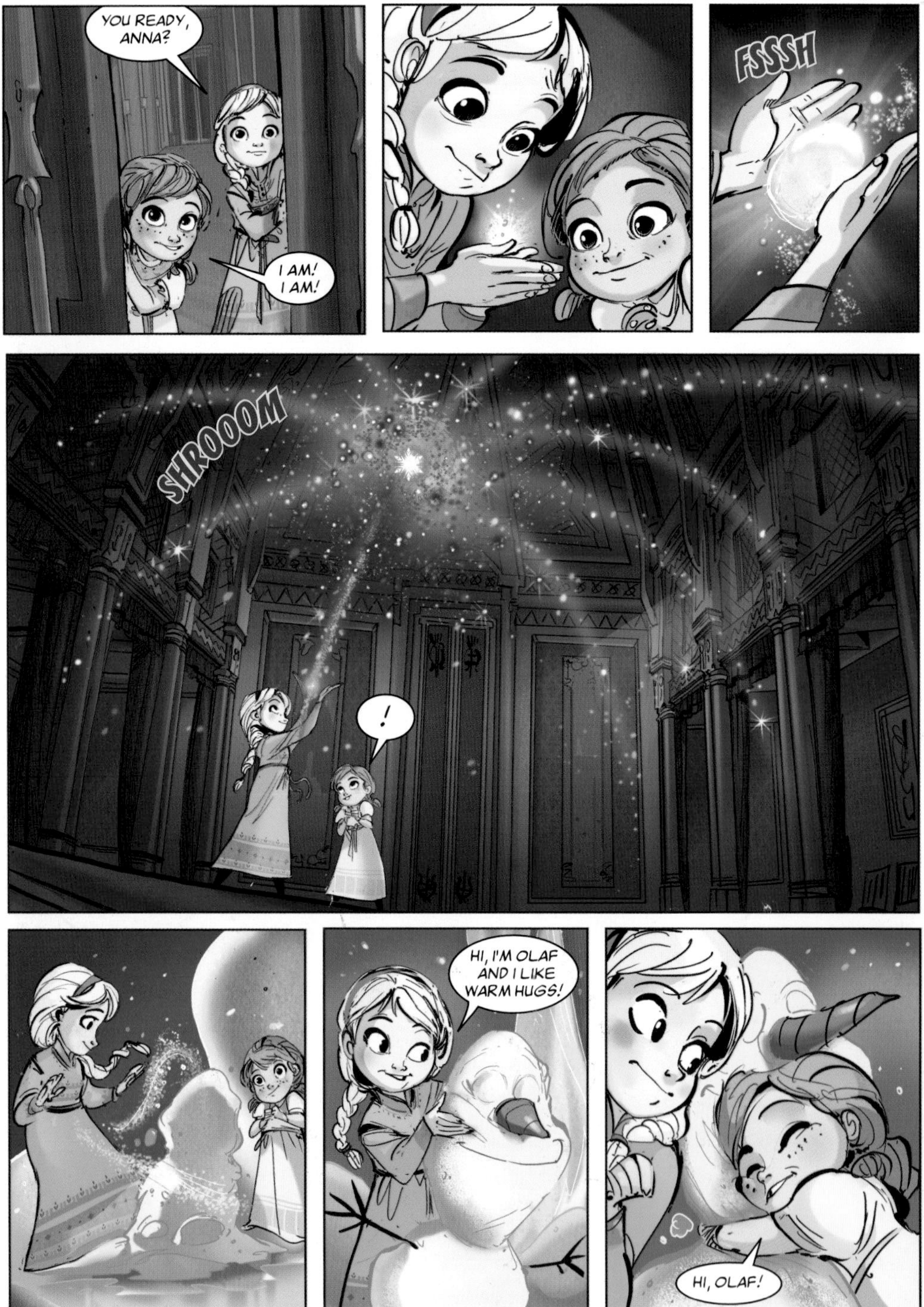
YOU READY, ANNA?
I AM! I AM!
FSSSH
SHROOOM
!
HI, I'M OLAF AND I LIKE WARM HUGS!
HI, OLAF!

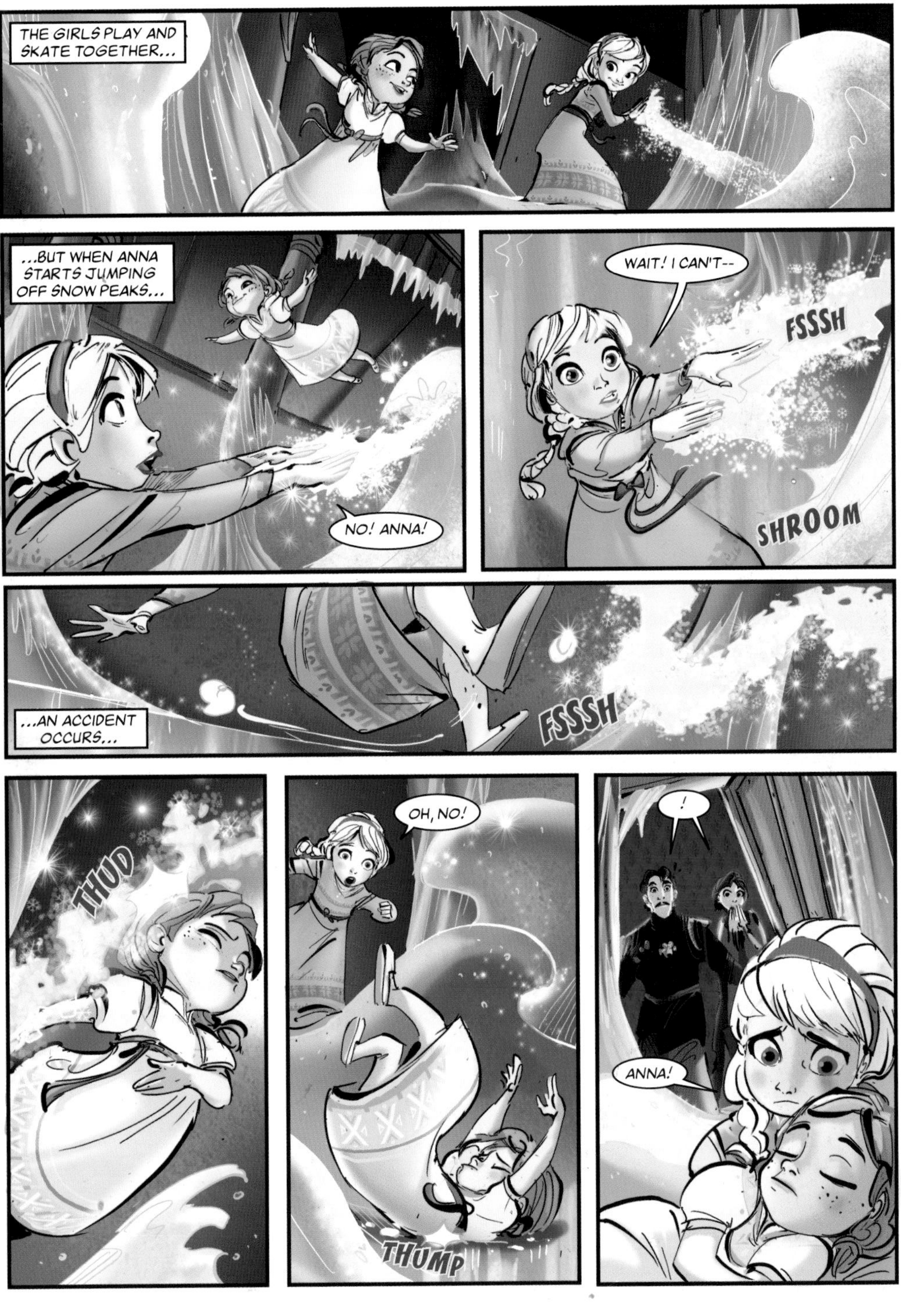
THE GIRLS PLAY AND SKATE TOGETHER...
...BUT WHEN ANNA STARTS JUMPING OFF SNOW PEAKS...
NO! ANNA!
WAIT! I CAN'T--
FSSSH
SHROOM
...AN ACCIDENT OCCURS...
FSSSH
THUD
OH, NO!
THUMP
!
ANNA!

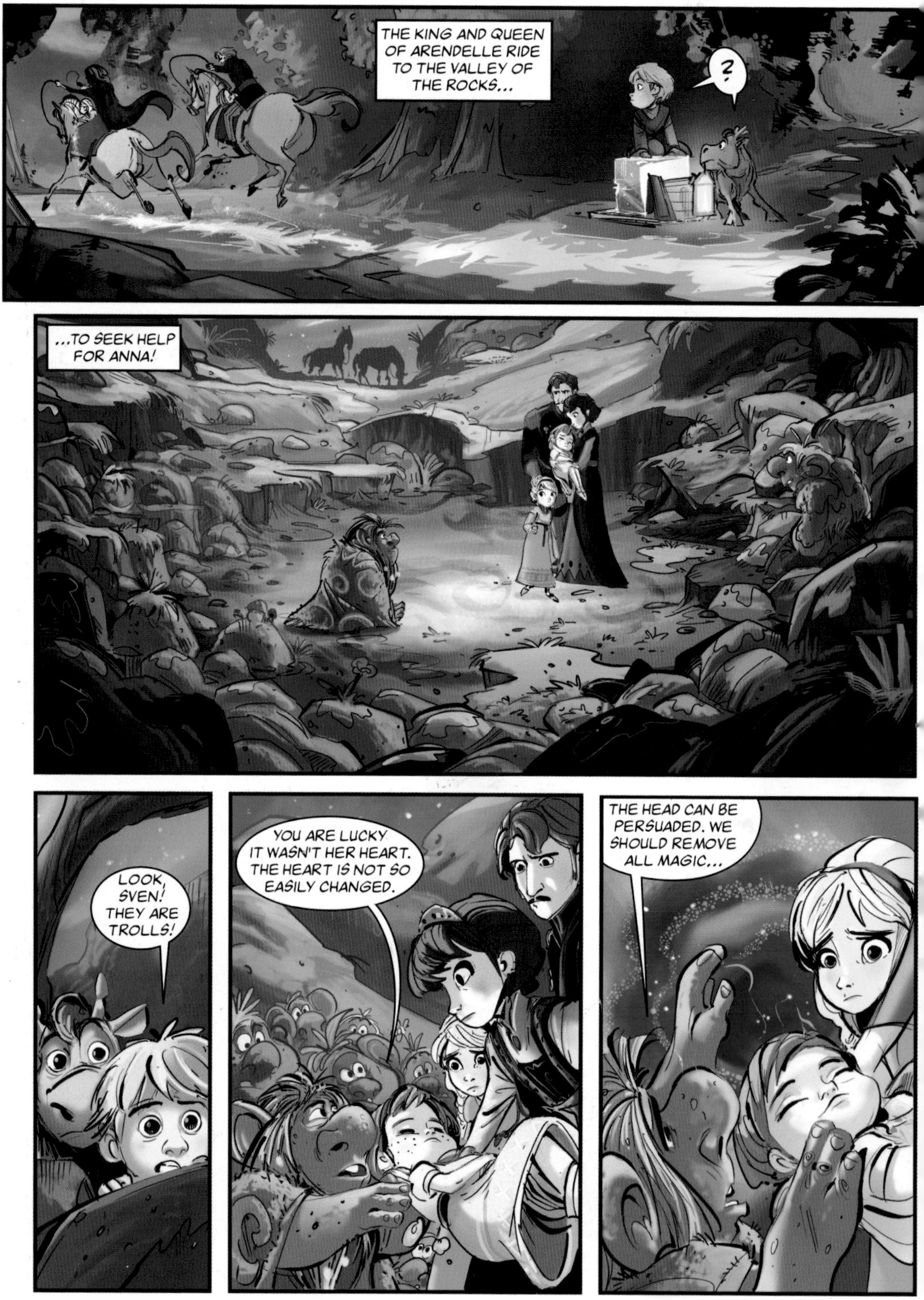
THE KING AND QUEEN OF ARENDELLE RIDE TO THE VALLEY OF THE ROCKS...
?
...TO SEEK HELP FOR ANNA!
LOOK, SVEN! THEY ARE TROLLS!
YOU ARE LUCKY IT WASN'T HER HEART. THE HEART IS NOT SO EASILY CHANGED.
THE HEAD CAN BE PERSUADED. WE SHOULD REMOVE ALL MAGIC...

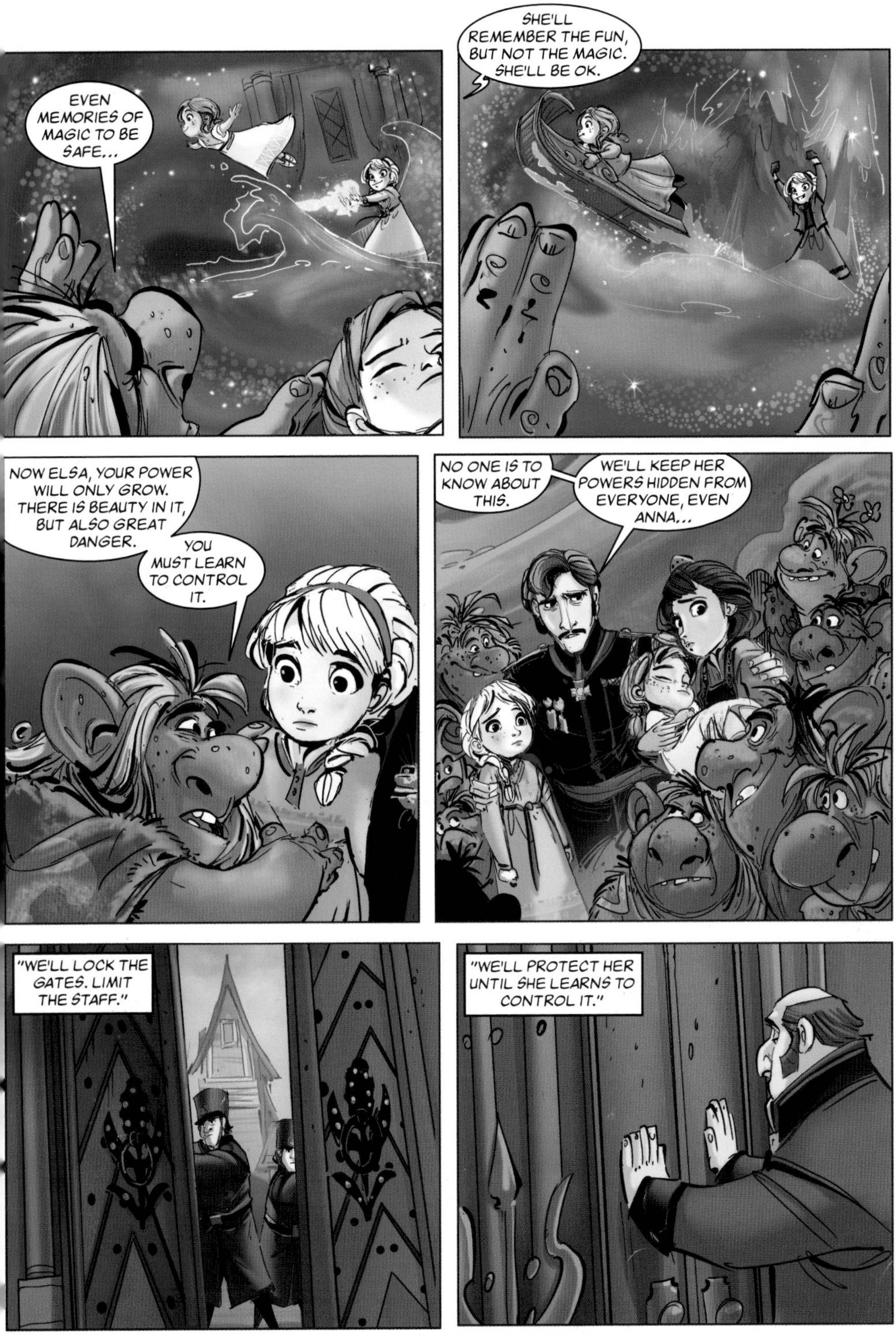
EVEN MEMORIES OF MAGIC TO BE SAFE...
SHE'LL REMEMBER THE FUN, BUT NOT THE MAGIC. SHE'LL BE OK.
NOW ELSA, YOUR POWER WILL ONLY GROW. THERE IS BEAUTY IN IT, BUT ALSO GREAT DANGER.
YOU MUST LEARN TO CONTROL IT.
NO ONE IS TO KNOW ABOUT THIS.
WE'LL KEEP HER POWERS HIDDEN FROM EVERYONE, EVEN ANNA...
"WE'LL LOCK THE GATES. LIMIT THE STAFF."
"WE'LL PROTECT HER UNTIL SHE LEARNS TO CONTROL IT."

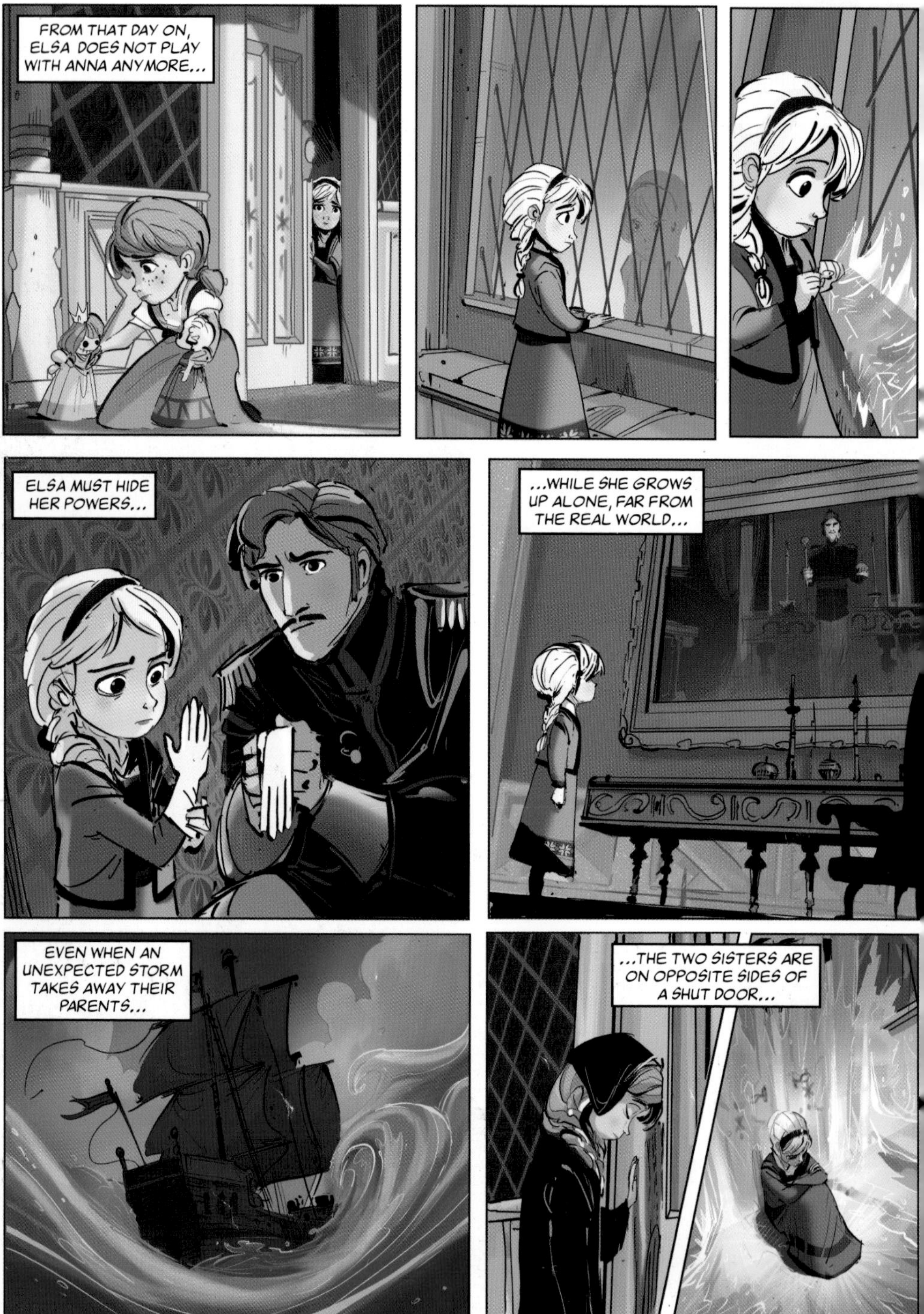
FROM THAT DAY ON, ELSA DOES NOT PLAY WITH ANNA ANYMORE...
ELSA MUST HIDE HER POWERS...
...WHILE SHE GROWS UP ALONE, FAR FROM THE REAL WORLD...
EVEN WHEN AN UNEXPECTED STORM TAKES AWAY THEIR PARENTS...
...THE TWO SISTERS ARE ON OPPOSITE SIDES OF A SHUT DOOR...

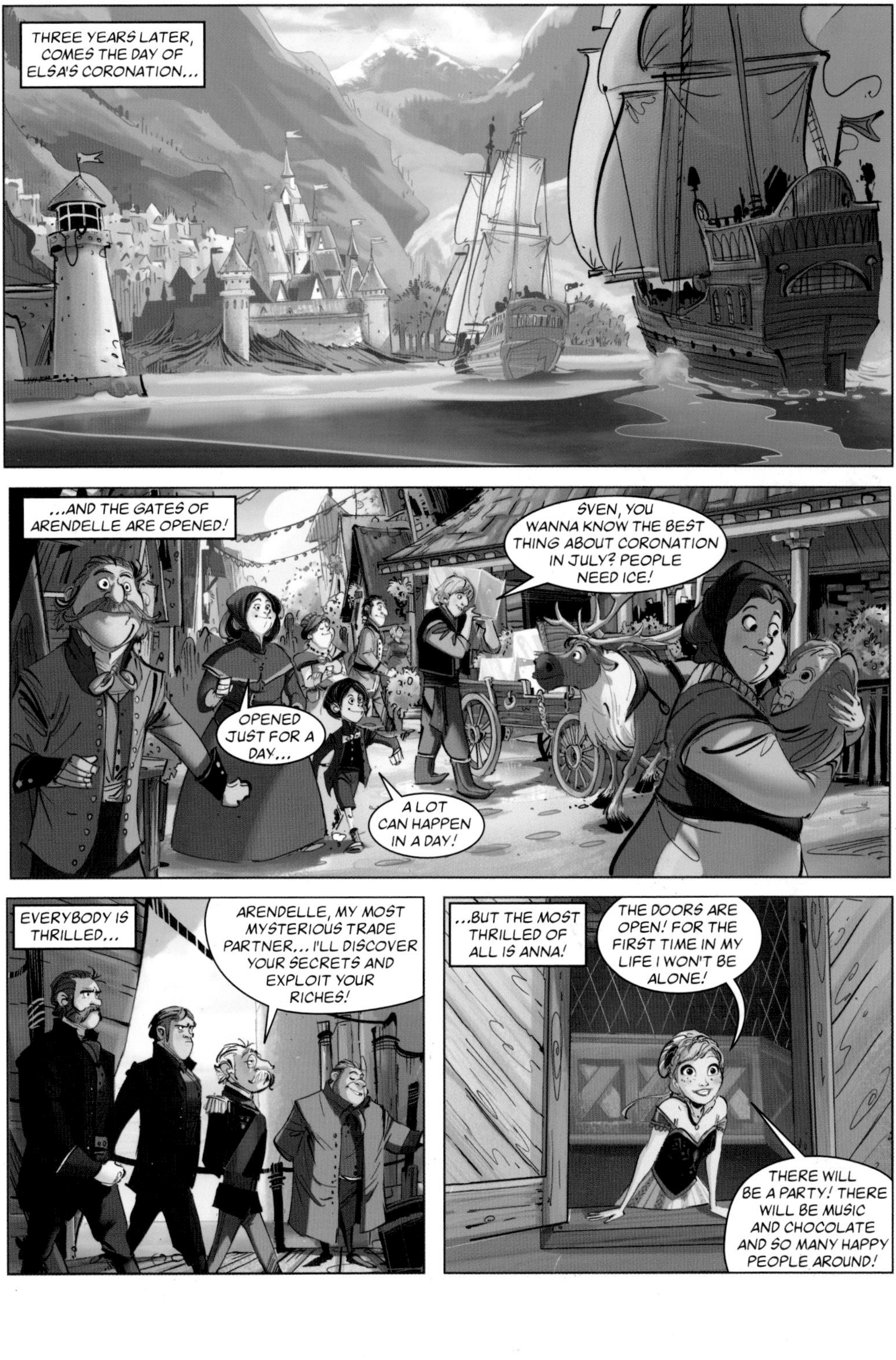
THREE YEARS LATER, COMES THE DAY OF ELSA'S CORONATION...
...AND THE GATES OF ARENDELLE ARE OPENED!
SVEN, YOU WANNA KNOW THE BEST THING ABOUT CORONATION IN JULY? PEOPLE NEED ICE!
OPENED JUST FOR A DAY...
A LOT CAN HAPPEN IN A DAY!
EVERYBODY IS THRILLED...
ARENDELLE, MY MOST MYSTERIOUS TRADE PARTNER... I'LL DISCOVER YOUR SECRETS AND EXPLOIT YOUR RICHES!
...BUT THE MOST THRILLED OF ALL IS ANNA!
THE DOORS ARE OPEN! FOR THE FIRST TIME IN MY LIFE I WON'T BE ALONE!
THERE WILL BE A PARTY! THERE WILL BE MUSIC AND CHOCOLATE AND SO MANY HAPPY PEOPLE AROUND!

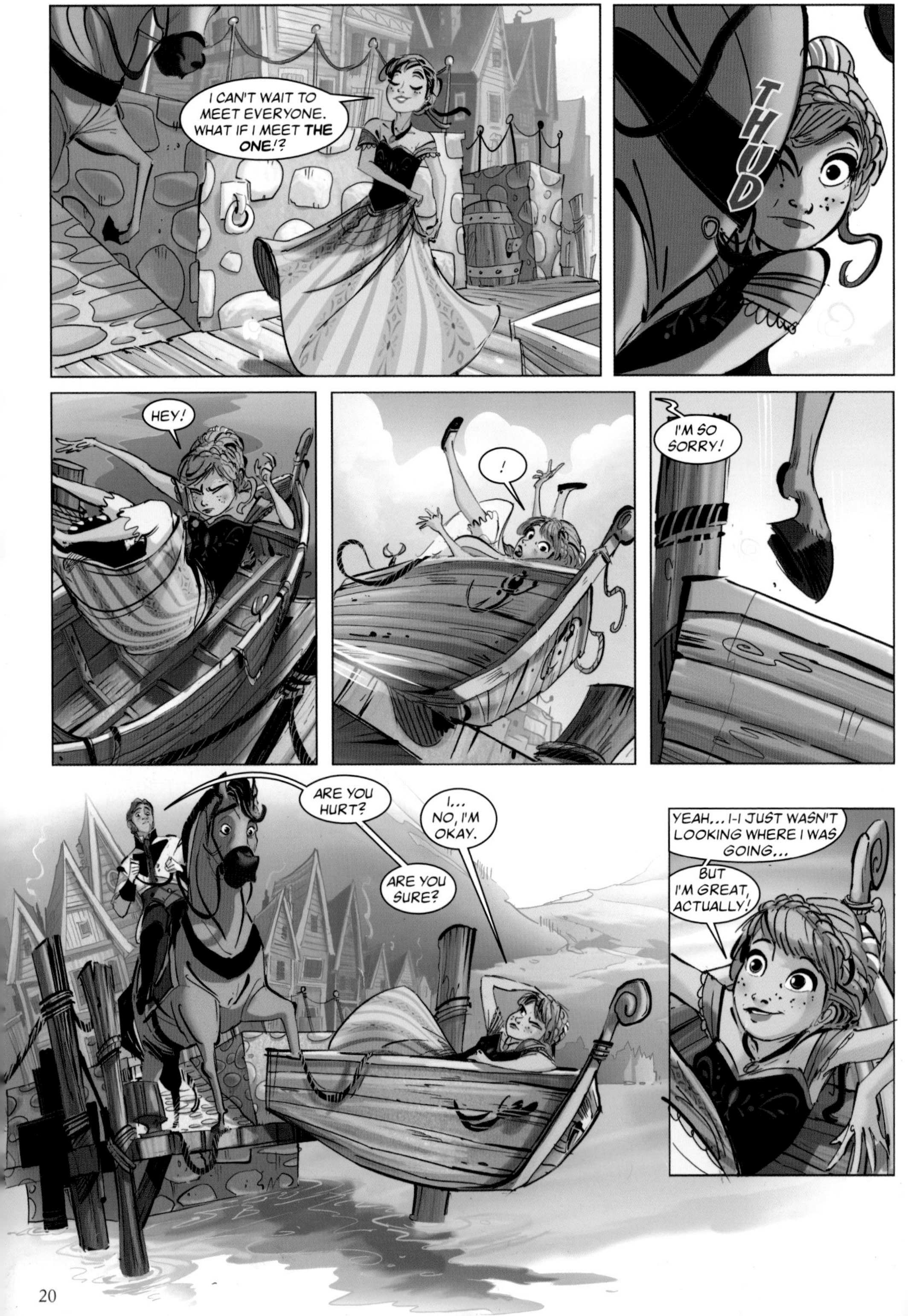

I CAN'T WAIT TO MEET EVERYONE. WHAT IF I MEET **THE ONE**!?
THUD
HEY!
!
I'M SO SORRY!
ARE YOU HURT?
I... NO, I'M OKAY.
ARE YOU SURE?
YEAH... I-I JUST WASN'T LOOKING WHERE I WAS GOING...
BUT I'M GREAT, ACTUALLY!

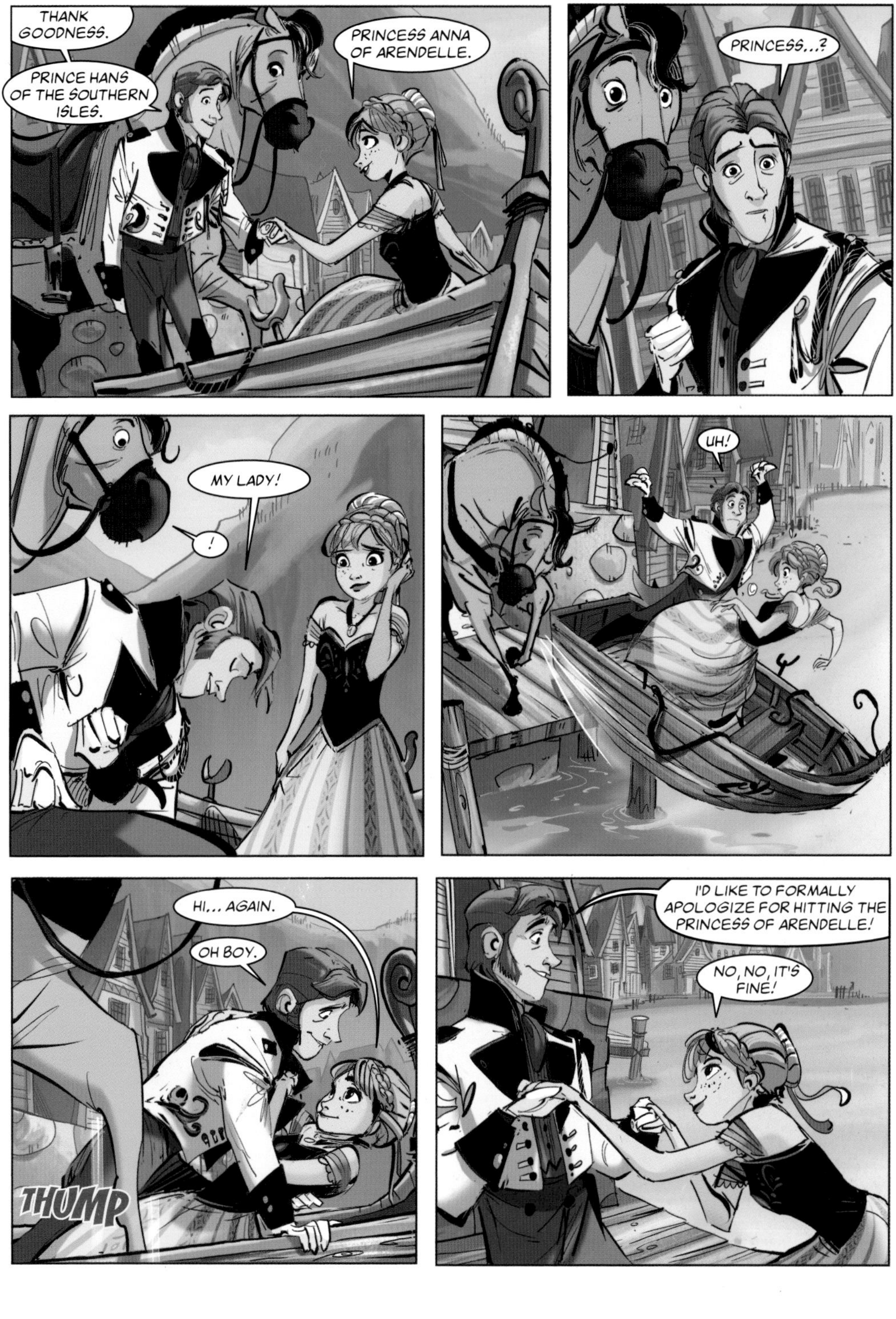
THANK GOODNESS.
PRINCE HANS OF THE SOUTHERN ISLES.
PRINCESS ANNA OF ARENDELLE.
PRINCESS...?
MY LADY!
!
UH!
HI... AGAIN.
OH BOY.
THUMP
I'D LIKE TO FORMALLY APOLOGIZE FOR HITTING THE PRINCESS OF ARENDELLE!
NO, NO, IT'S FINE!

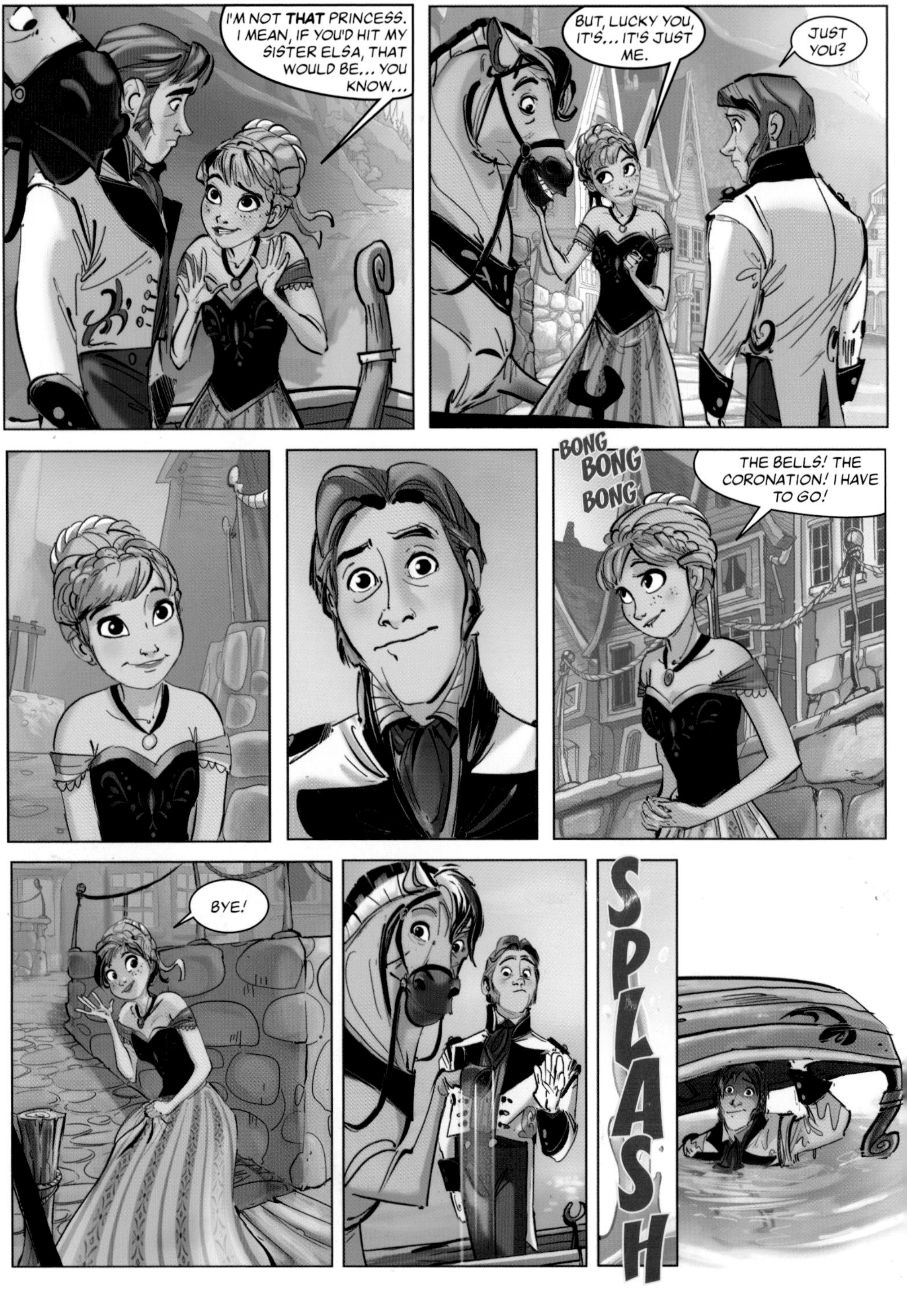
I'M NOT **THAT** PRINCESS. I MEAN, IF YOU'D HIT MY SISTER ELSA, THAT WOULD BE... YOU KNOW...
BUT, LUCKY YOU, IT'S... IT'S JUST ME.
JUST YOU?
BONG BONG BONG
THE BELLS! THE CORONATION! I HAVE TO GO!
BYE!
SPLASH

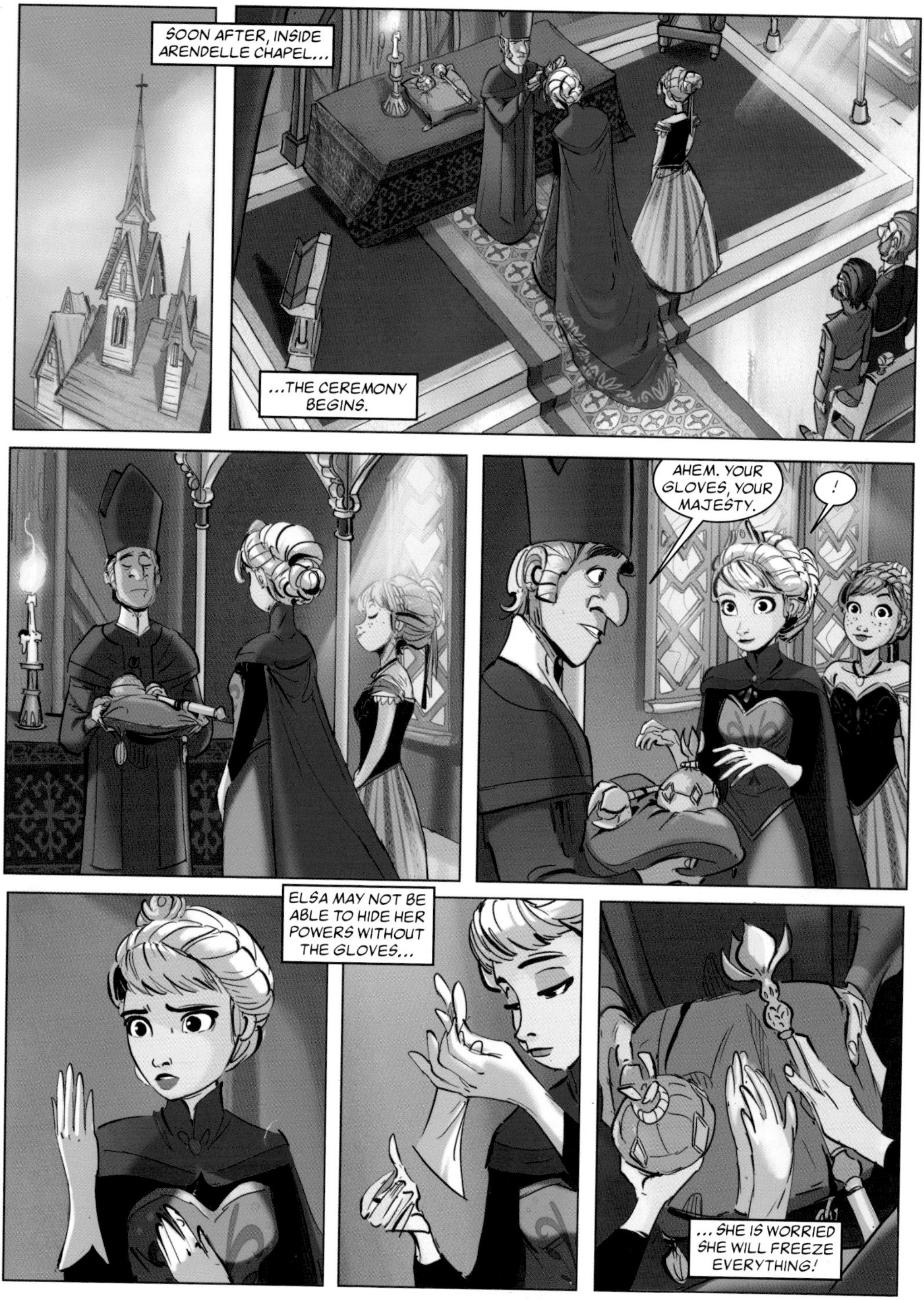
SOON AFTER, INSIDE ARENDELLE CHAPEL...
...THE CEREMONY BEGINS.
AHEM. YOUR GLOVES, YOUR MAJESTY.
!
ELSA MAY NOT BE ABLE TO HIDE HER POWERS WITHOUT THE GLOVES...
...SHE IS WORRIED SHE WILL FREEZE EVERYTHING!

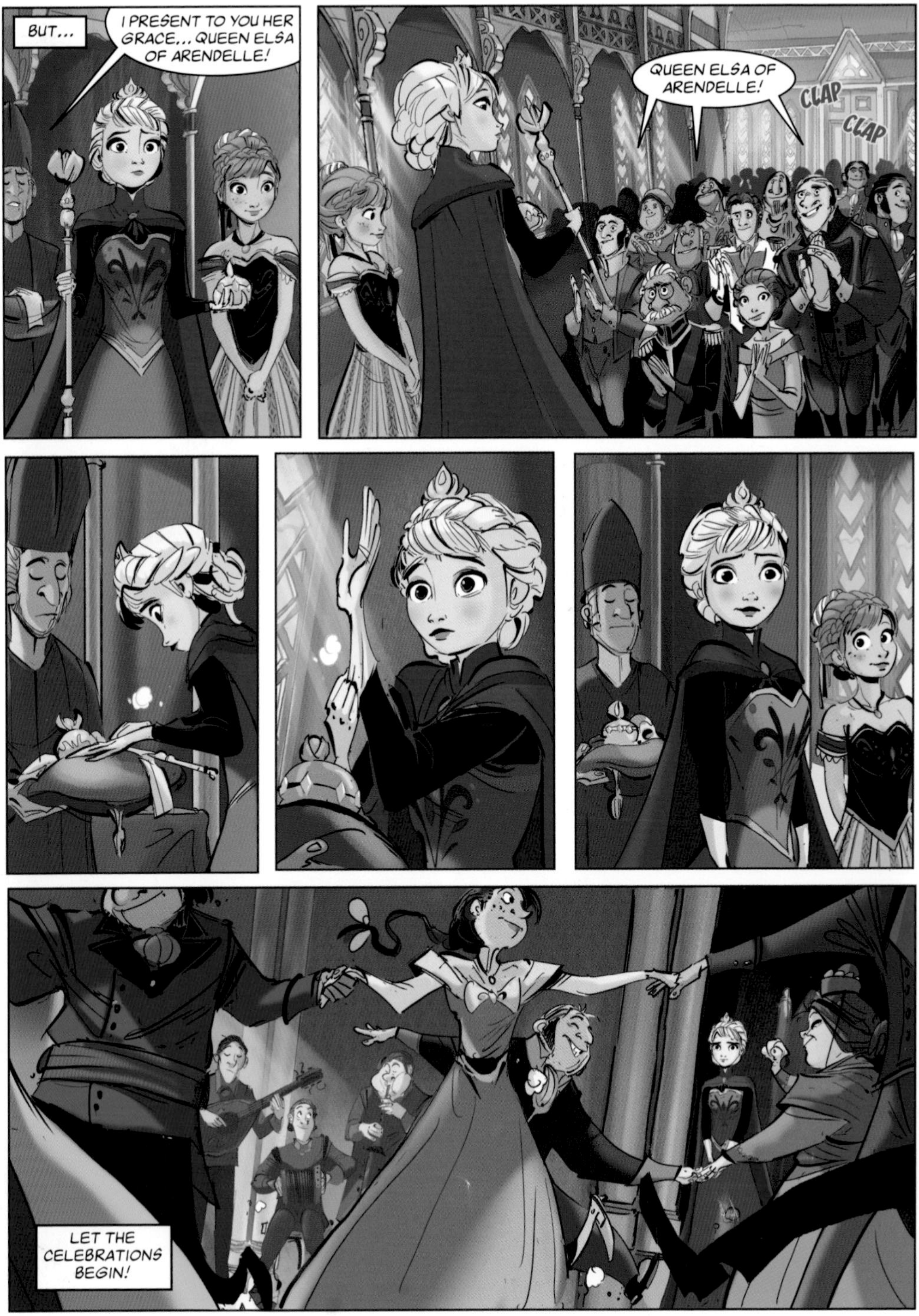
BUT...
I PRESENT TO YOU HER GRACE... QUEEN ELSA OF ARENDELLE!
QUEEN ELSA OF ARENDELLE!
CLAP
CLAP
LET THE CELEBRATIONS BEGIN!

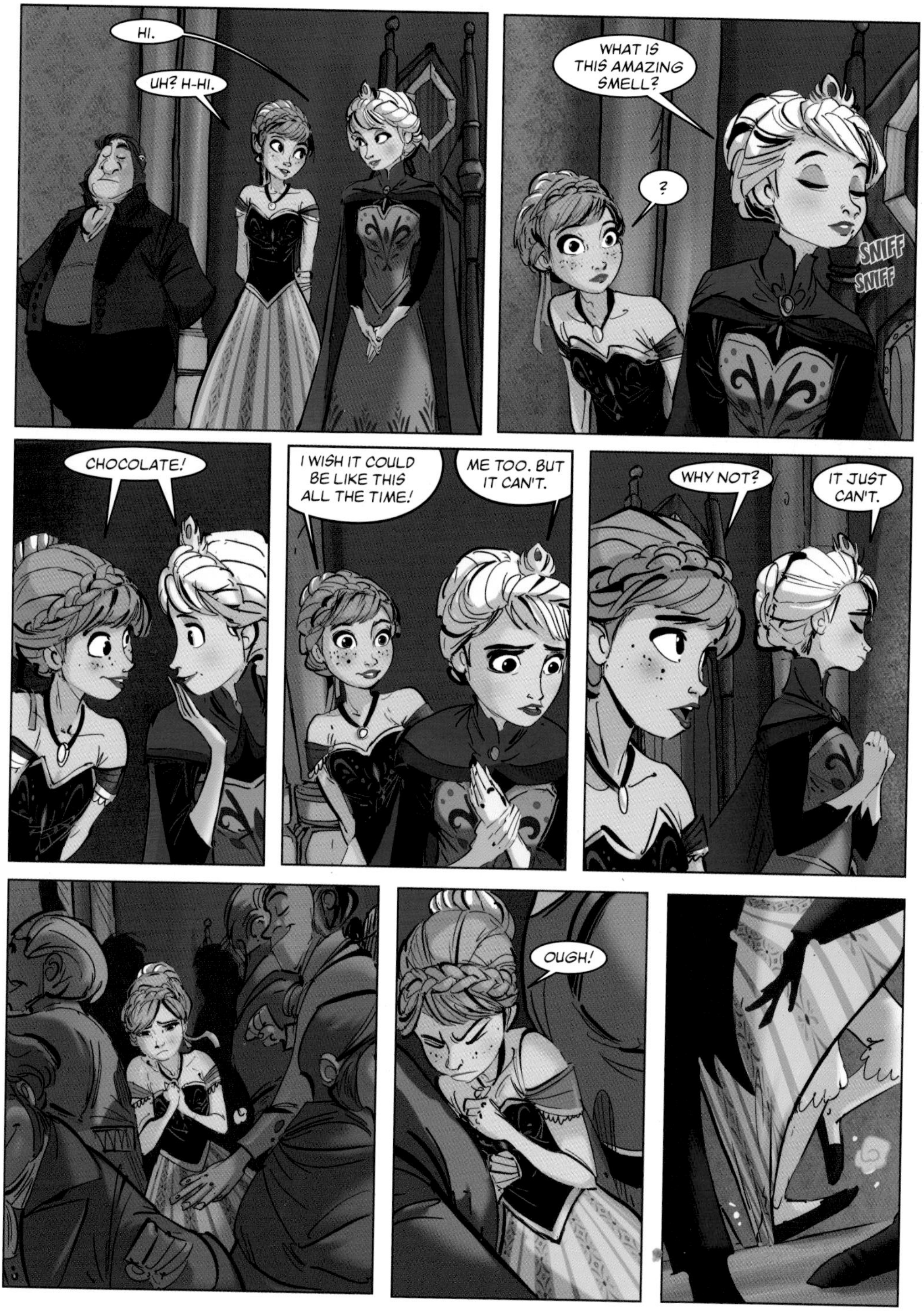
HI.
UH? H-HI.
WHAT IS THIS AMAZING SMELL?
?
SNIFF
SNIFF
CHOCOLATE!
I WISH IT COULD BE LIKE THIS ALL THE TIME!
ME TOO. BUT IT CAN'T.
WHY NOT?
IT JUST CAN'T.
OUGH!

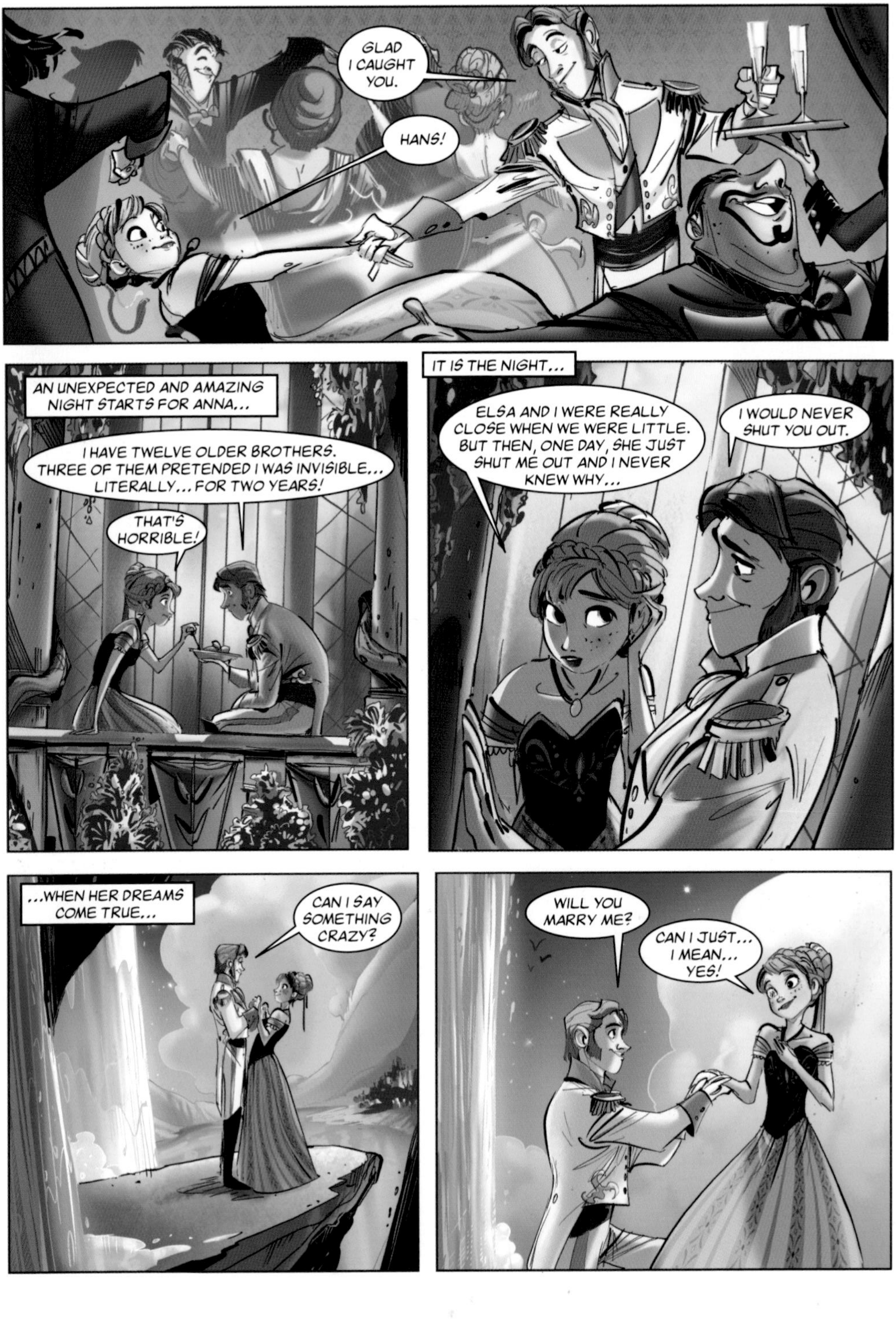
GLAD I CAUGHT YOU.
HANS!
AN UNEXPECTED AND AMAZING NIGHT STARTS FOR ANNA...
I HAVE TWELVE OLDER BROTHERS. THREE OF THEM PRETENDED I WAS INVISIBLE... LITERALLY... FOR TWO YEARS!
THAT'S HORRIBLE!
IT IS THE NIGHT...
ELSA AND I WERE REALLY CLOSE WHEN WE WERE LITTLE. BUT THEN, ONE DAY, SHE JUST SHUT ME OUT AND I NEVER KNEW WHY...
I WOULD NEVER SHUT YOU OUT.
...WHEN HER DREAMS COME TRUE...
CAN I SAY SOMETHING CRAZY?
WILL YOU MARRY ME?
CAN I JUST... I MEAN... YES!

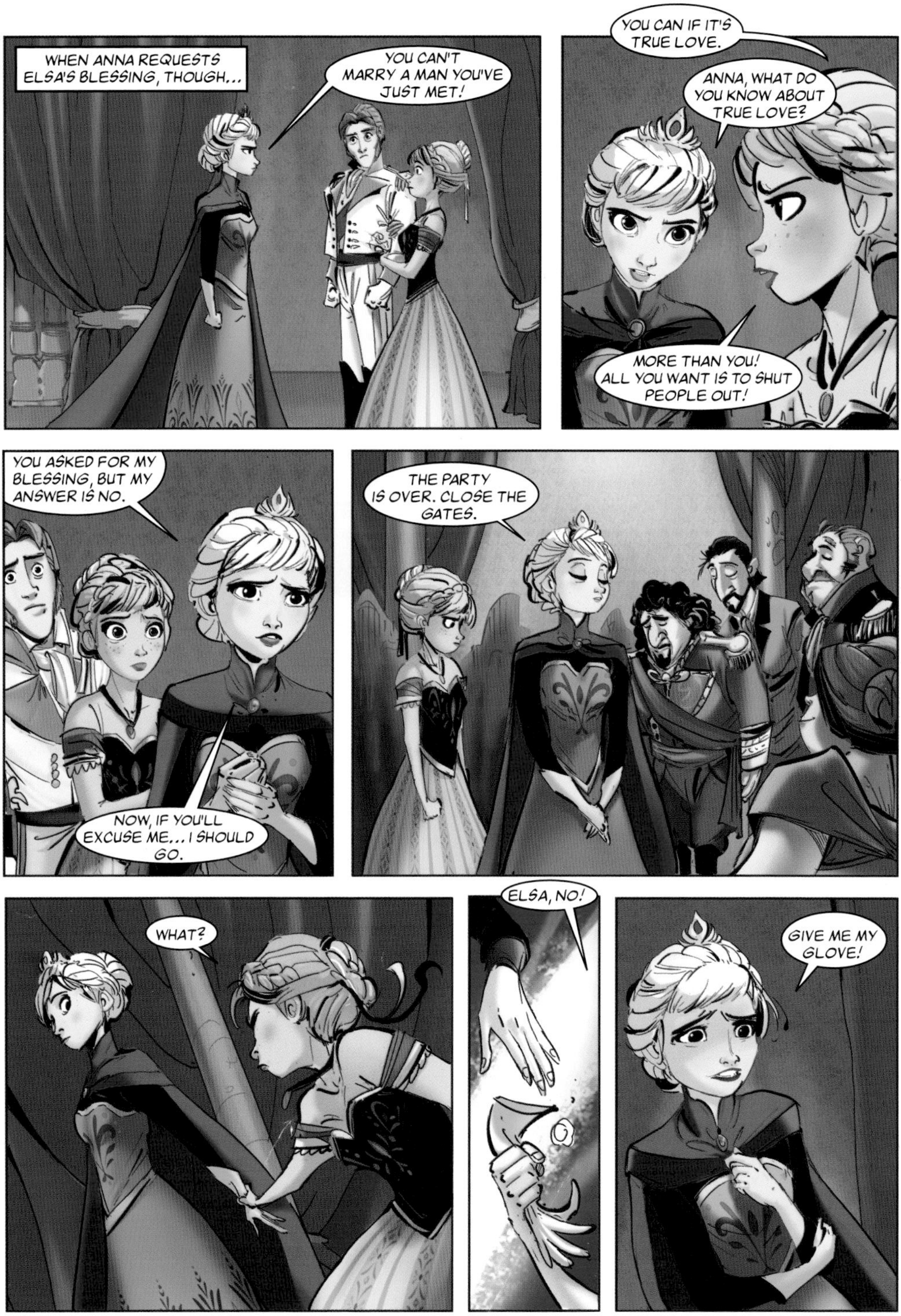
WHEN ANNA REQUESTS ELSA'S BLESSING, THOUGH...
YOU CAN'T MARRY A MAN YOU'VE JUST MET!
YOU CAN IF IT'S TRUE LOVE.
ANNA, WHAT DO YOU KNOW ABOUT TRUE LOVE?
MORE THAN YOU! ALL YOU WANT IS TO SHUT PEOPLE OUT!
YOU ASKED FOR MY BLESSING, BUT MY ANSWER IS NO.
NOW, IF YOU'LL EXCUSE ME... I SHOULD GO.
THE PARTY IS OVER. CLOSE THE GATES.
WHAT?
ELSA, NO!
GIVE ME MY GLOVE!

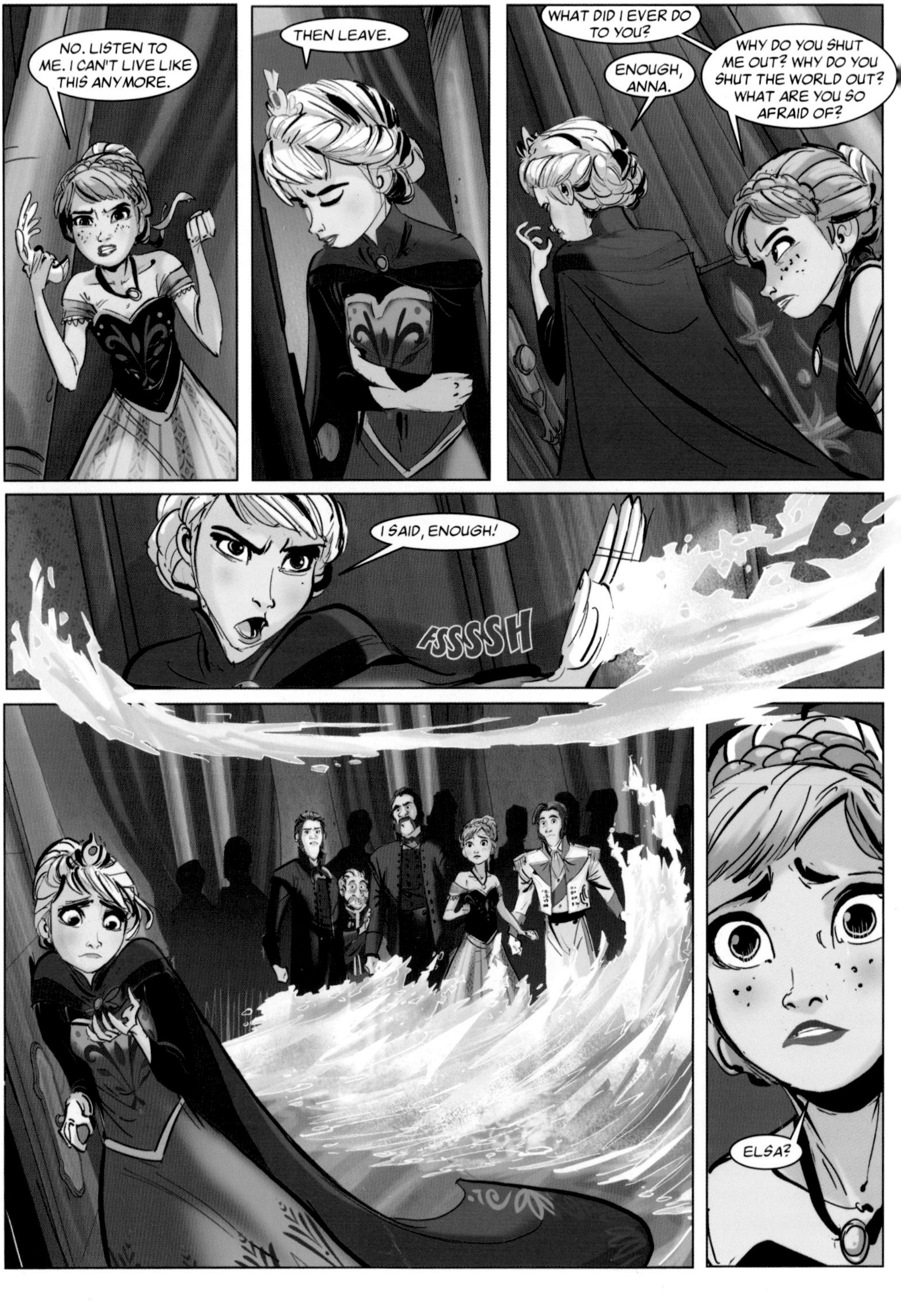
NO. LISTEN TO ME. I CAN'T LIVE LIKE THIS ANYMORE.
THEN LEAVE.
WHAT DID I EVER DO TO YOU?
ENOUGH, ANNA.
WHY DO YOU SHUT ME OUT? WHY DO YOU SHUT THE WORLD OUT? WHAT ARE YOU SO AFRAID OF?
I SAID, ENOUGH!
FSSSSH
ELSA?

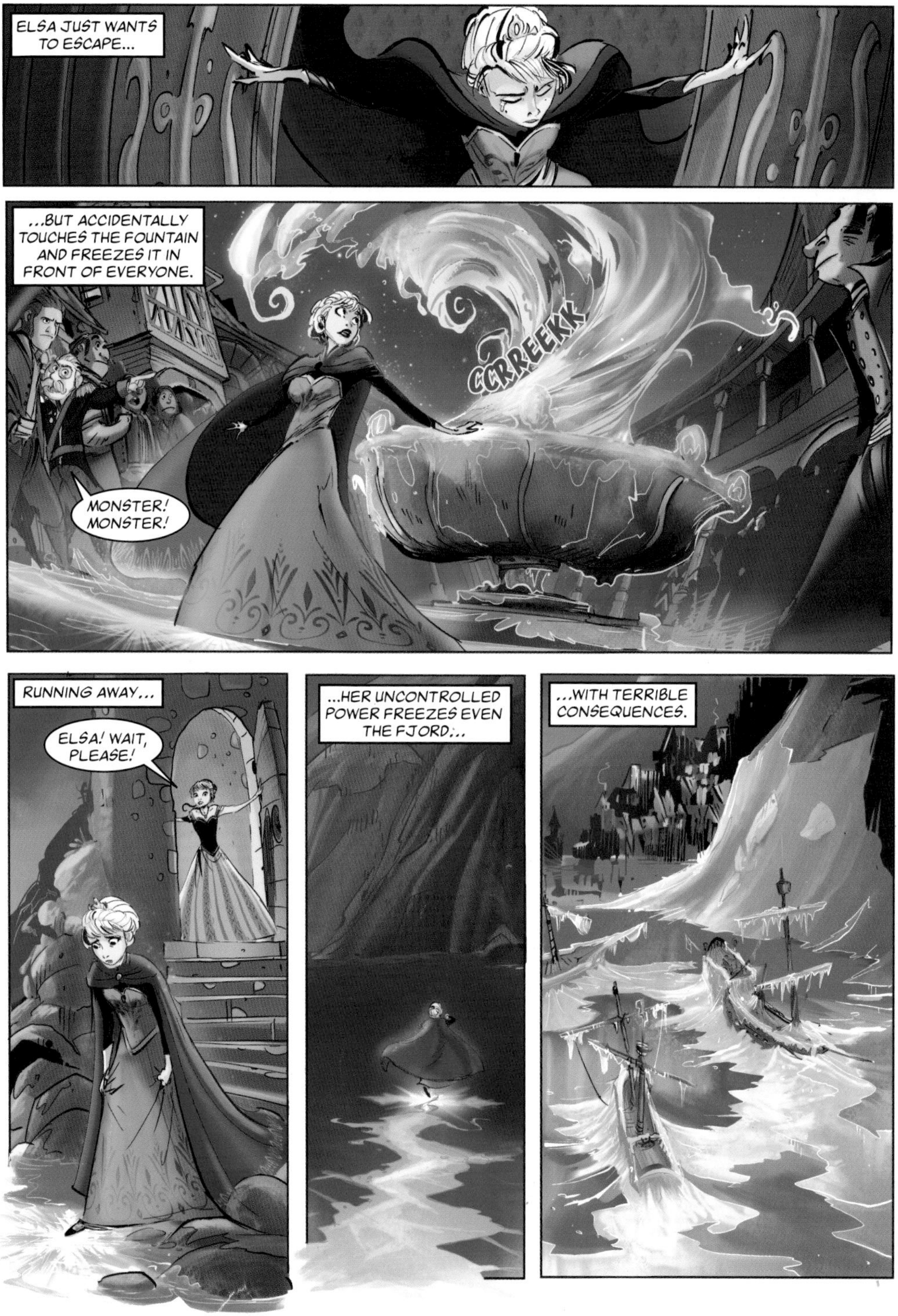
ELSA JUST WANTS TO ESCAPE...
...BUT ACCIDENTALLY TOUCHES THE FOUNTAIN AND FREEZES IT IN FRONT OF EVERYONE.
CCRREEKK
MONSTER! MONSTER!
RUNNING AWAY...
ELSA! WAIT, PLEASE!
...HER UNCONTROLLED POWER FREEZES EVEN THE FJORD...
...WITH TERRIBLE CONSEQUENCES.

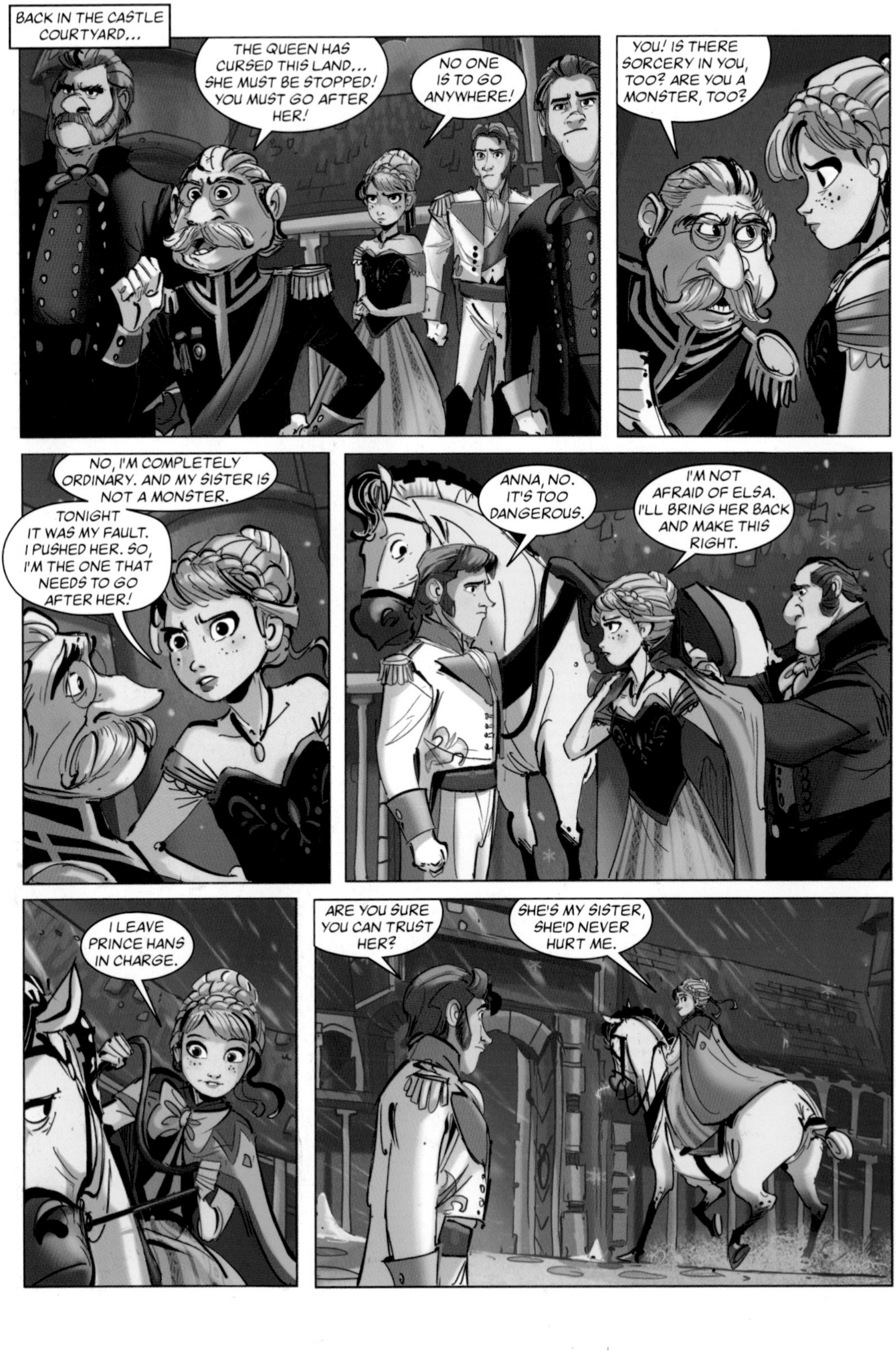
BACK IN THE CASTLE COURTYARD...
THE QUEEN HAS CURSED THIS LAND... SHE MUST BE STOPPED! YOU MUST GO AFTER HER!
NO ONE IS TO GO ANYWHERE!
YOU! IS THERE SORCERY IN YOU, TOO? ARE YOU A MONSTER, TOO?
NO, I'M COMPLETELY ORDINARY. AND MY SISTER IS NOT A MONSTER.
TONIGHT IT WAS MY FAULT. I PUSHED HER. SO, I'M THE ONE THAT NEEDS TO GO AFTER HER!
ANNA, NO. IT'S TOO DANGEROUS.
I'M NOT AFRAID OF ELSA. I'LL BRING HER BACK AND MAKE THIS RIGHT.
I LEAVE PRINCE HANS IN CHARGE.
ARE YOU SURE YOU CAN TRUST HER?
SHE'S MY SISTER, SHE'D NEVER HURT ME.

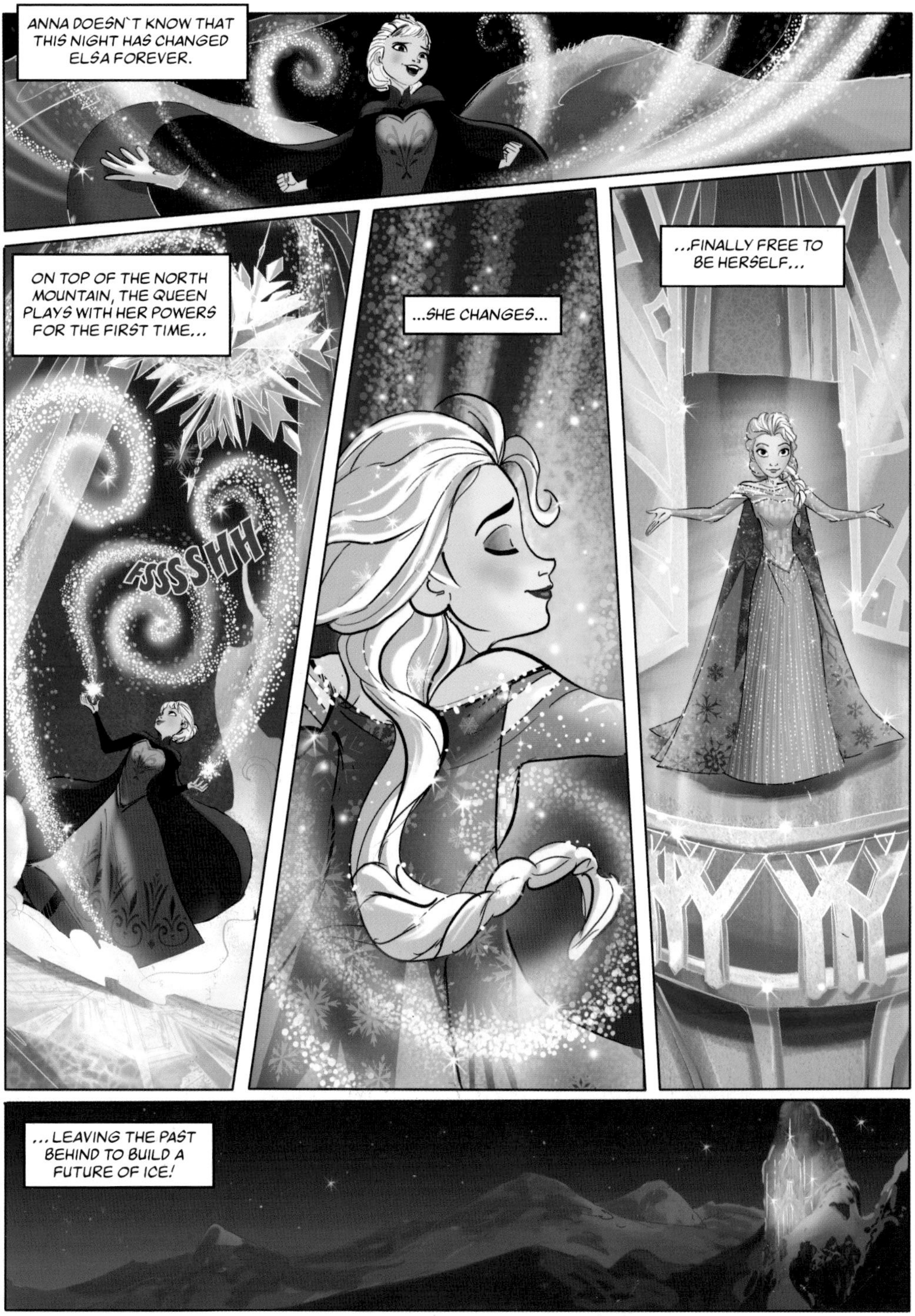
ANNA DOESN'T KNOW THAT THIS NIGHT HAS CHANGED ELSA FOREVER.
ON TOP OF THE NORTH MOUNTAIN, THE QUEEN PLAYS WITH HER POWERS FOR THE FIRST TIME...
FSSSSHH
...SHE CHANGES...
...FINALLY FREE TO BE HERSELF...
...LEAVING THE PAST BEHIND TO BUILD A FUTURE OF ICE!

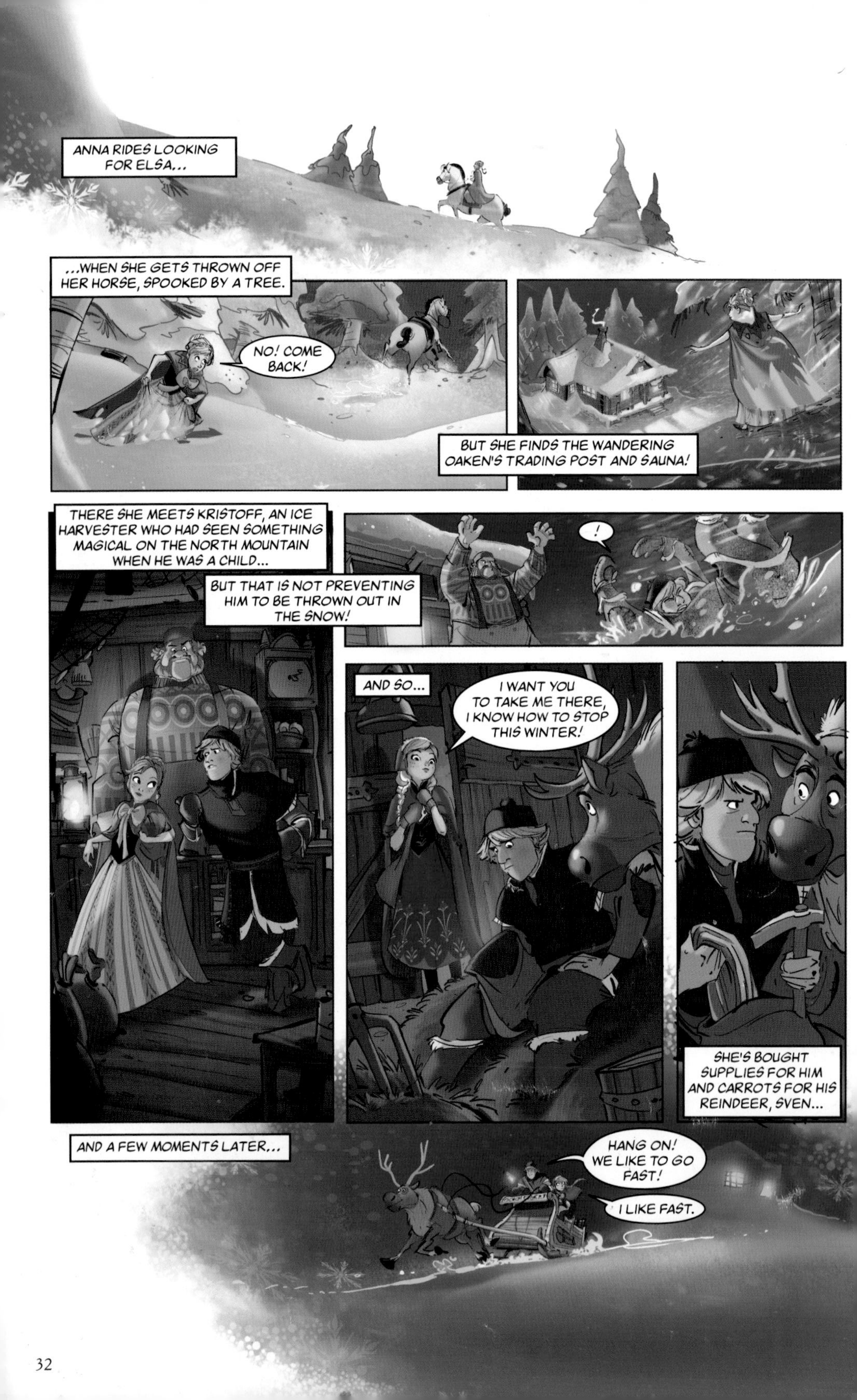
ANNA RIDES LOOKING FOR ELSA...
...WHEN SHE GETS THROWN OFF HER HORSE, SPOOKED BY A TREE.
NO! COME BACK!
BUT SHE FINDS THE WANDERING OAKEN'S TRADING POST AND SAUNA!
THERE SHE MEETS KRISTOFF, AN ICE HARVESTER WHO HAD SEEN SOMETHING MAGICAL ON THE NORTH MOUNTAIN WHEN HE WAS A CHILD...
BUT THAT IS NOT PREVENTING HIM TO BE THROWN OUT IN THE SNOW!
!
AND SO...
I WANT YOU TO TAKE ME THERE, I KNOW HOW TO STOP THIS WINTER!
SHE'S BOUGHT SUPPLIES FOR HIM AND CARROTS FOR HIS REINDEER, SVEN...
AND A FEW MOMENTS LATER...
HANG ON! WE LIKE TO GO FAST!
I LIKE FAST.

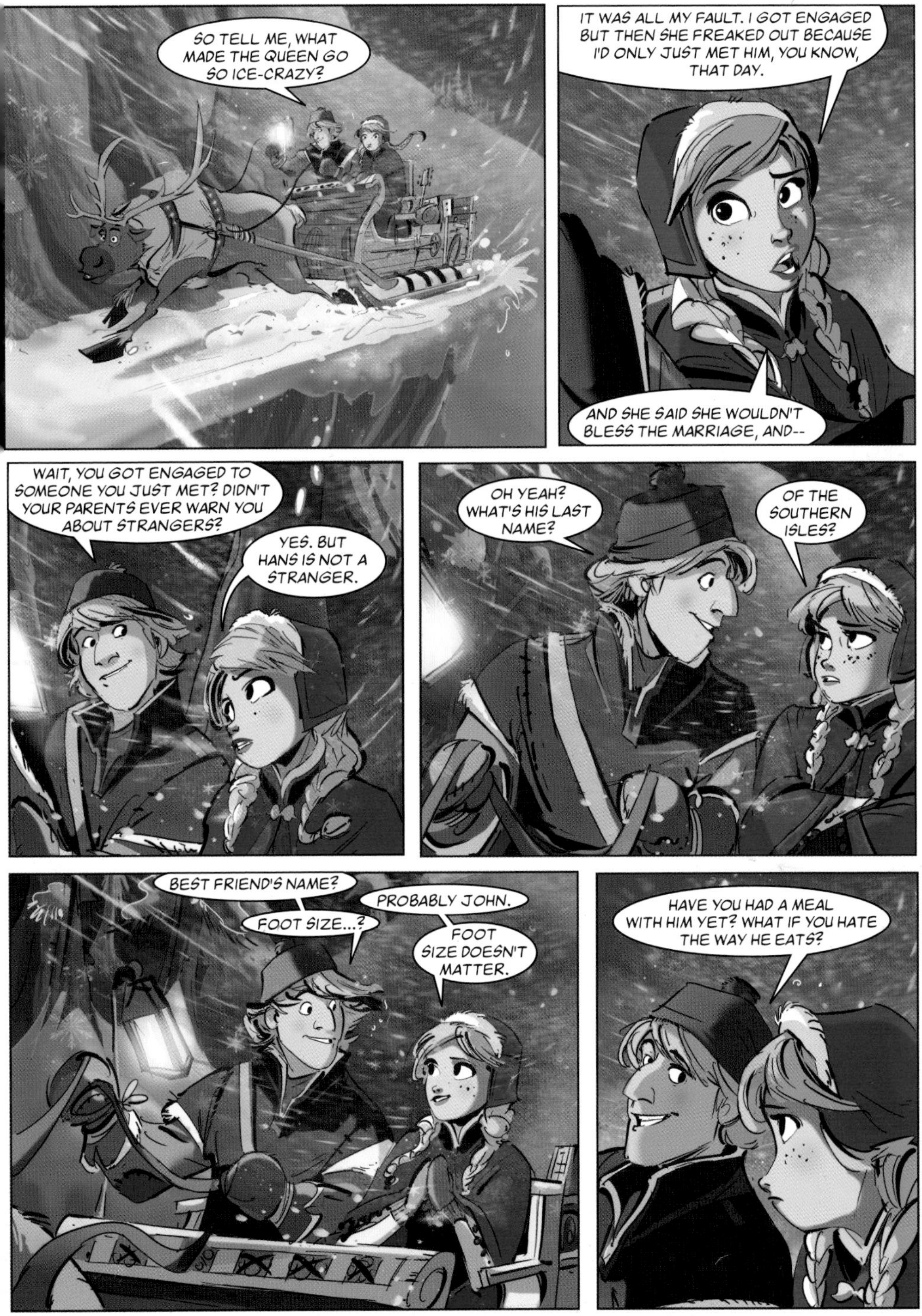
SO TELL ME, WHAT MADE THE QUEEN GO SO ICE-CRAZY?
IT WAS ALL MY FAULT. I GOT ENGAGED BUT THEN SHE FREAKED OUT BECAUSE I'D ONLY JUST MET HIM, YOU KNOW, THAT DAY.
AND SHE SAID SHE WOULDN'T BLESS THE MARRIAGE, AND--
WAIT, YOU GOT ENGAGED TO SOMEONE YOU JUST MET? DIDN'T YOUR PARENTS EVER WARN YOU ABOUT STRANGERS?
YES. BUT HANS IS NOT A STRANGER.
OH YEAH? WHAT'S HIS LAST NAME?
OF THE SOUTHERN ISLES?
BEST FRIEND'S NAME?
PROBABLY JOHN.
FOOT SIZE...?
FOOT SIZE DOESN'T MATTER.
HAVE YOU HAD A MEAL WITH HIM YET? WHAT IF YOU HATE THE WAY HE EATS?

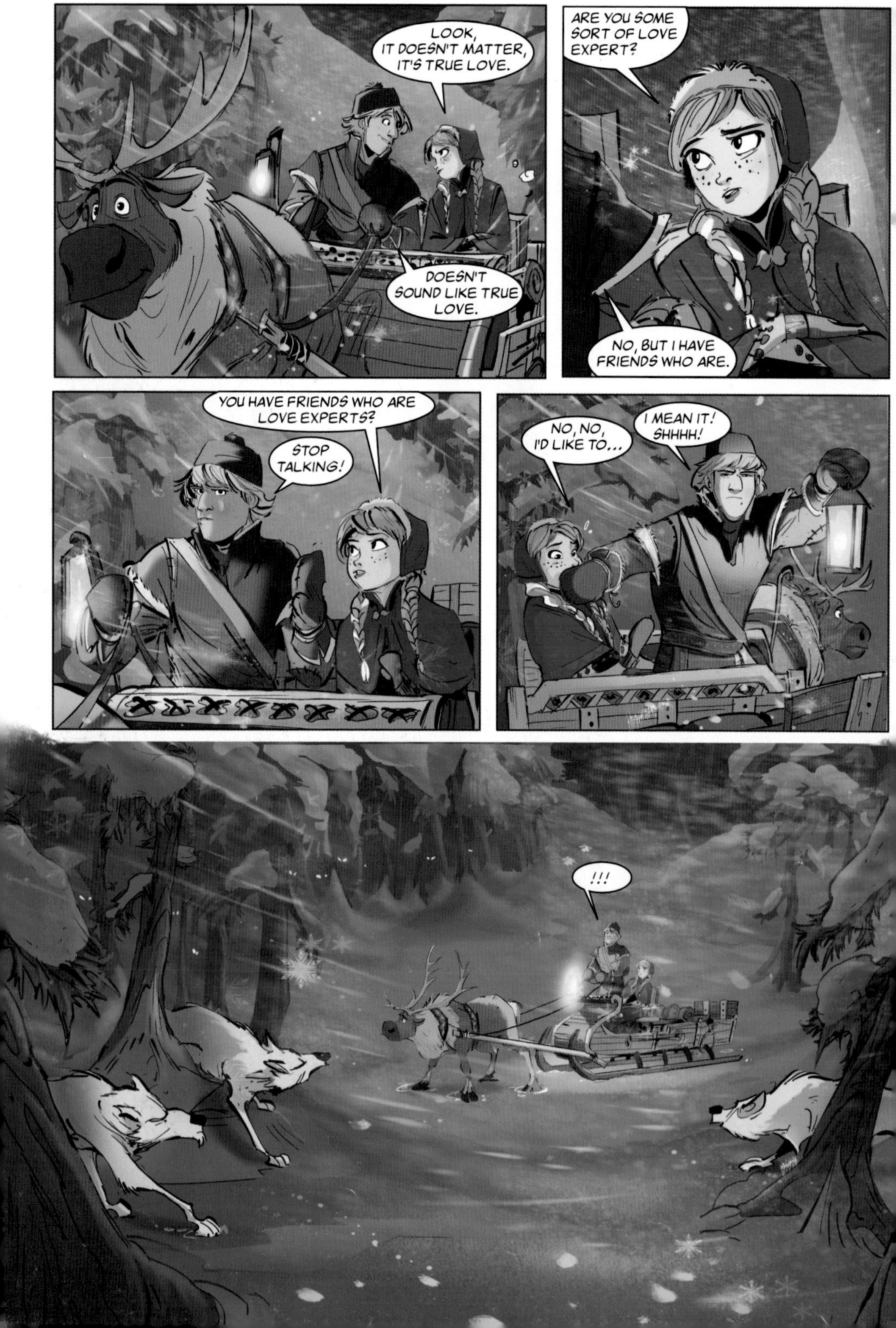
LOOK, IT DOESN'T MATTER, IT'S TRUE LOVE.
DOESN'T SOUND LIKE TRUE LOVE.
ARE YOU SOME SORT OF LOVE EXPERT?
NO, BUT I HAVE FRIENDS WHO ARE.
YOU HAVE FRIENDS WHO ARE LOVE EXPERTS?
STOP TALKING!
NO, NO, I'D LIKE TO...
I MEAN IT! SHHHH!
!!!

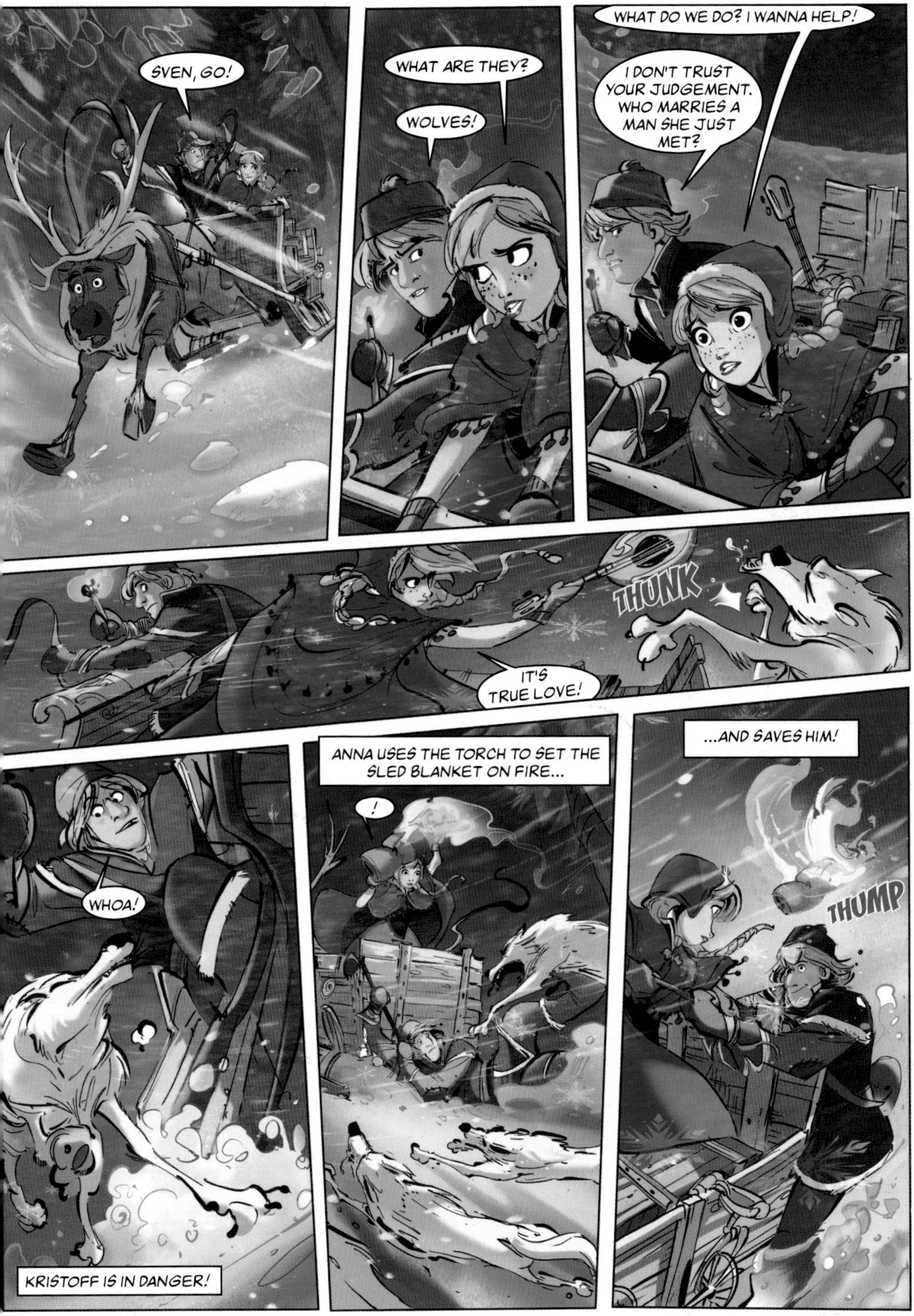
SVEN, GO!
WHAT ARE THEY?
WOLVES!
WHAT DO WE DO? I WANNA HELP!
I DON'T TRUST YOUR JUDGEMENT. WHO MARRIES A MAN SHE JUST MET?
THUNK
IT'S TRUE LOVE!
WHOA!
KRISTOFF IS IN DANGER!
ANNA USES THE TORCH TO SET THE SLED BLANKET ON FIRE...
!
...AND SAVES HIM!
THUMP

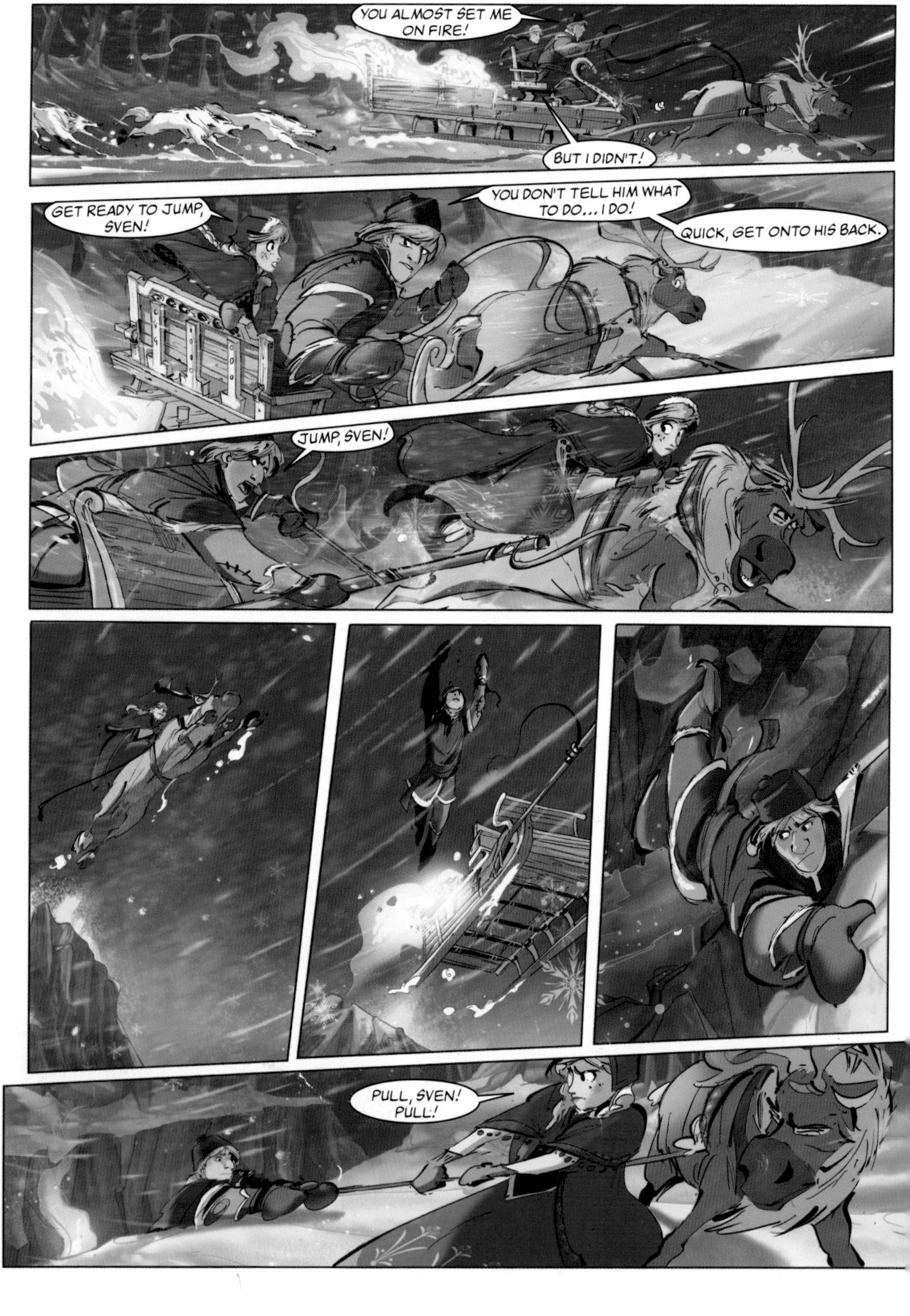
YOU ALMOST SET ME ON FIRE!
BUT I DIDN'T!
GET READY TO JUMP, SVEN!
YOU DON'T TELL HIM WHAT TO DO... I DO!
QUICK, GET ONTO HIS BACK.
JUMP, SVEN!
PULL, SVEN! PULL!

I'LL REPLACE YOUR SLED, AND EVERYTHING IN IT.

AND I UNDERSTAND IF YOU DON'T WANT TO HELP ME ANYMORE...

OF COURSE I DON'T WANT TO HELP HER ANYMORE. IN FACT, THIS WHOLE THING HAS RUINED ME FOR HELPING ANYONE EVER AGAIN.

"SHE'LL DIE ON HER OWN," SAYS KRISTOFF, PRETENDING TO SPEAK FOR SVEN.

ALTHOUGH KRISTOFF THINKS HE CAN LIVE WITH THAT...

...HE CAN'T IN THE END.

WAIT THERE. WE'RE COMING!

YOU ARE?

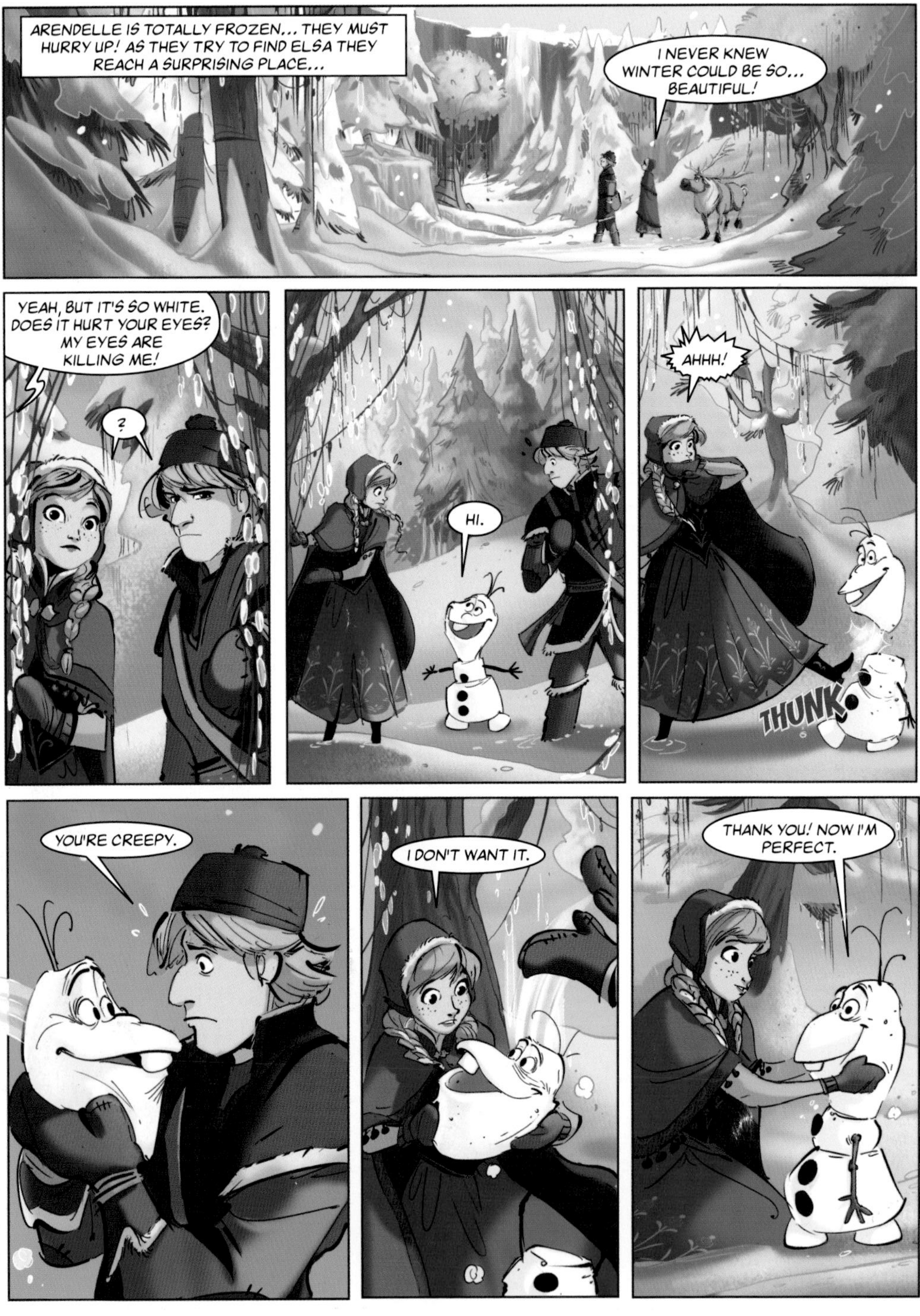
ARENDELLE IS TOTALLY FROZEN... THEY MUST HURRY UP! AS THEY TRY TO FIND ELSA THEY REACH A SURPRISING PLACE...
I NEVER KNEW WINTER COULD BE SO... BEAUTIFUL!
YEAH, BUT IT'S SO WHITE. DOES IT HURT YOUR EYES? MY EYES ARE KILLING ME!
?
HI.
AHHH!
THUNK
YOU'RE CREEPY.
I DON'T WANT IT.
THANK YOU! NOW I'M PERFECT.

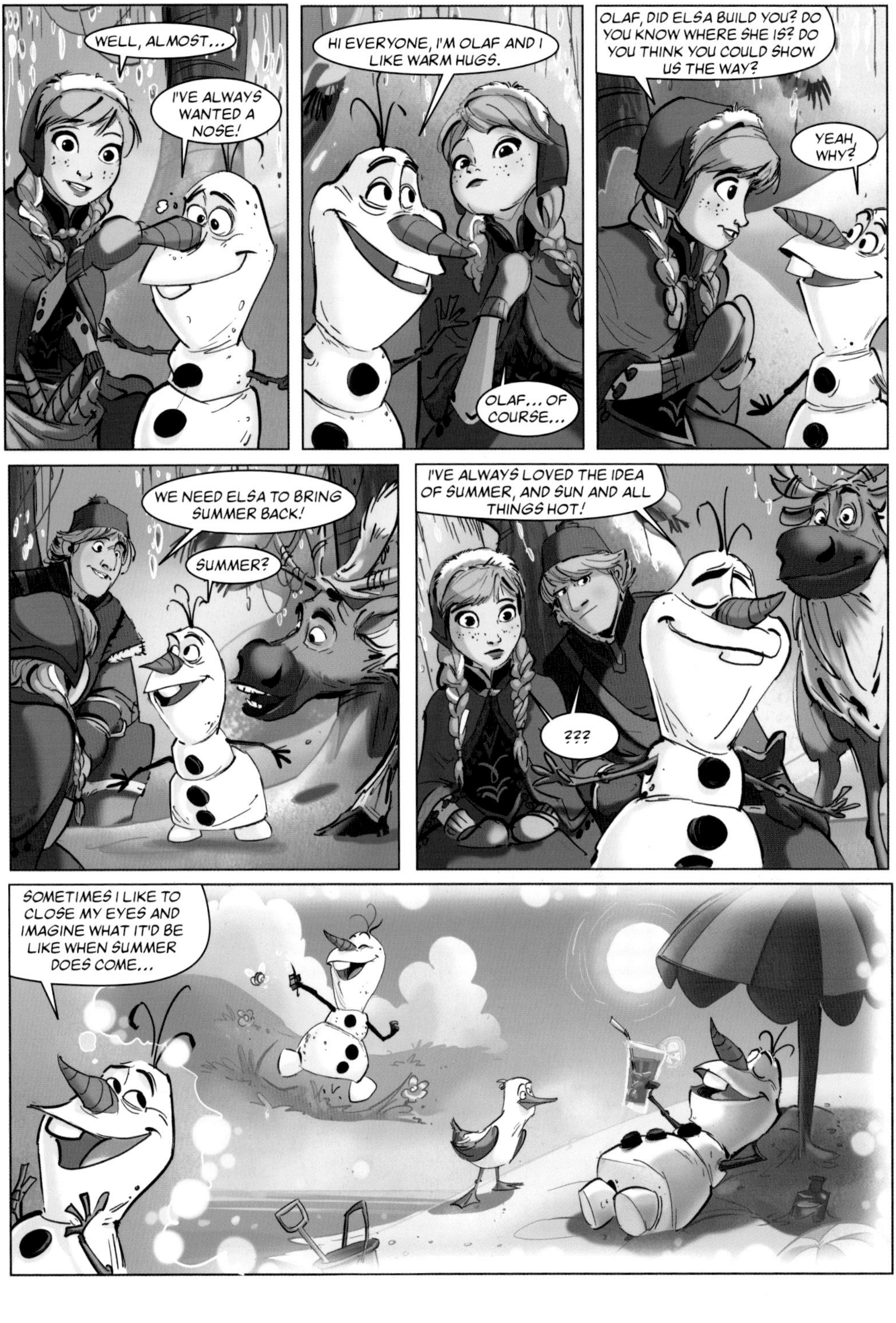
WELL, ALMOST...
I'VE ALWAYS WANTED A NOSE!
HI EVERYONE, I'M OLAF AND I LIKE WARM HUGS.
OLAF... OF COURSE...
OLAF, DID ELSA BUILD YOU? DO YOU KNOW WHERE SHE IS? DO YOU THINK YOU COULD SHOW US THE WAY?
YEAH, WHY?
WE NEED ELSA TO BRING SUMMER BACK!
SUMMER?
I'VE ALWAYS LOVED THE IDEA OF SUMMER, AND SUN AND ALL THINGS HOT!
???
SOMETIMES I LIKE TO CLOSE MY EYES AND IMAGINE WHAT IT'D BE LIKE WHEN SUMMER DOES COME...

SO, COME ON! LET'S GO BRING SUMMER BACK!

WHILE THE FOUR OF THEM START THEIR WALK TOWARDS ELSA'S PALACE...

...ANNA'S HORSE REACHES ARENDELLE!

PRINCESS ANNA IS IN TROUBLE... I NEED VOLUNTEERS TO GO WITH ME TO FIND HER!

I VOLUNTEER TWO MEN, M'LORD!

SHOULD YOU ENCOUNTER THE QUEEN, BE PREPARED TO PUT AN END TO THIS WINTER. DO YOU UNDERSTAND?

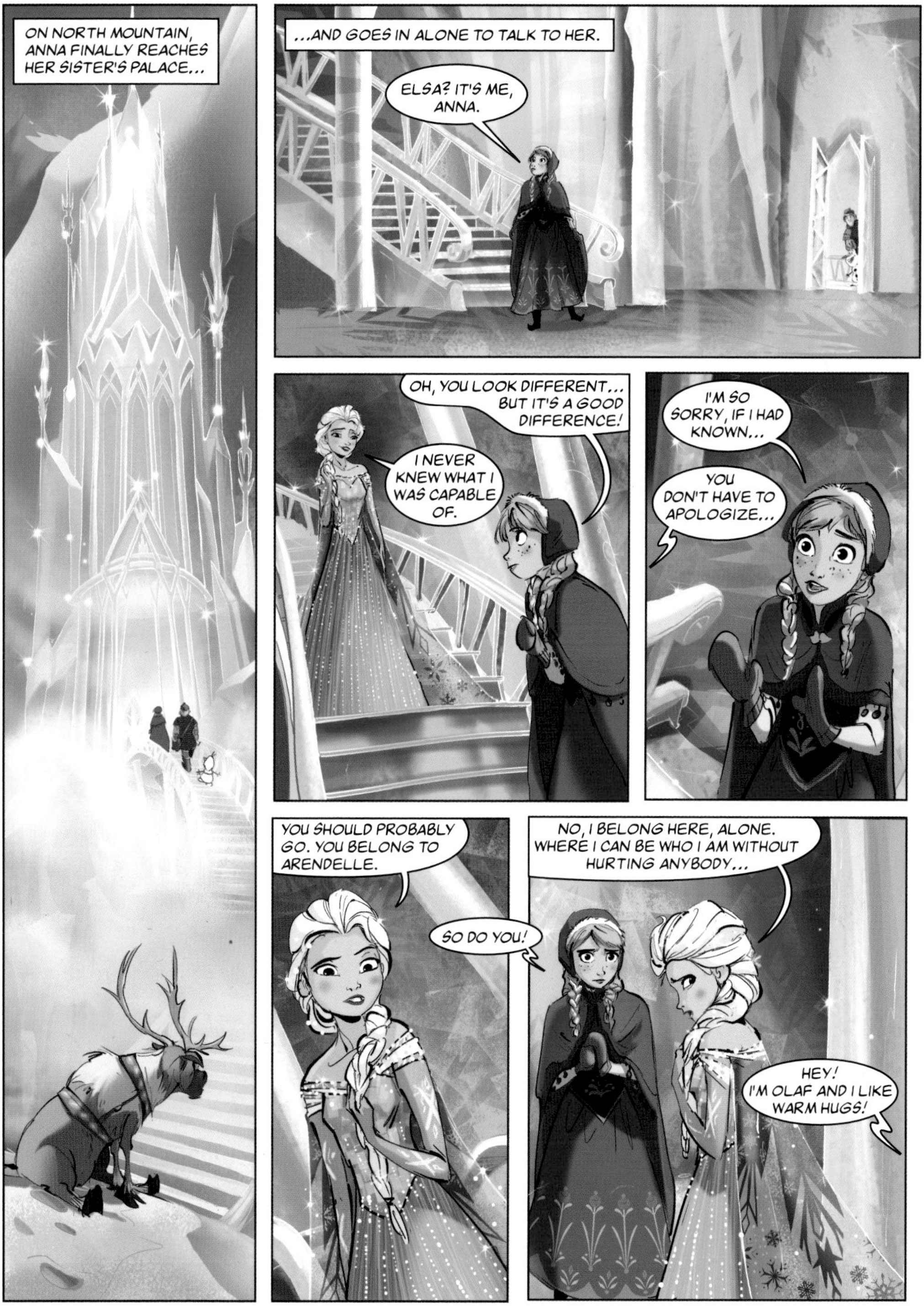
ON NORTH MOUNTAIN, ANNA FINALLY REACHES HER SISTER'S PALACE...
...AND GOES IN ALONE TO TALK TO HER.
ELSA? IT'S ME, ANNA.
OH, YOU LOOK DIFFERENT... BUT IT'S A GOOD DIFFERENCE!
I NEVER KNEW WHAT I WAS CAPABLE OF.
I'M SO SORRY, IF I HAD KNOWN...
YOU DON'T HAVE TO APOLOGIZE...
YOU SHOULD PROBABLY GO. YOU BELONG TO ARENDELLE.
SO DO YOU!
NO, I BELONG HERE, ALONE. WHERE I CAN BE WHO I AM WITHOUT HURTING ANYBODY...
HEY! I'M OLAF AND I LIKE WARM HUGS!

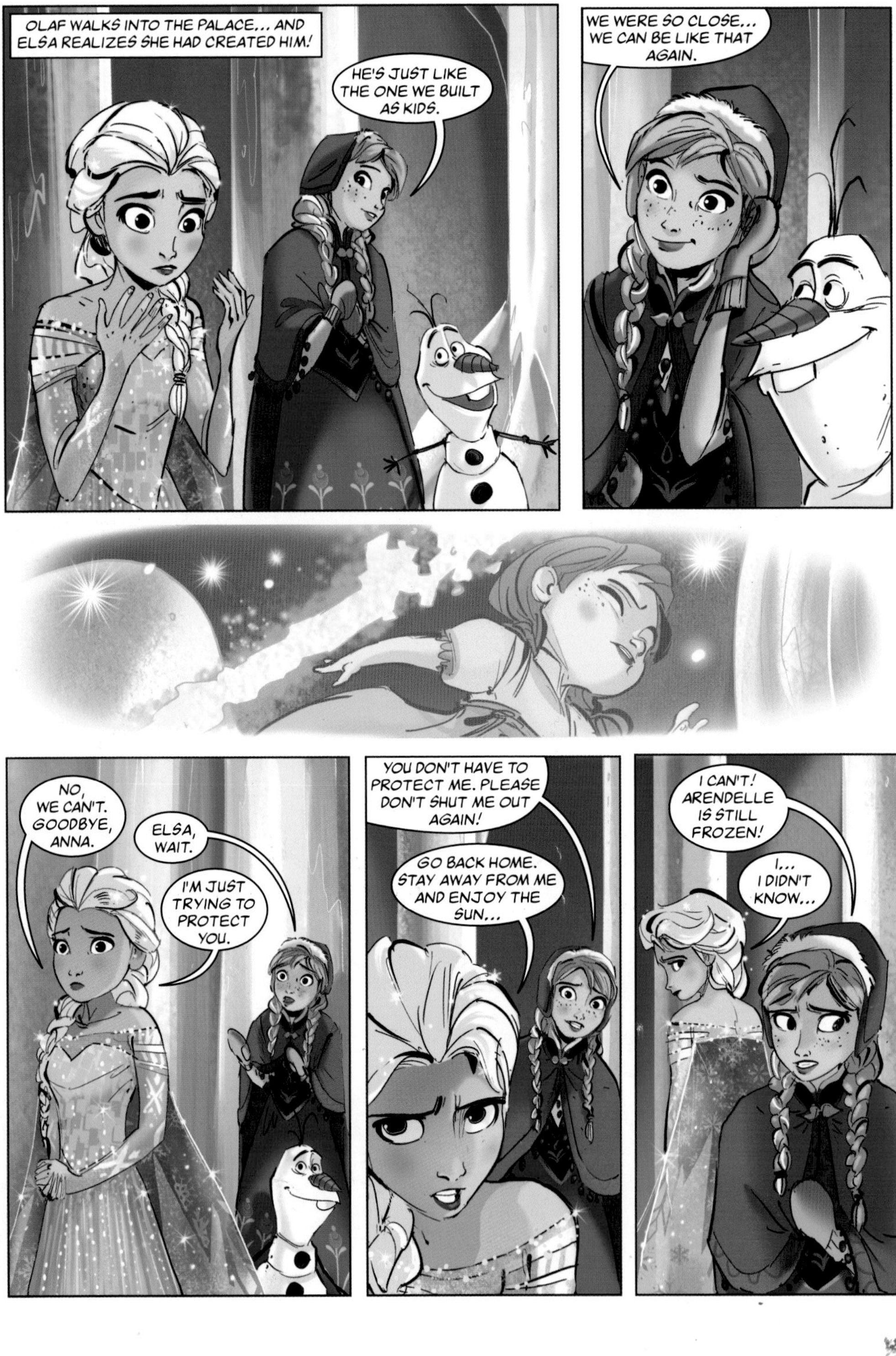

OLAF WALKS INTO THE PALACE... AND ELSA REALIZES SHE HAD CREATED HIM!
HE'S JUST LIKE THE ONE WE BUILT AS KIDS.
WE WERE SO CLOSE... WE CAN BE LIKE THAT AGAIN.
NO, WE CAN'T. GOODBYE, ANNA.
ELSA, WAIT.
I'M JUST TRYING TO PROTECT YOU.
YOU DON'T HAVE TO PROTECT ME. PLEASE DON'T SHUT ME OUT AGAIN!
GO BACK HOME. STAY AWAY FROM ME AND ENJOY THE SUN...
I CAN'T! ARENDELLE IS STILL FROZEN!
I... I DIDN'T KNOW...

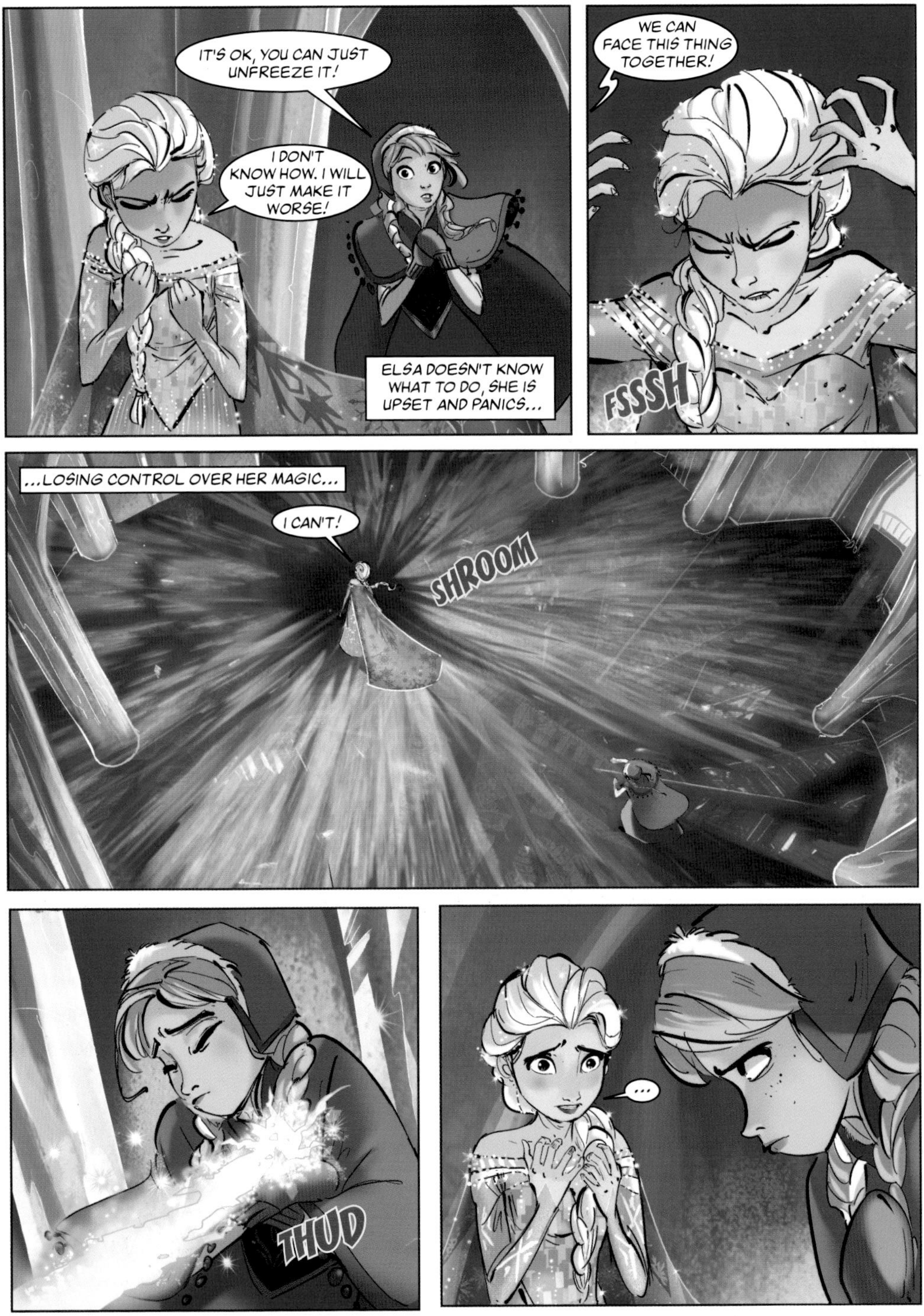
IT'S OK, YOU CAN JUST UNFREEZE IT!
I DON'T KNOW HOW. I WILL JUST MAKE IT WORSE!
ELSA DOESN'T KNOW WHAT TO DO, SHE IS UPSET AND PANICS...
WE CAN FACE THIS THING TOGETHER!
FSSSH
...LOSING CONTROL OVER HER MAGIC...
I CAN'T!
SHROOM
THUD
...

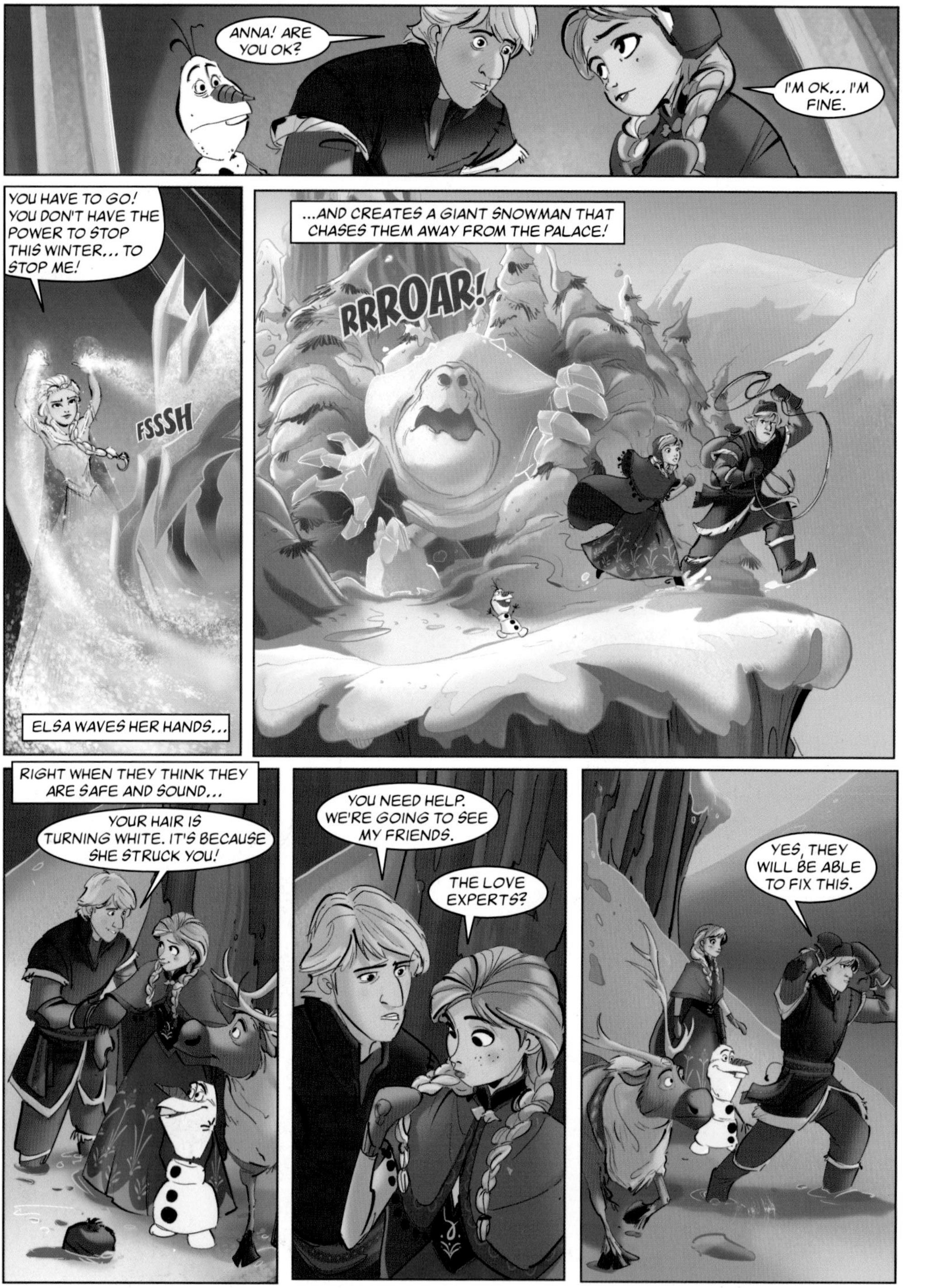
ANNA! ARE YOU OK?
I'M OK... I'M FINE.
YOU HAVE TO GO! YOU DON'T HAVE THE POWER TO STOP THIS WINTER... TO STOP ME!
FSSSH
ELSA WAVES HER HANDS...
...AND CREATES A GIANT SNOWMAN THAT CHASES THEM AWAY FROM THE PALACE!
RRROAR!
RIGHT WHEN THEY THINK THEY ARE SAFE AND SOUND...
YOUR HAIR IS TURNING WHITE. IT'S BECAUSE SHE STRUCK YOU!
YOU NEED HELP. WE'RE GOING TO SEE MY FRIENDS.
THE LOVE EXPERTS?
YES, THEY WILL BE ABLE TO FIX THIS.

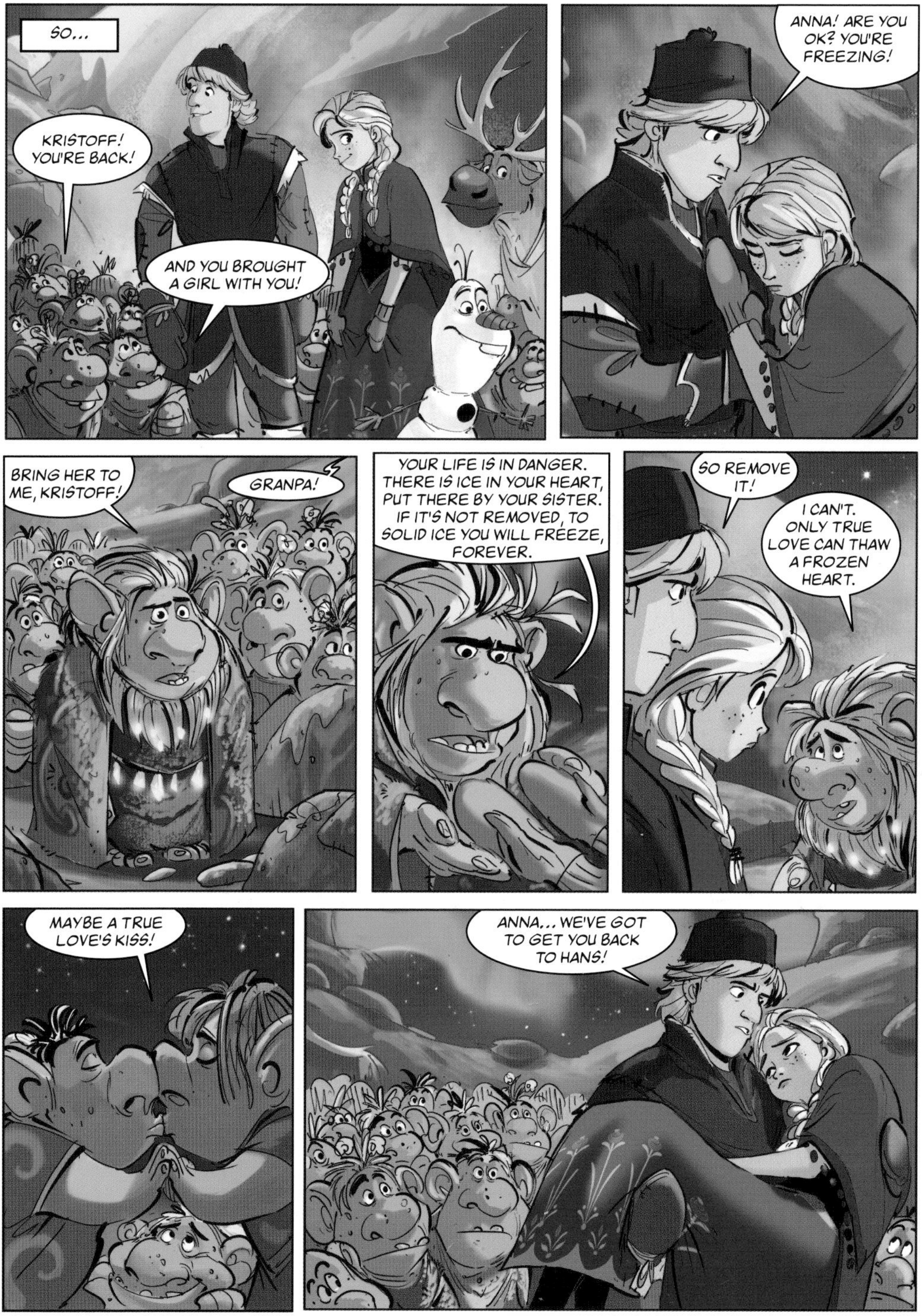
SO...
KRISTOFF! YOU'RE BACK!
AND YOU BROUGHT A GIRL WITH YOU!
ANNA! ARE YOU OK? YOU'RE FREEZING!
BRING HER TO ME, KRISTOFF!
GRANPA!
YOUR LIFE IS IN DANGER. THERE IS ICE IN YOUR HEART, PUT THERE BY YOUR SISTER. IF IT'S NOT REMOVED, TO SOLID ICE YOU WILL FREEZE, FOREVER.
SO REMOVE IT!
I CAN'T. ONLY TRUE LOVE CAN THAW A FROZEN HEART.
MAYBE A TRUE LOVE'S KISS!
ANNA... WE'VE GOT TO GET YOU BACK TO HANS!

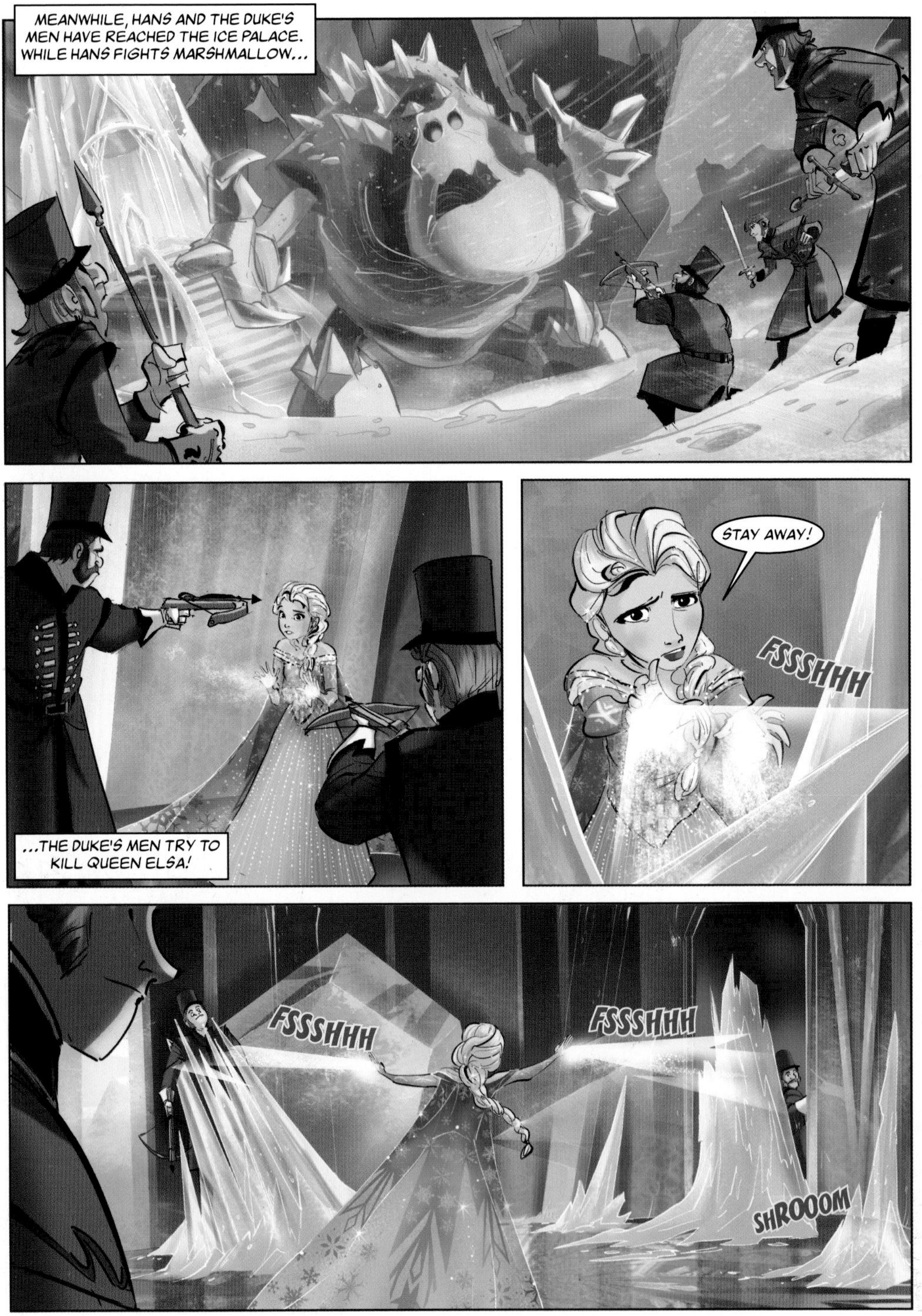
MEANWHILE, HANS AND THE DUKE'S MEN HAVE REACHED THE ICE PALACE. WHILE HANS FIGHTS MARSHMALLOW...
...THE DUKE'S MEN TRY TO KILL QUEEN ELSA!
STAY AWAY!
FSSSHHH
FSSSHHH
FSSSHHH
SHROOOM

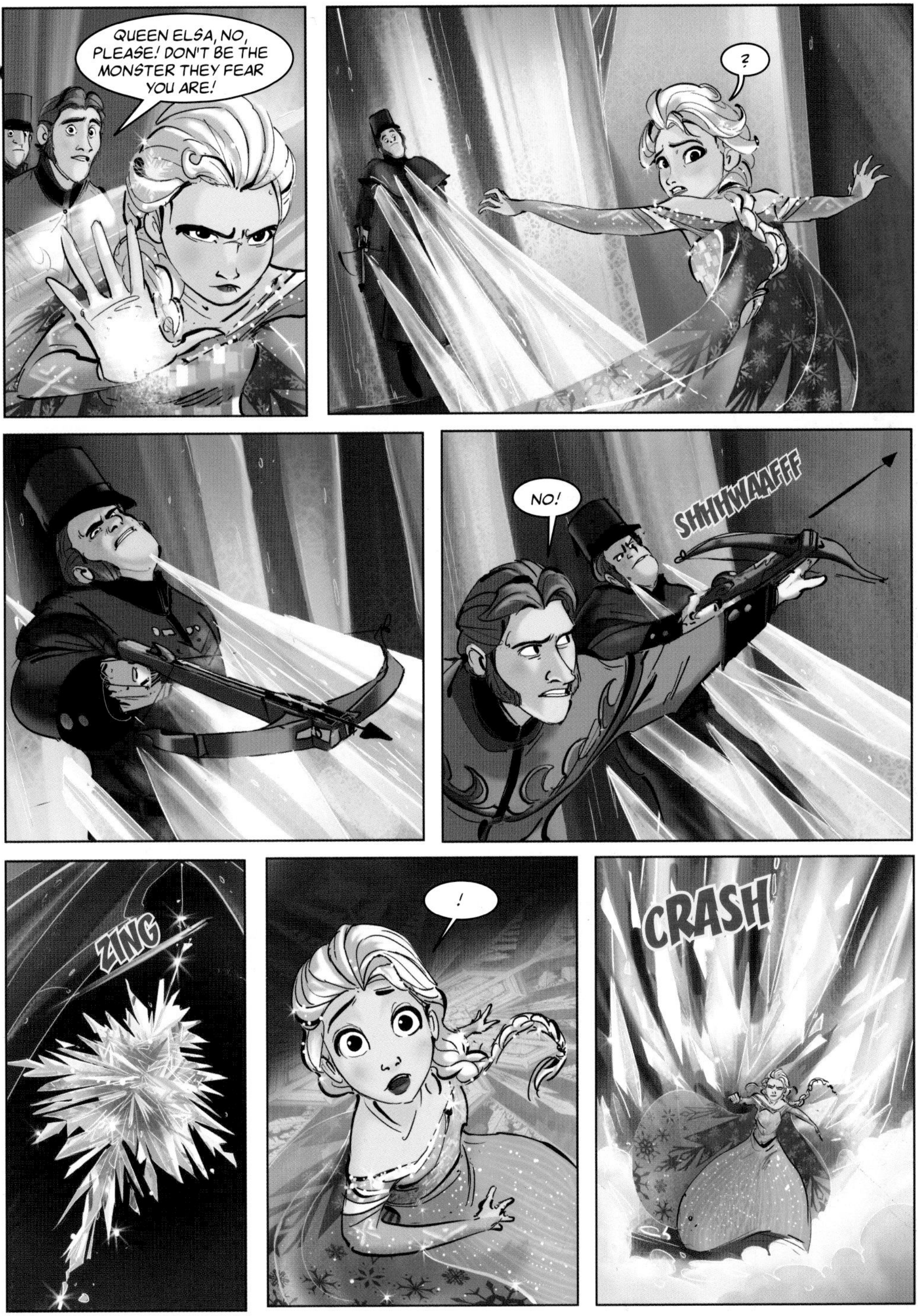
QUEEN ELSA, NO, PLEASE! DON'T BE THE MONSTER THEY FEAR YOU ARE!
?
NO!
SHHHWAAFFF
ZING
!
CRASH

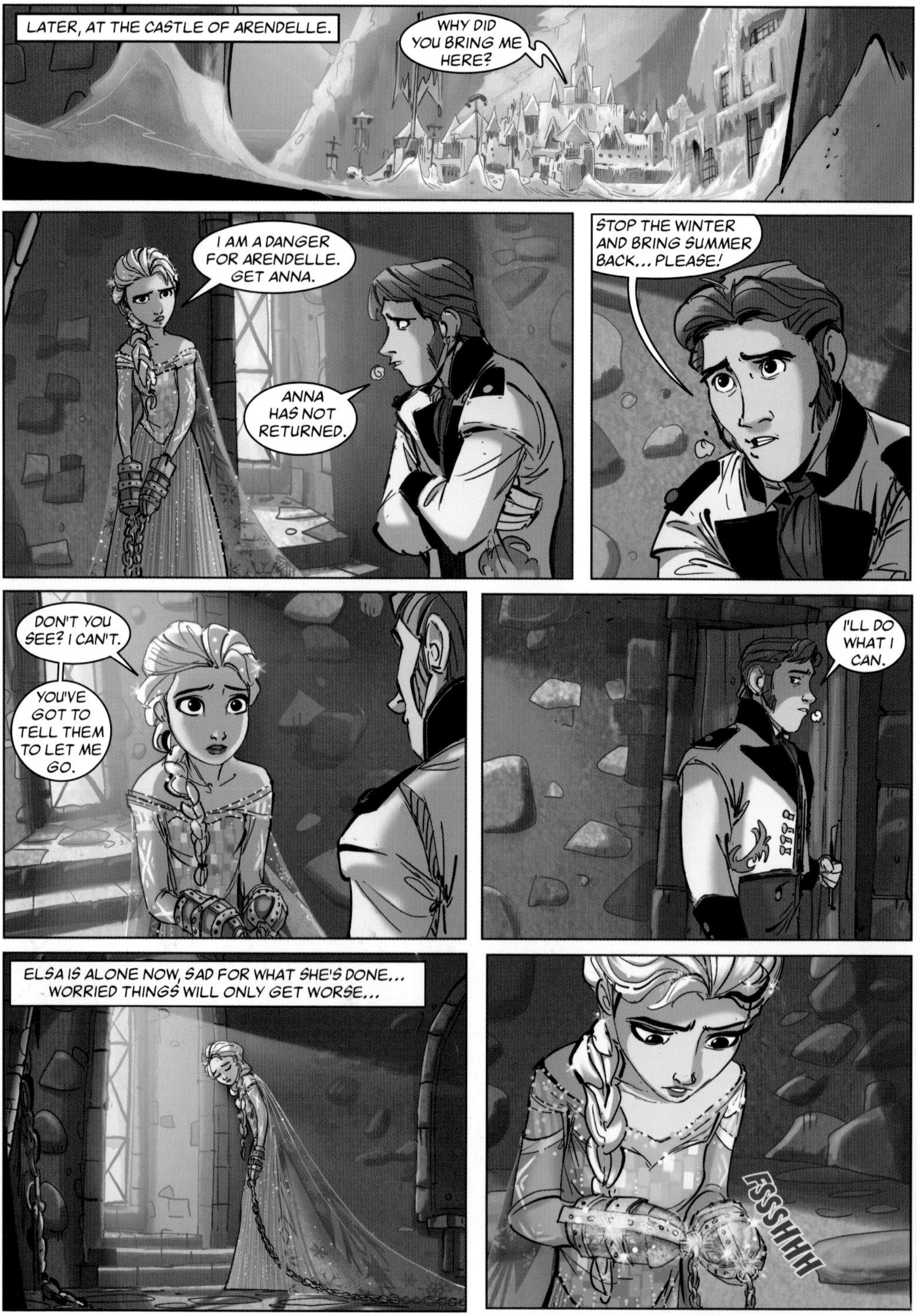
LATER, AT THE CASTLE OF ARENDELLE.
WHY DID YOU BRING ME HERE?
I AM A DANGER FOR ARENDELLE. GET ANNA.
ANNA HAS NOT RETURNED.
STOP THE WINTER AND BRING SUMMER BACK... PLEASE!
DON'T YOU SEE? I CAN'T.
YOU'VE GOT TO TELL THEM TO LET ME GO.
I'LL DO WHAT I CAN.
ELSA IS ALONE NOW, SAD FOR WHAT SHE'S DONE...
WORRIED THINGS WILL ONLY GET WORSE...
FSSSHHH

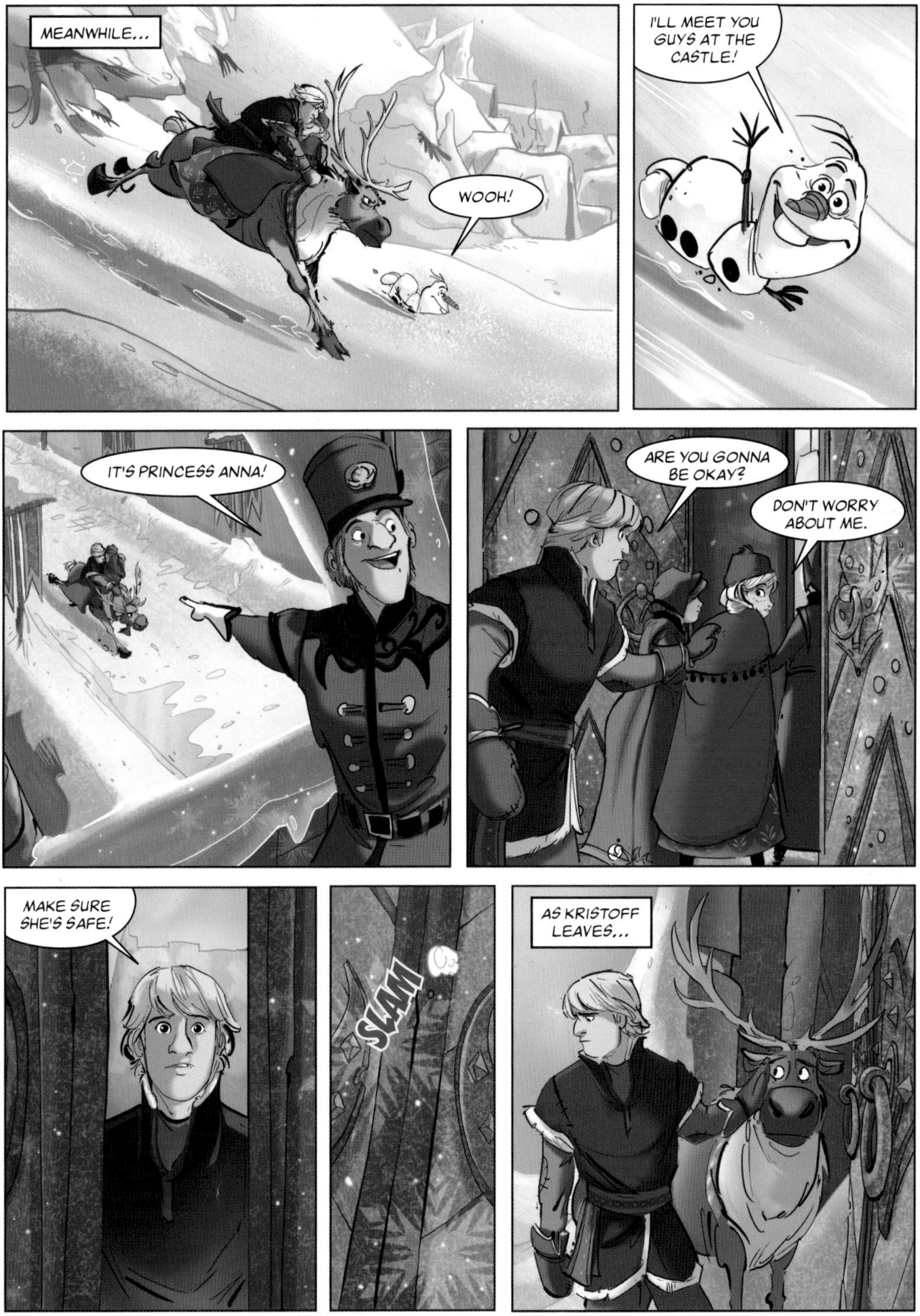
MEANWHILE...
WOOH!
I'LL MEET YOU GUYS AT THE CASTLE!
IT'S PRINCESS ANNA!
ARE YOU GONNA BE OKAY?
DON'T WORRY ABOUT ME.
MAKE SURE SHE'S SAFE!
SLAM
AS KRISTOFF LEAVES...

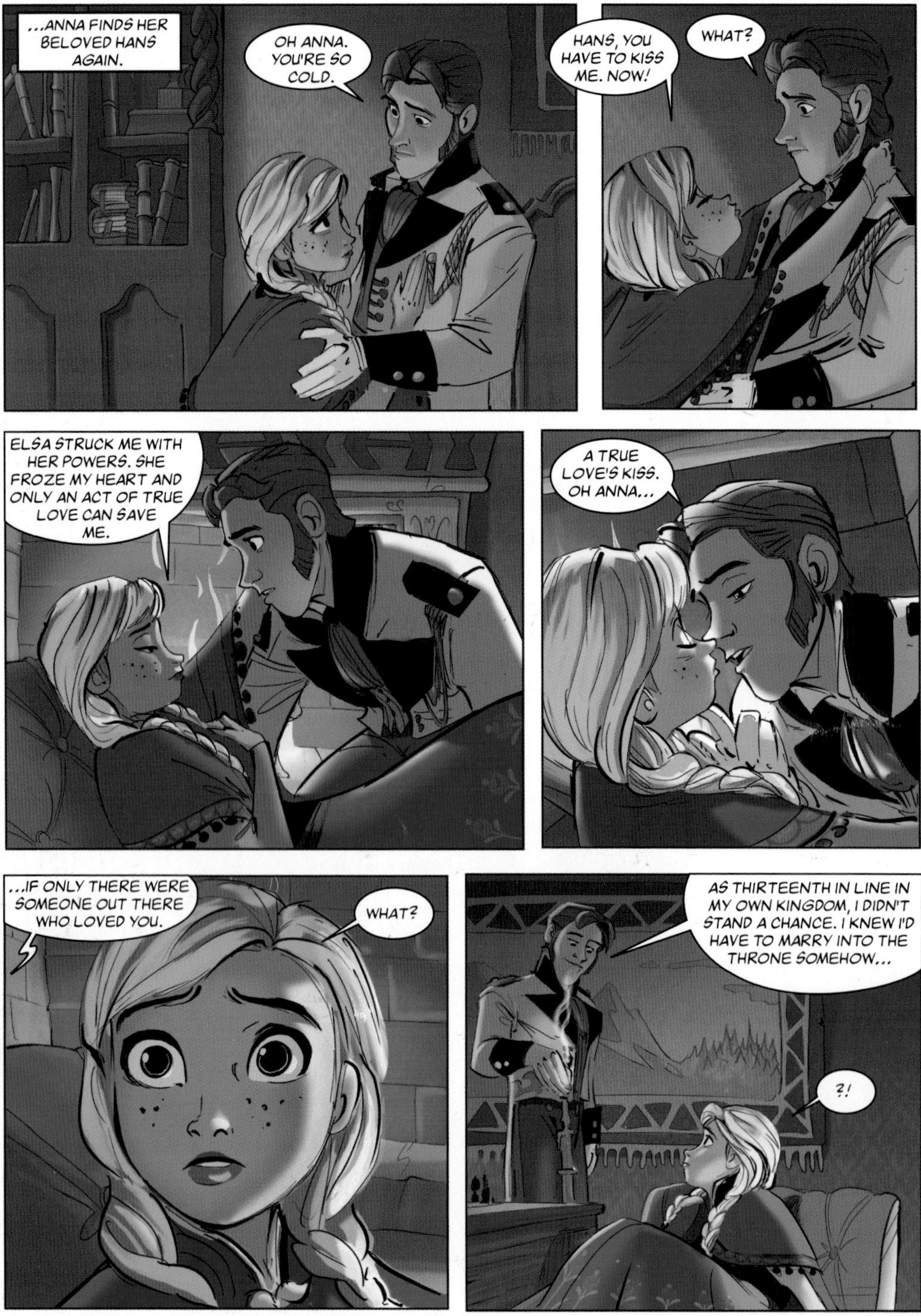
...ANNA FINDS HER BELOVED HANS AGAIN.
OH ANNA. YOU'RE SO COLD.
HANS, YOU HAVE TO KISS ME. NOW!
WHAT?
ELSA STRUCK ME WITH HER POWERS. SHE FROZE MY HEART AND ONLY AN ACT OF TRUE LOVE CAN SAVE ME.
A TRUE LOVE'S KISS. OH ANNA...
...IF ONLY THERE WERE SOMEONE OUT THERE WHO LOVED YOU.
WHAT?
AS THIRTEENTH IN LINE IN MY OWN KINGDOM, I DIDN'T STAND A CHANCE. I KNEW I'D HAVE TO MARRY INTO THE THRONE SOMEHOW...
?!

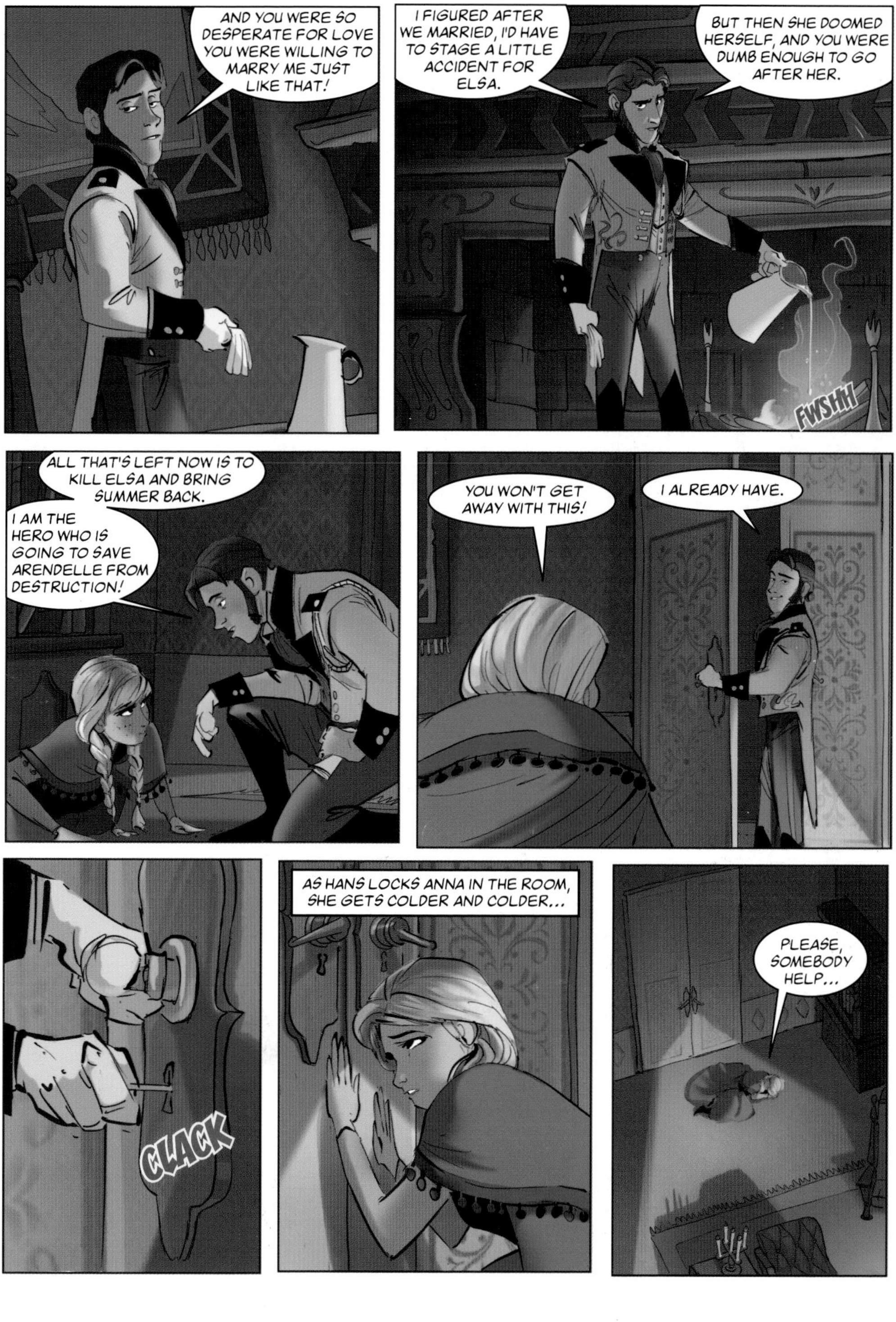
AND YOU WERE SO DESPERATE FOR LOVE YOU WERE WILLING TO MARRY ME JUST LIKE THAT!
I FIGURED AFTER WE MARRIED, I'D HAVE TO STAGE A LITTLE ACCIDENT FOR ELSA.
BUT THEN SHE DOOMED HERSELF, AND YOU WERE DUMB ENOUGH TO GO AFTER HER.
FWSHH
ALL THAT'S LEFT NOW IS TO KILL ELSA AND BRING SUMMER BACK.
I AM THE HERO WHO IS GOING TO SAVE ARENDELLE FROM DESTRUCTION!
YOU WON'T GET AWAY WITH THIS!
I ALREADY HAVE.
CLACK
AS HANS LOCKS ANNA IN THE ROOM, SHE GETS COLDER AND COLDER...
PLEASE, SOMEBODY HELP...

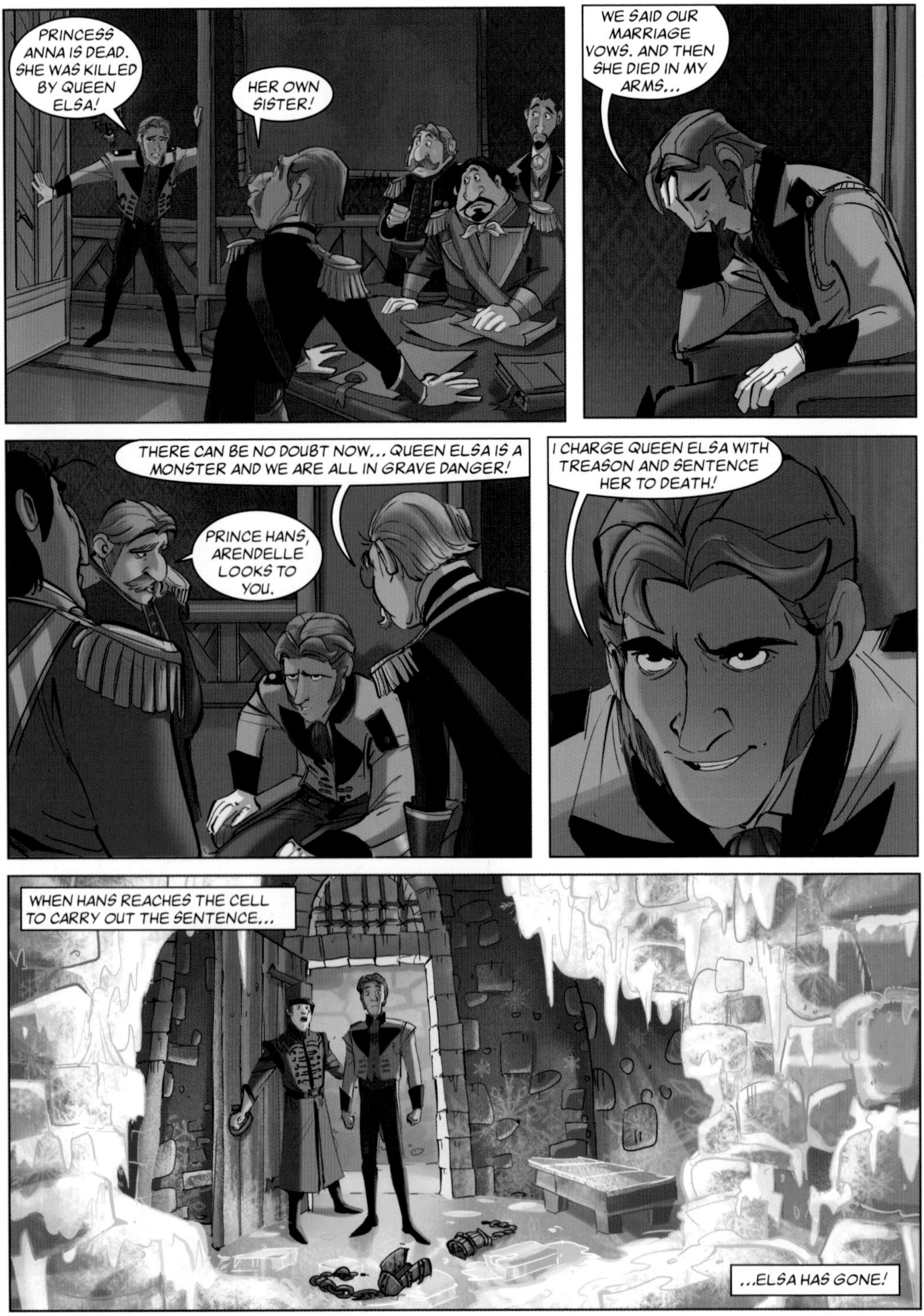
PRINCESS ANNA IS DEAD. SHE WAS KILLED BY QUEEN ELSA!
HER OWN SISTER!
WE SAID OUR MARRIAGE VOWS. AND THEN SHE DIED IN MY ARMS...
THERE CAN BE NO DOUBT NOW... QUEEN ELSA IS A MONSTER AND WE ARE ALL IN GRAVE DANGER!
PRINCE HANS, ARENDELLE LOOKS TO YOU.
I CHARGE QUEEN ELSA WITH TREASON AND SENTENCE HER TO DEATH!
WHEN HANS REACHES THE CELL TO CARRY OUT THE SENTENCE...
...ELSA HAS GONE!

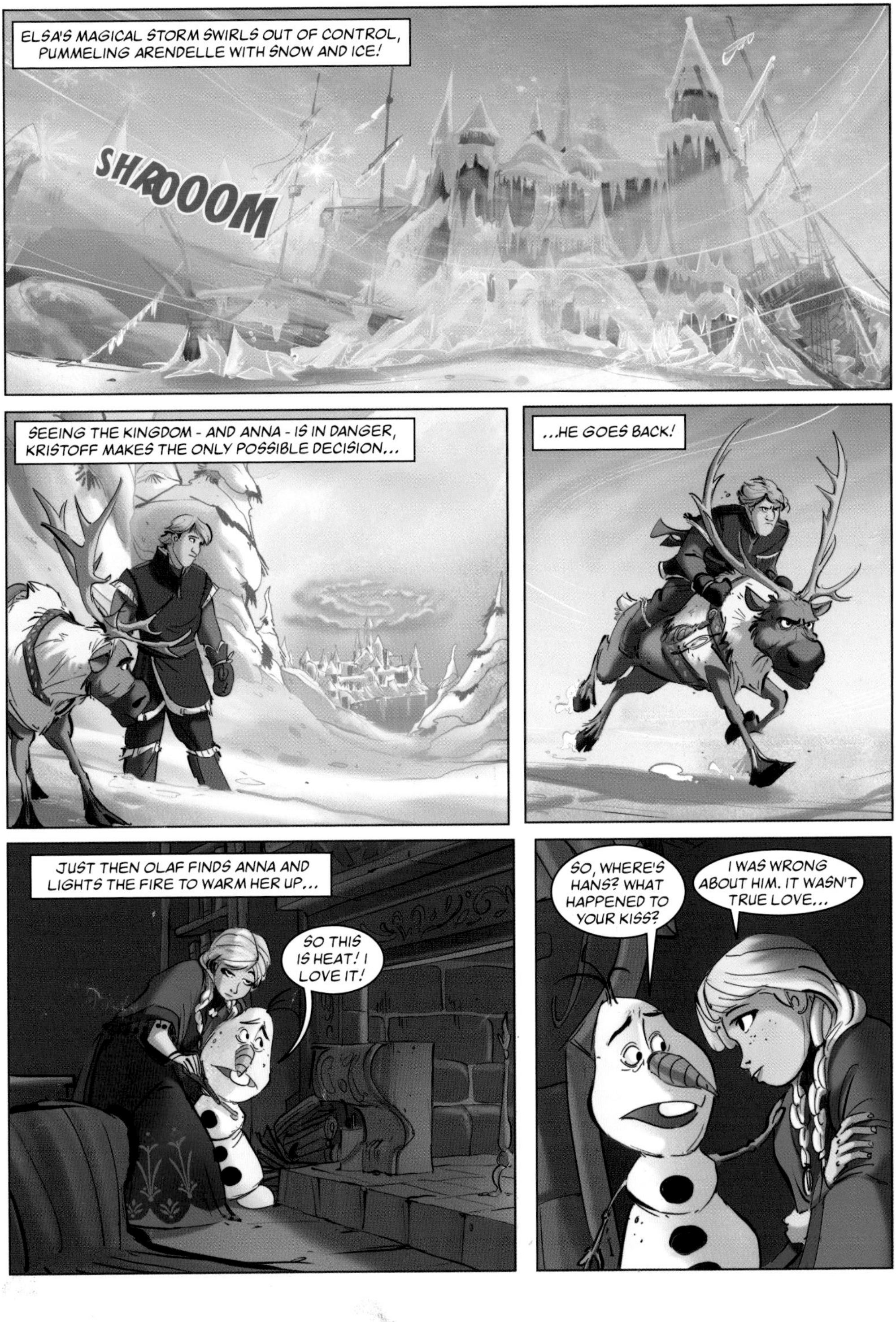
ELSA'S MAGICAL STORM SWIRLS OUT OF CONTROL, PUMMELING ARENDELLE WITH SNOW AND ICE!
SHROOOM
SEEING THE KINGDOM - AND ANNA - IS IN DANGER, KRISTOFF MAKES THE ONLY POSSIBLE DECISION...
...HE GOES BACK!
JUST THEN OLAF FINDS ANNA AND LIGHTS THE FIRE TO WARM HER UP...
SO THIS IS HEAT! I LOVE IT!
SO, WHERE'S HANS? WHAT HAPPENED TO YOUR KISS?
I WAS WRONG ABOUT HIM. IT WASN'T TRUE LOVE...

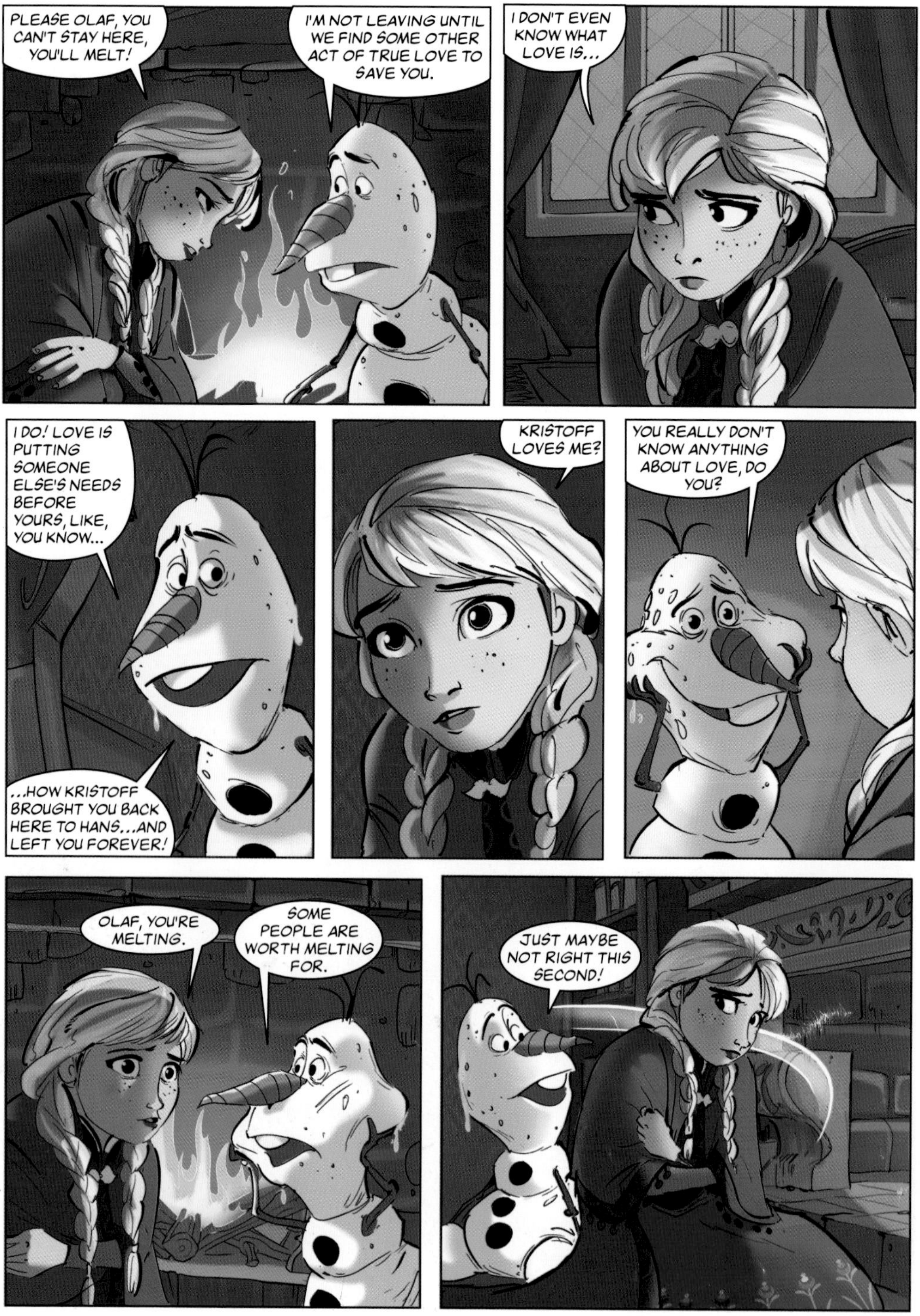
PLEASE OLAF, YOU CAN'T STAY HERE, YOU'LL MELT!
I'M NOT LEAVING UNTIL WE FIND SOME OTHER ACT OF TRUE LOVE TO SAVE YOU.
I DON'T EVEN KNOW WHAT LOVE IS...
I DO! LOVE IS PUTTING SOMEONE ELSE'S NEEDS BEFORE YOURS, LIKE, YOU KNOW...
...HOW KRISTOFF BROUGHT YOU BACK HERE TO HANS...AND LEFT YOU FOREVER!
KRISTOFF LOVES ME?
YOU REALLY DON'T KNOW ANYTHING ABOUT LOVE, DO YOU?
OLAF, YOU'RE MELTING.
SOME PEOPLE ARE WORTH MELTING FOR.
JUST MAYBE NOT RIGHT THIS SECOND!

SUDDENLY A WINDOW BLOWS OPEN AND WHEN OLAF RUNS TO CLOSE IT...

SWOOSH

BAM

?

CRACK

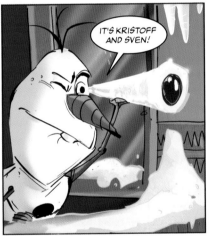

IT'S KRISTOFF AND SVEN!

THEY'RE COMING BACK THIS WAY!

I GUESS I WAS WRONG. I GUESS KRISTOFF DOESN'T LOVE YOU ENOUGH TO LEAVE YOU BEHIND!

HELP ME UP, OLAF. PLEASE. I NEED TO GET TO KRISTOFF.

WHY?

OH, I KNOW WHY. THERE'S YOUR TRUE LOVE, RIGHT THERE...

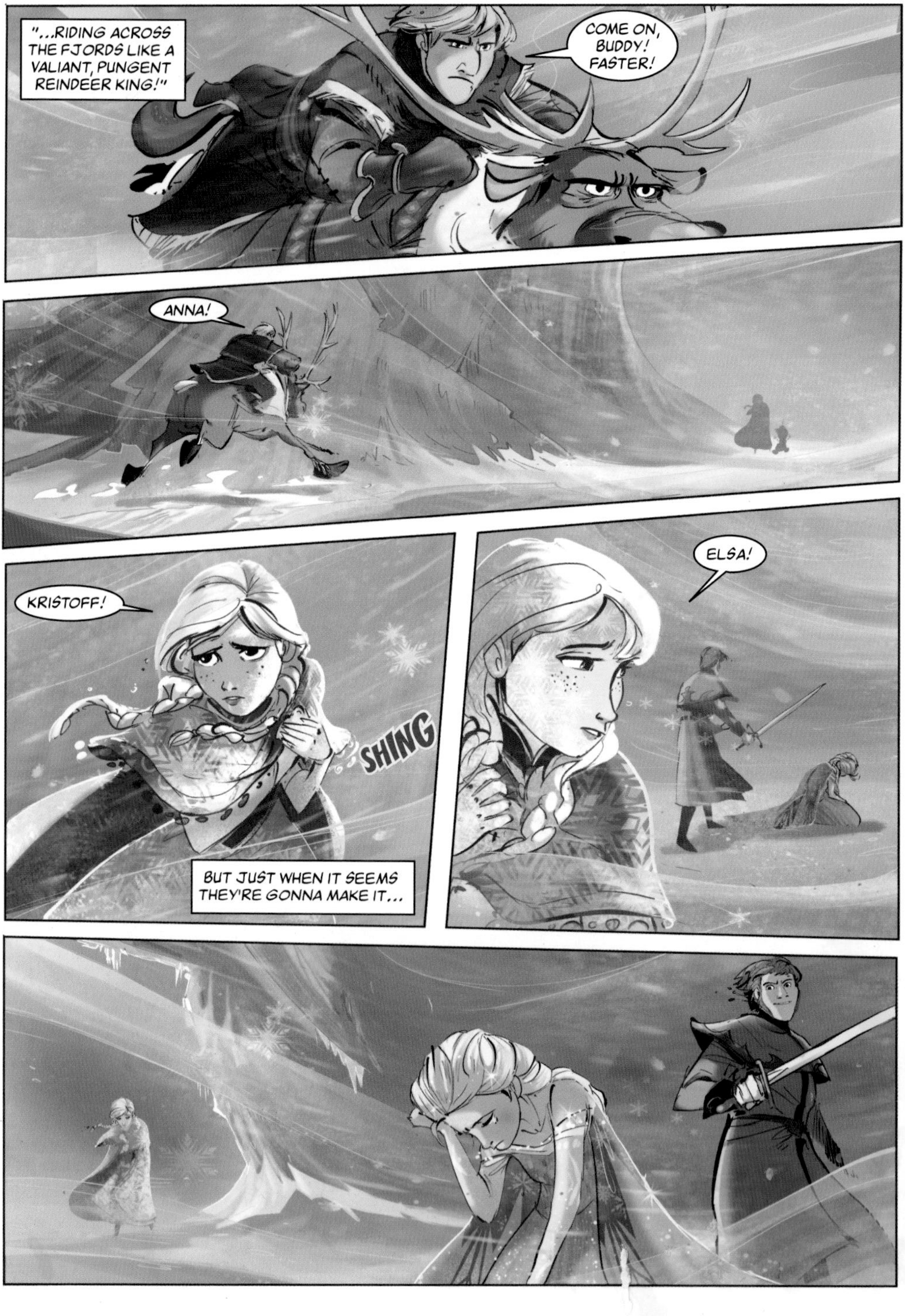
"...RIDING ACROSS THE FJORDS LIKE A VALIANT, PUNGENT REINDEER KING!"
COME ON, BUDDY! FASTER!
ANNA!
KRISTOFF!
SHING
BUT JUST WHEN IT SEEMS THEY'RE GONNA MAKE IT...
ELSA!

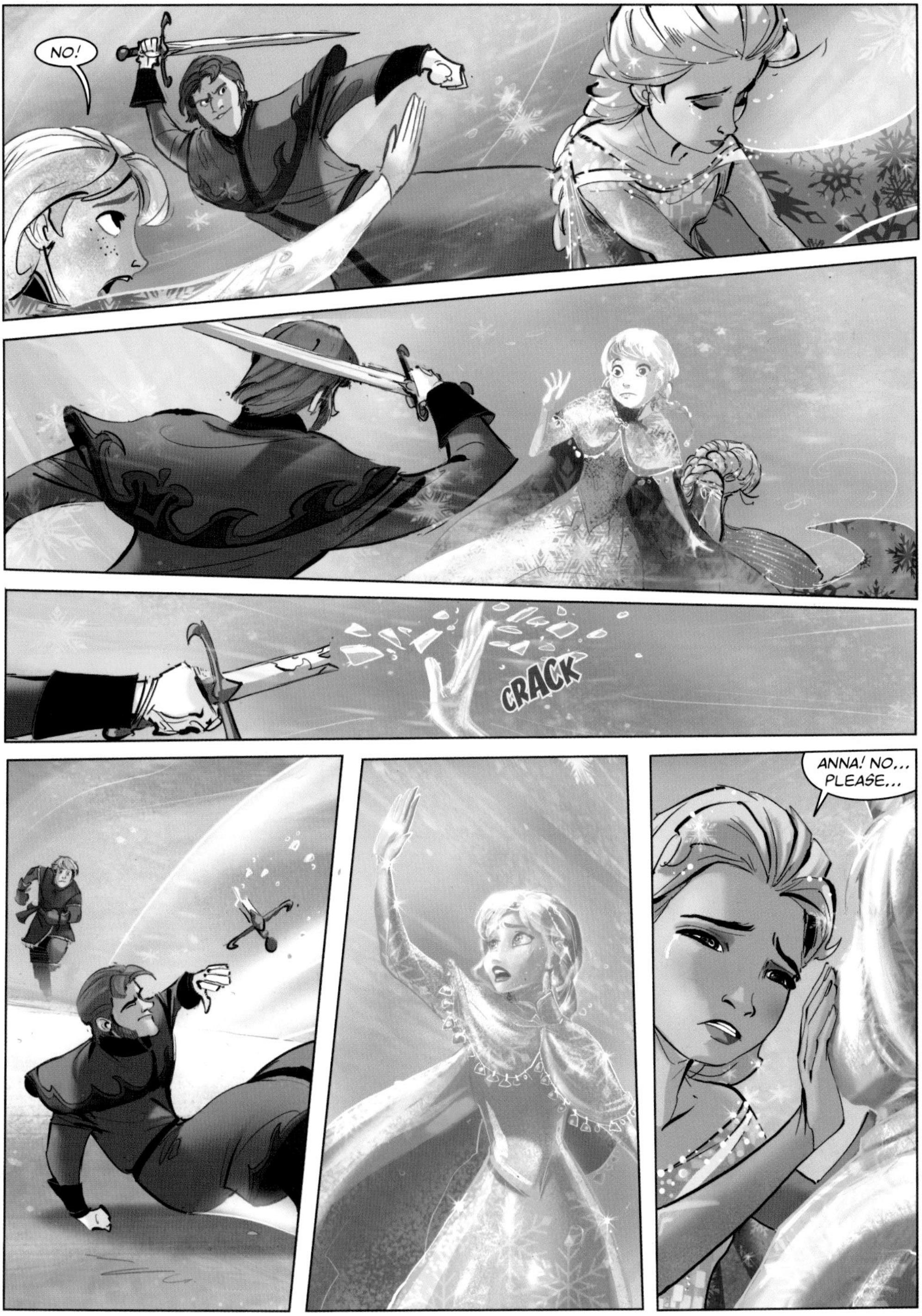
NO!
CRACK
ANNA! NO... PLEASE...

IN THE SILENCE OF THE FJORD, EVERYONE LOOKS AT ANNA, FROZEN SOLID...

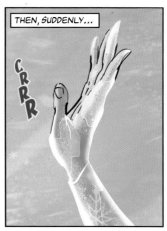

THEN, SUDDENLY...

CRRR

...THE ICE MELTS...

CRRR

...AND ANNA COMES BACK TO LIFE AGAIN!

YOU SACRIFICED YOURSELF FOR ME?

I LOVE YOU...

AN ACT OF TRUE LOVE WILL THAW A FROZEN HEART!

LOVE WILL THAW... LOVE, OF COURSE!

FWIIIS

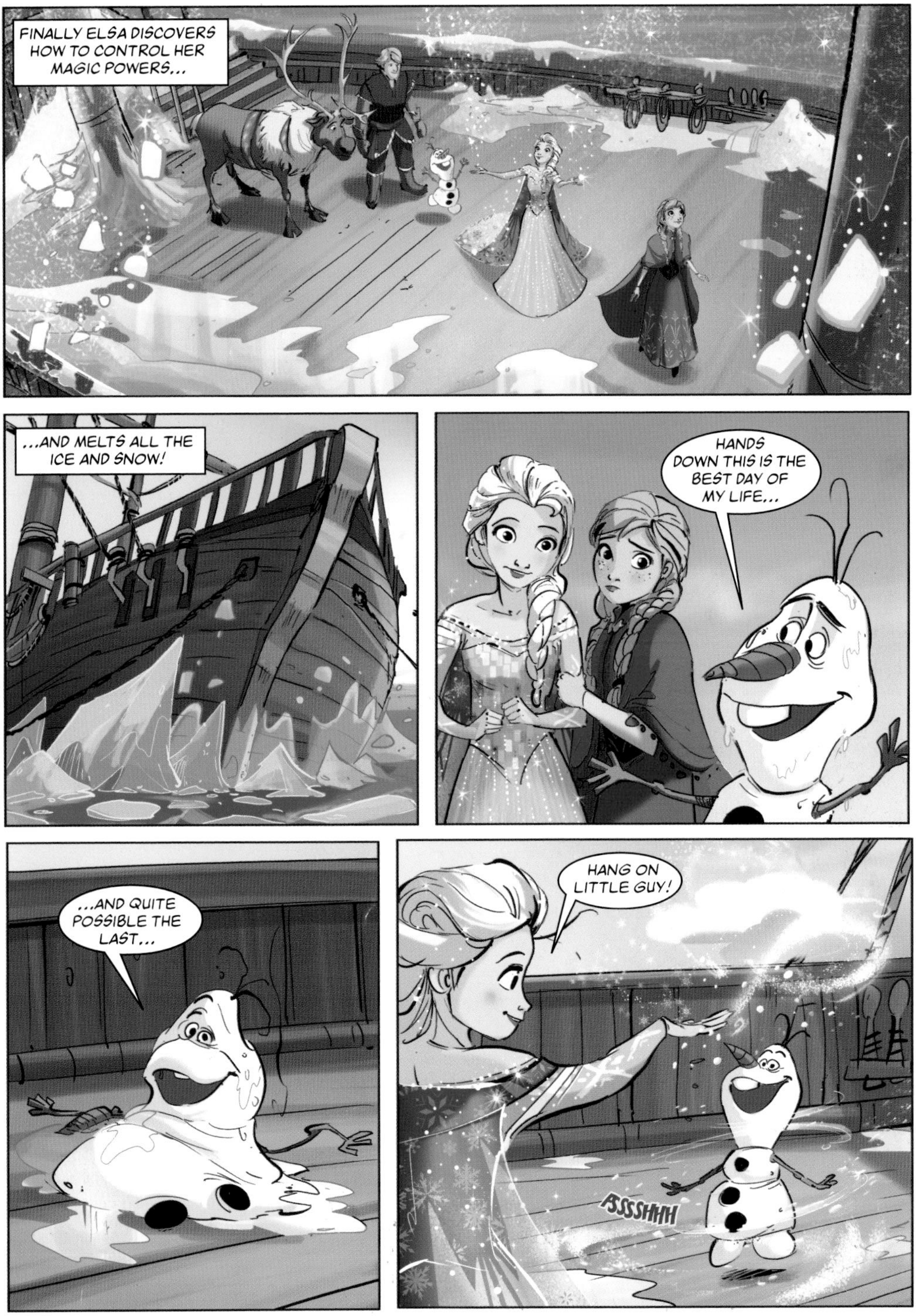
FINALLY ELSA DISCOVERS HOW TO CONTROL HER MAGIC POWERS...
...AND MELTS ALL THE ICE AND SNOW!
HANDS DOWN THIS IS THE BEST DAY OF MY LIFE...
...AND QUITE POSSIBLE THE LAST...
HANG ON LITTLE GUY!
PSSSSHHH

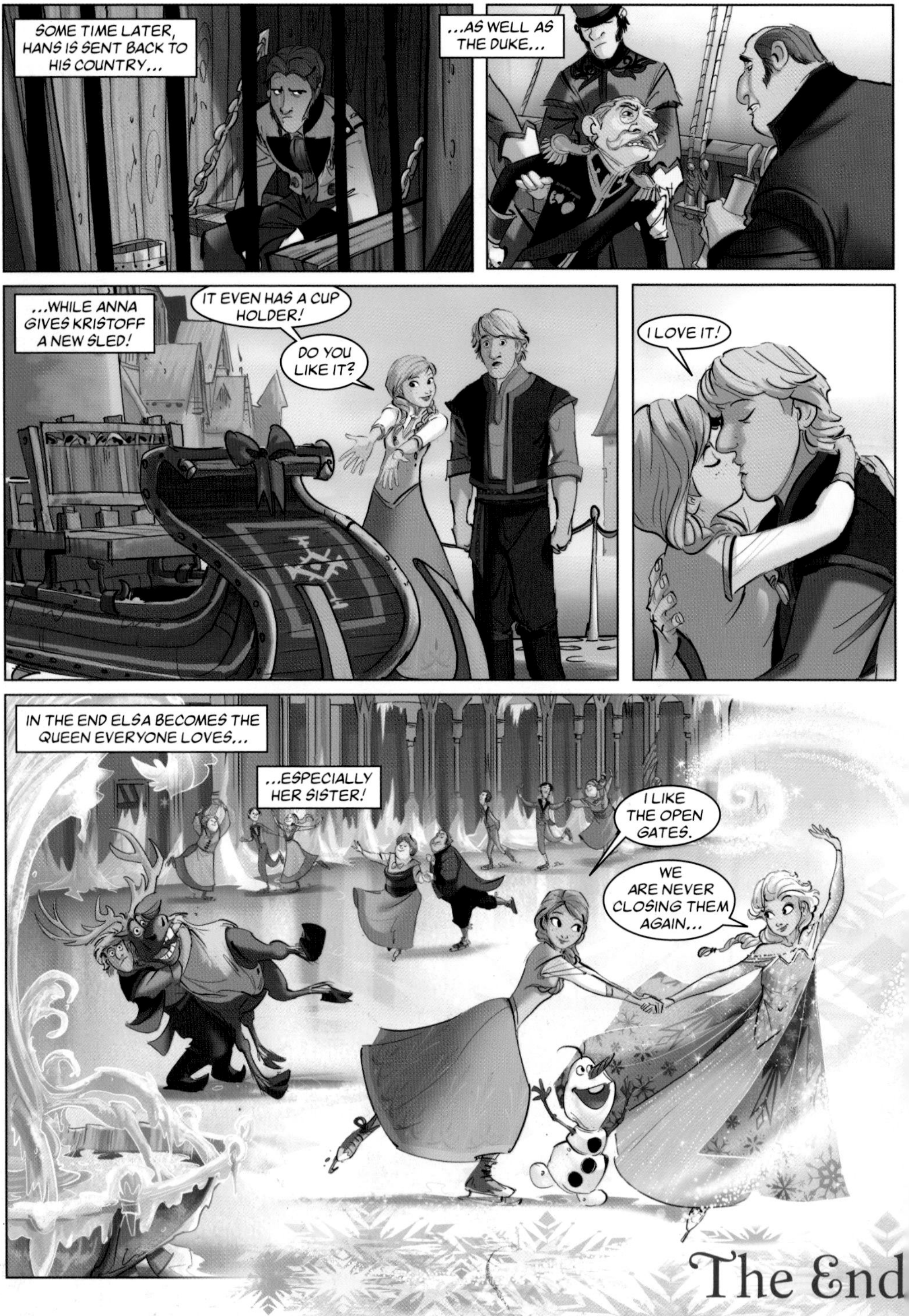
SOME TIME LATER, HANS IS SENT BACK TO HIS COUNTRY...
...AS WELL AS THE DUKE...
...WHILE ANNA GIVES KRISTOFF A NEW SLED!
IT EVEN HAS A CUP HOLDER!
DO YOU LIKE IT?
I LOVE IT!
IN THE END ELSA BECOMES THE QUEEN EVERYONE LOVES...
...ESPECIALLY HER SISTER!
I LIKE THE OPEN GATES.
WE ARE NEVER CLOSING THEM AGAIN...
The End

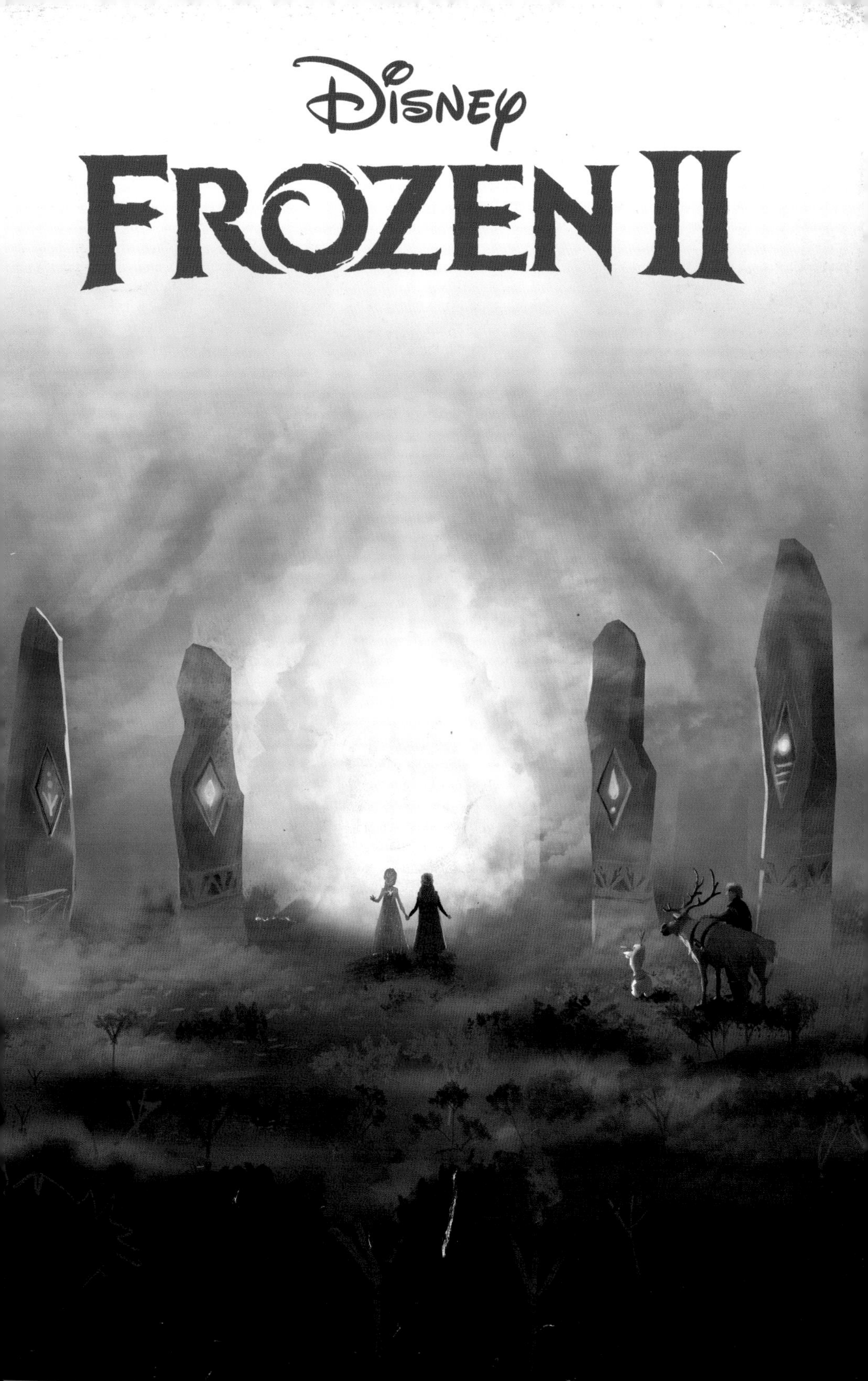
Disney
FROZEN II

ARENDELLE AND THE

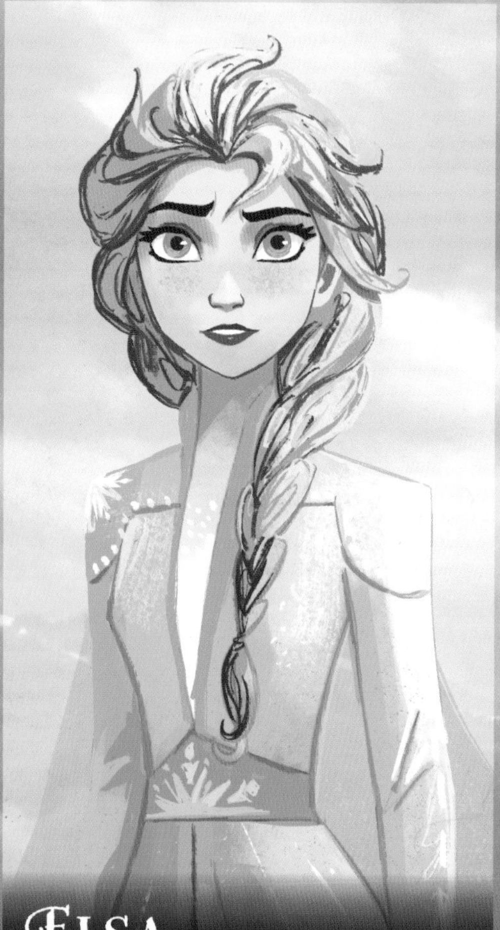

ELSA

Elsa, the Queen of Arendelle, works hard to keep her kingdom safe. She is grateful to be accepted by the people of Arendelle, but she still wonders why she was born with the ability to create ice and snow—powers which have grown and evolved over the years. When she begins hearing a strange voice calling her North, she senses that change is coming. After they are mysteriously pushed out of their kingdom, Elsa and her friends embark on a quest to an uncharted land in search of answers.

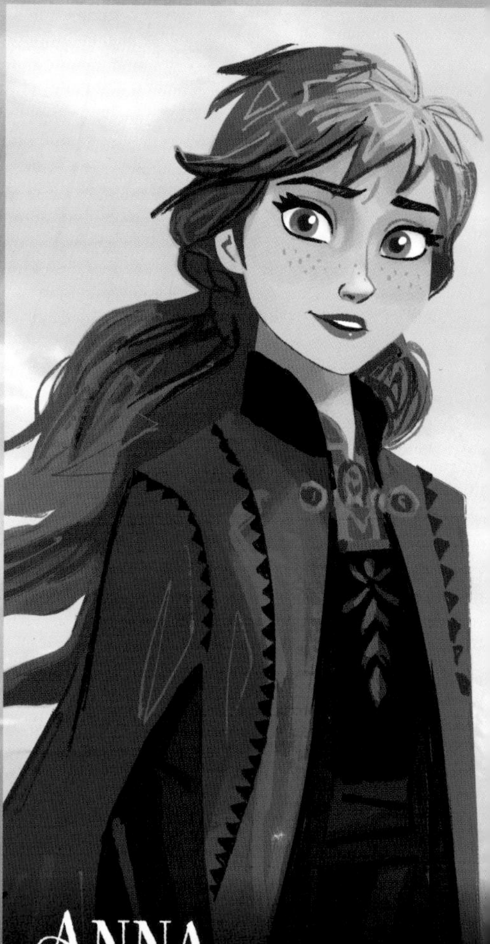

ANNA

Free spirited, courageous, and loving, Anna sees the good and the wonder in everything. She chooses to have an optimistic outlook on life and is always ready to take on an adventure, especially if it means helping someone she loves. Now that she has reconnected with her sister, Elsa, Anna is determined not to lose her again.

ENCHANTED FOREST

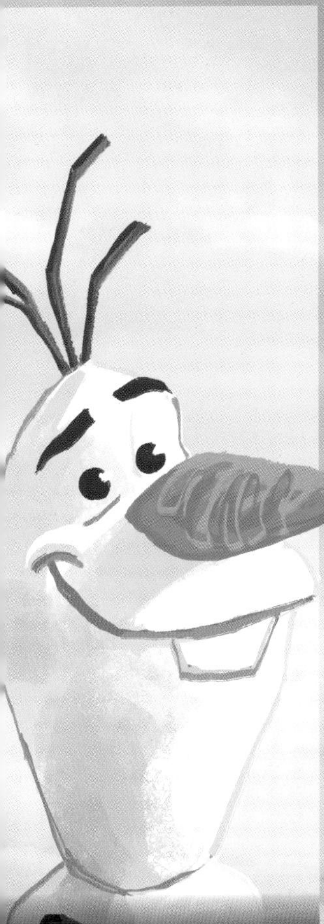

OLAF

Ever since he was created by Elsa, Olaf has loved meeting new people and learning about the world around him. Now that he has learned to read, his questions have grown bigger and more philosophical. Olaf is thrilled to explore his surroundings alongside his friends and is up for any new adventure.

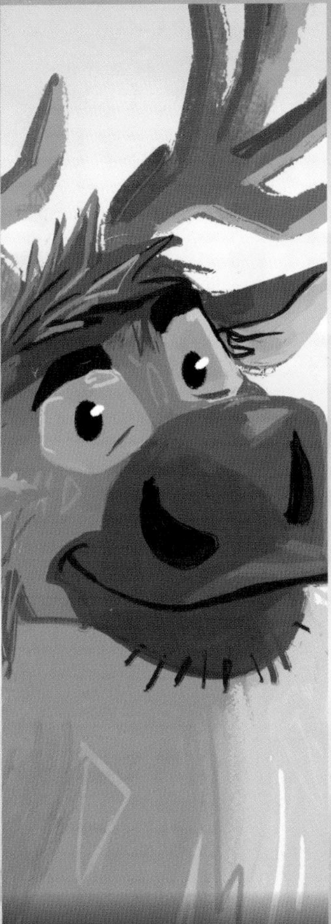

SVEN

Kristoff's best friend and conscience. He's great for bouncing ideas off of, even if Kristoff *does* do most of the talking. He is very loyal, and is always there for those in need. Kristoff will always be thankful for Sven's advice and to have such a great friend by his side.

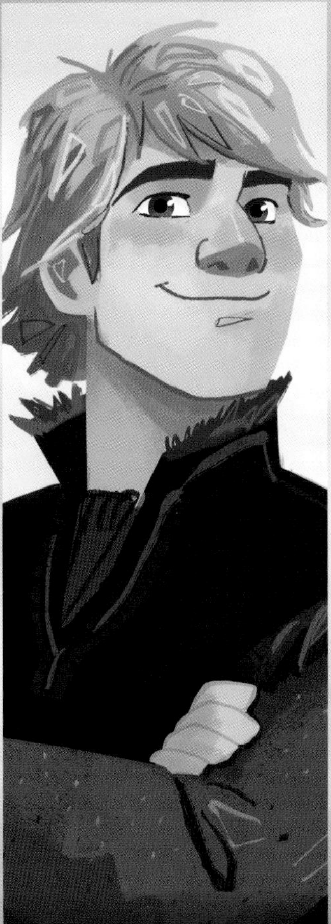

KRISTOFF

This mountain man's world was turned upside down by Anna, and now he's ready to take their relationship to the next level. But after Anna's disastrous relationship with Hans, he respects that Anna does not want to rush things and allows her to take her time. However, when her commitment to Elsa keeps putting Anna in danger, he will do anything not to lose her.

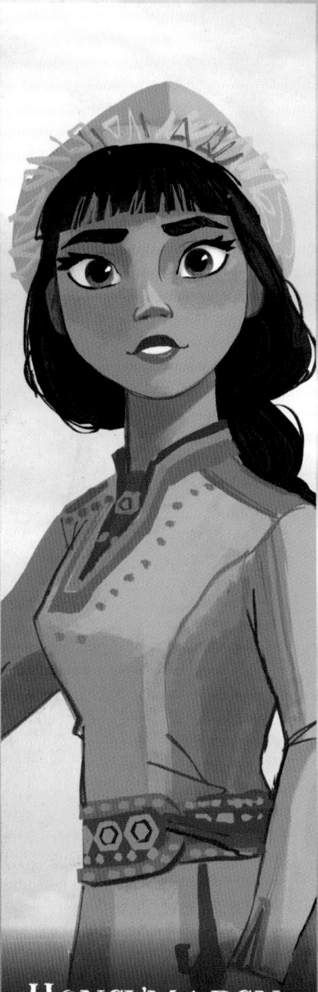

Honeymaren

Bold and brave, Honeymaren longs to move beyond the conflicts of the past and the Enchanted Forest. She shares her knowledge of the magic of nature with Elsa, helping her along on her journey to find her destiny.

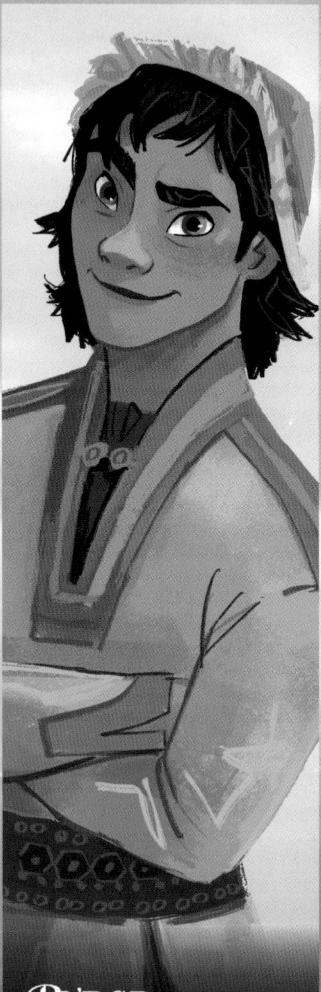

Ryder

Like his sister, Honeymaren, Ryder yearns to see the world outside the Enchanted Forest. He embraces life and handles conflict with wit and a disarming smile. Ryder loves reindeer almost as much as Kristoff.

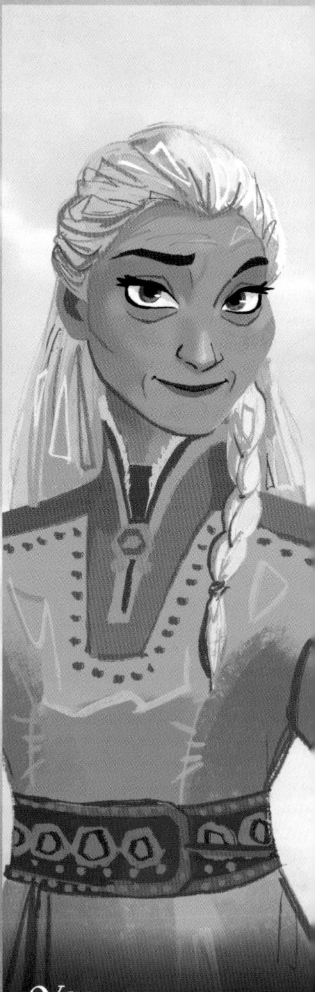

Yelana

Yelana, the wise and protective Northuldra elder, has a deep connection to nature. After witnessing that Elsa is connected to it as well, she encourages Elsa to listen when it speaks.

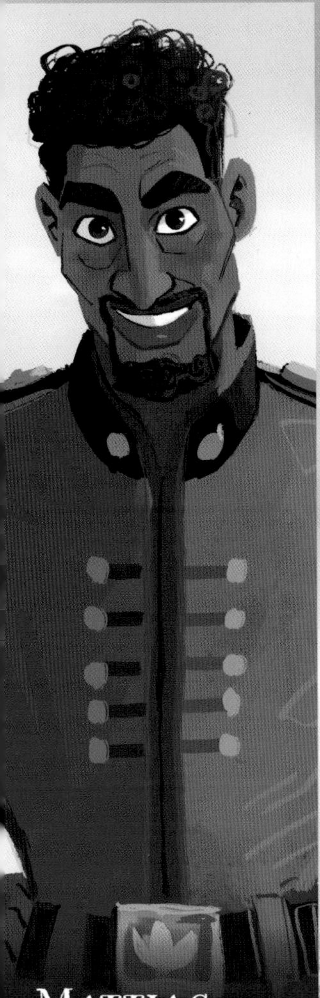

Mattias

Once a loyal protector of Arendelle and guard to Prince Agnarr, Lieutenant Destin Mattias has been living in the Enchanted Forest for over thirty years, ever since the battle. But even after all this time, he has never forgotten where he came from and his sworn duty to protect Arendelle.

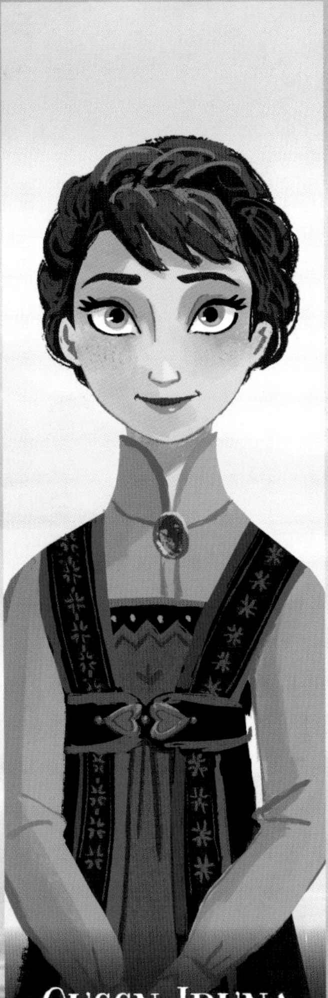

Queen Iduna

The Queen of Arendelle and wife to King Agnarr, Iduna loves her daughters and longs to protect them at all costs. She can't help but wonder if the secrets of her past may hold the answer to why Elsa was born with powers.

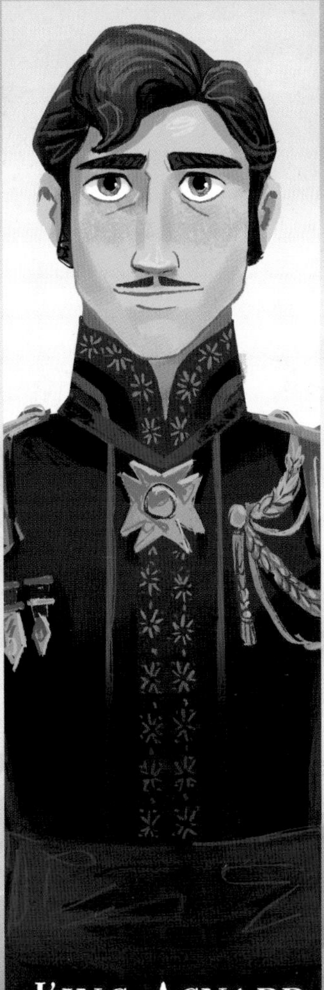

King Agnarr

As a child, the prince of Arendelle, Agnarr, traveled to the Enchanted Forest with his father, King Runeard, for a celebration with the Northuldra. When battle broke out, he was mysteriously rescued and always wondered who saved him. He does his best to prepare his family for what the future holds, warning Anna and Elsa that the past may return.

"... I believe whoever
is calling me is good."
—Elsa

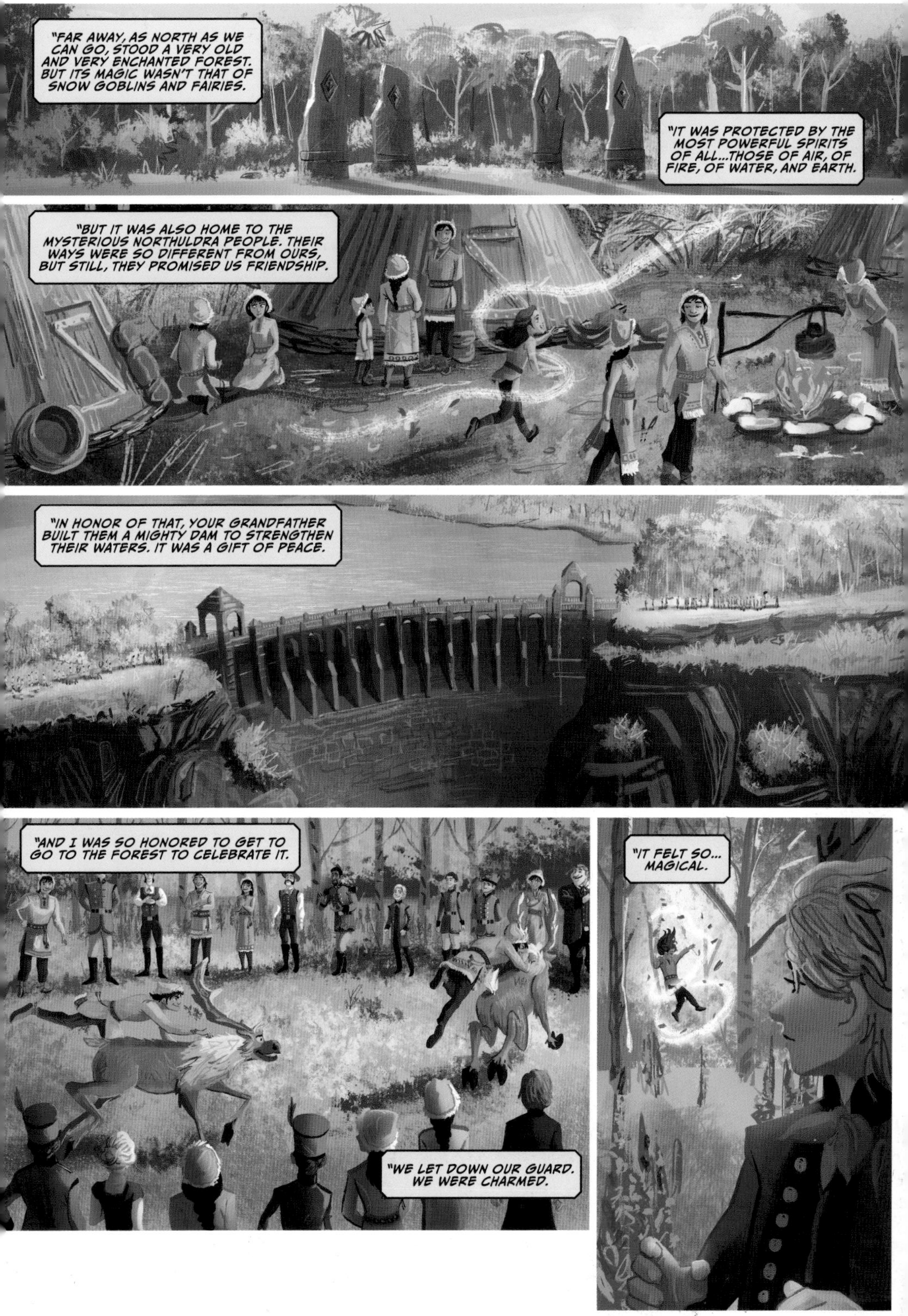
"FAR AWAY, AS NORTH AS WE CAN GO, STOOD A VERY OLD AND VERY ENCHANTED FOREST. BUT ITS MAGIC WASN'T THAT OF SNOW GOBLINS AND FAIRIES.
"IT WAS PROTECTED BY THE MOST POWERFUL SPIRITS OF ALL...THOSE OF AIR, OF FIRE, OF WATER, AND EARTH.
"BUT IT WAS ALSO HOME TO THE MYSTERIOUS NORTHULDRA PEOPLE. THEIR WAYS WERE SO DIFFERENT FROM OURS, BUT STILL, THEY PROMISED US FRIENDSHIP.
"IN HONOR OF THAT, YOUR GRANDFATHER BUILT THEM A MIGHTY DAM TO STRENGTHEN THEIR WATERS. IT WAS A GIFT OF PEACE.
"AND I WAS SO HONORED TO GET TO GO TO THE FOREST TO CELEBRATE IT.
"WE LET DOWN OUR GUARD. WE WERE CHARMED.
"IT FELT SO... MAGICAL.

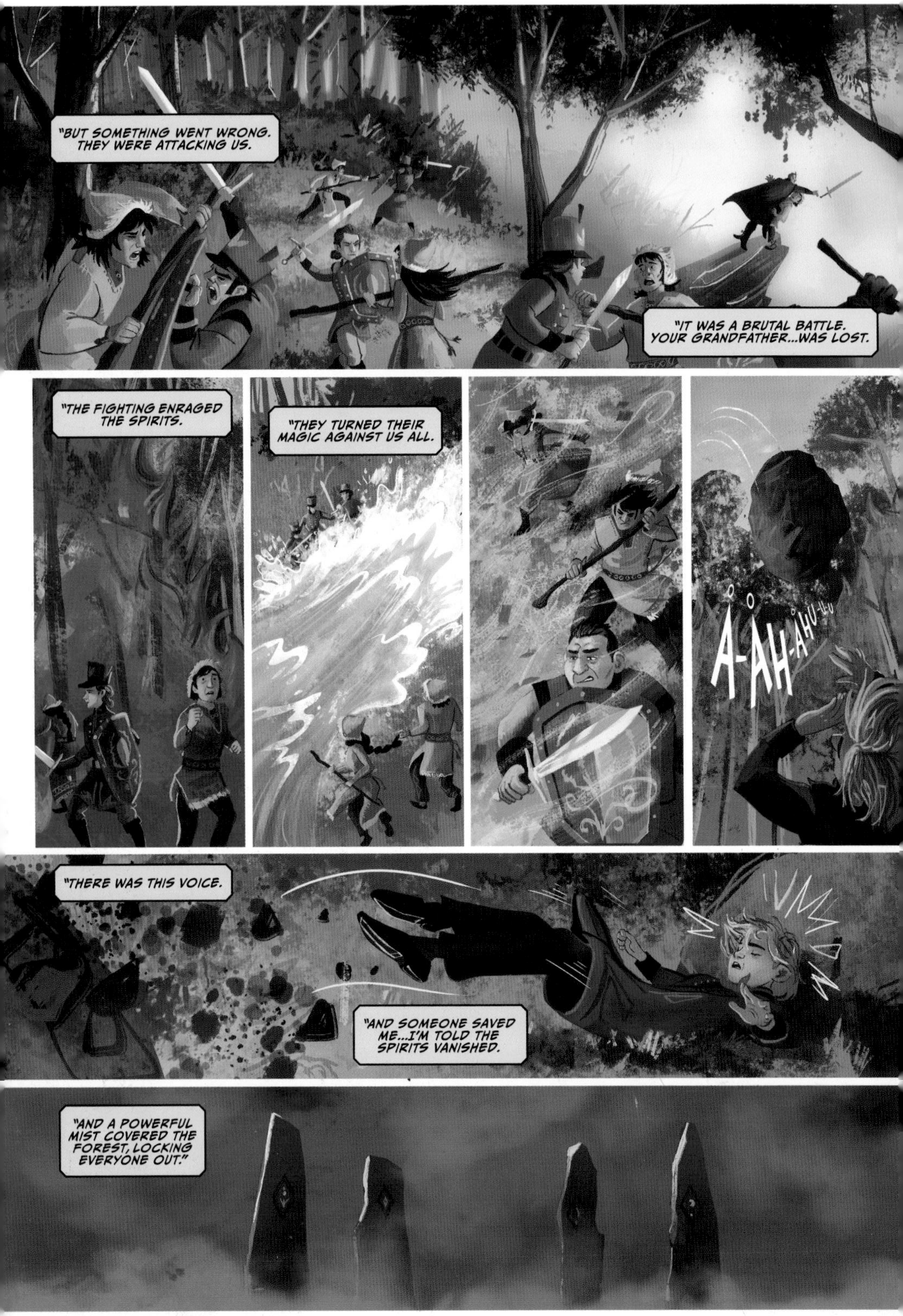
"BUT SOMETHING WENT WRONG. THEY WERE ATTACKING US.
"IT WAS A BRUTAL BATTLE. YOUR GRANDFATHER...WAS LOST.
"THE FIGHTING ENRAGED THE SPIRITS.
"THEY TURNED THEIR MAGIC AGAINST US ALL.
A-AH-AHU-UU
"THERE WAS THIS VOICE.
"AND SOMEONE SAVED ME...I'M TOLD THE SPIRITS VANISHED.
"AND A POWERFUL MIST COVERED THE FOREST, LOCKING EVERYONE OUT."

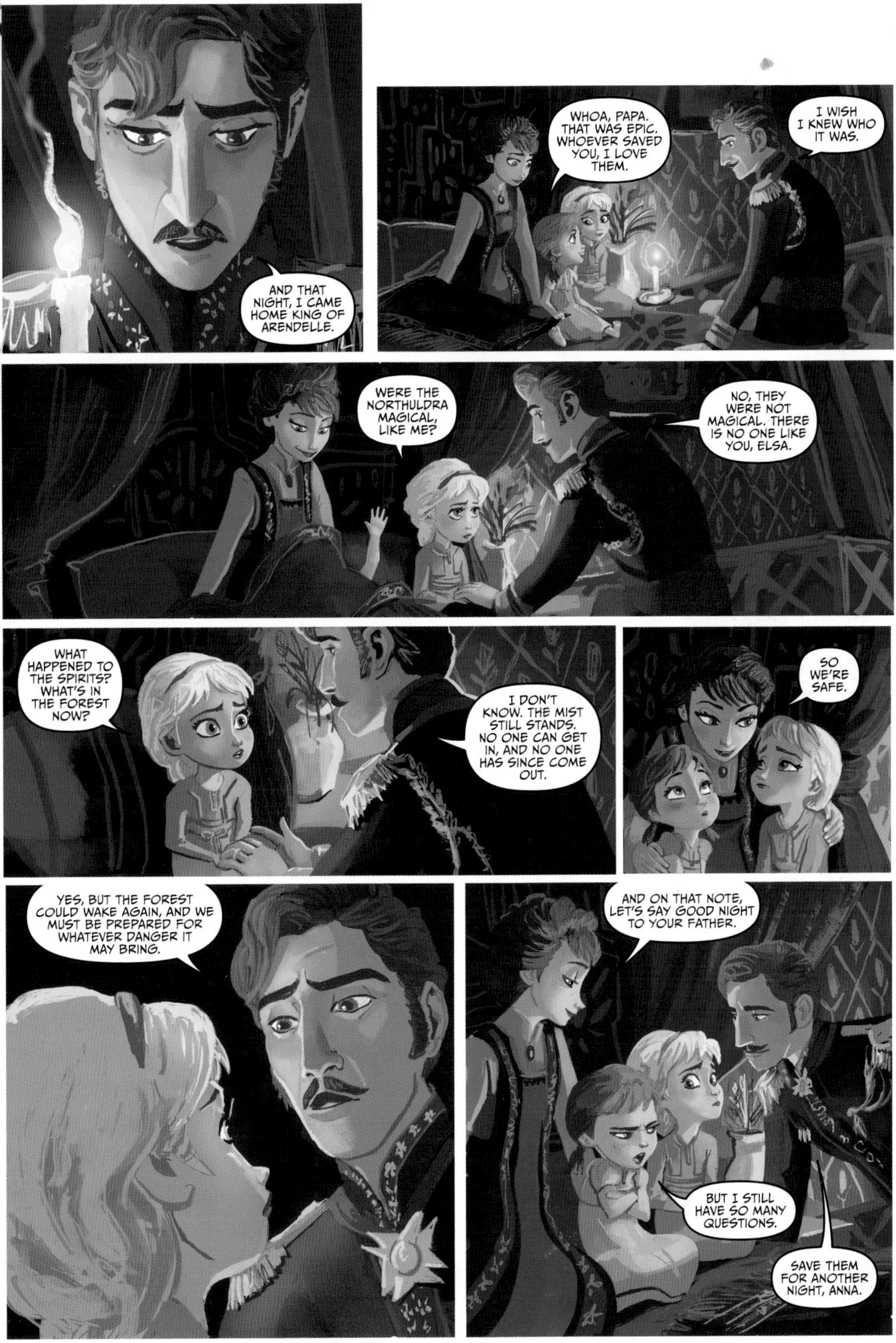
AND THAT NIGHT, I CAME HOME KING OF ARENDELLE.
WHOA, PAPA. THAT WAS EPIC. WHOEVER SAVED YOU, I LOVE THEM.
I WISH I KNEW WHO IT WAS.
WERE THE NORTHULDRA MAGICAL, LIKE ME?
NO, THEY WERE NOT MAGICAL. THERE IS NO ONE LIKE YOU, ELSA.
WHAT HAPPENED TO THE SPIRITS? WHAT'S IN THE FOREST NOW?
I DON'T KNOW. THE MIST STILL STANDS. NO ONE CAN GET IN, AND NO ONE HAS SINCE COME OUT.
SO WE'RE SAFE.
YES, BUT THE FOREST COULD WAKE AGAIN, AND WE MUST BE PREPARED FOR WHATEVER DANGER IT MAY BRING.
AND ON THAT NOTE, LET'S SAY GOOD NIGHT TO YOUR FATHER.
BUT I STILL HAVE SO MANY QUESTIONS.
SAVE THEM FOR ANOTHER NIGHT, ANNA.

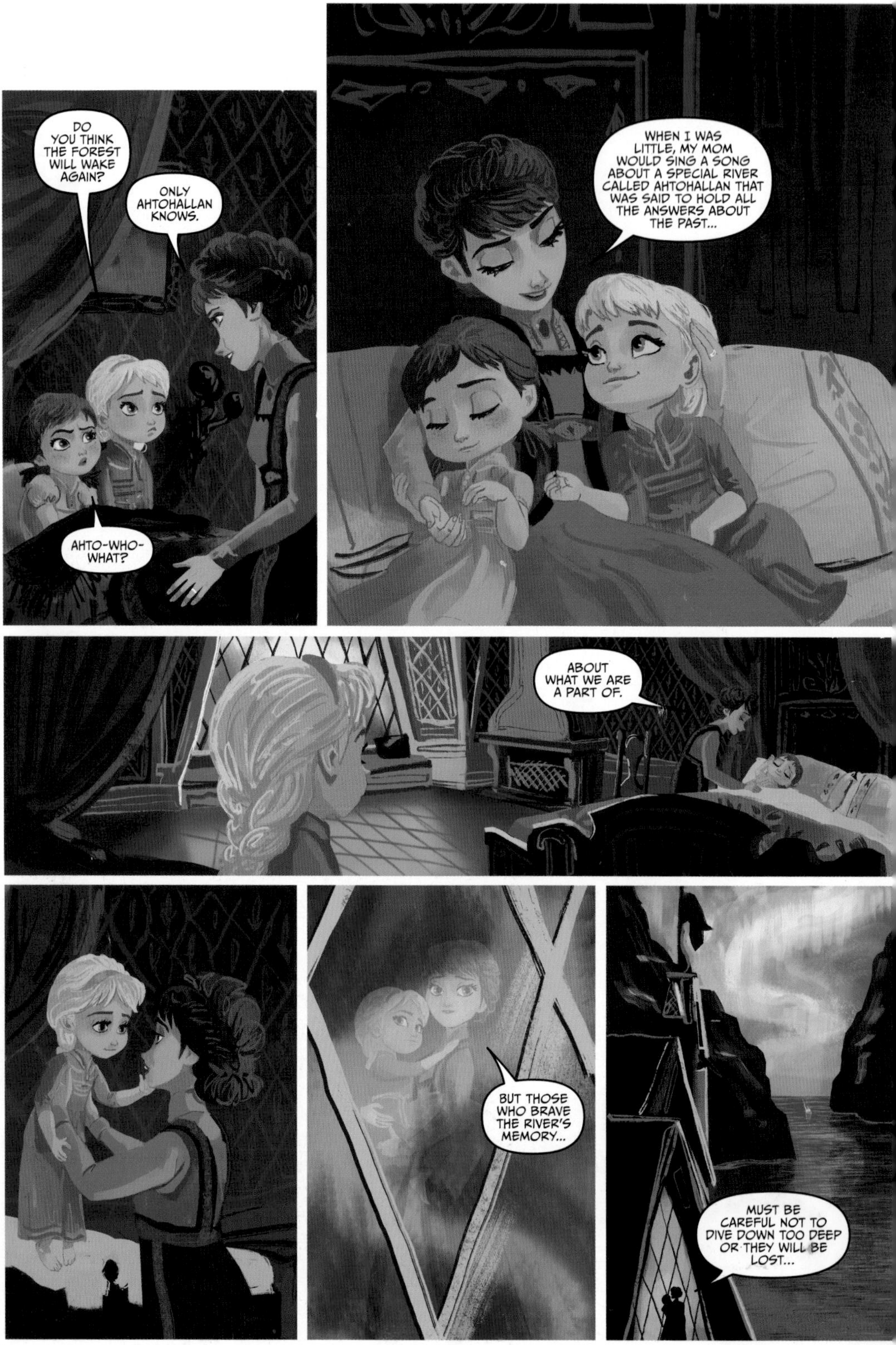
DO YOU THINK THE FOREST WILL WAKE AGAIN?
ONLY AHTOHALLAN KNOWS.
AHTO-WHO-WHAT?
WHEN I WAS LITTLE, MY MOM WOULD SING A SONG ABOUT A SPECIAL RIVER CALLED AHTOHALLAN THAT WAS SAID TO HOLD ALL THE ANSWERS ABOUT THE PAST...
ABOUT WHAT WE ARE A PART OF.
BUT THOSE WHO BRAVE THE RIVER'S MEMORY...
MUST BE CAREFUL NOT TO DIVE DOWN TOO DEEP OR THEY WILL BE LOST...

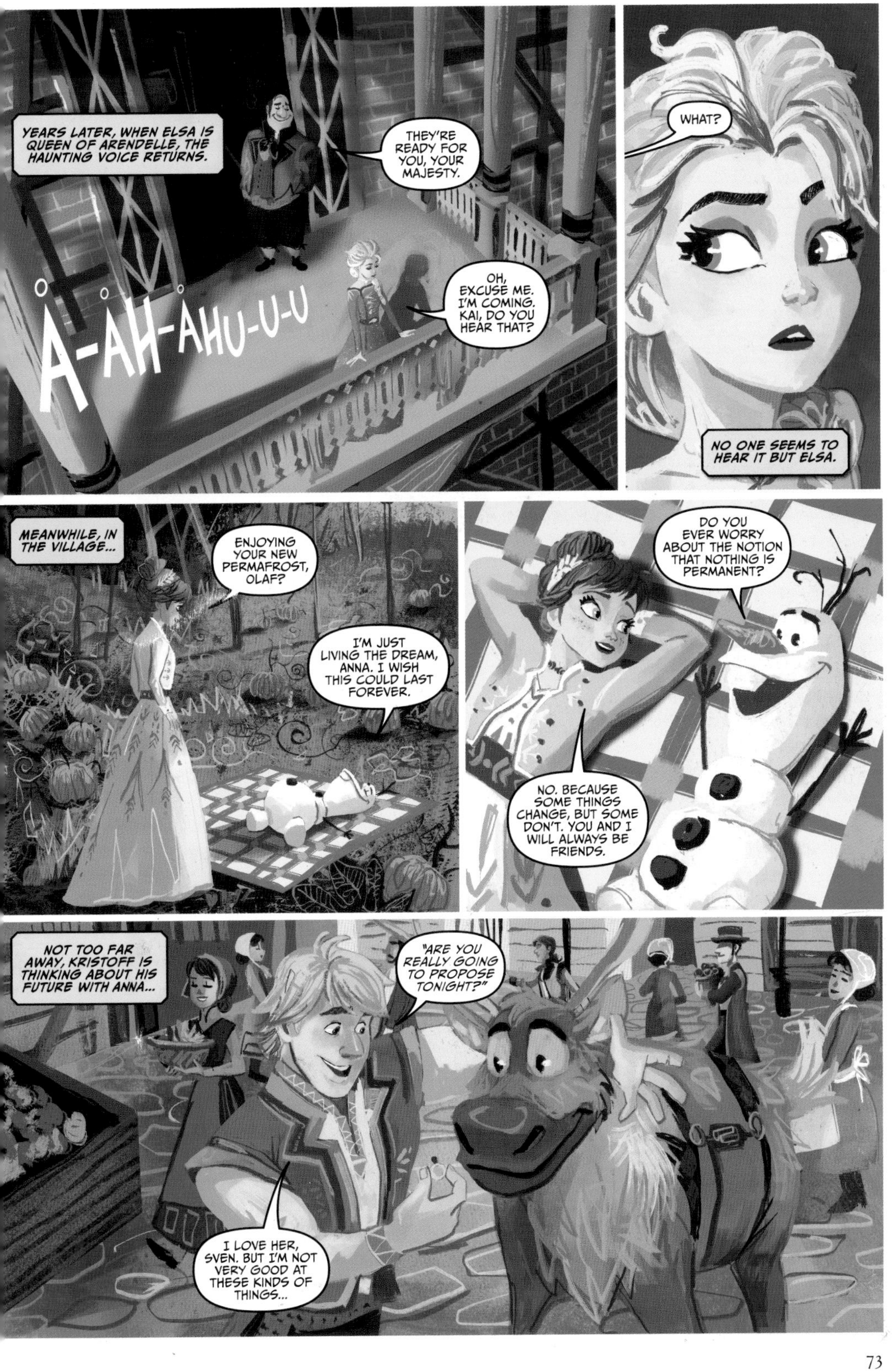
YEARS LATER, WHEN ELSA IS QUEEN OF ARENDELLE, THE HAUNTING VOICE RETURNS.
THEY'RE READY FOR YOU, YOUR MAJESTY.
A-AH-AHU-U-U
OH, EXCUSE ME. I'M COMING. KAI, DO YOU HEAR THAT?
WHAT?
NO ONE SEEMS TO HEAR IT BUT ELSA.
MEANWHILE, IN THE VILLAGE...
ENJOYING YOUR NEW PERMAFROST, OLAF?
I'M JUST LIVING THE DREAM, ANNA. I WISH THIS COULD LAST FOREVER.
DO YOU EVER WORRY ABOUT THE NOTION THAT NOTHING IS PERMANENT?
NO. BECAUSE SOME THINGS CHANGE, BUT SOME DON'T. YOU AND I WILL ALWAYS BE FRIENDS.
NOT TOO FAR AWAY, KRISTOFF IS THINKING ABOUT HIS FUTURE WITH ANNA...
"ARE YOU REALLY GOING TO PROPOSE TONIGHT?"
I LOVE HER, SVEN. BUT I'M NOT VERY GOOD AT THESE KINDS OF THINGS...

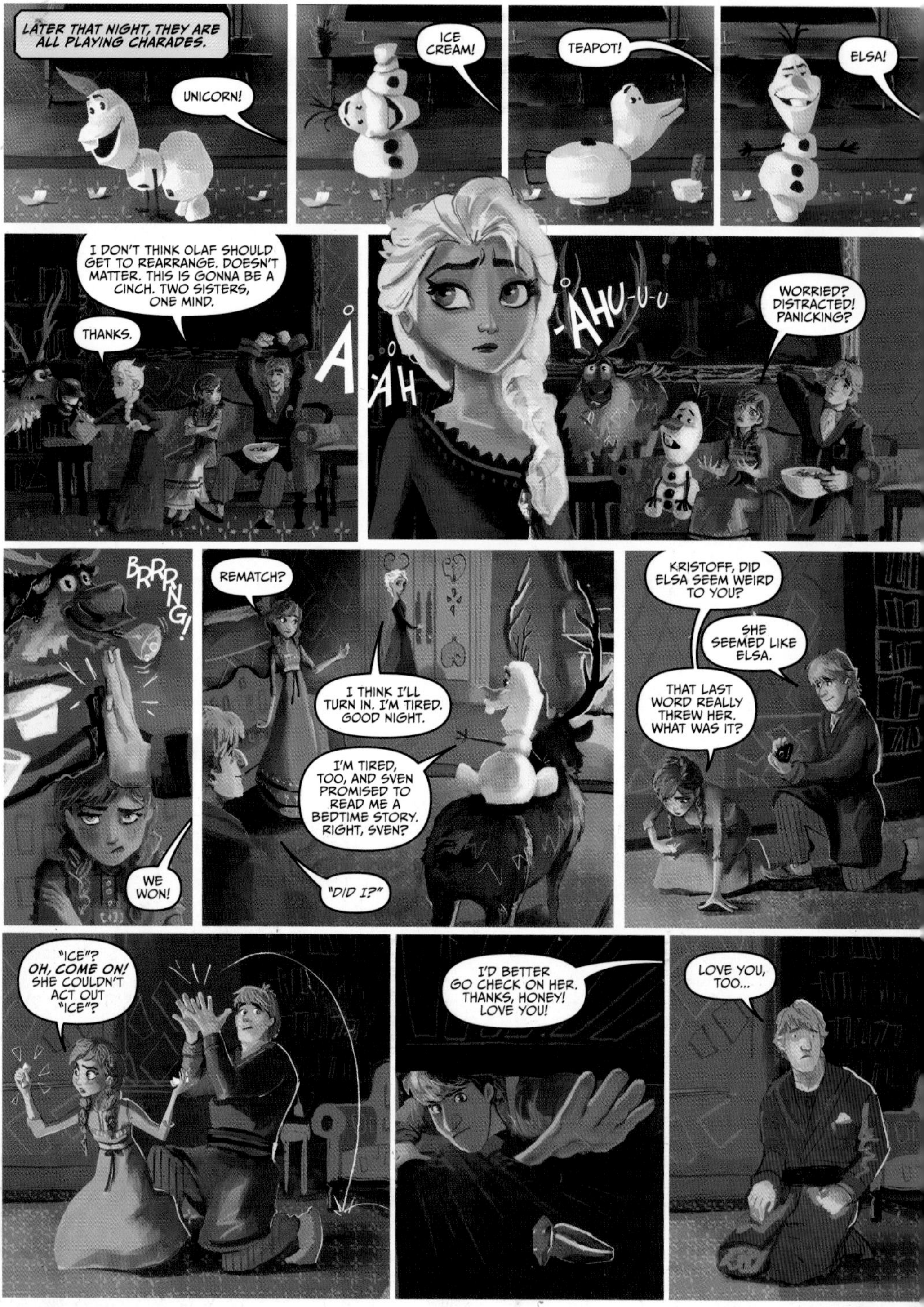
LATER THAT NIGHT, THEY ARE ALL PLAYING CHARADES.
UNICORN!
ICE CREAM!
TEAPOT!
ELSA!
I DON'T THINK OLAF SHOULD GET TO REARRANGE. DOESN'T MATTER. THIS IS GONNA BE A CINCH. TWO SISTERS, ONE MIND.
THANKS.
AAAH
AHU-U-U
WORRIED? DISTRACTED! PANICKING?
BRRRNG!
WE WON!
REMATCH?
I THINK I'LL TURN IN. I'M TIRED. GOOD NIGHT.
I'M TIRED, TOO, AND SVEN PROMISED TO READ ME A BEDTIME STORY. RIGHT, SVEN?
"DID I?"
KRISTOFF, DID ELSA SEEM WEIRD TO YOU?
SHE SEEMED LIKE ELSA.
THAT LAST WORD REALLY THREW HER. WHAT WAS IT?
"ICE"? OH, COME ON! SHE COULDN'T ACT OUT "ICE"?
I'D BETTER GO CHECK ON HER. THANKS, HONEY! LOVE YOU!
LOVE YOU, TOO...

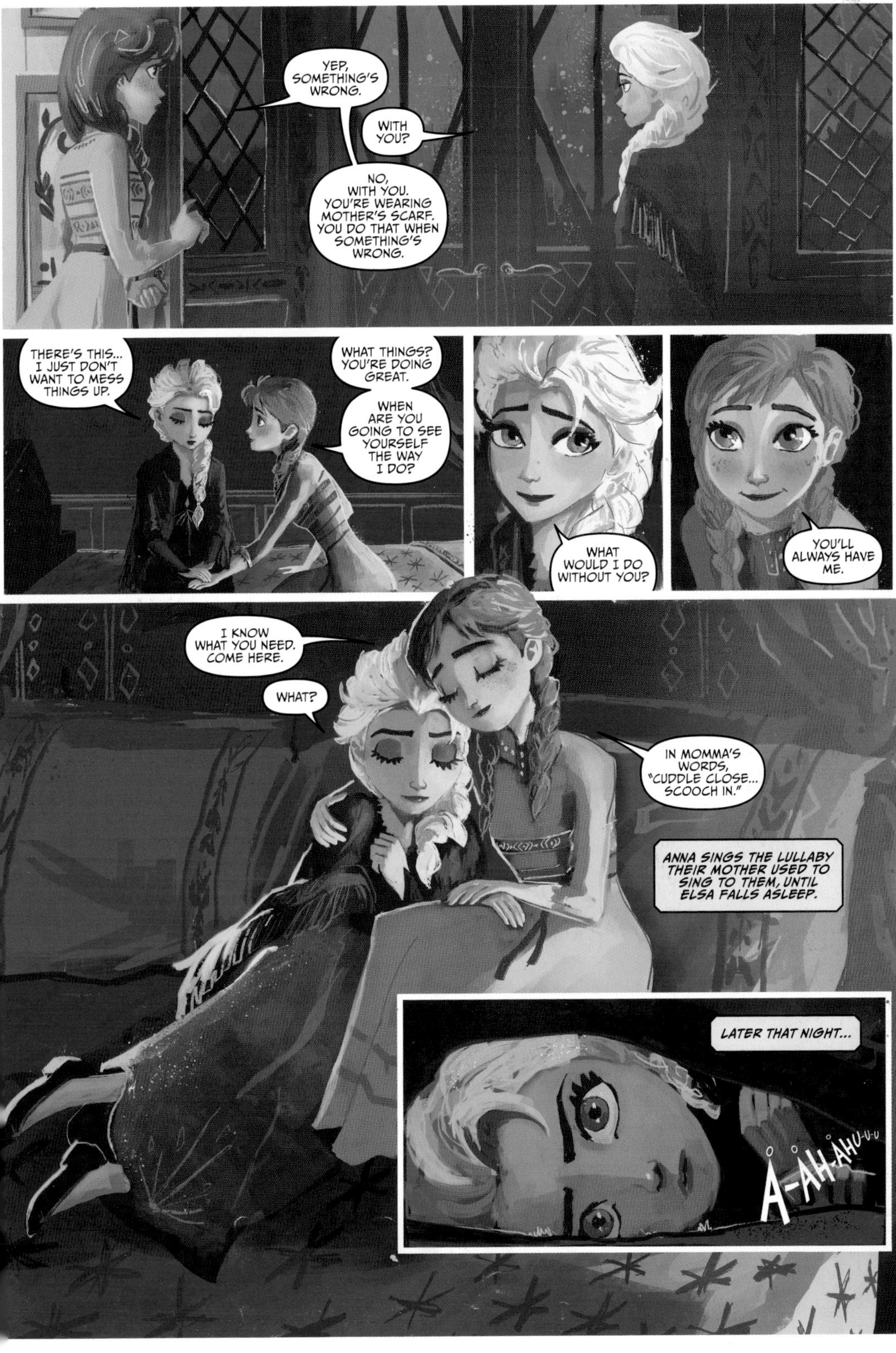
YEP, SOMETHING'S WRONG.
WITH YOU?
NO, WITH YOU. YOU'RE WEARING MOTHER'S SCARF. YOU DO THAT WHEN SOMETHING'S WRONG.
THERE'S THIS... I JUST DON'T WANT TO MESS THINGS UP.
WHAT THINGS? YOU'RE DOING GREAT.
WHEN ARE YOU GOING TO SEE YOURSELF THE WAY I DO?
WHAT WOULD I DO WITHOUT YOU?
YOU'LL ALWAYS HAVE ME.
I KNOW WHAT YOU NEED. COME HERE.
WHAT?
IN MOMMA'S WORDS, "CUDDLE CLOSE... SCOOCH IN."
ANNA SINGS THE LULLABY THEIR MOTHER USED TO SING TO THEM, UNTIL ELSA FALLS ASLEEP.
LATER THAT NIGHT...
A-AH-AH-AHU-U-U

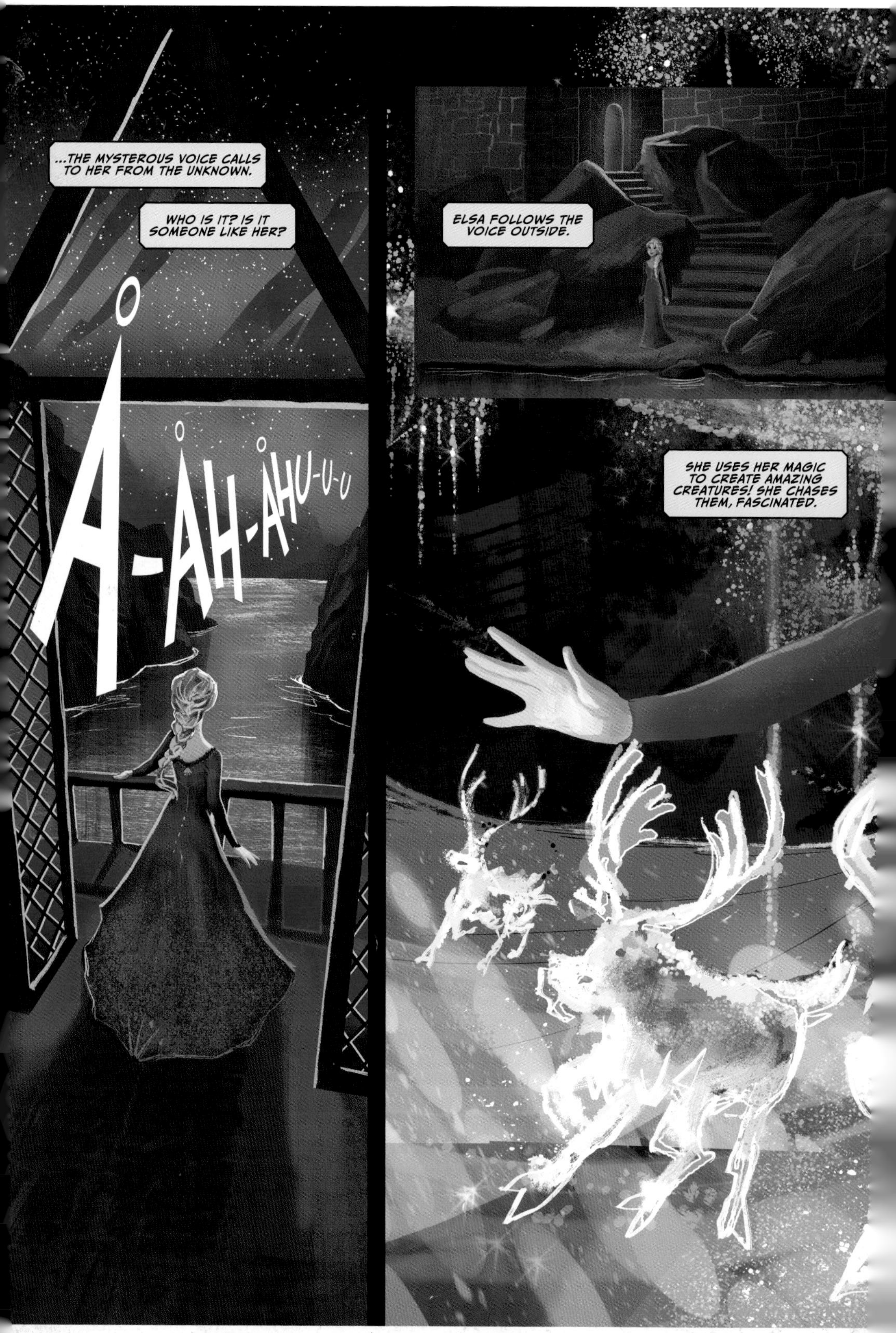
...THE MYSTEROUS VOICE CALLS TO HER FROM THE UNKNOWN.
WHO IS IT? IS IT SOMEONE LIKE HER?
Å-ÅH-ÅHU-U-U
ELSA FOLLOWS THE VOICE OUTSIDE.
SHE USES HER MAGIC TO CREATE AMAZING CREATURES! SHE CHASES THEM, FASCINATED.

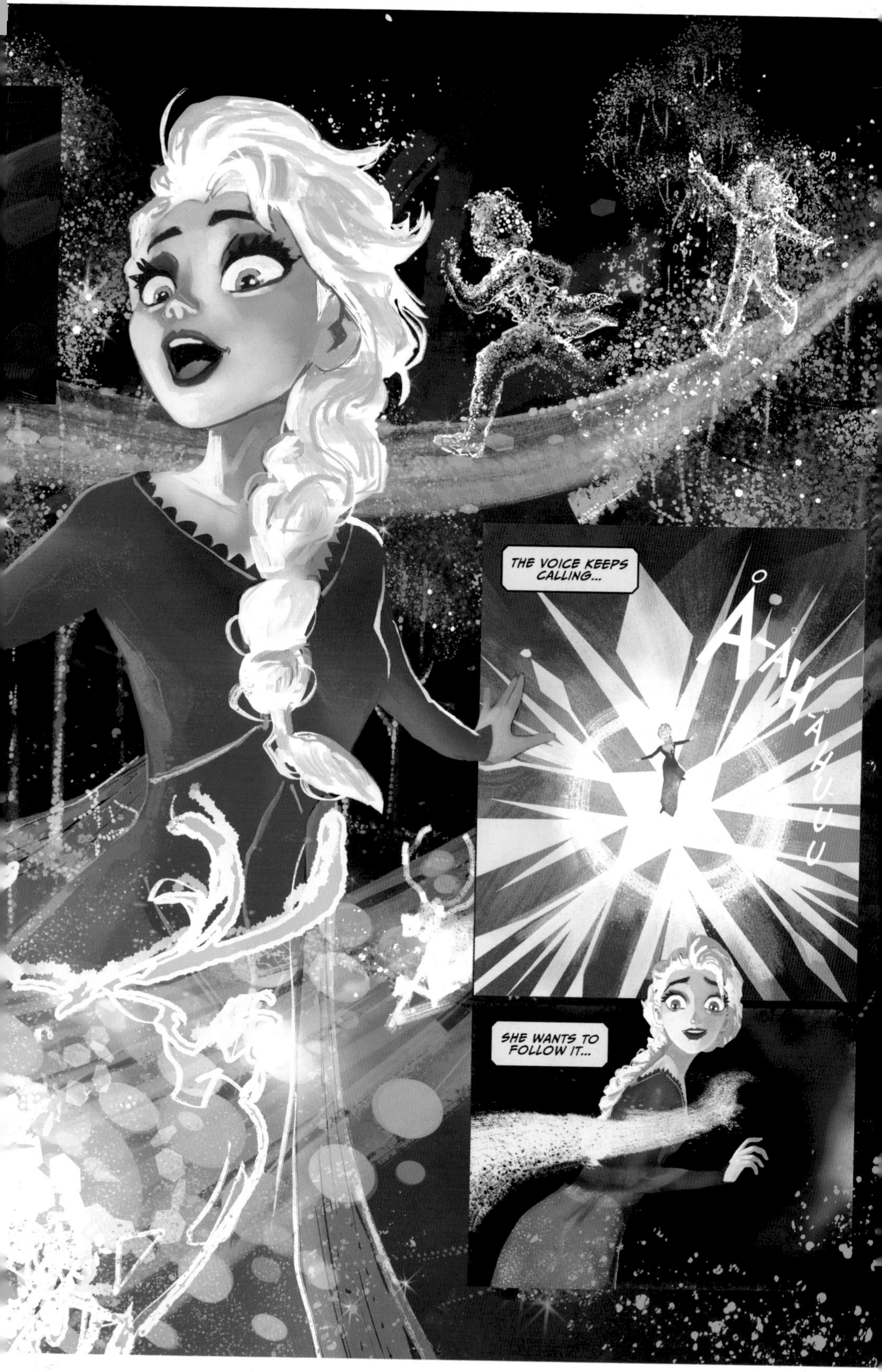
THE VOICE KEEPS CALLING...
A-AH-AH-AH-UU
SHE WANTS TO FOLLOW IT...

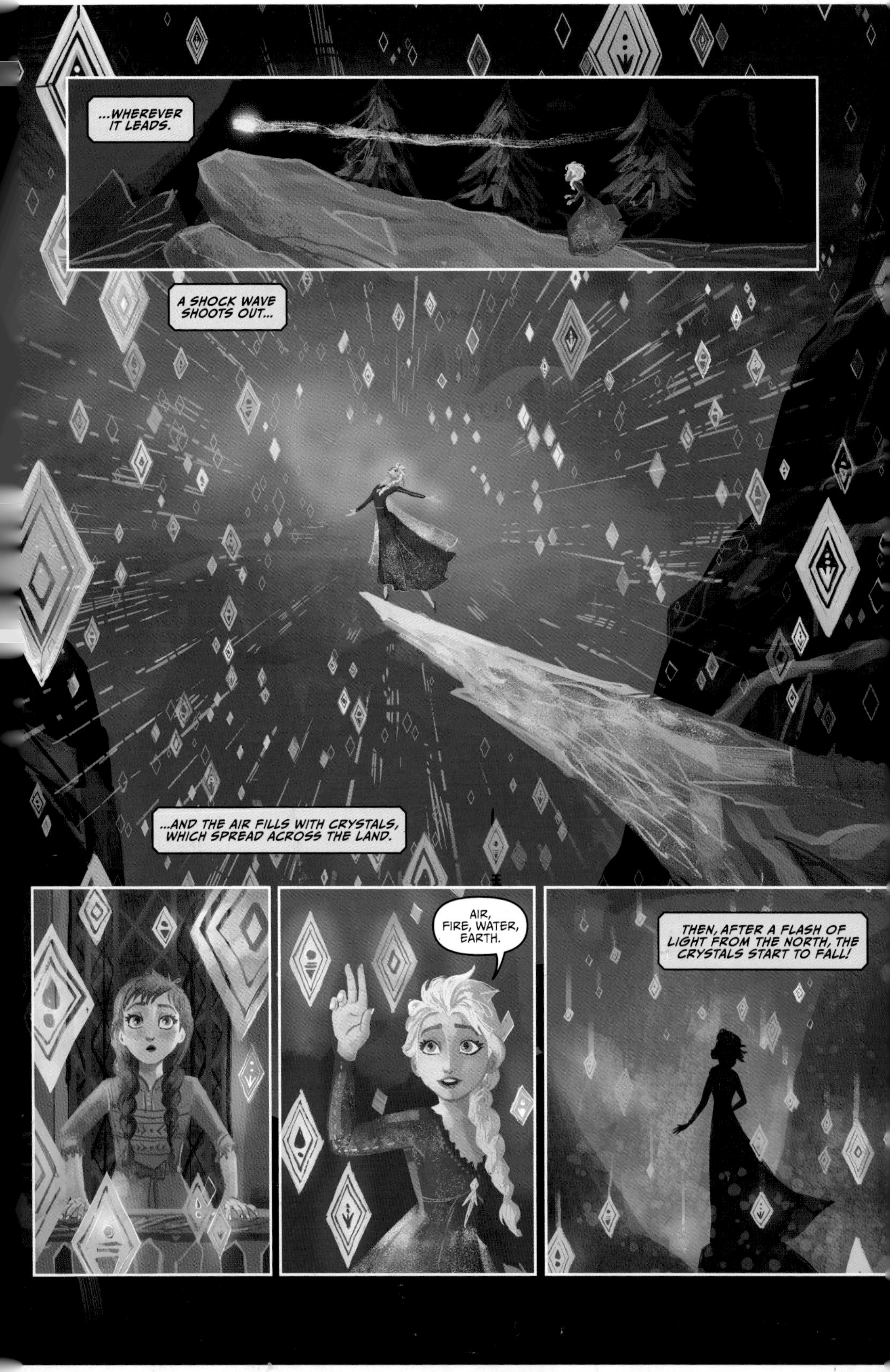
...WHEREVER IT LEADS.
A SHOCK WAVE SHOOTS OUT...
...AND THE AIR FILLS WITH CRYSTALS, WHICH SPREAD ACROSS THE LAND.
AIR, FIRE, WATER, EARTH.
THEN, AFTER A FLASH OF LIGHT FROM THE NORTH, THE CRYSTALS START TO FALL!

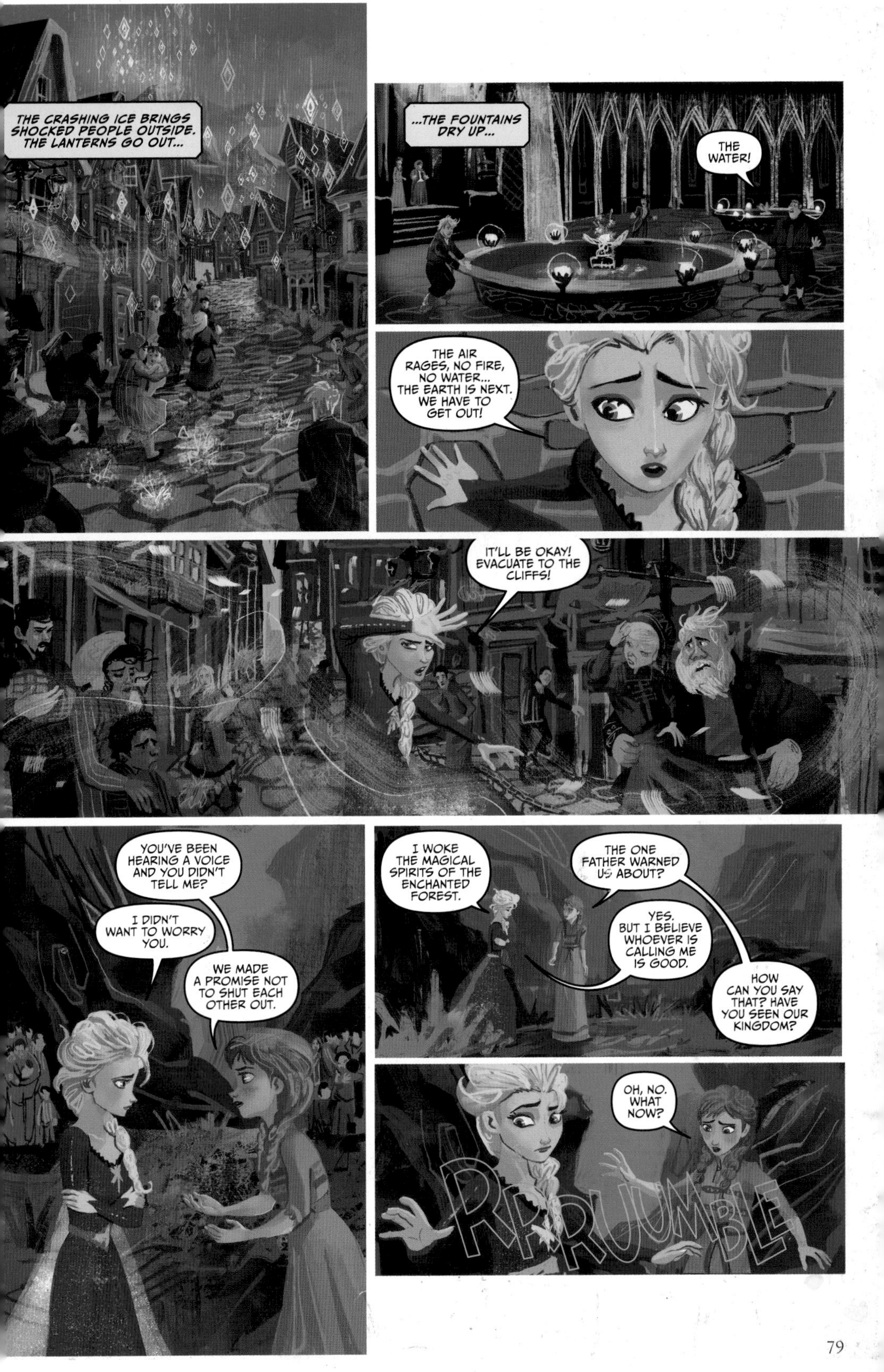
THE CRASHING ICE BRINGS SHOCKED PEOPLE OUTSIDE. THE LANTERNS GO OUT...
...THE FOUNTAINS DRY UP...
THE WATER!
THE AIR RAGES, NO FIRE, NO WATER... THE EARTH HAS NEXT. WE HAVE TO GET OUT!
IT'LL BE OKAY! EVACUATE TO THE CLIFFS!
YOU'VE BEEN HEARING A VOICE AND YOU DIDN'T TELL ME?
I DIDN'T WANT TO WORRY YOU.
WE MADE A PROMISE NOT TO SHUT EACH OTHER OUT.
I WOKE THE MAGICAL SPIRITS OF THE ENCHANTED FOREST.
THE ONE FATHER WARNED US ABOUT?
YES. BUT I BELIEVE WHOEVER IS CALLING ME IS GOOD.
HOW CAN YOU SAY THAT? HAVE YOU SEEN OUR KINGDOM?
OH, NO. WHAT NOW?
RRRUUMBLE

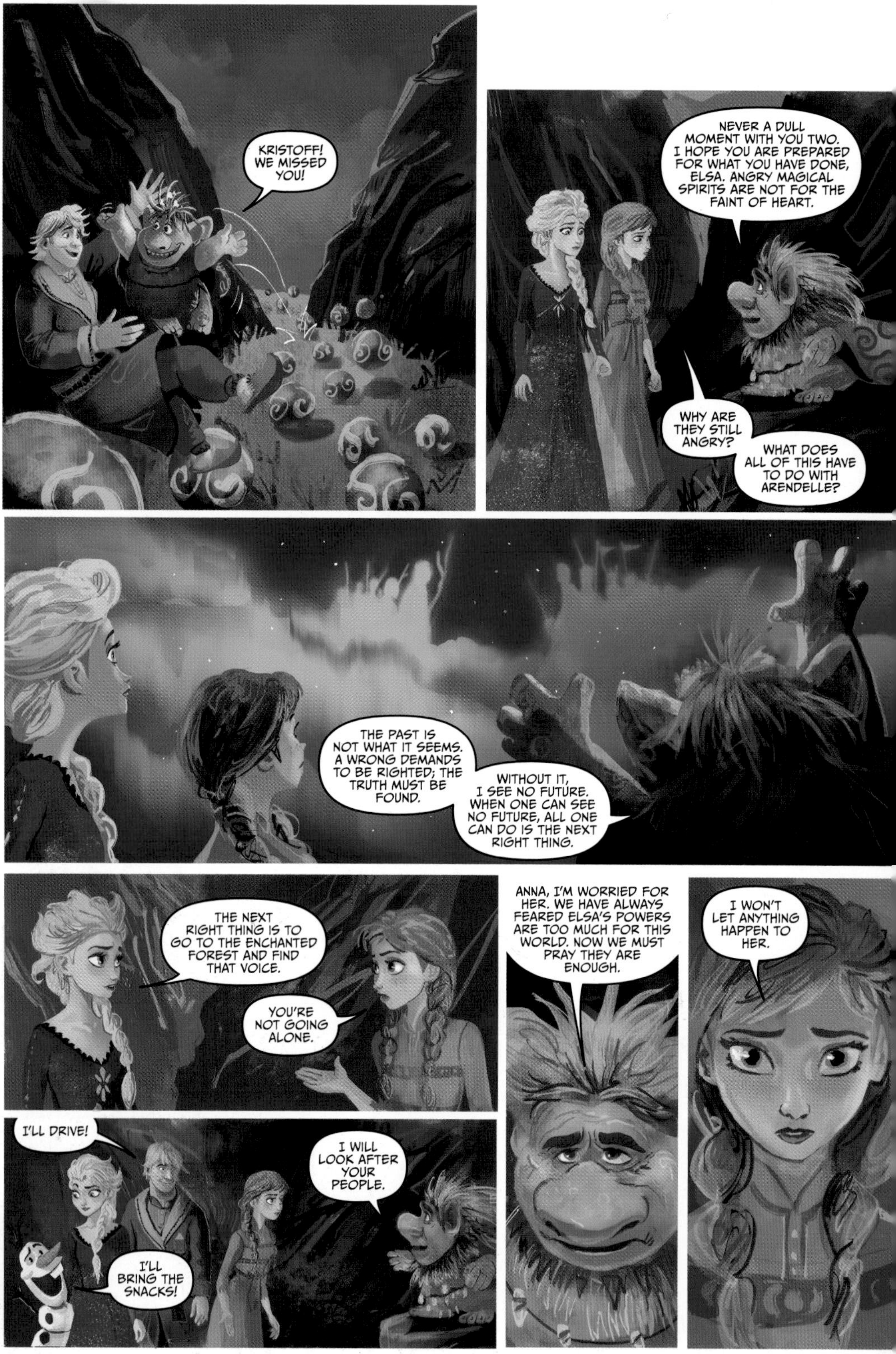
KRISTOFF! WE MISSED YOU!
NEVER A DULL MOMENT WITH YOU TWO. I HOPE YOU ARE PREPARED FOR WHAT YOU HAVE DONE, ELSA. ANGRY MAGICAL SPIRITS ARE NOT FOR THE FAINT OF HEART.
WHY ARE THEY STILL ANGRY?
WHAT DOES ALL OF THIS HAVE TO DO WITH ARENDELLE?
THE PAST IS NOT WHAT IT SEEMS. A WRONG DEMANDS TO BE RIGHTED; THE TRUTH MUST BE FOUND.
WITHOUT IT, I SEE NO FUTURE. WHEN ONE CAN SEE NO FUTURE, ALL ONE CAN DO IS THE NEXT RIGHT THING.
THE NEXT RIGHT THING IS TO GO TO THE ENCHANTED FOREST AND FIND THAT VOICE.
YOU'RE NOT GOING ALONE.
I'LL DRIVE!
I'LL BRING THE SNACKS!
I WILL LOOK AFTER YOUR PEOPLE.
ANNA, I'M WORRIED FOR HER. WE HAVE ALWAYS FEARED ELSA'S POWERS ARE TOO MUCH FOR THIS WORLD. NOW WE MUST PRAY THEY ARE ENOUGH.
I WON'T LET ANYTHING HAPPEN TO HER.

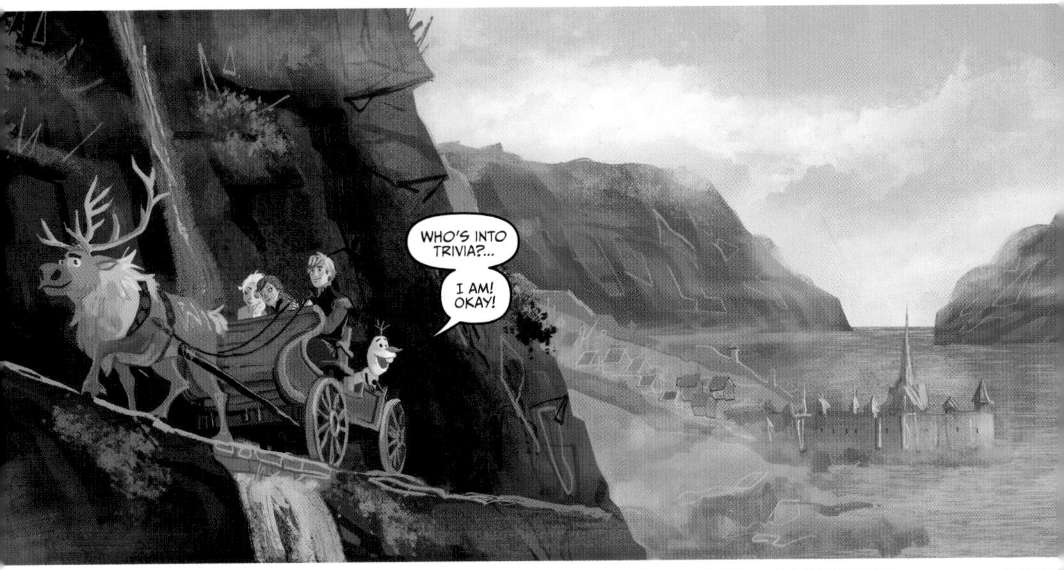
WHO'S INTO TRIVIA?...
I AM! OKAY!
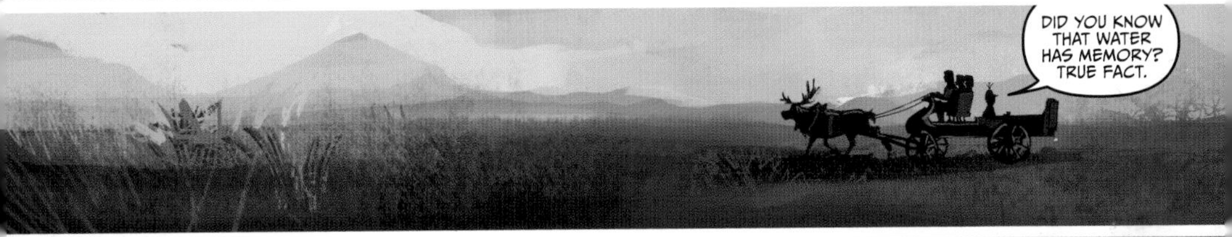
DID YOU KNOW THAT WATER HAS MEMORY? TRUE FACT.
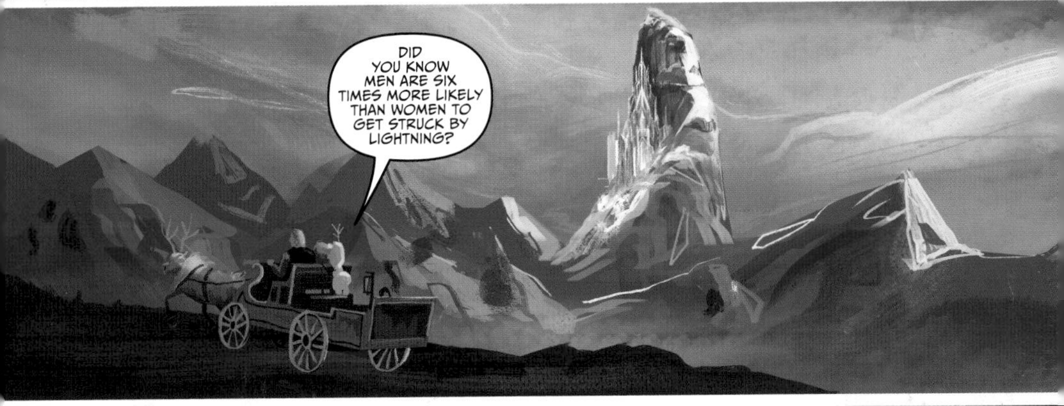
DID YOU KNOW MEN ARE SIX TIMES MORE LIKELY THAN WOMEN TO GET STRUCK BY LIGHTNING?
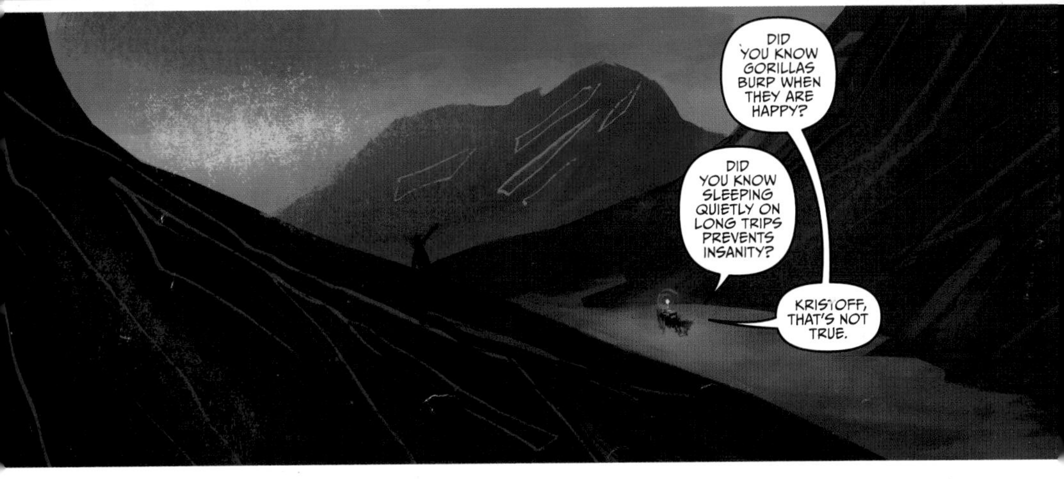
DID YOU KNOW GORILLAS BURP WHEN THEY ARE HAPPY?
DID YOU KNOW SLEEPING QUIETLY ON LONG TRIPS PREVENTS INSANITY?
KRISTOFF, THAT'S NOT TRUE.

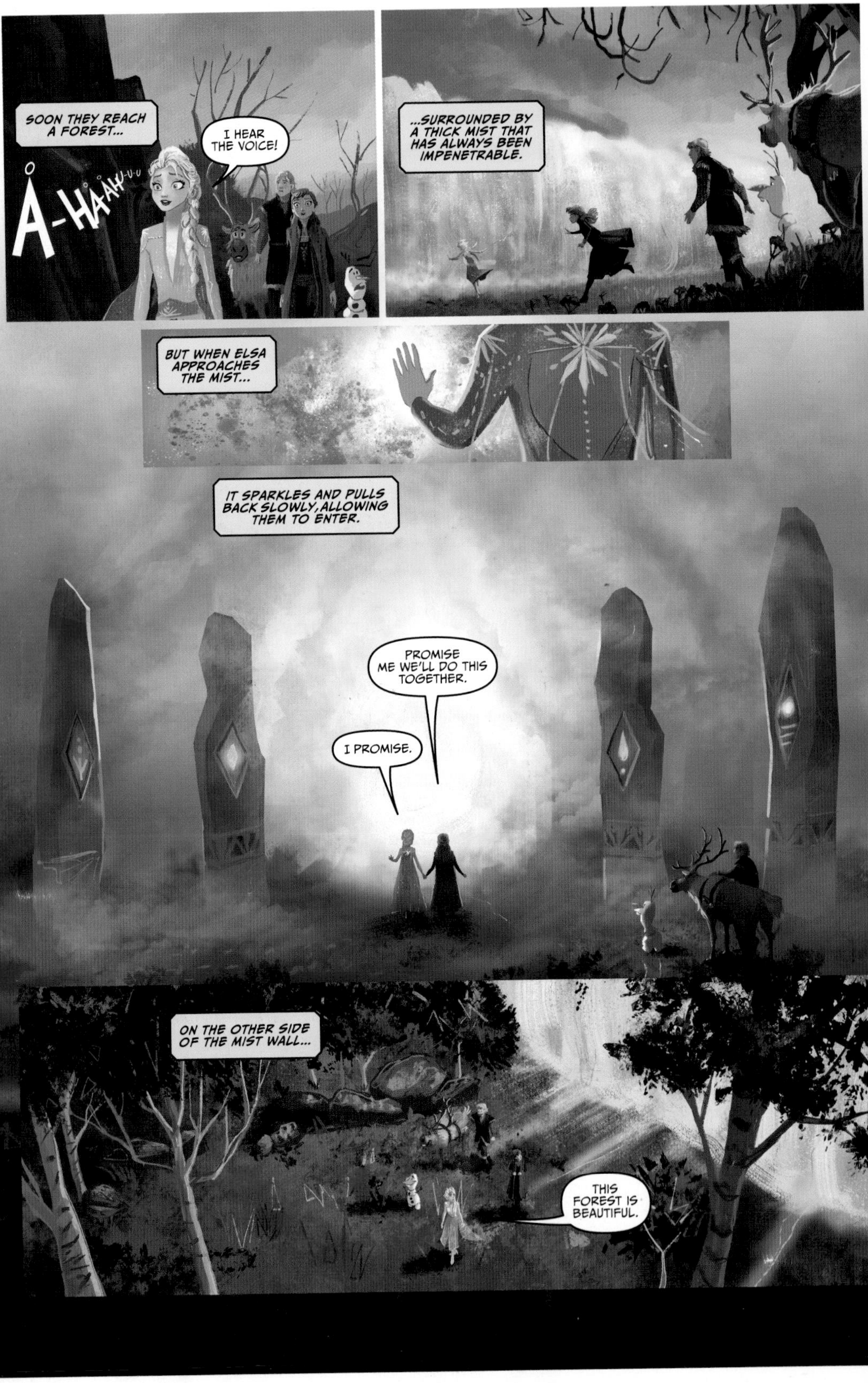
SOON THEY REACH A FOREST...
Å-HÅÅH-U-U
I HEAR THE VOICE!
...SURROUNDED BY A THICK MIST THAT HAS ALWAYS BEEN IMPENETRABLE.
BUT WHEN ELSA APPROACHES THE MIST...
IT SPARKLES AND PULLS BACK SLOWLY, ALLOWING THEM TO ENTER.
PROMISE ME WE'LL DO THIS TOGETHER.
I PROMISE.
ON THE OTHER SIDE OF THE MIST WALL...
THIS FOREST IS BEAUTIFUL.

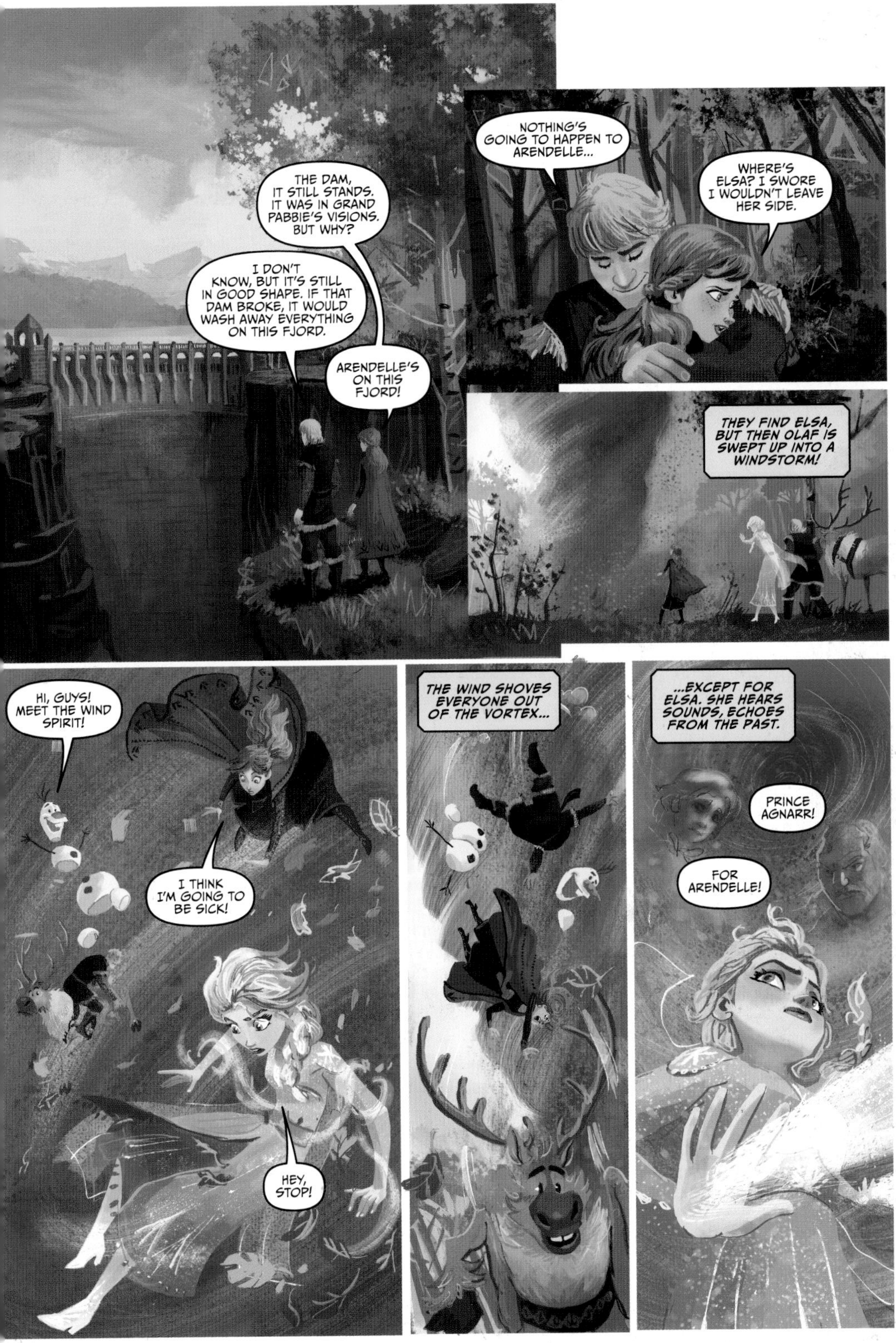
THE DAM, IT STILL STANDS. IT WAS IN GRAND PABBIE'S VISIONS. BUT WHY?
I DON'T KNOW, BUT IT'S STILL IN GOOD SHAPE. IF THAT DAM BROKE, IT WOULD WASH AWAY EVERYTHING ON THIS FJORD.
ARENDELLE'S ON THIS FJORD!
NOTHING'S GOING TO HAPPEN TO ARENDELLE...
WHERE'S ELSA? I SWORE I WOULDN'T LEAVE HER SIDE.
THEY FIND ELSA, BUT THEN OLAF IS SWEPT UP INTO A WINDSTORM!
HI, GUYS! MEET THE WIND SPIRIT!
I THINK I'M GOING TO BE SICK!
HEY, STOP!
THE WIND SHOVES EVERYONE OUT OF THE VORTEX...
...EXCEPT FOR ELSA. SHE HEARS SOUNDS, ECHOES FROM THE PAST.
PRINCE AGNARR!
FOR ARENDELLE!

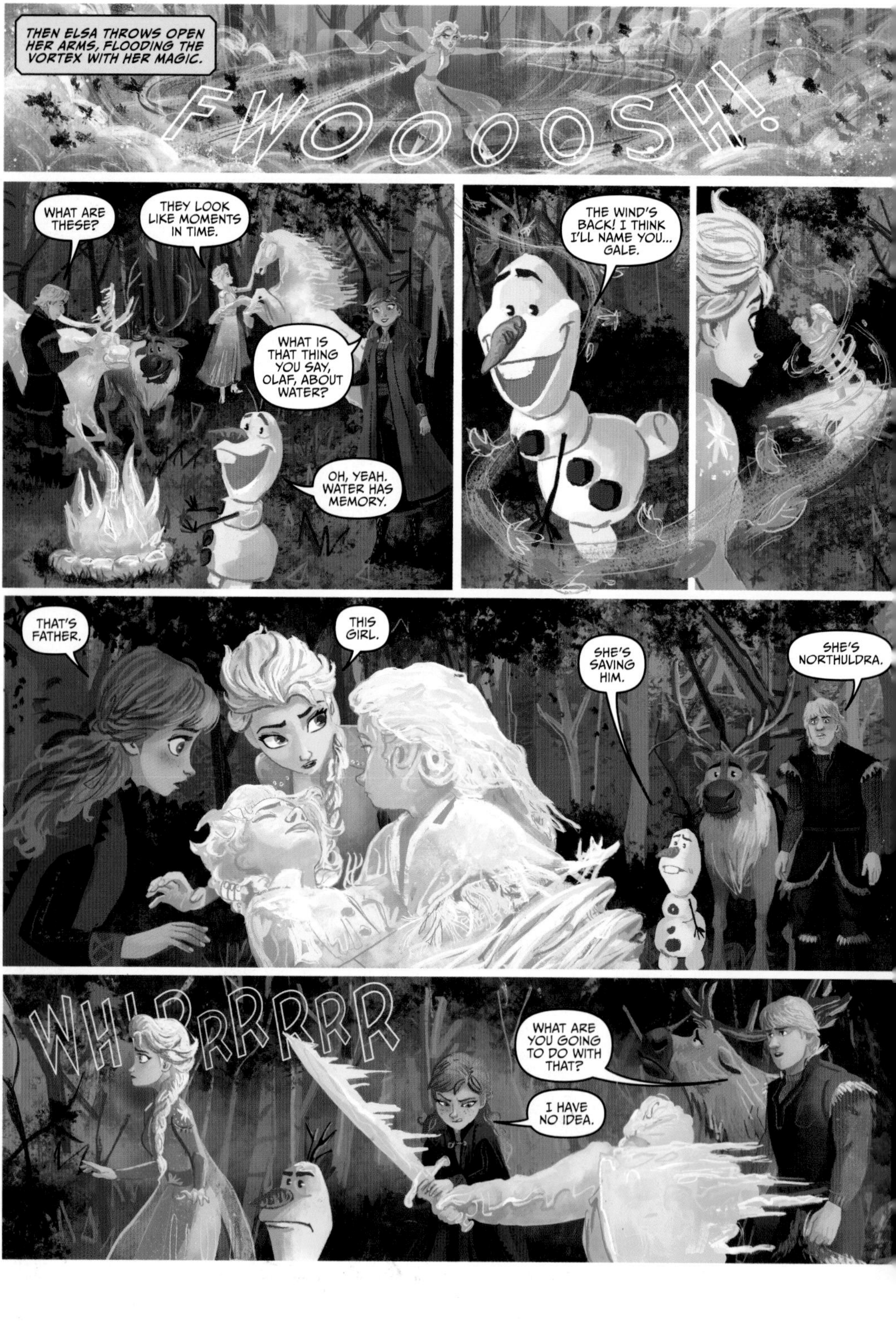
THEN ELSA THROWS OPEN HER ARMS, FLOODING THE VORTEX WITH HER MAGIC.
FWOOOOSH!
WHAT ARE THESE?
THEY LOOK LIKE MOMENTS IN TIME.
WHAT IS THAT THING YOU SAY, OLAF, ABOUT WATER?
OH, YEAH. WATER HAS MEMORY.
THE WIND'S BACK! I THINK I'LL NAME YOU... GALE.
THAT'S FATHER.
THIS GIRL.
SHE'S SAVING HIM.
SHE'S NORTHULDRA.
WHIRRRRRR
WHAT ARE YOU GOING TO DO WITH THAT?
I HAVE NO IDEA.

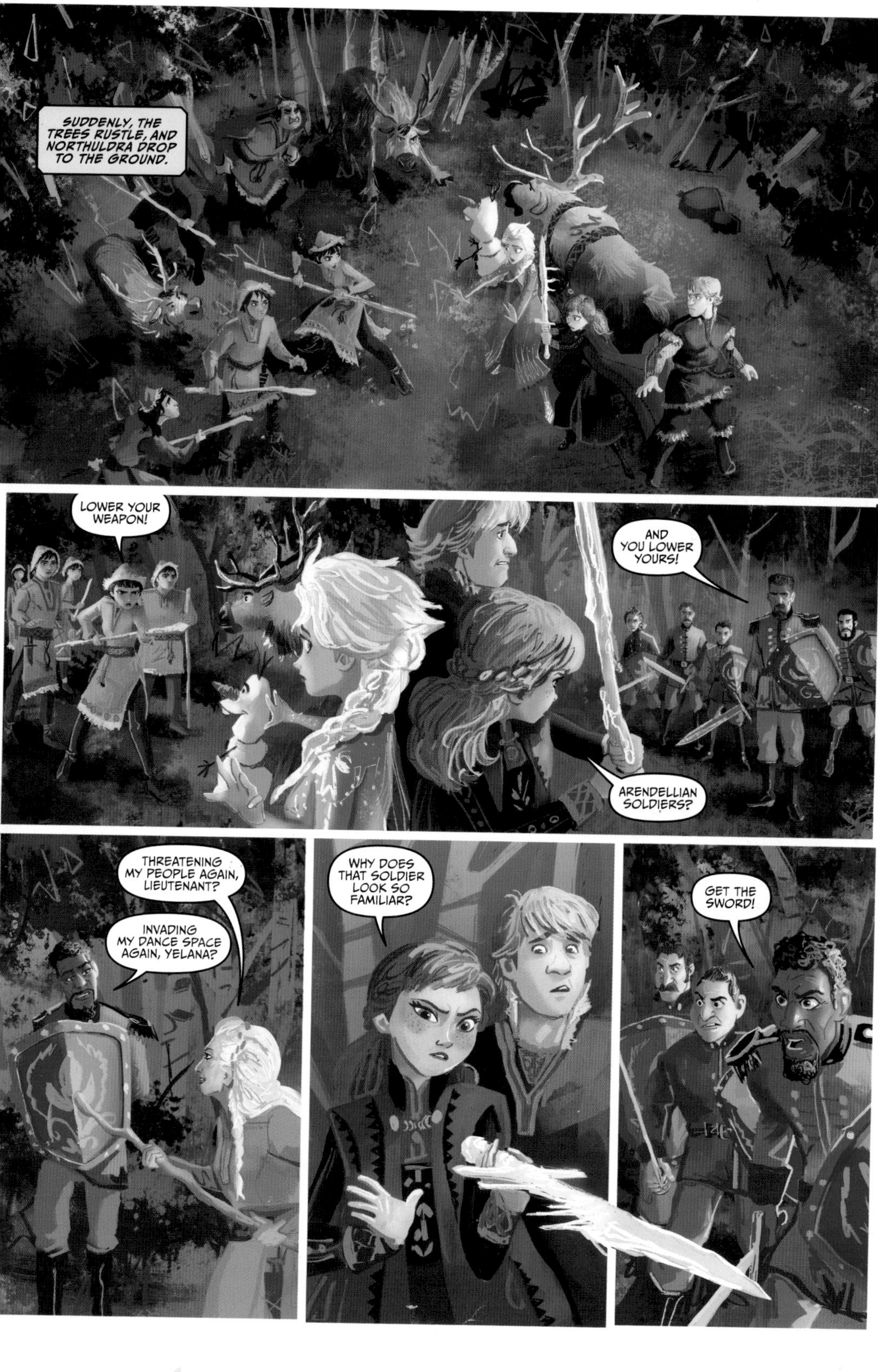
SUDDENLY, THE TREES RUSTLE, AND NORTHULDRA DROP TO THE GROUND.
LOWER YOUR WEAPON!
AND YOU LOWER YOURS!
ARENDELLIAN SOLDIERS?
THREATENING MY PEOPLE AGAIN, LIEUTENANT?
INVADING MY DANCE SPACE AGAIN, YELANA?
WHY DOES THAT SOLDIER LOOK SO FAMILIAR?
GET THE SWORD!

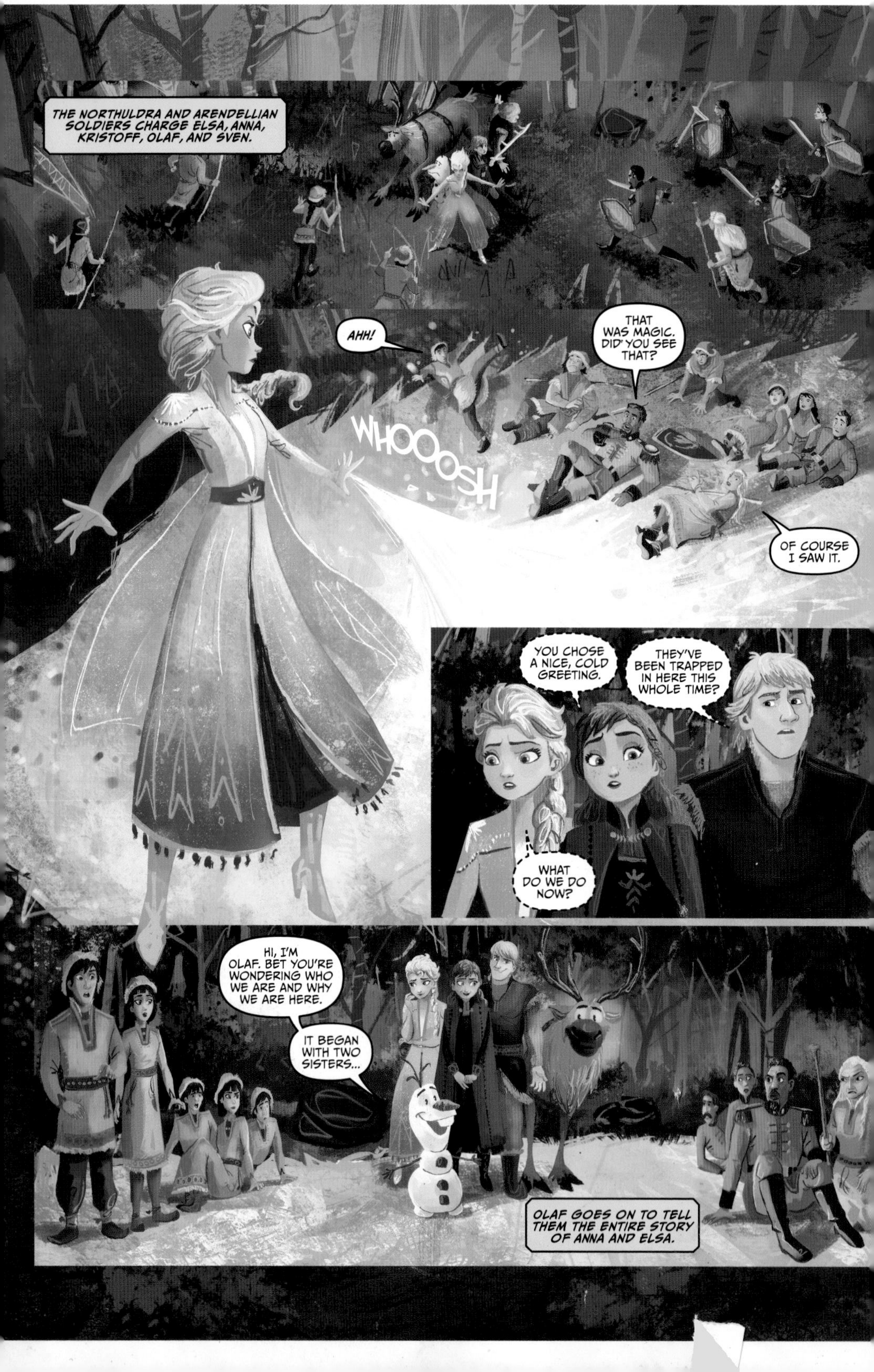
THE NORTHULDRA AND ARENDELLIAN SOLDIERS CHARGE ELSA, ANNA, KRISTOFF, OLAF, AND SVEN.
AHH!
THAT WAS MAGIC. DID YOU SEE THAT?
WHOOOOSH
OF COURSE I SAW IT.
YOU CHOSE A NICE, COLD GREETING.
THEY'VE BEEN TRAPPED IN HERE THIS WHOLE TIME?
WHAT DO WE DO NOW?
HI, I'M OLAF. BET YOU'RE WONDERING WHO WE ARE AND WHY WE ARE HERE.
IT BEGAN WITH TWO SISTERS...
OLAF GOES ON TO TELL THEM THE ENTIRE STORY OF ANNA AND ELSA.

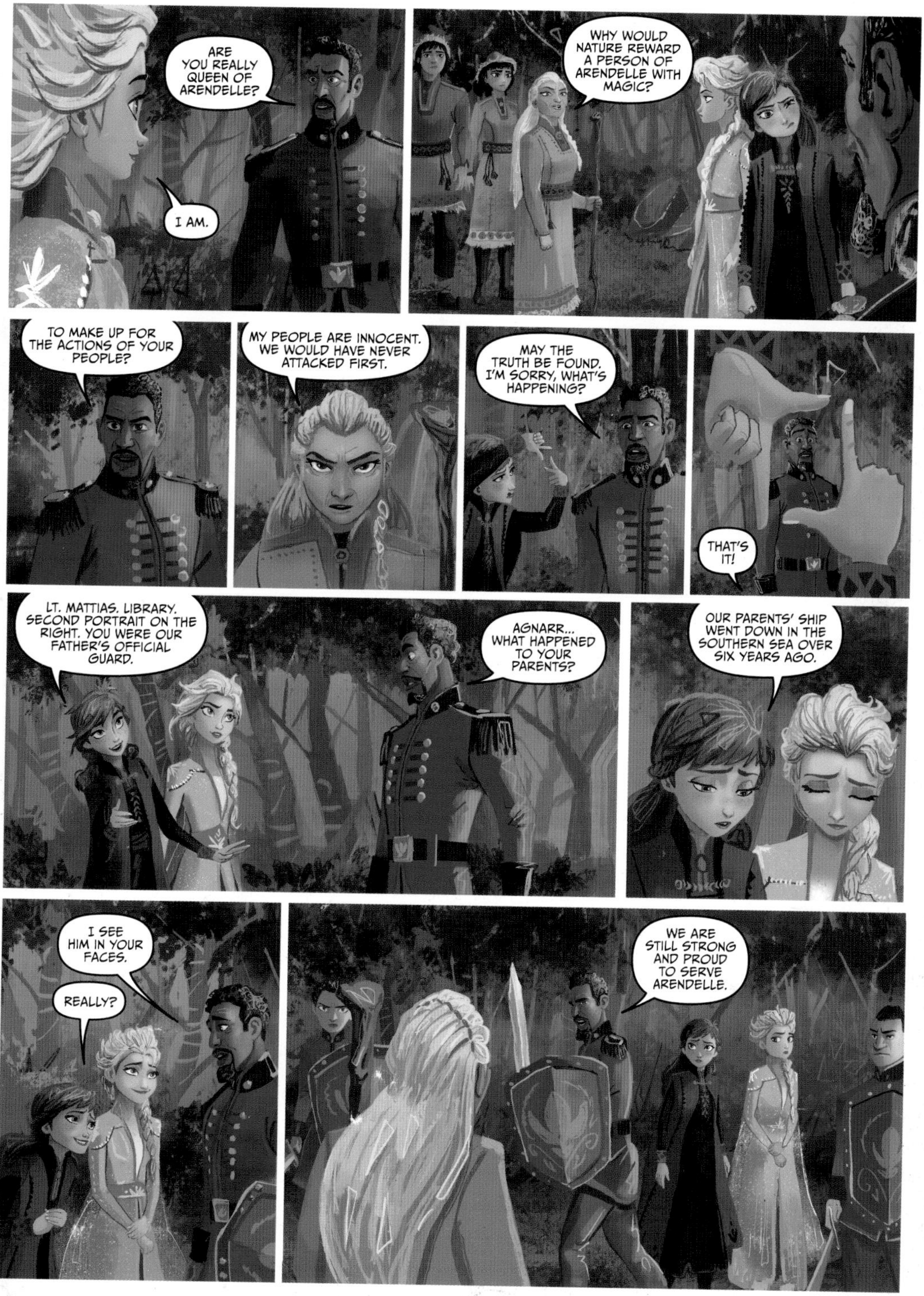
ARE YOU REALLY QUEEN OF ARENDELLE?
I AM.
WHY WOULD NATURE REWARD A PERSON OF ARENDELLE WITH MAGIC?
TO MAKE UP FOR THE ACTIONS OF YOUR PEOPLE?
MY PEOPLE ARE INNOCENT. WE WOULD HAVE NEVER ATTACKED FIRST.
MAY THE TRUTH BE FOUND. I'M SORRY, WHAT'S HAPPENING?
THAT'S IT!
LT. MATTIAS. LIBRARY. SECOND PORTRAIT ON THE RIGHT. YOU WERE OUR FATHER'S OFFICIAL GUARD.
AGNARR... WHAT HAPPENED TO YOUR PARENTS?
OUR PARENTS' SHIP WENT DOWN IN THE SOUTHERN SEA OVER SIX YEARS AGO.
I SEE HIM IN YOUR FACES.
REALLY?
WE ARE STILL STRONG AND PROUD TO SERVE ARENDELLE.

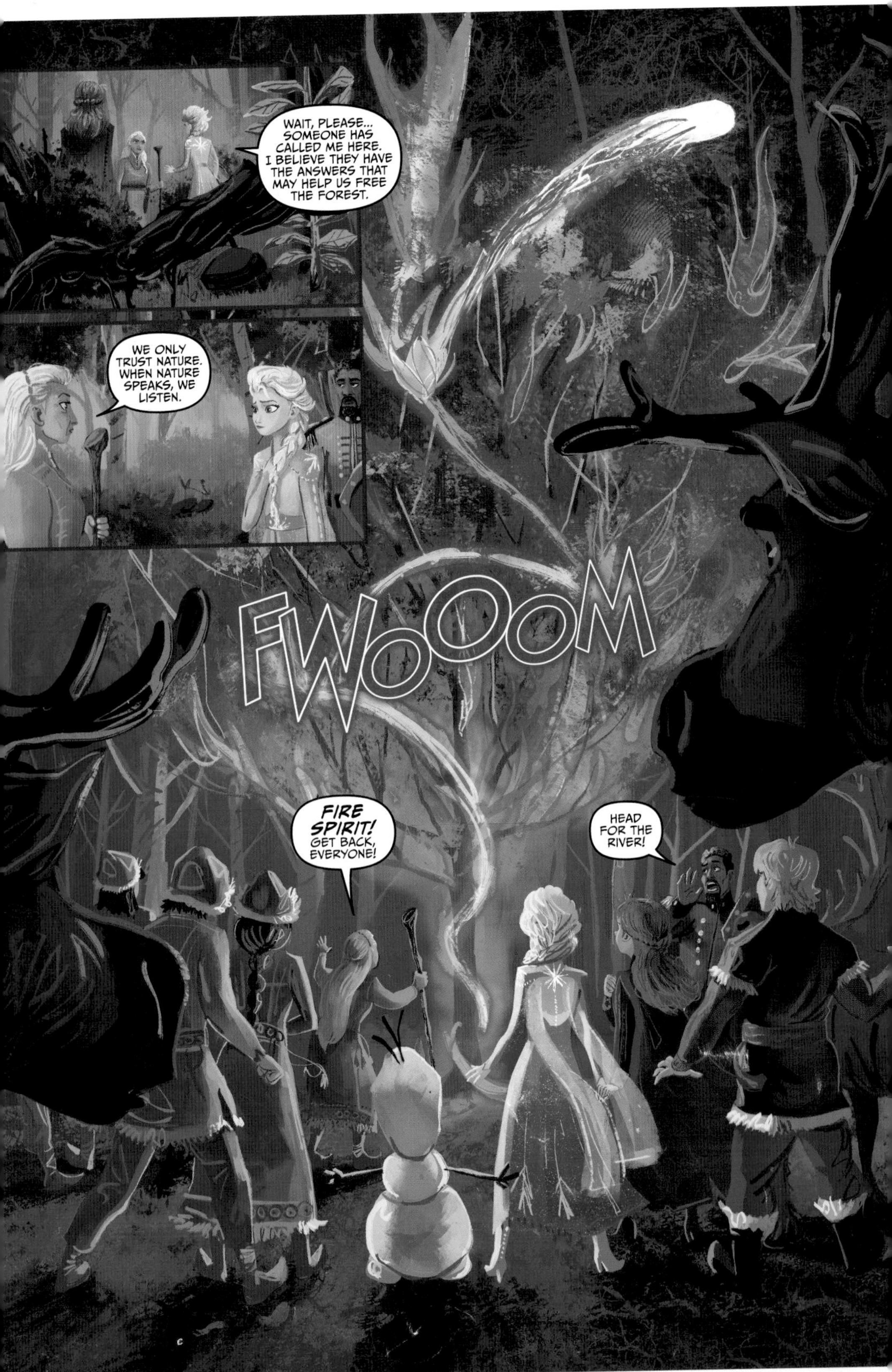
WAIT, PLEASE... SOMEONE HAS CALLED ME HERE. I BELIEVE THEY HAVE THE ANSWERS THAT MAY HELP US FREE THE FOREST.
WE ONLY TRUST NATURE. WHEN NATURE SPEAKS, WE LISTEN.
FWOOOOM
FIRE SPIRIT! GET BACK, EVERYONE!
HEAD FOR THE RIVER!

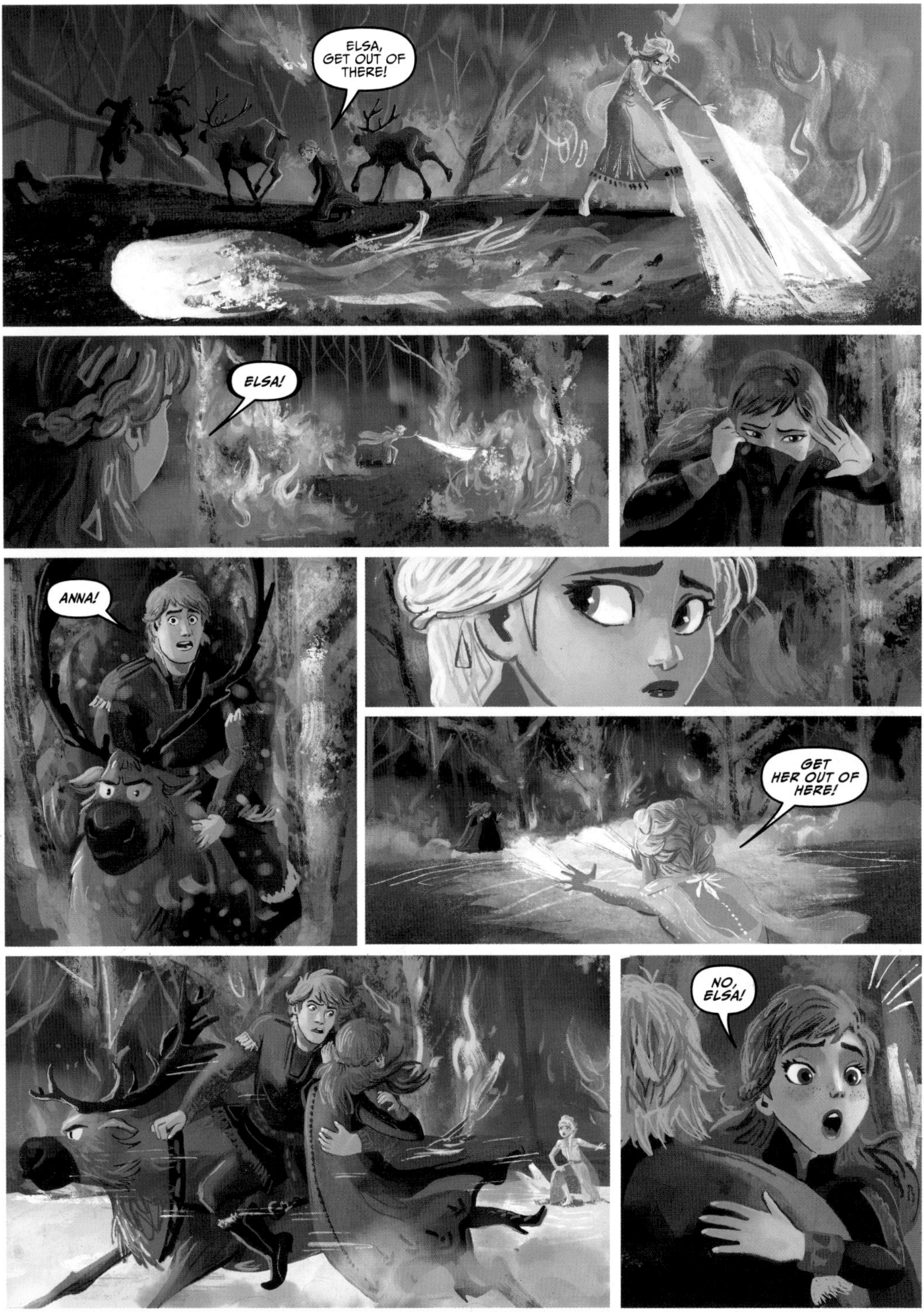
ELSA, GET OUT OF THERE!
ELSA!
ANNA!
GET HER OUT OF HERE!
NO, ELSA!

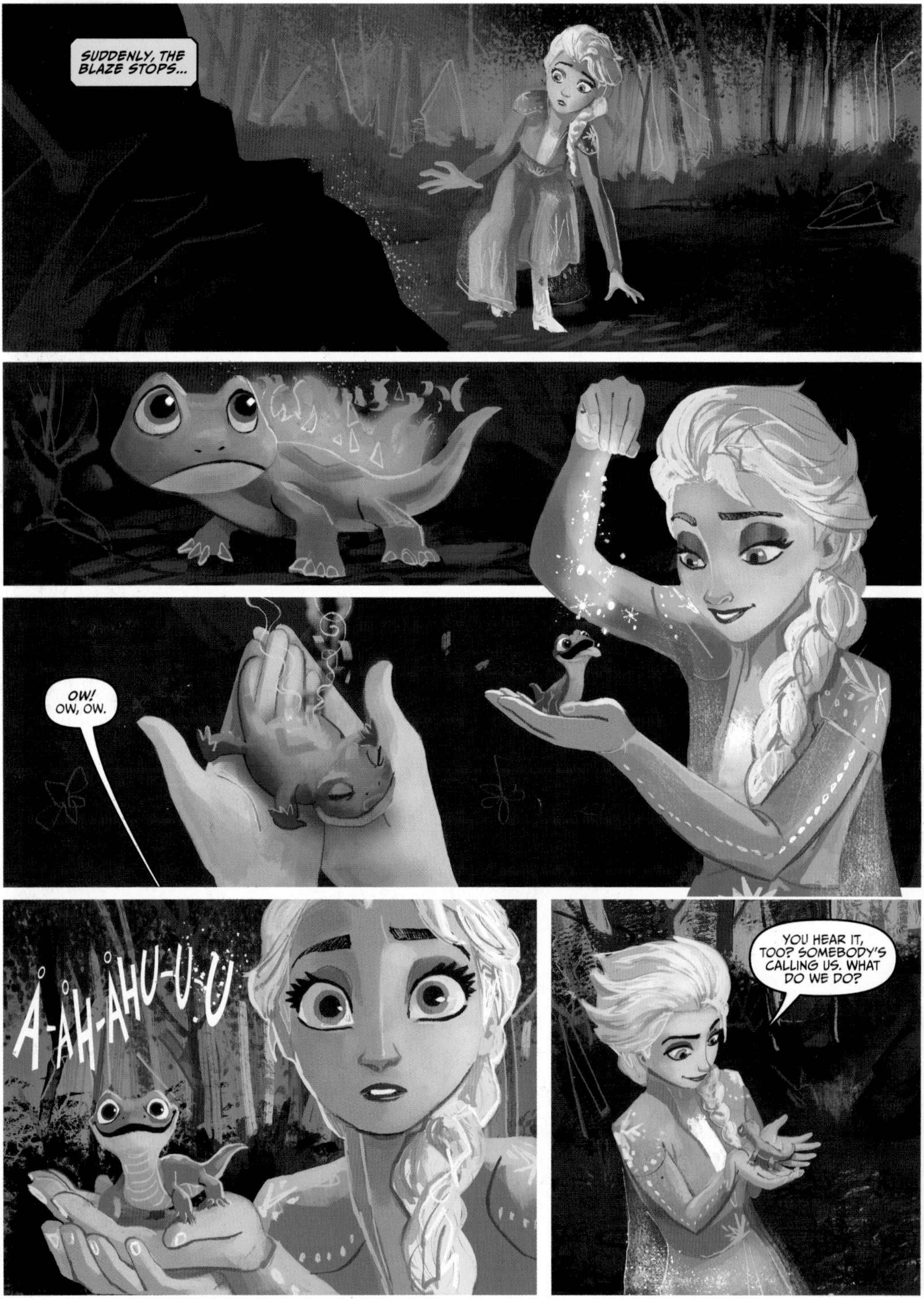
SUDDENLY, THE BLAZE STOPS...
OW! OW, OW.
Å-ÅH-ÅHU-U-U
YOU HEAR IT, TOO? SOMEBODY'S CALLING US. WHAT DO WE DO?

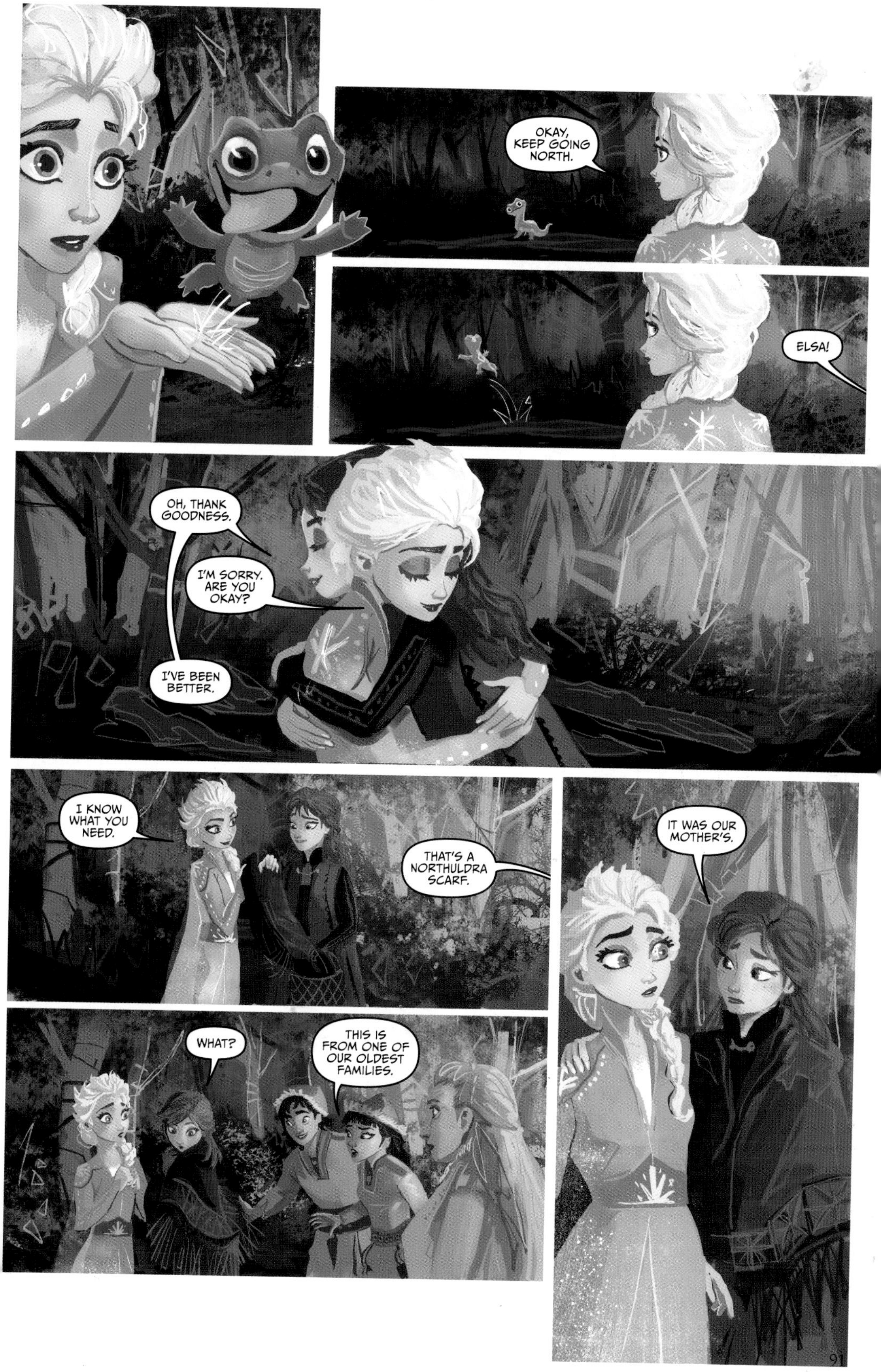
OKAY, KEEP GOING NORTH.
ELSA!
OH, THANK GOODNESS.
I'M SORRY. ARE YOU OKAY?
I'VE BEEN BETTER.
I KNOW WHAT YOU NEED.
THAT'S A NORTHULDRA SCARF.
WHAT?
THIS IS FROM ONE OF OUR OLDEST FAMILIES.
IT WAS OUR MOTHER'S.

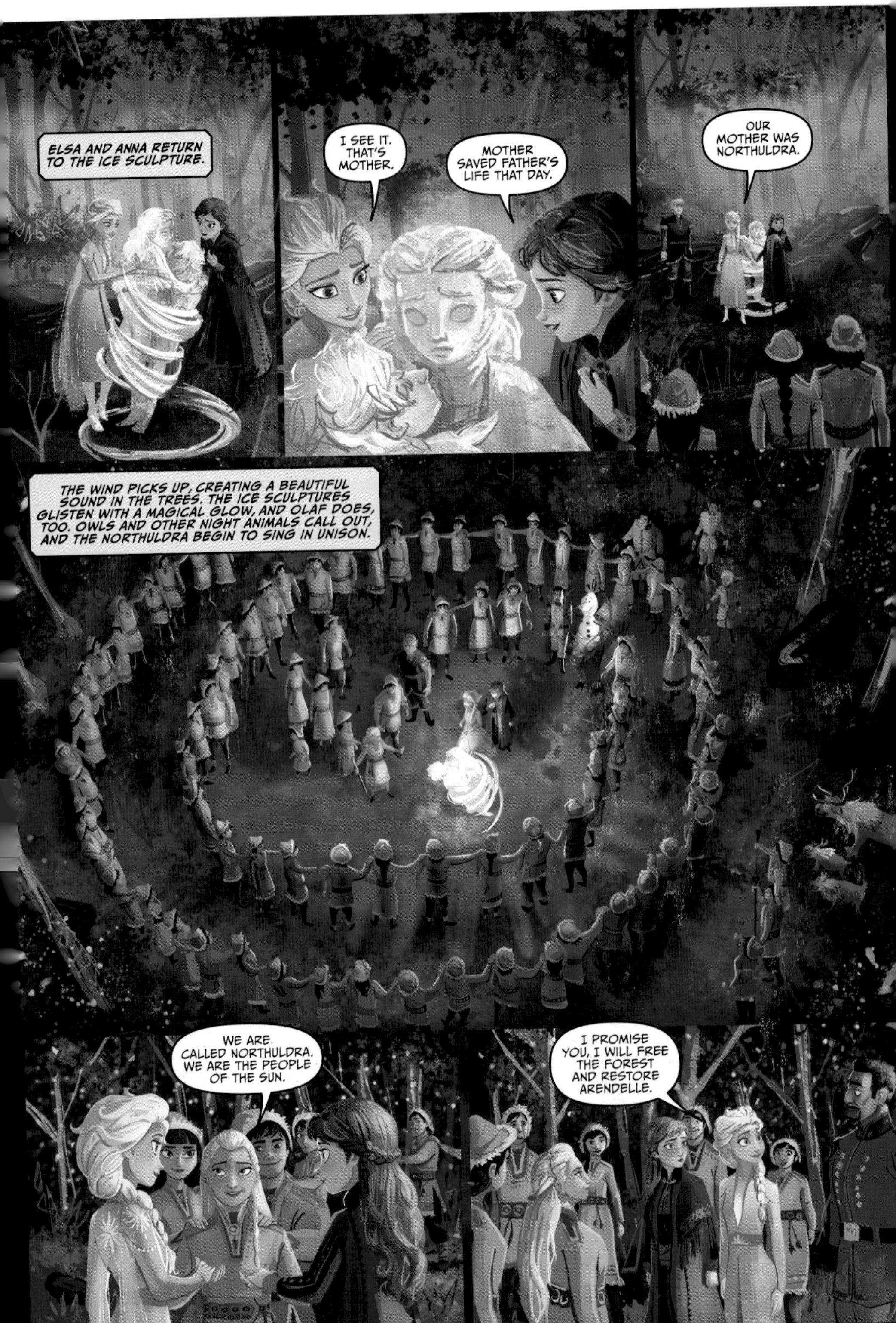
ELSA AND ANNA RETURN TO THE ICE SCULPTURE.
I SEE IT. THAT'S MOTHER.
MOTHER SAVED FATHER'S LIFE THAT DAY.
OUR MOTHER WAS NORTHULDRA.
THE WIND PICKS UP, CREATING A BEAUTIFUL SOUND IN THE TREES. THE ICE SCULPTURES GLISTEN WITH A MAGICAL GLOW, AND OLAF DOES, TOO. OWLS AND OTHER NIGHT ANIMALS CALL OUT, AND THE NORTHULDRA BEGIN TO SING IN UNISON.
WE ARE CALLED NORTHULDRA. WE ARE THE PEOPLE OF THE SUN.
I PROMISE YOU, I WILL FREE THE FOREST AND RESTORE ARENDELLE.

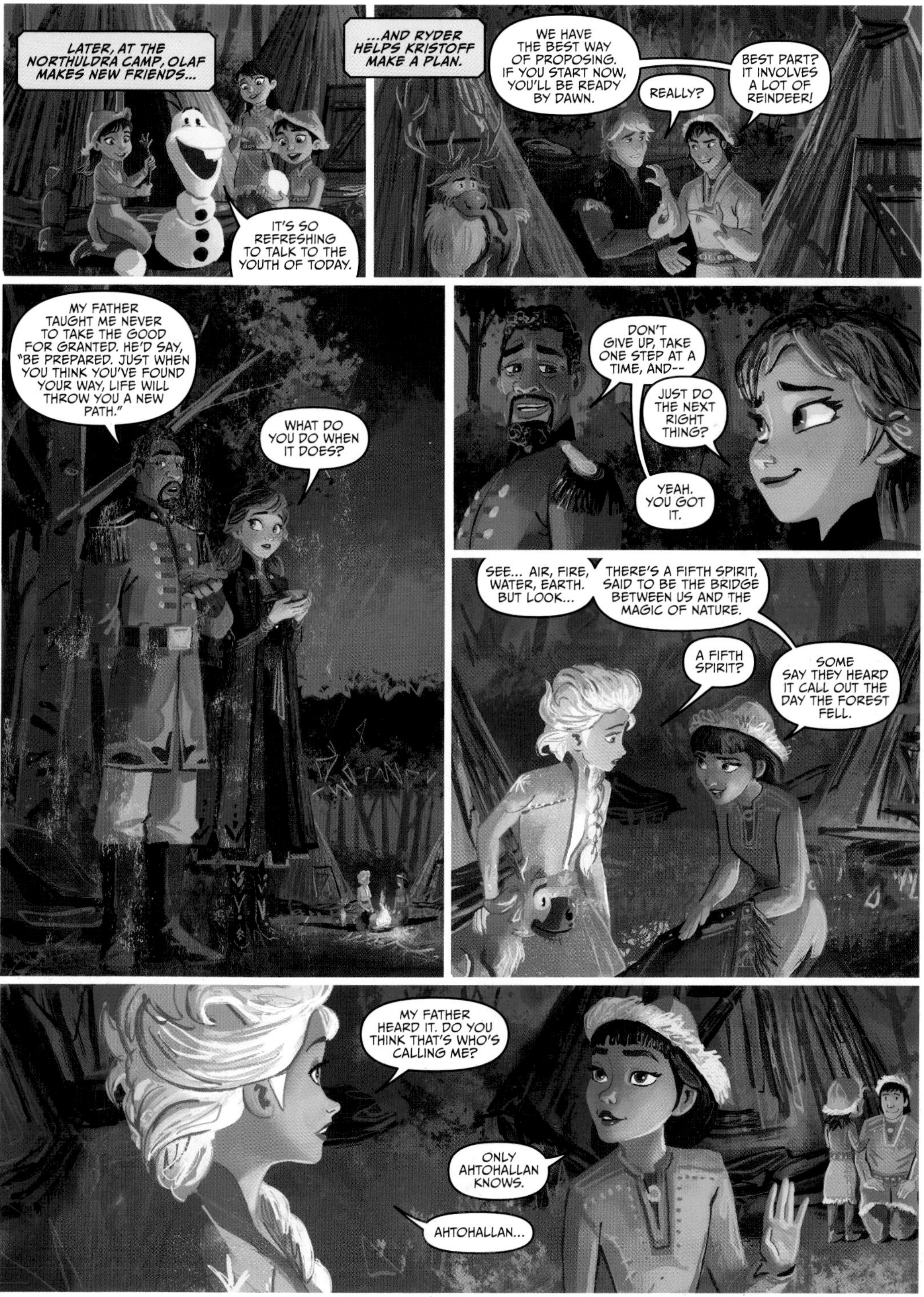
LATER, AT THE NORTHULDRA CAMP, OLAF MAKES NEW FRIENDS...
IT'S SO REFRESHING TO TALK TO THE YOUTH OF TODAY.
...AND RYDER HELPS KRISTOFF MAKE A PLAN.
WE HAVE THE BEST WAY OF PROPOSING. IF YOU START NOW, YOU'LL BE READY BY DAWN.
BEST PART? IT INVOLVES A LOT OF REINDEER!
REALLY?
MY FATHER TAUGHT ME NEVER TO TAKE THE GOOD FOR GRANTED. HE'D SAY, "BE PREPARED. JUST WHEN YOU THINK YOU'VE FOUND YOUR WAY, LIFE WILL THROW YOU A NEW PATH."
WHAT DO YOU DO WHEN IT DOES?
DON'T GIVE UP, TAKE ONE STEP AT A TIME, AND--
JUST DO THE NEXT RIGHT THING?
YEAH. YOU GOT IT.
SEE... AIR, FIRE, WATER, EARTH. BUT LOOK...
THERE'S A FIFTH SPIRIT, SAID TO BE THE BRIDGE BETWEEN US AND THE MAGIC OF NATURE.
A FIFTH SPIRIT?
SOME SAY THEY HEARD IT CALL OUT THE DAY THE FOREST FELL.
MY FATHER HEARD IT. DO YOU THINK THAT'S WHO'S CALLING ME?
ONLY AHTOHALLAN KNOWS.
AHTOHALLAN...

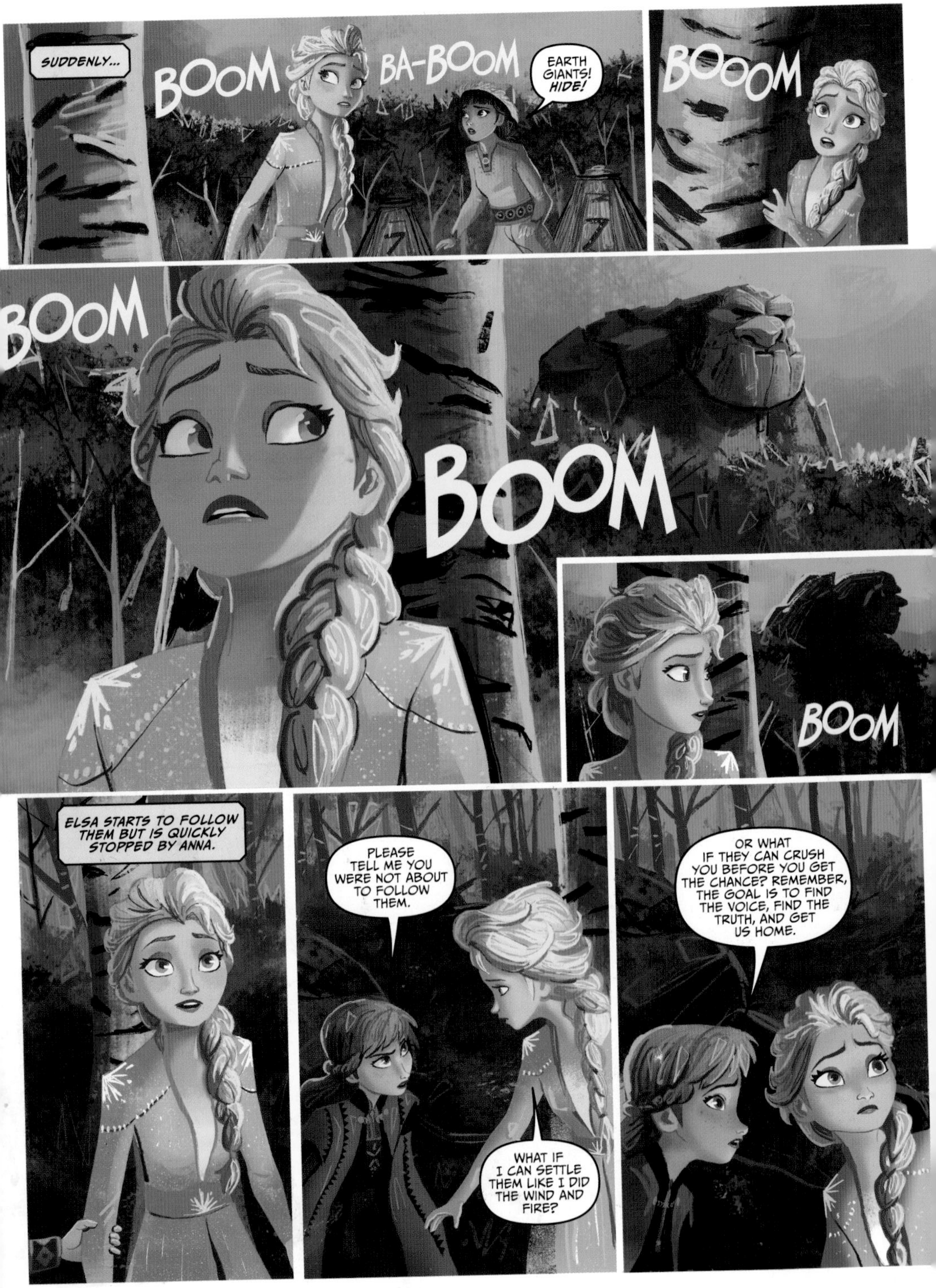
SUDDENLY...
BOOM
BA-BOOM
EARTH GIANTS! HIDE!
BOOOM
BOOM
BOOM
BOOM
ELSA STARTS TO FOLLOW THEM BUT IS QUICKLY STOPPED BY ANNA.
PLEASE TELL ME YOU WERE NOT ABOUT TO FOLLOW THEM.
WHAT IF I CAN SETTLE THEM LIKE I DID THE WIND AND FIRE?
OR WHAT IF THEY CAN CRUSH YOU BEFORE YOU GET THE CHANCE? REMEMBER, THE GOAL IS TO FIND THE VOICE, FIND THE TRUTH, AND GET US HOME.

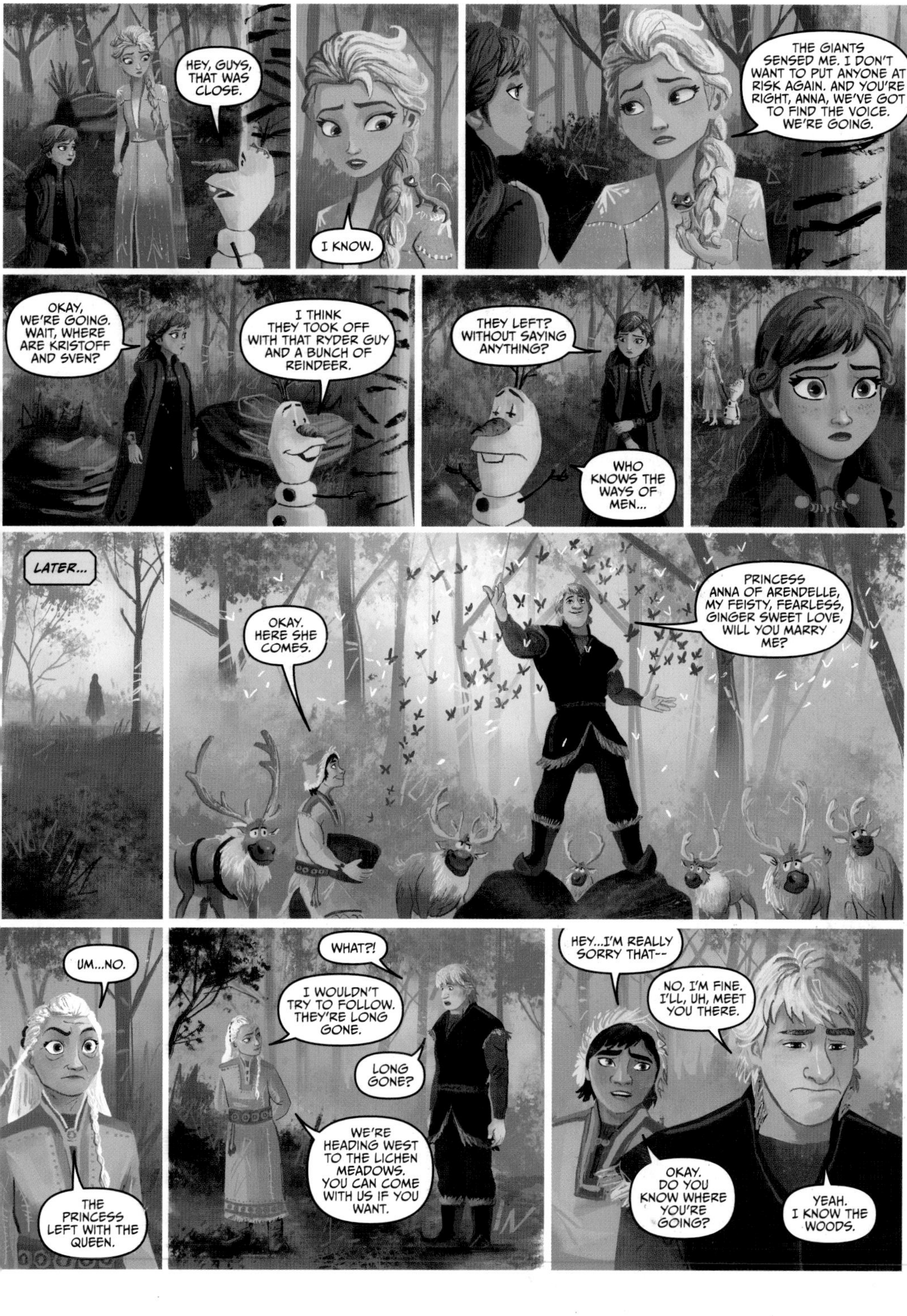
HEY, GUYS, THAT WAS CLOSE.
I KNOW.
THE GIANTS SENSED ME. I DON'T WANT TO PUT ANYONE AT RISK AGAIN. AND YOU'RE RIGHT, ANNA, WE'VE GOT TO FIND THE VOICE. WE'RE GOING.
OKAY, WE'RE GOING. WAIT, WHERE ARE KRISTOFF AND SVEN?
I THINK THEY TOOK OFF WITH THAT RYDER GUY AND A BUNCH OF REINDEER.
THEY LEFT? WITHOUT SAYING ANYTHING?
WHO KNOWS THE WAYS OF MEN...
LATER...
OKAY. HERE SHE COMES.
PRINCESS ANNA OF ARENDELLE, MY FEISTY, FEARLESS, GINGER SWEET LOVE, WILL YOU MARRY ME?
UM...NO.
THE PRINCESS LEFT WITH THE QUEEN.
WHAT?!
I WOULDN'T TRY TO FOLLOW. THEY'RE LONG GONE.
LONG GONE?
WE'RE HEADING WEST TO THE LICHEN MEADOWS. YOU CAN COME WITH US IF YOU WANT.
HEY...I'M REALLY SORRY THAT--
NO, I'M FINE. I'LL, UH, MEET YOU THERE.
OKAY. DO YOU KNOW WHERE YOU'RE GOING?
YEAH. I KNOW THE WOODS.

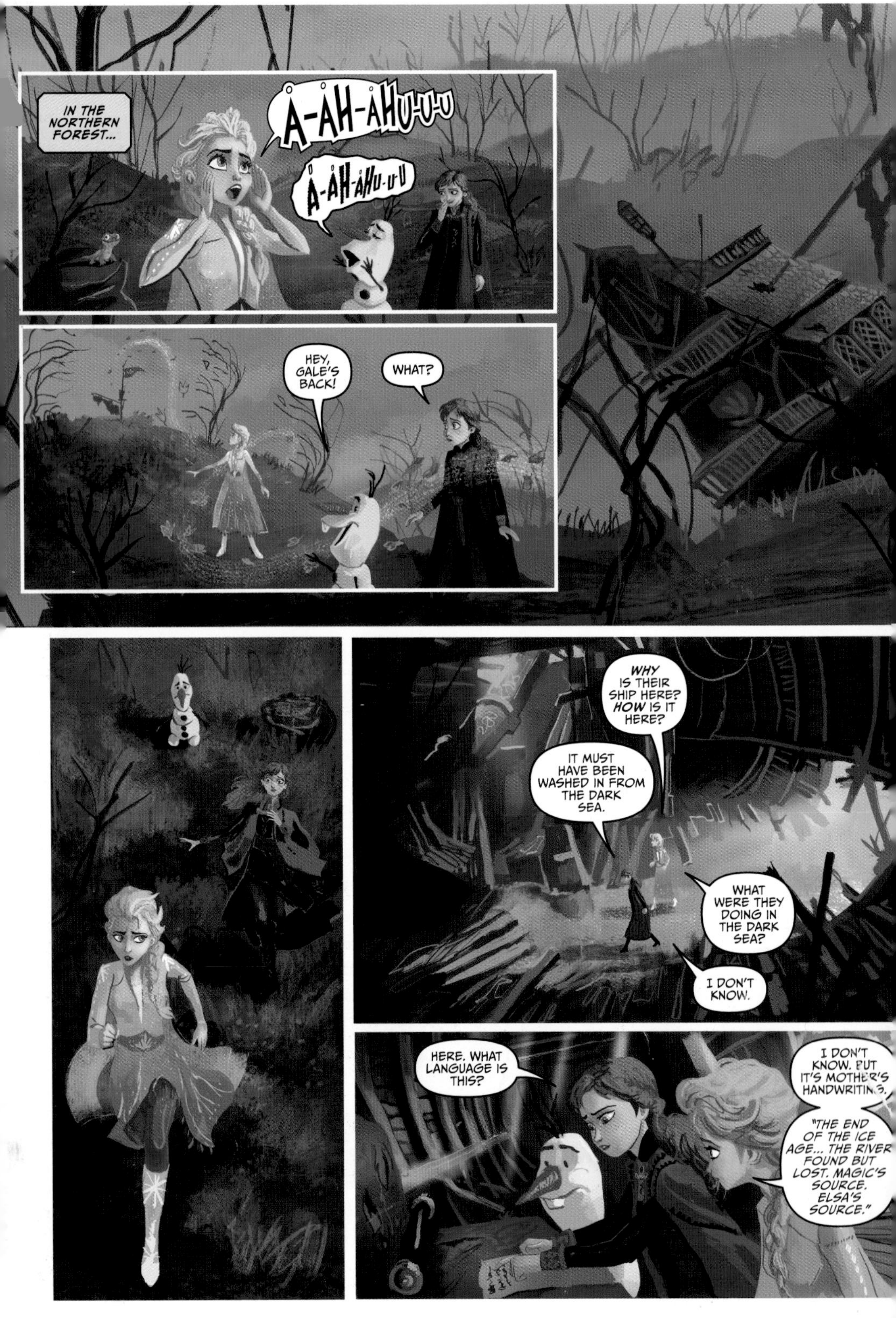
IN THE NORTHERN FOREST...
Å-ÅH-ÅHU-U-U
Å-ÅH-ÅHU-U-U
HEY, GALE'S BACK!
WHAT?
WHY IS THEIR SHIP HERE? HOW IS IT HERE?
IT MUST HAVE BEEN WASHED IN FROM THE DARK SEA.
WHAT WERE THEY DOING IN THE DARK SEA?
I DON'T KNOW.
HERE. WHAT LANGUAGE IS THIS?
I DON'T KNOW. BUT IT'S MOTHER'S HANDWRITING.
"THE END OF THE ICE AGE... THE RIVER FOUND BUT LOST. MAGIC'S SOURCE. ELSA'S SOURCE."

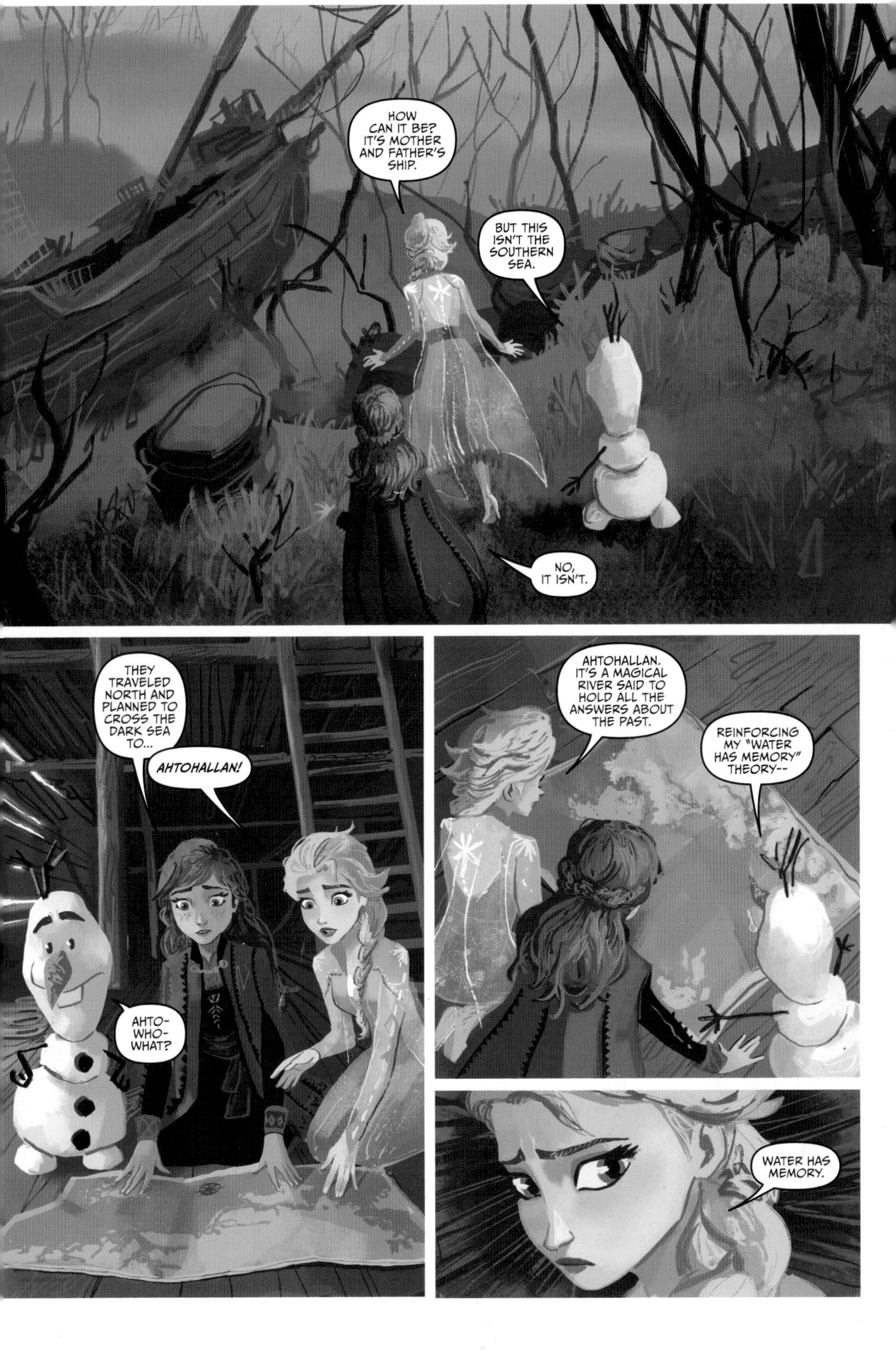
HOW CAN IT BE? IT'S MOTHER AND FATHER'S SHIP.
BUT THIS ISN'T THE SOUTHERN SEA.
NO, IT ISN'T.
THEY TRAVELED NORTH AND PLANNED TO CROSS THE DARK SEA TO...
AHTOHALLAN!
AHTO-WHO-WHAT?
AHTOHALLAN. IT'S A MAGICAL RIVER SAID TO HOLD ALL THE ANSWERS ABOUT THE PAST.
REINFORCING MY "WATER HAS MEMORY" THEORY--
WATER HAS MEMORY.

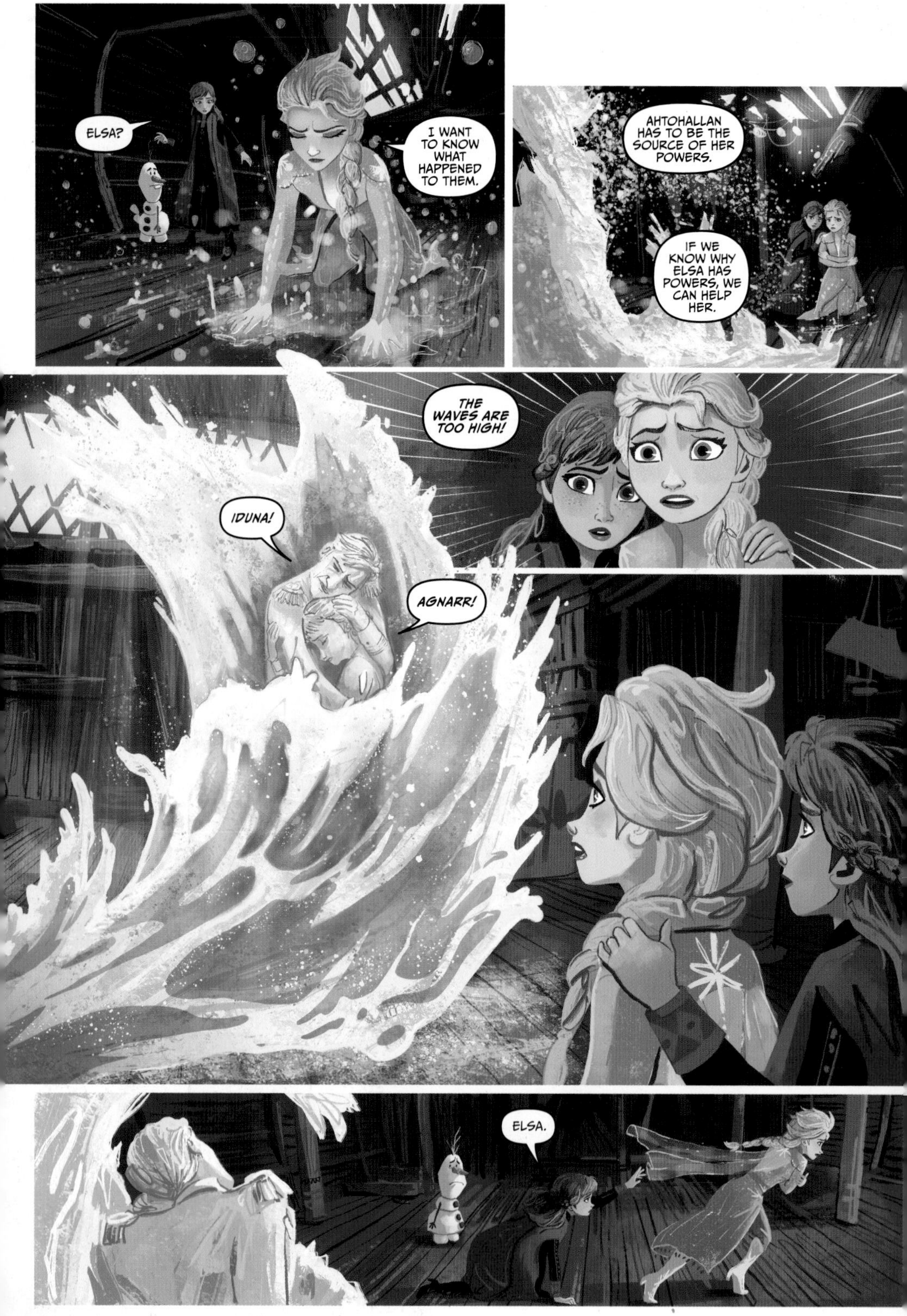
ELSA?
I WANT TO KNOW WHAT HAPPENED TO THEM.
AHTOHALLAN HAS TO BE THE SOURCE OF HER POWERS.
IF WE KNOW WHY ELSA HAS POWERS, WE CAN HELP HER.
THE WAVES ARE TOO HIGH!
IDUNA!
AGNARR!
ELSA.

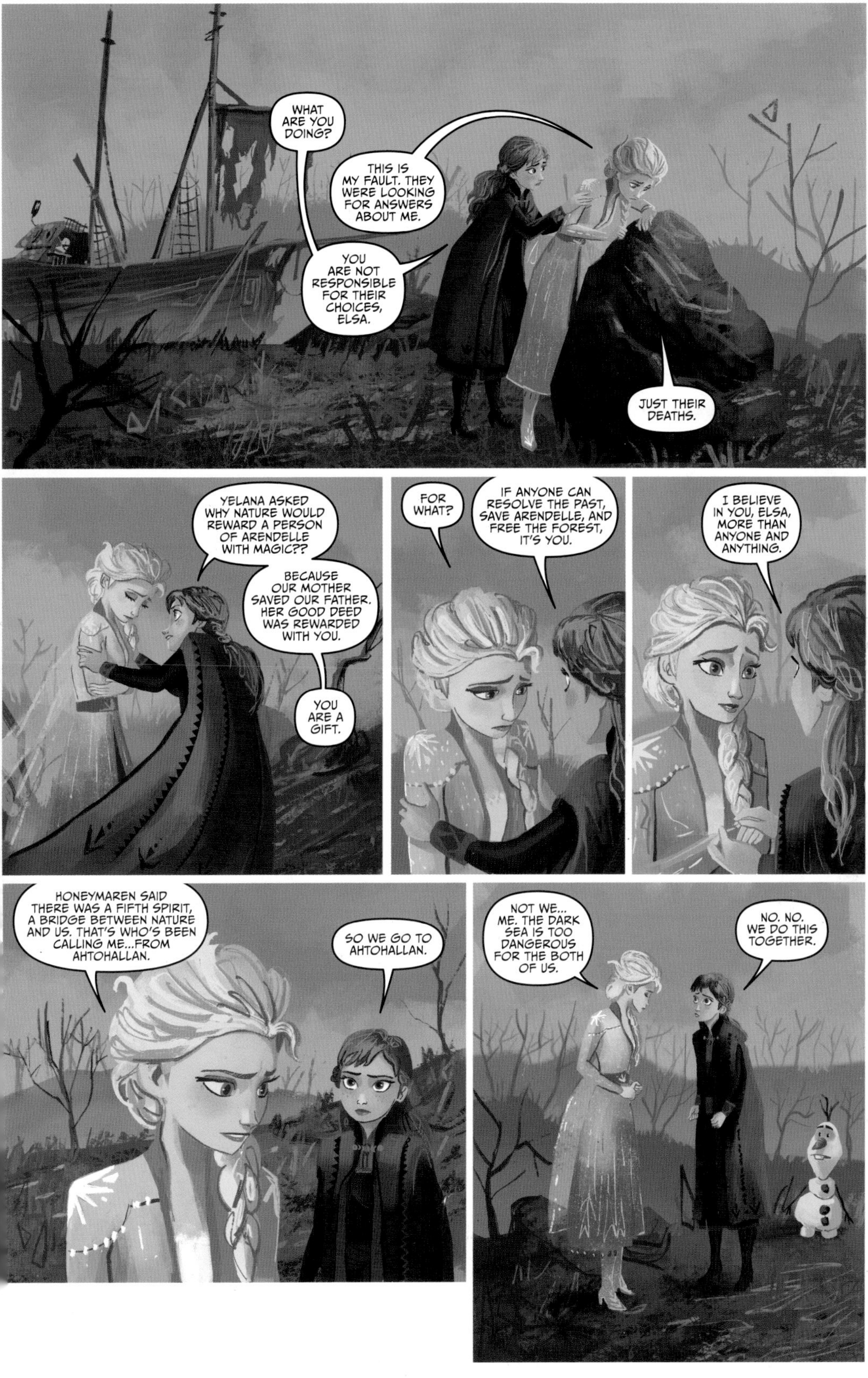
WHAT ARE YOU DOING?
THIS IS MY FAULT. THEY WERE LOOKING FOR ANSWERS ABOUT ME.
YOU ARE NOT RESPONSIBLE FOR THEIR CHOICES, ELSA.
JUST THEIR DEATHS.
YELANA ASKED WHY NATURE WOULD REWARD A PERSON OF ARENDELLE WITH MAGIC??
BECAUSE OUR MOTHER SAVED OUR FATHER. HER GOOD DEED WAS REWARDED WITH YOU.
YOU ARE A GIFT.
FOR WHAT?
IF ANYONE CAN RESOLVE THE PAST, SAVE ARENDELLE, AND FREE THE FOREST, IT'S YOU.
I BELIEVE IN YOU, ELSA, MORE THAN ANYONE AND ANYTHING.
HONEYMAREN SAID THERE WAS A FIFTH SPIRIT, A BRIDGE BETWEEN NATURE AND US. THAT'S WHO'S BEEN CALLING ME...FROM AHTOHALLAN.
SO WE GO TO AHTOHALLAN.
NOT WE... ME. THE DARK SEA IS TOO DANGEROUS FOR THE BOTH OF US.
NO. NO. WE DO THIS TOGETHER.

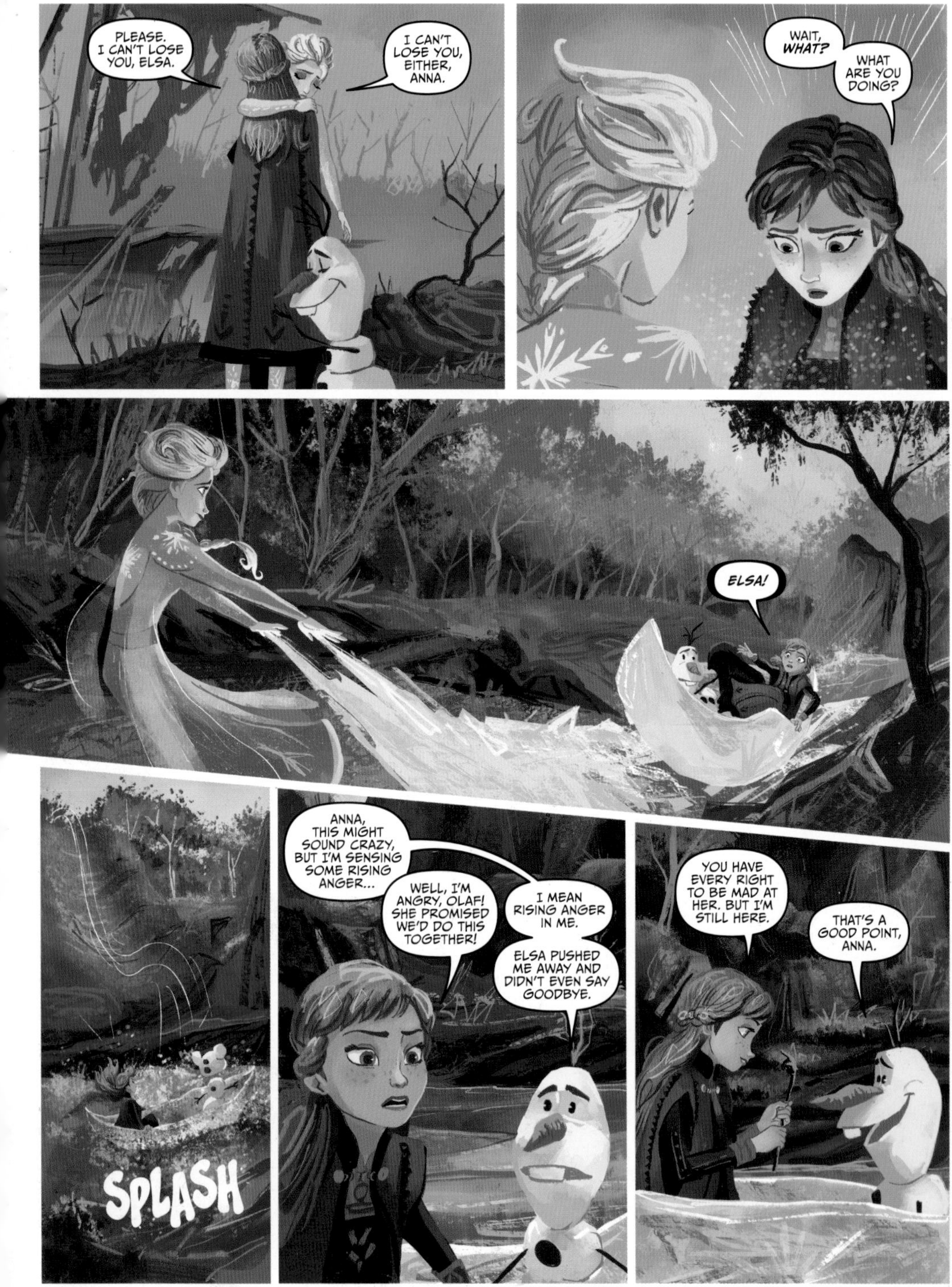
PLEASE. I CAN'T LOSE YOU, ELSA.
I CAN'T LOSE YOU, EITHER, ANNA.
WAIT, WHAT?
WHAT ARE YOU DOING?
ELSA!
SPLASH
ANNA, THIS MIGHT SOUND CRAZY, BUT I'M SENSING SOME RISING ANGER...
WELL, I'M ANGRY, OLAF! SHE PROMISED WE'D DO THIS TOGETHER!
I MEAN RISING ANGER IN ME.
ELSA PUSHED ME AWAY AND DIDN'T EVEN SAY GOODBYE.
YOU HAVE EVERY RIGHT TO BE MAD AT HER. BUT I'M STILL HERE.
THAT'S A GOOD POINT, ANNA.

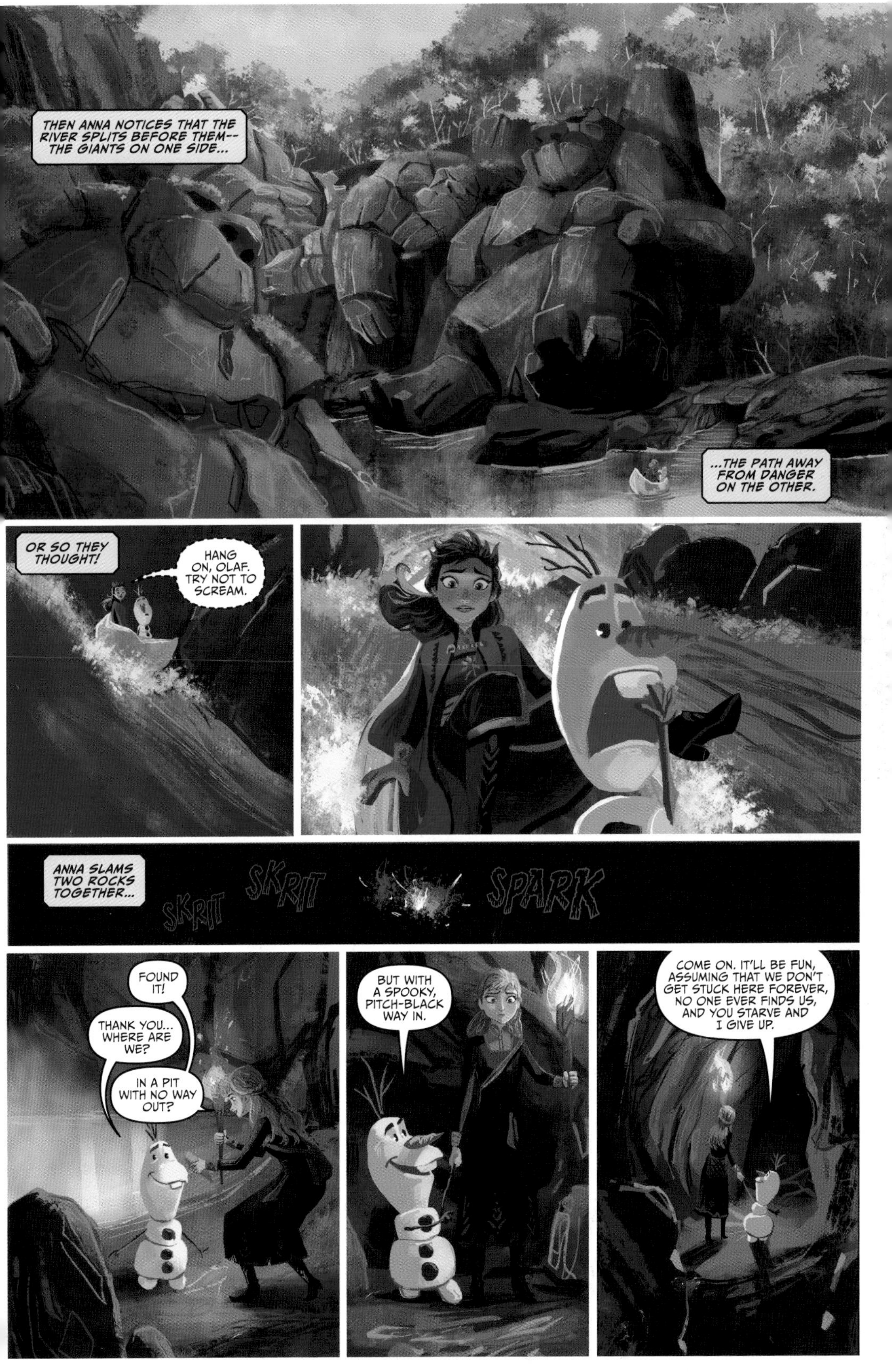
THEN ANNA NOTICES THAT THE RIVER SPLITS BEFORE THEM-- THE GIANTS ON ONE SIDE...
...THE PATH AWAY FROM DANGER ON THE OTHER.
OR SO THEY THOUGHT!
HANG ON, OLAF. TRY NOT TO SCREAM.
ANNA SLAMS TWO ROCKS TOGETHER...
SKRIT
SKRIT
SPARK
FOUND IT!
THANK YOU... WHERE ARE WE?
IN A PIT WITH NO WAY OUT?
BUT WITH A SPOOKY, PITCH-BLACK WAY IN.
COME ON. IT'LL BE FUN, ASSUMING THAT WE DON'T GET STUCK HERE FOREVER, NO ONE EVER FINDS US, AND YOU STARVE AND I GIVE UP.

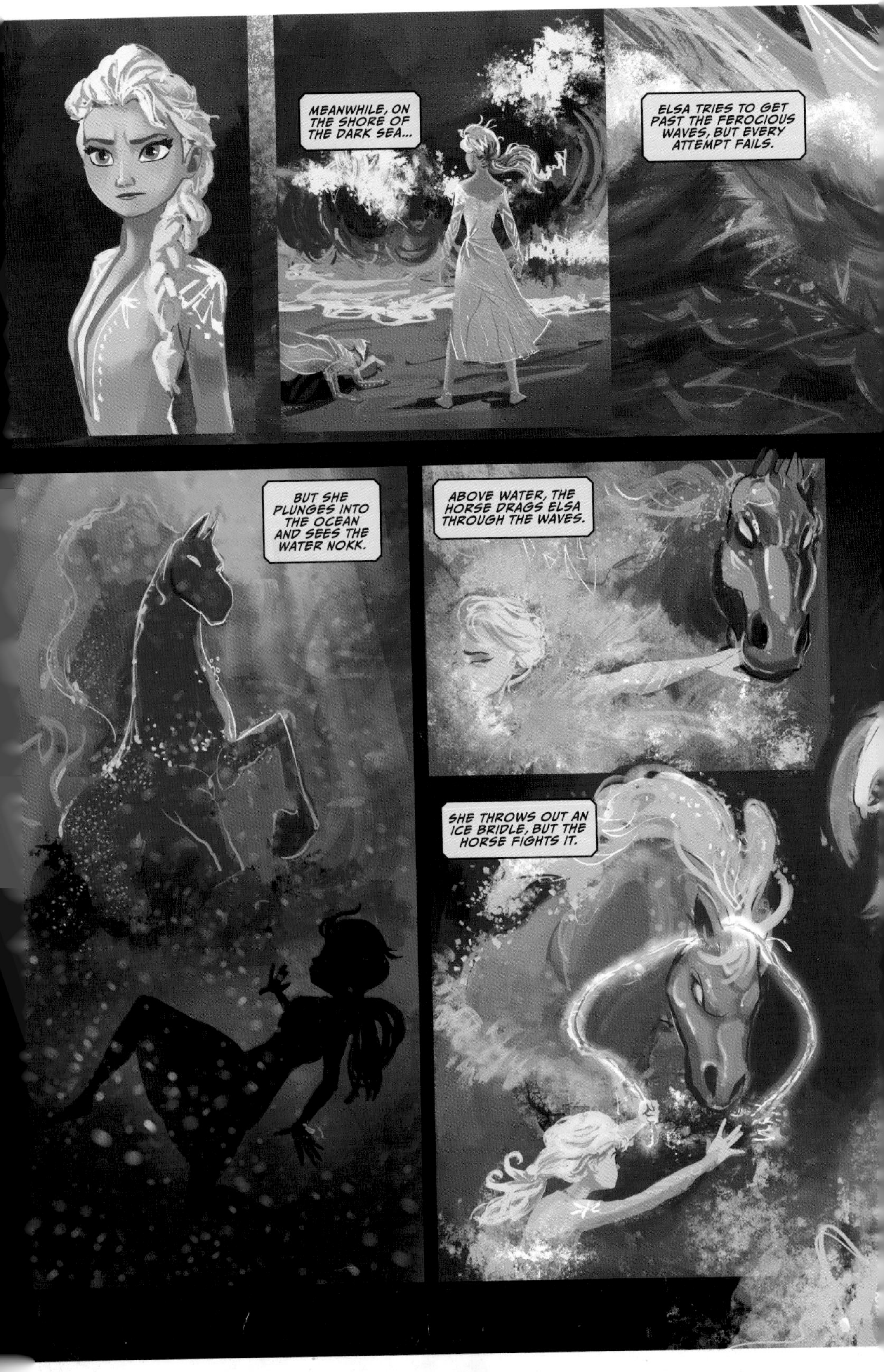
MEANWHILE, ON THE SHORE OF THE DARK SEA...
ELSA TRIES TO GET PAST THE FEROCIOUS WAVES, BUT EVERY ATTEMPT FAILS.
BUT SHE PLUNGES INTO THE OCEAN AND SEES THE WATER NOKK.
ABOVE WATER, THE HORSE DRAGS ELSA THROUGH THE WAVES.
SHE THROWS OUT AN ICE BRIDLE, BUT THE HORSE FIGHTS IT.

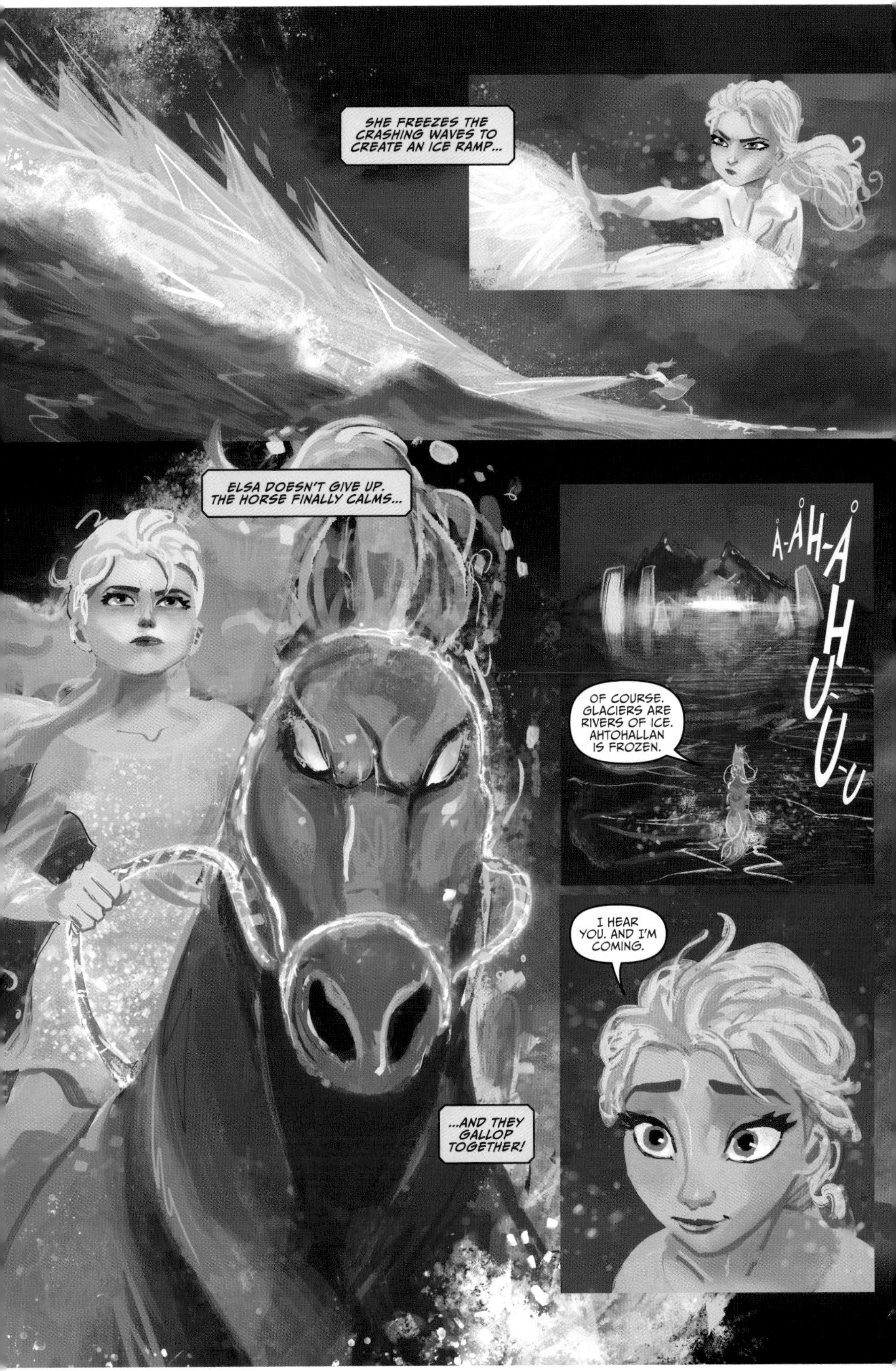

SHE FREEZES THE CRASHING WAVES TO CREATE AN ICE RAMP...
ELSA DOESN'T GIVE UP. THE HORSE FINALLY CALMS...
...AND THEY GALLOP TOGETHER!
Å-ÅH-ÅHU-U-U
OF COURSE. GLACIERS ARE RIVERS OF ICE. AHTOHALLAN IS FROZEN.
I HEAR YOU. AND I'M COMING.

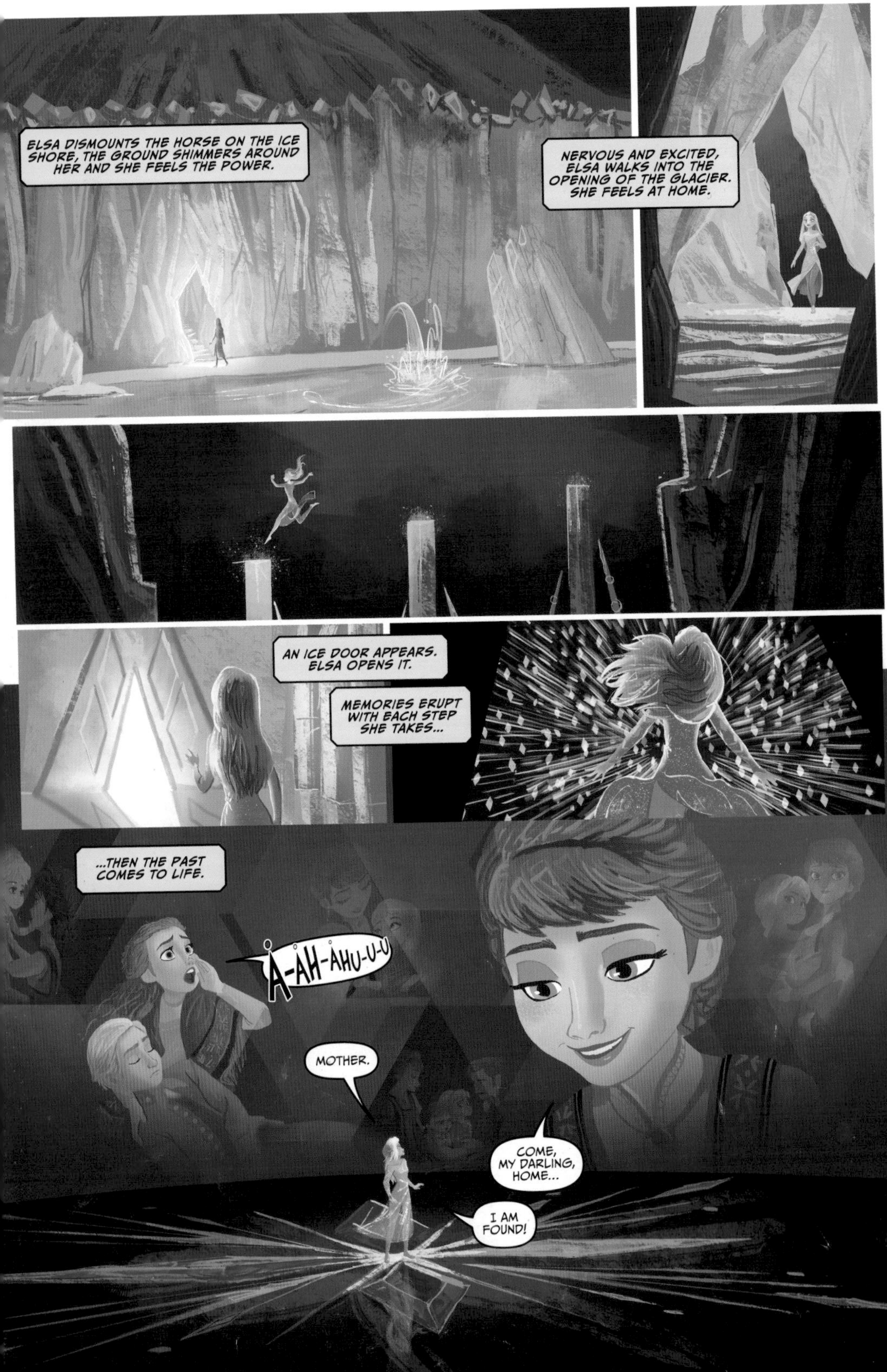
ELSA DISMOUNTS THE HORSE ON THE ICE SHORE, THE GROUND SHIMMERS AROUND HER AND SHE FEELS THE POWER.
NERVOUS AND EXCITED, ELSA WALKS INTO THE OPENING OF THE GLACIER. SHE FEELS AT HOME.
AN ICE DOOR APPEARS. ELSA OPENS IT.
MEMORIES ERUPT WITH EACH STEP SHE TAKES...
...THEN THE PAST COMES TO LIFE.
Å-AH-AHU-U-U
MOTHER.
COME, MY DARLING, HOME...
I AM FOUND!

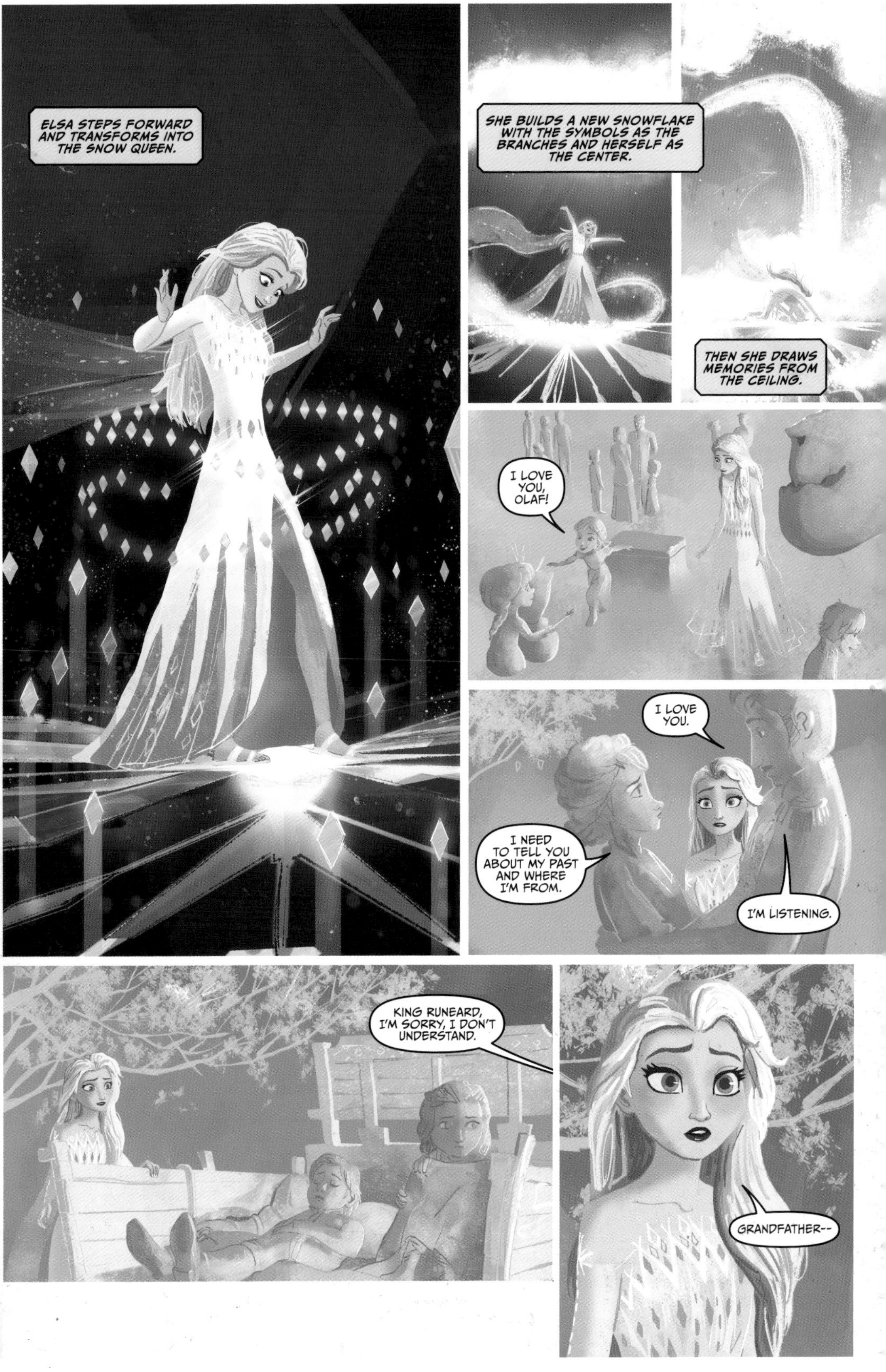
ELSA STEPS FORWARD AND TRANSFORMS INTO THE SNOW QUEEN.
SHE BUILDS A NEW SNOWFLAKE WITH THE SYMBOLS AS THE BRANCHES AND HERSELF AS THE CENTER.
THEN SHE DRAWS MEMORIES FROM THE CEILING.
I LOVE YOU, OLAF!
I LOVE YOU.
I NEED TO TELL YOU ABOUT MY PAST AND WHERE I'M FROM.
I'M LISTENING.
KING RUNEARD, I'M SORRY, I DON'T UNDERSTAND.
GRANDFATHER--

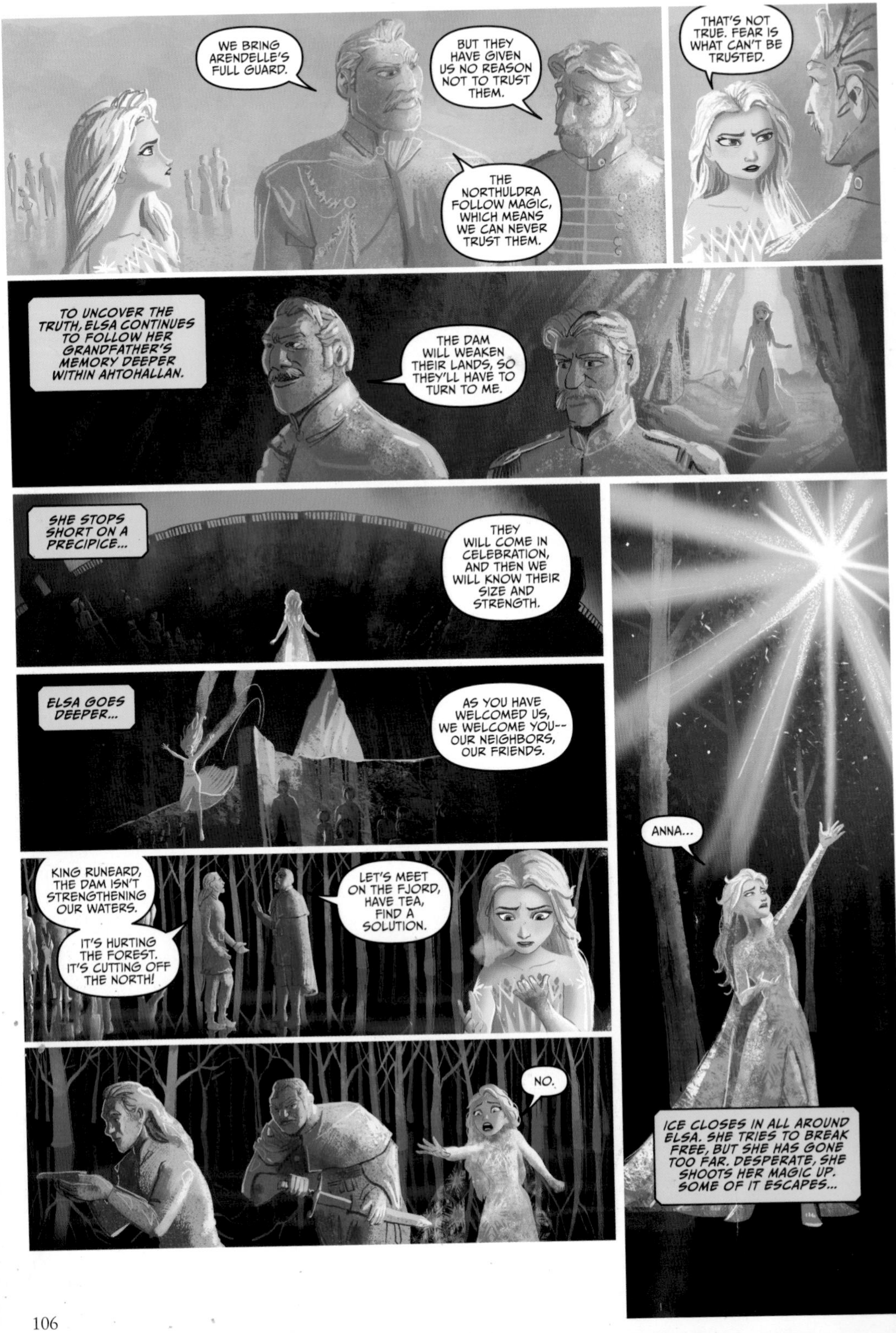
WE BRING ARENDELLE'S FULL GUARD.
BUT THEY HAVE GIVEN US NO REASON NOT TO TRUST THEM.
THE NORTHULDRA FOLLOW MAGIC, WHICH MEANS WE CAN NEVER TRUST THEM.
THAT'S NOT TRUE. FEAR IS WHAT CAN'T BE TRUSTED.
TO UNCOVER THE TRUTH, ELSA CONTINUES TO FOLLOW HER GRANDFATHER'S MEMORY DEEPER WITHIN AHTOHALLAN.
THE DAM WILL WEAKEN THEIR LANDS, SO THEY'LL HAVE TO TURN TO ME.
SHE STOPS SHORT ON A PRECIPICE...
THEY WILL COME IN CELEBRATION, AND THEN WE WILL KNOW THEIR SIZE AND STRENGTH.
ELSA GOES DEEPER...
AS YOU HAVE WELCOMED US, WE WELCOME YOU-- OUR NEIGHBORS, OUR FRIENDS.
KING RUNEARD, THE DAM ISN'T STRENGTHENING OUR WATERS.
IT'S HURTING THE FOREST. IT'S CUTTING OFF THE NORTH!
LET'S MEET ON THE FJORD, HAVE TEA, FIND A SOLUTION.
NO.
ANNA...
ICE CLOSES IN ALL AROUND ELSA. SHE TRIES TO BREAK FREE, BUT SHE HAS GONE TOO FAR. DESPERATE, SHE SHOOTS HER MAGIC UP. SOME OF IT ESCAPES...

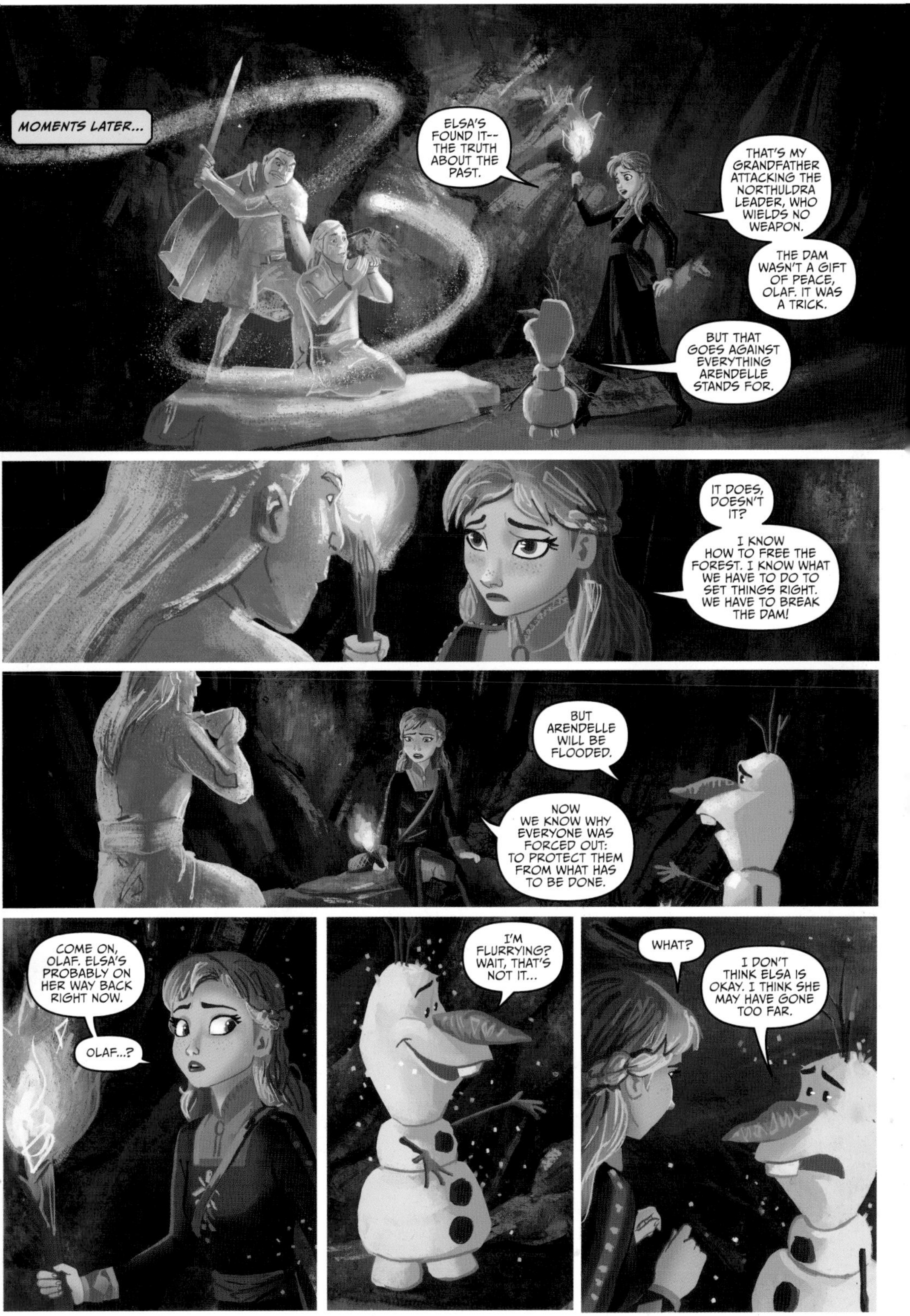
MOMENTS LATER...
ELSA'S FOUND IT-- THE TRUTH ABOUT THE PAST.
THAT'S MY GRANDFATHER ATTACKING THE NORTHULDRA LEADER, WHO WIELDS NO WEAPON.
THE DAM WASN'T A GIFT OF PEACE, OLAF. IT WAS A TRICK.
BUT THAT GOES AGAINST EVERYTHING ARENDELLE STANDS FOR.
IT DOES, DOESN'T IT?
I KNOW HOW TO FREE THE FOREST. I KNOW WHAT WE HAVE TO DO TO SET THINGS RIGHT. WE HAVE TO BREAK THE DAM!
BUT ARENDELLE WILL BE FLOODED.
NOW WE KNOW WHY EVERYONE WAS FORCED OUT: TO PROTECT THEM FROM WHAT HAS TO BE DONE.
COME ON, OLAF. ELSA'S PROBABLY ON HER WAY BACK RIGHT NOW.
OLAF...?
I'M FLURRYING? WAIT, THAT'S NOT IT...
WHAT?
I DON'T THINK ELSA IS OKAY. I THINK SHE MAY HAVE GONE TOO FAR.

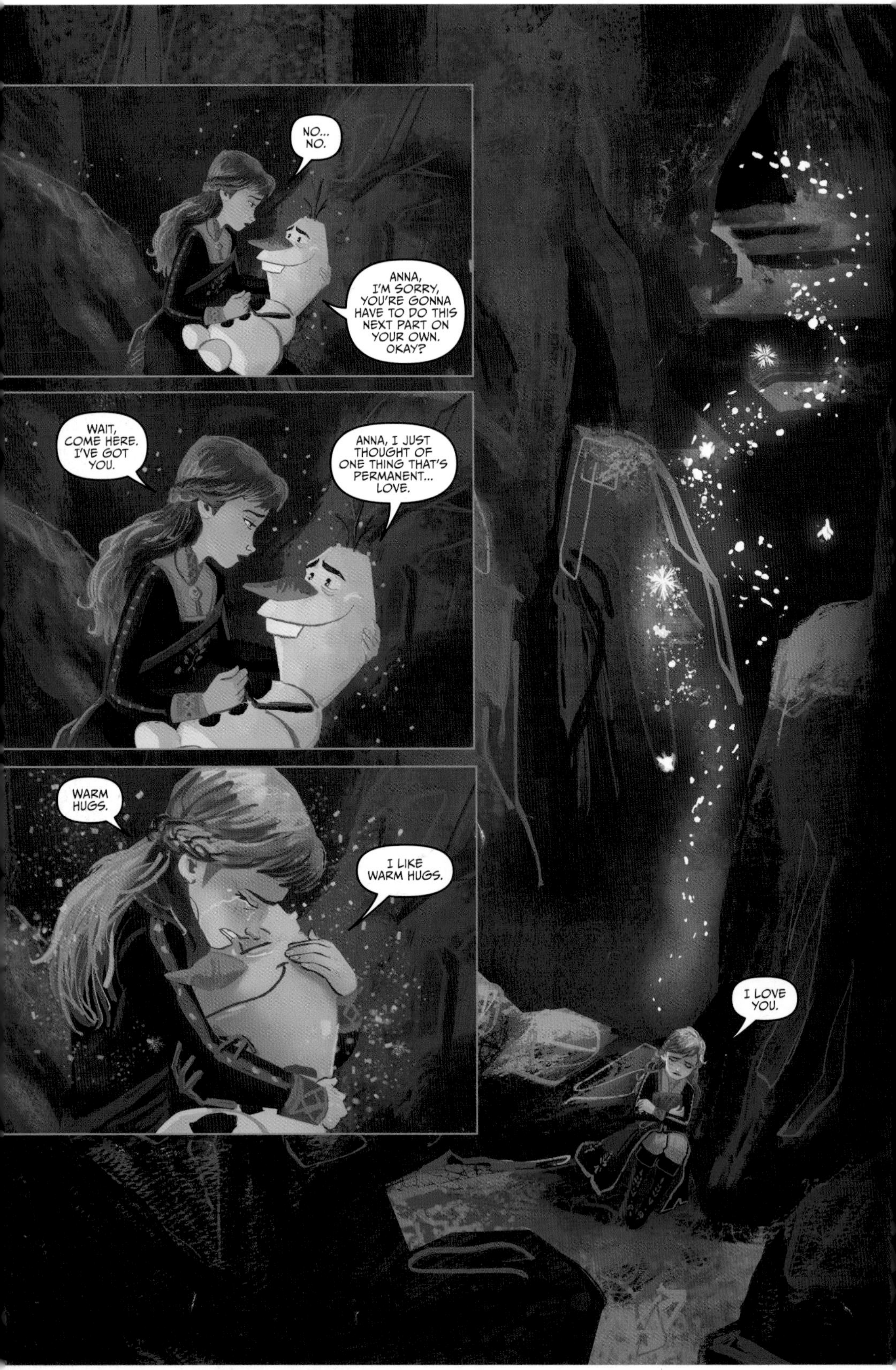
NO... NO.
ANNA, I'M SORRY, YOU'RE GONNA HAVE TO DO THIS NEXT PART ON YOUR OWN. OKAY?
WAIT, COME HERE. I'VE GOT YOU.
ANNA, I JUST THOUGHT OF ONE THING THAT'S PERMANENT... LOVE.
WARM HUGS.
I LIKE WARM HUGS.
I LOVE YOU.

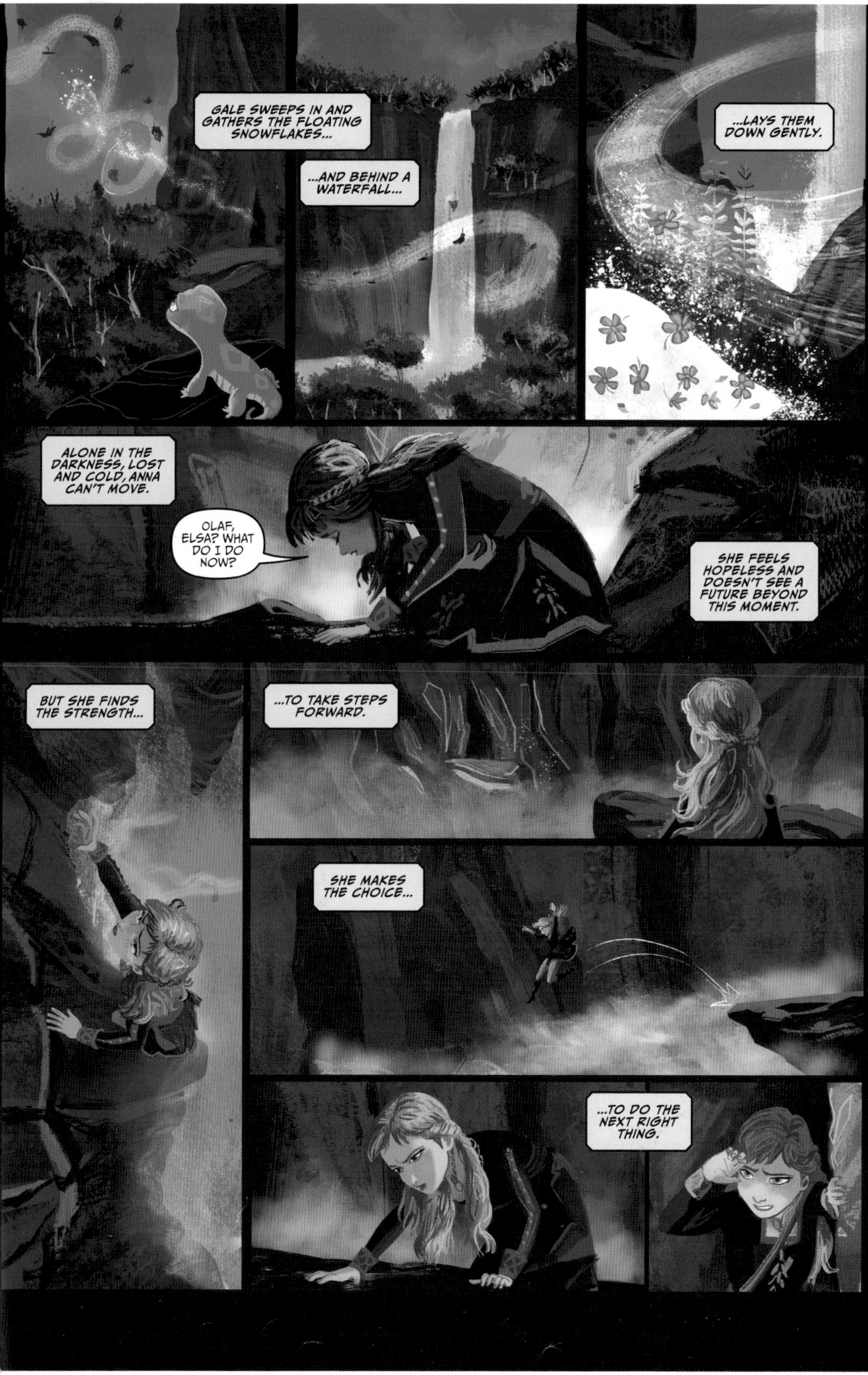
GALE SWEEPS IN AND GATHERS THE FLOATING SNOWFLAKES...
...AND BEHIND A WATERFALL...
...LAYS THEM DOWN GENTLY.
ALONE IN THE DARKNESS, LOST AND COLD, ANNA CAN'T MOVE.
OLAF, ELSA? WHAT DO I DO NOW?
SHE FEELS HOPELESS AND DOESN'T SEE A FUTURE BEYOND THIS MOMENT.
BUT SHE FINDS THE STRENGTH...
...TO TAKE STEPS FORWARD.
SHE MAKES THE CHOICE...
...TO DO THE NEXT RIGHT THING.

AFTER EMERGING FROM THE PIT, ANNA KNOWS WHAT SHE MUST DO TO MAKE THINGS RIGHT.

SHE RUNS TO THE RIVER WHERE THE EARTH GIANTS ARE ASLEEP ON THE SHORE.

WAKE UP!

WAKE UP!

OVER HERE! COME AND GET ME. COME ON!

BOOM BOOM

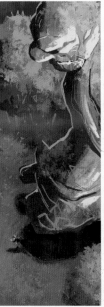

KRISTOFF!

I'M HERE... WHAT DO YOU NEED?

TO GET TO THE DAM!

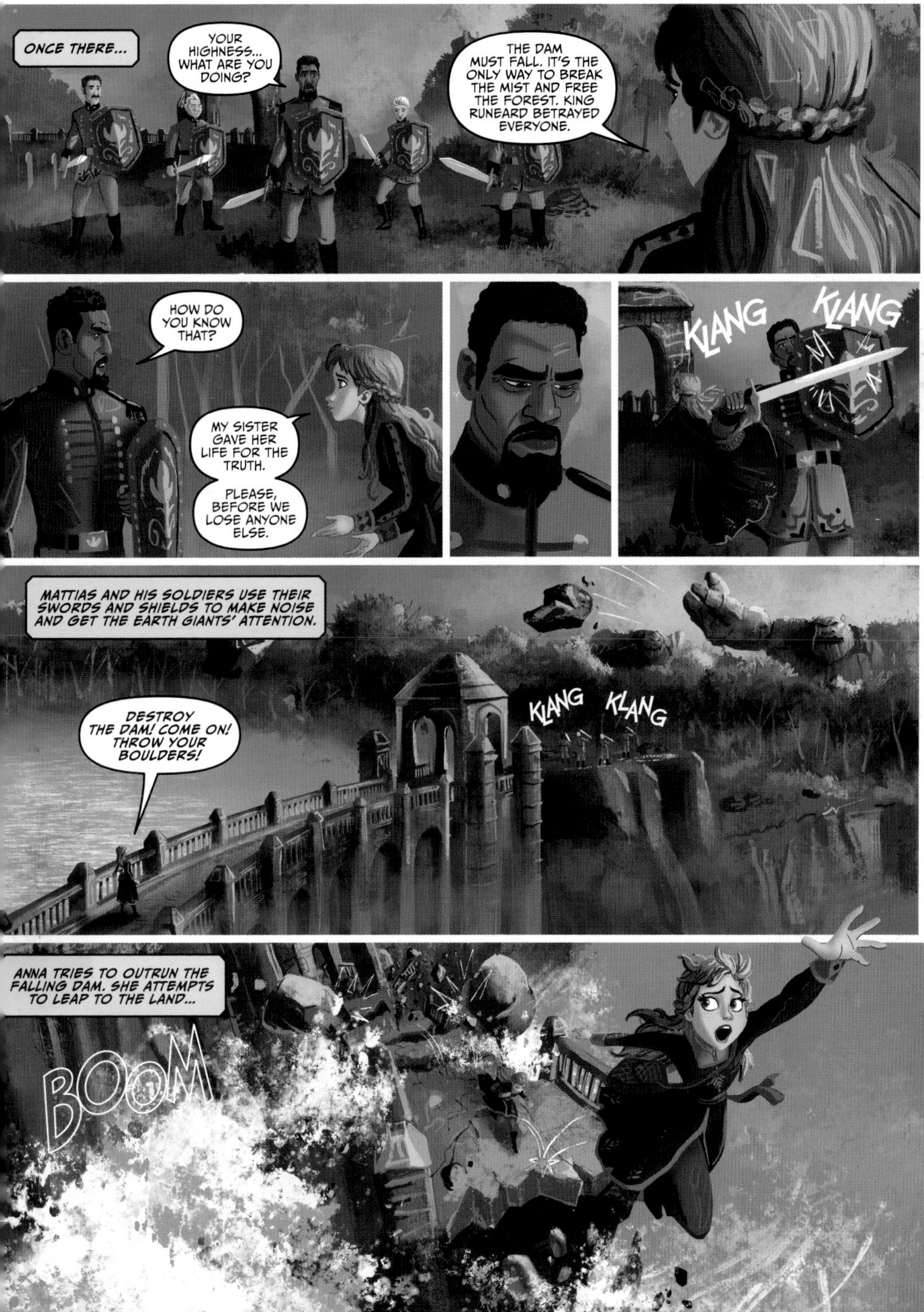
ONCE THERE...
YOUR HIGHNESS... WHAT ARE YOU DOING?
THE DAM MUST FALL. IT'S THE ONLY WAY TO BREAK THE MIST AND FREE THE FOREST. KING RUNEARD BETRAYED EVERYONE.
HOW DO YOU KNOW THAT?
MY SISTER GAVE HER LIFE FOR THE TRUTH.
PLEASE, BEFORE WE LOSE ANYONE ELSE.
KLANG
KLANG
MATTIAS AND HIS SOLDIERS USE THEIR SWORDS AND SHIELDS TO MAKE NOISE AND GET THE EARTH GIANTS' ATTENTION.
DESTROY THE DAM! COME ON! THROW YOUR BOULDERS!
KLANG
KLANG
ANNA TRIES TO OUTRUN THE FALLING DAM. SHE ATTEMPTS TO LEAP TO THE LAND...
BOOM

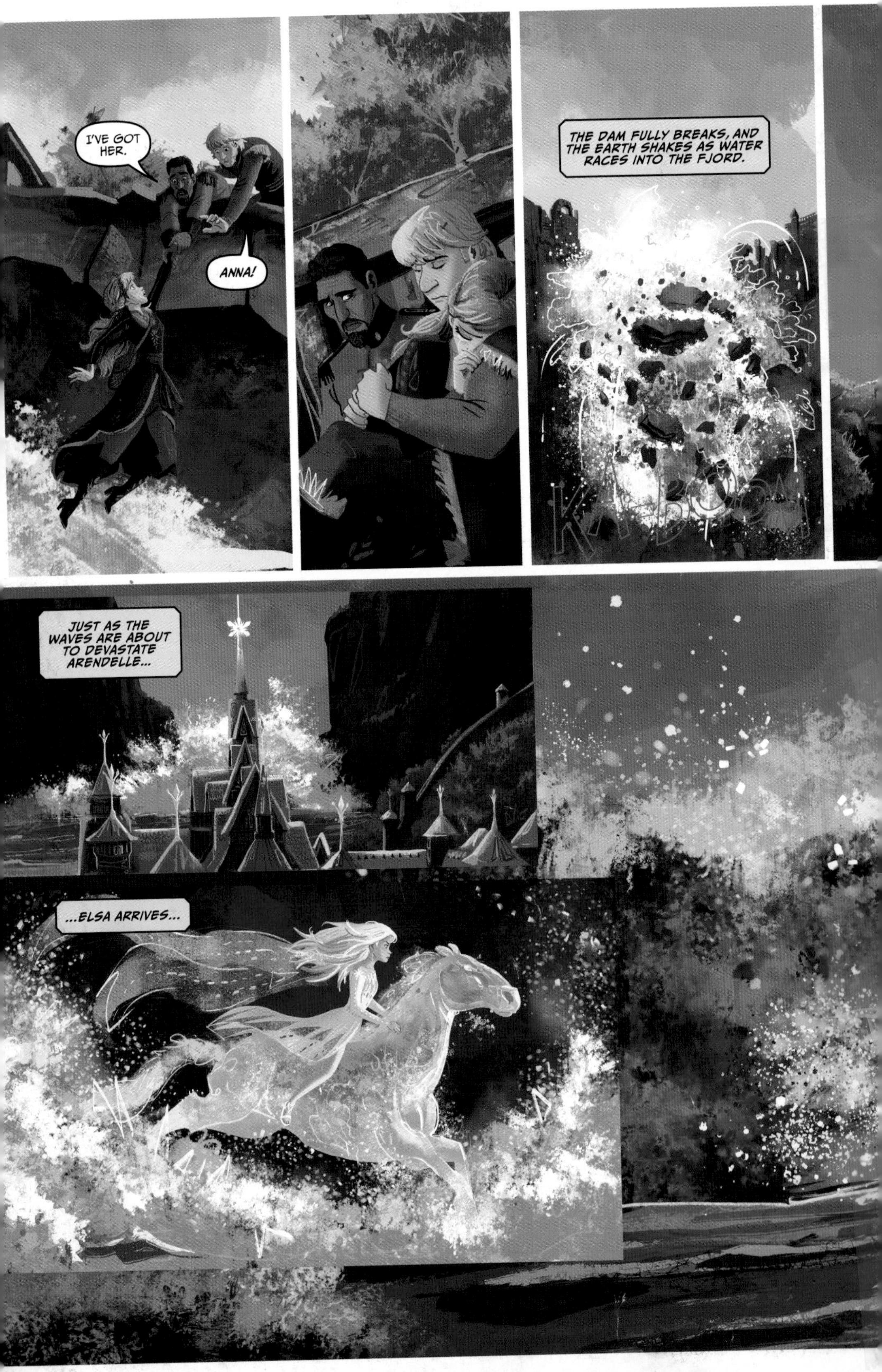
I'VE GOT HER.
ANNA!
THE DAM FULLY BREAKS, AND THE EARTH SHAKES AS WATER RACES INTO THE FJORD.
KA-BOOM!
JUST AS THE WAVES ARE ABOUT TO DEVASTATE ARENDELLE...
...ELSA ARRIVES...

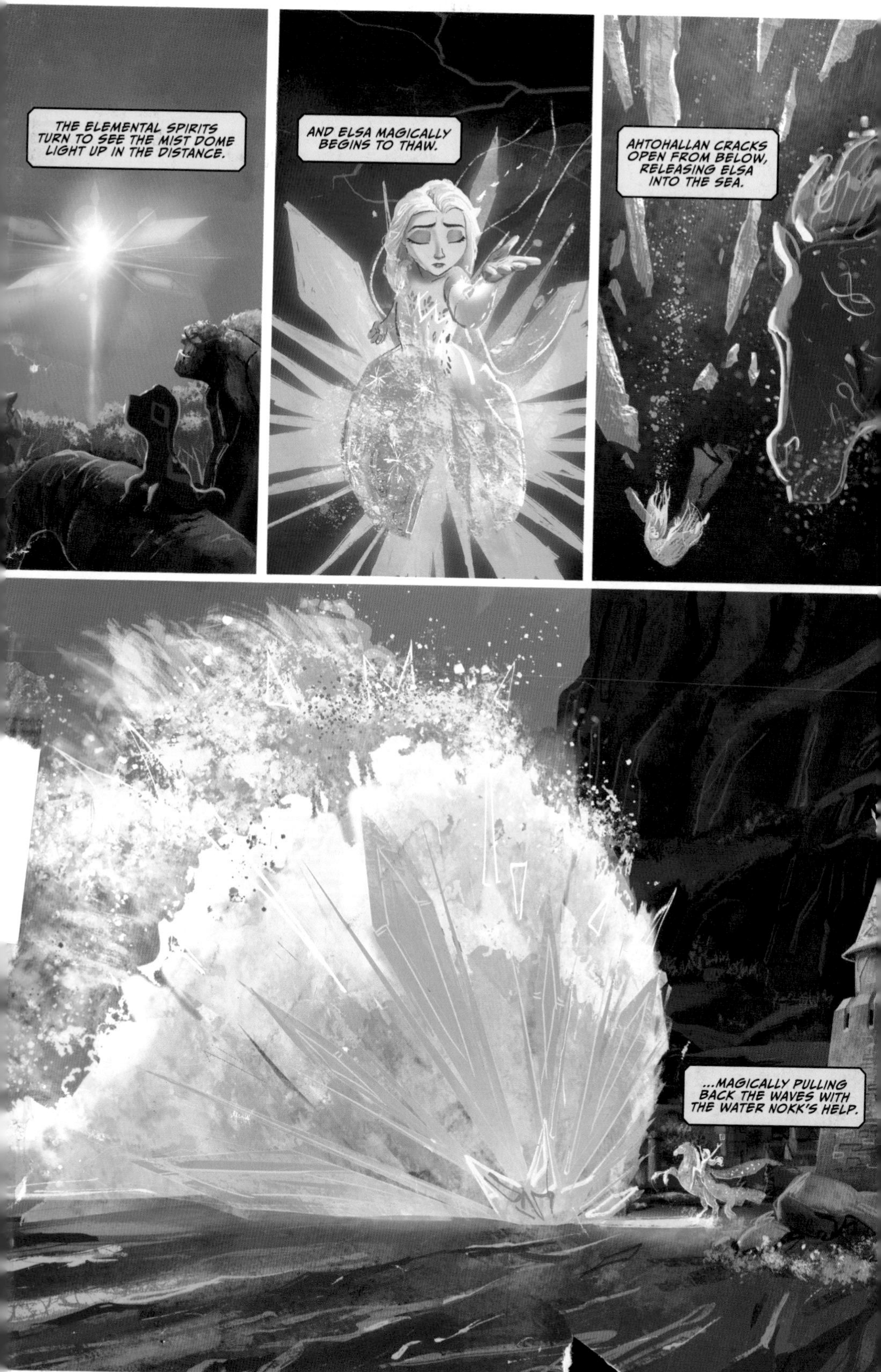
THE ELEMENTAL SPIRITS TURN TO SEE THE MIST DOME LIGHT UP IN THE DISTANCE.
AND ELSA MAGICALLY BEGINS TO THAW.
AHTOHALLAN CRACKS OPEN FROM BELOW, RELEASING ELSA INTO THE SEA.
...MAGICALLY PULLING BACK THE WAVES WITH THE WATER NOKK'S HELP.

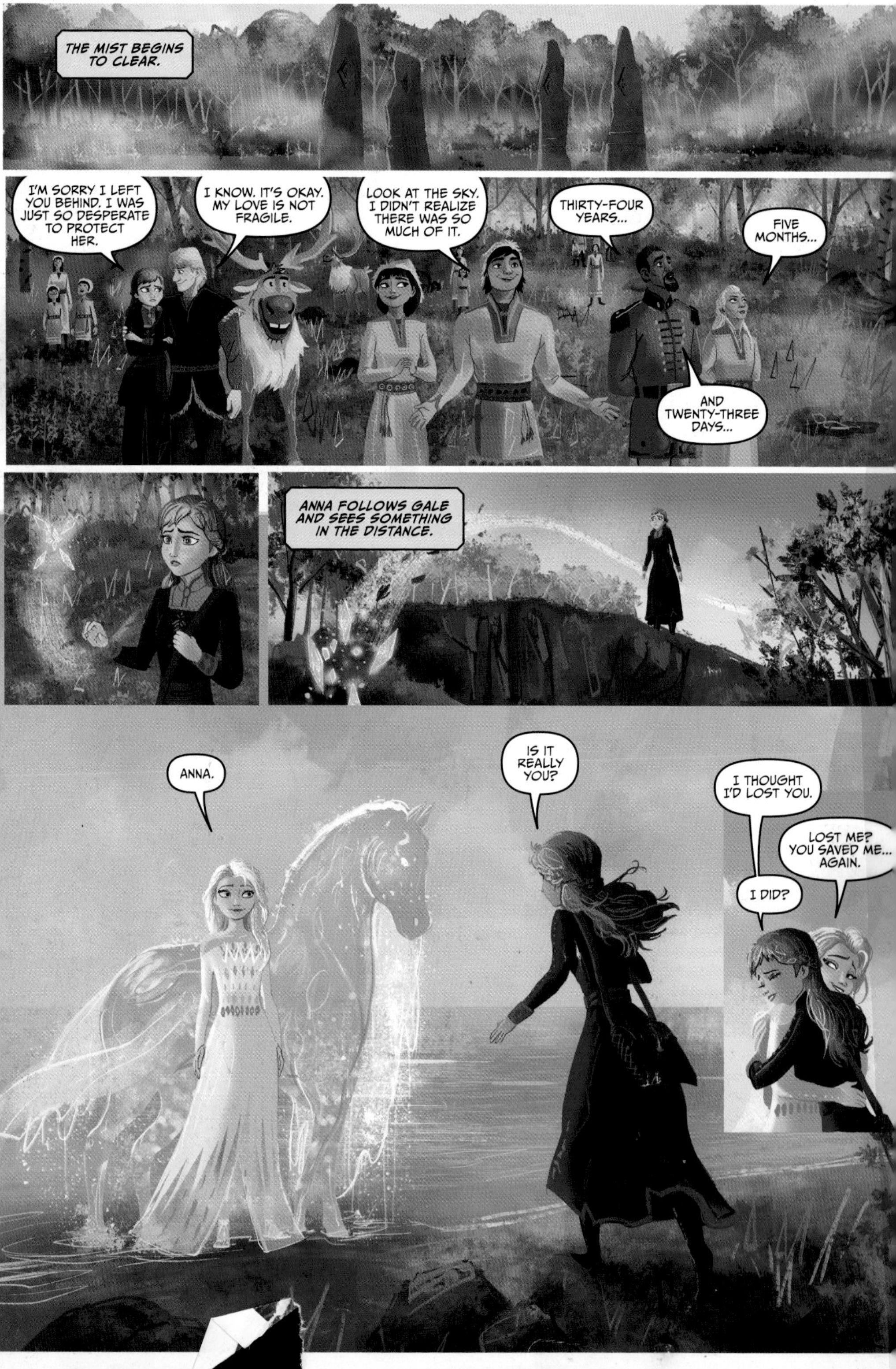
THE MIST BEGINS TO CLEAR.
I'M SORRY I LEFT YOU BEHIND. I WAS JUST SO DESPERATE TO PROTECT HER.
I KNOW. IT'S OKAY. MY LOVE IS NOT FRAGILE.
LOOK AT THE SKY. I DIDN'T REALIZE THERE WAS SO MUCH OF IT.
THIRTY-FOUR YEARS...
FIVE MONTHS...
AND TWENTY-THREE DAYS...
ANNA FOLLOWS GALE AND SEES SOMETHING IN THE DISTANCE.
ANNA.
IS IT REALLY YOU?
I THOUGHT I'D LOST YOU.
LOST ME? YOU SAVED ME... AGAIN.
I DID?

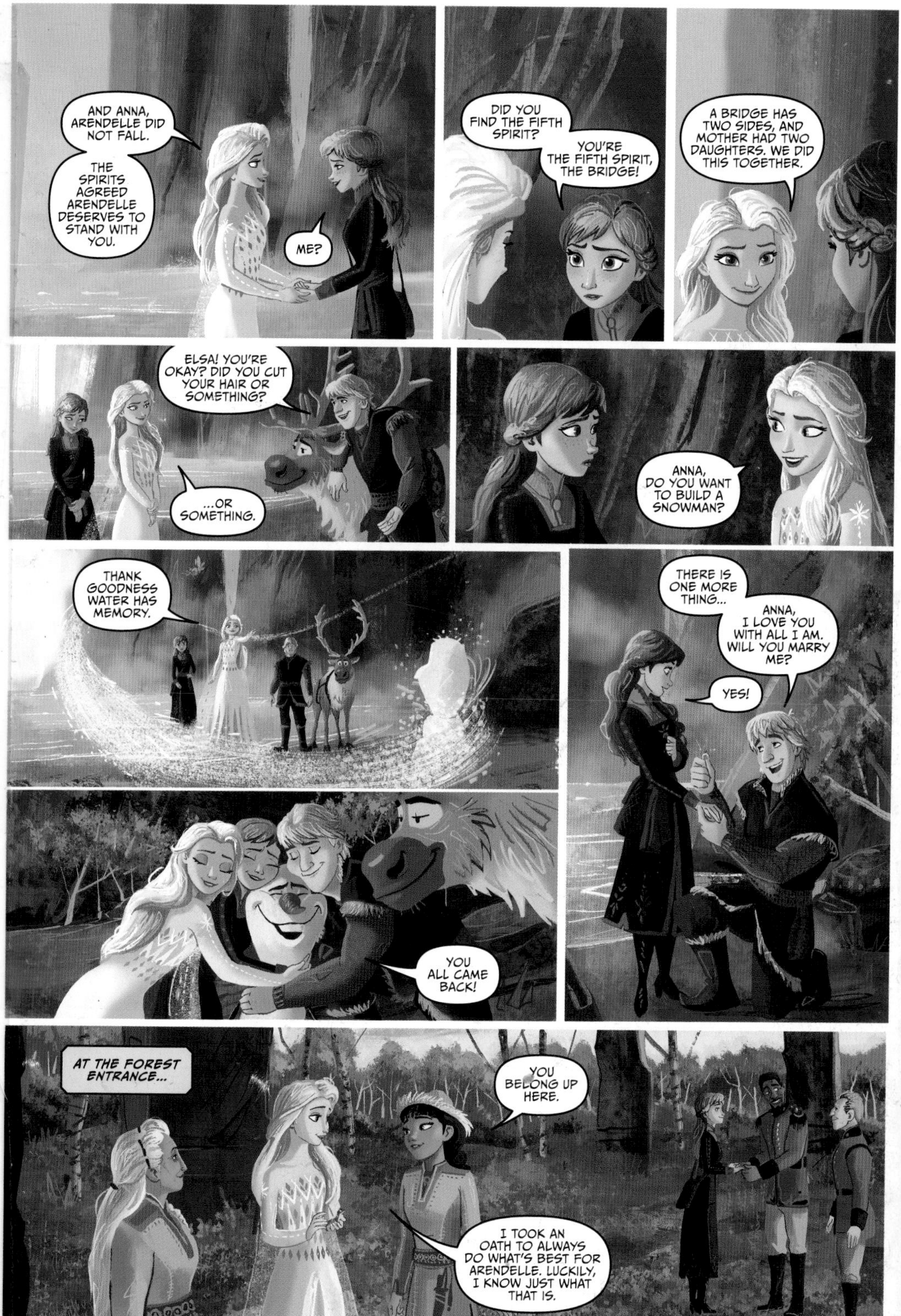
AND ANNA, ARENDELLE DID NOT FALL.
THE SPIRITS AGREED ARENDELLE DESERVES TO STAND WITH YOU.
ME?
DID YOU FIND THE FIFTH SPIRIT?
YOU'RE THE FIFTH SPIRIT, THE BRIDGE!
A BRIDGE HAS TWO SIDES, AND MOTHER HAD TWO DAUGHTERS. WE DID THIS TOGETHER.
ELSA! YOU'RE OKAY? DID YOU CUT YOUR HAIR OR SOMETHING?
...OR SOMETHING.
ANNA, DO YOU WANT TO BUILD A SNOWMAN?
THANK GOODNESS WATER HAS MEMORY.
YOU ALL CAME BACK!
THERE IS ONE MORE THING...
ANNA, I LOVE YOU WITH ALL I AM. WILL YOU MARRY ME?
YES!
AT THE FOREST ENTRANCE...
YOU BELONG UP HERE.
I TOOK AN OATH TO ALWAYS DO WHAT'S BEST FOR ARENDELLE. LUCKILY, I KNOW JUST WHAT THAT IS.

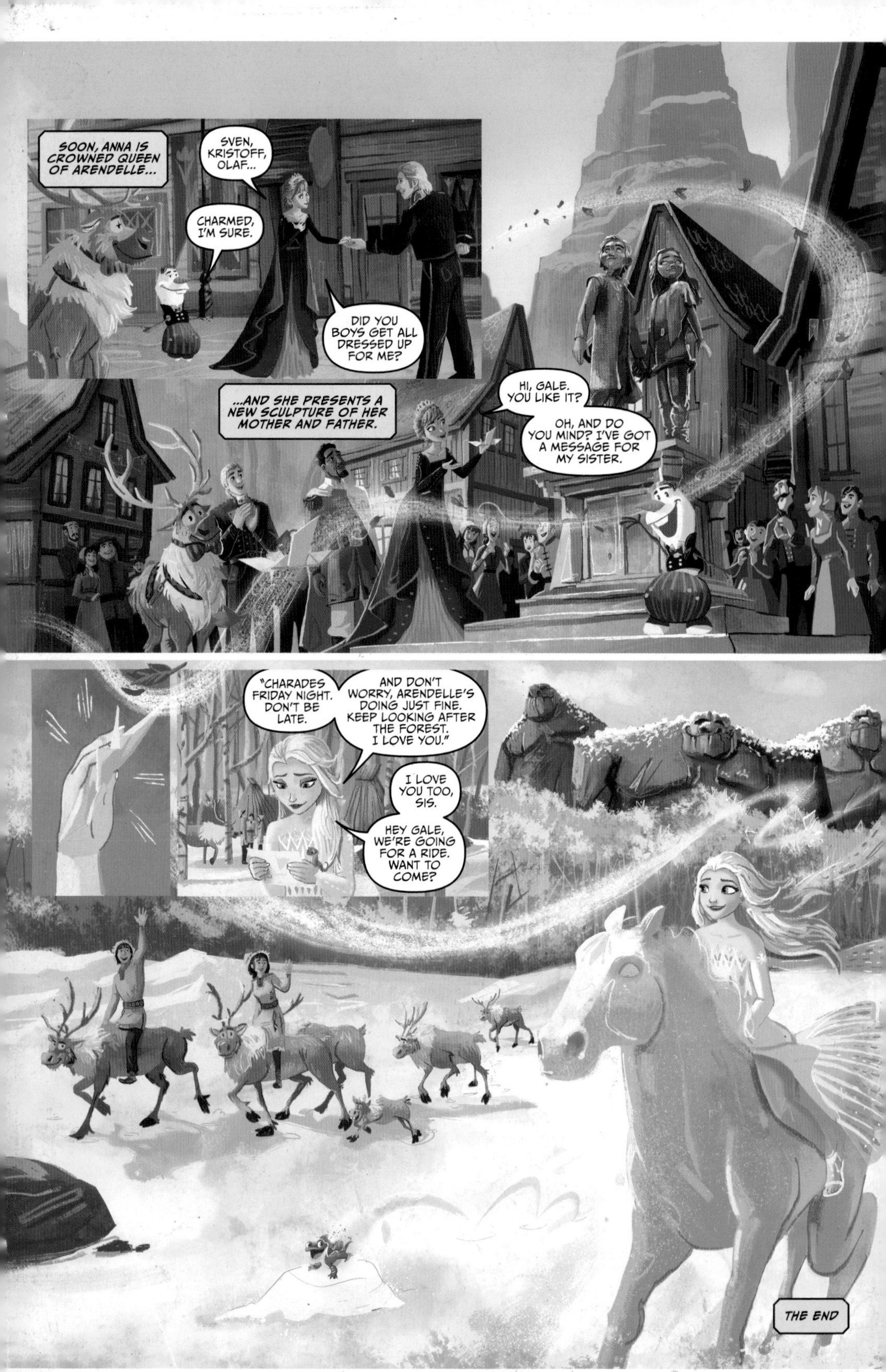
SOON, ANNA IS CROWNED QUEEN OF ARENDELLE...
SVEN, KRISTOFF, OLAF...
CHARMED, I'M SURE.
DID YOU BOYS GET ALL DRESSED UP FOR ME?
...AND SHE PRESENTS A NEW SCULPTURE OF HER MOTHER AND FATHER.
HI, GALE. YOU LIKE IT?
OH, AND DO YOU MIND? I'VE GOT A MESSAGE FOR MY SISTER.
"CHARADES FRIDAY NIGHT. DON'T BE LATE.
AND DON'T WORRY, ARENDELLE'S DOING JUST FINE. KEEP LOOKING AFTER THE FOREST. I LOVE YOU."
I LOVE YOU TOO, SIS.
HEY GALE, WE'RE GOING FOR A RIDE. WANT TO COME?
THE END

Looking for Disney *Frozen*?

$10.99 each!

Disney
FROZEN
BREAKING BOUNDARIES

Disney Frozen: Breaking Boundaries
978-1-50671-051-8

Anna, Elsa, and friends have a quest to fulfill, mysteries to solve, and peace to restore!

Disney
FROZEN
REUNION ROAD

Disney Frozen: Reunion Road
978-1-50671-270-3

Elsa and Anna gather friends and family for an unforgettable trip to a harvest festival in the neighboring kingdom of Snoob!

Disney
FROZEN
THE HERO WITHIN

Disney Frozen: The Hero Within
978-1-50671-269-7

Anna, Elsa, Kristoff, Sven, Olaf, and new friend Hedda, deal with bullies and the harsh environment of the Forbidden Land!

Disney
FROZEN
TRUE TREASURE

Disney Frozen: True Treasure
978-1-50671-705-0

A lead-in story to Disney *Frozen 2*. Elsa and Anna embark on an adventure searching for clues to uncover a lost message from their mother.

Disney
FROZEN
ADVENTURES
FLURRIES OF FUN

Disney Frozen Adventures: Flurries of Fun
978-1-50671-470-7

Disney
FROZEN
ADVENTURES
SNOWY STORIES

Disney Frozen Adventures: Snowy Stories
978-1-50671-471-4

Disney
FROZEN
ADVENTURES
ICE AND MAGIC

Disney Frozen Adventures: Ice and Magic
978-1-50671-472-1

Collections of short comics stories expanding on the world of Disney *Frozen*!

AVAILABLE AT YOUR LOCAL COMICS SHOP OR BOOKSTORE!
TO FIND A COMICS SHOP IN YOUR AREA, VISIT COMICSHOPLOCATOR.COM

For more information or to order direct, visit DarkHorse.com

The **u**nforgettable tale of *Disney The Little Mermaid*,
told through the perspective of Ariel herself!

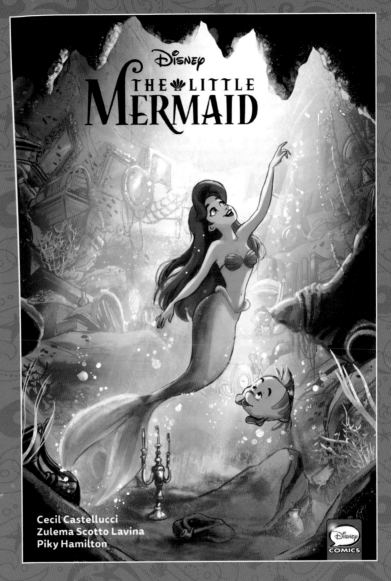

Dive into the heart and mind of Ariel as her
world changes before her eyes—her life, and life
under the sea, will never be the same.

978-1-50671-572-8 | $12.99

DISNEY•PIXAR'S INCREDIBLES 2!

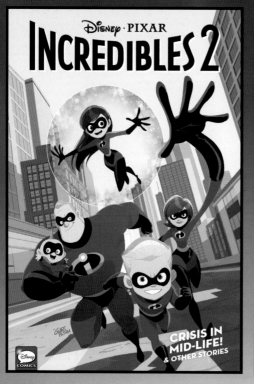

Disney · PIXAR
INCREDIBLES 2
CRISIS IN MID-LIFE!
& OTHER STORIES
DISNEY COMICS

Disney · PIXAR
INCREDIBLES 2
SECRET IDENTITIES
DISNEY COMICS

Disney · PIXAR

INCREDIBLES 2

CRISIS IN MID-LIFE! & OTHER STORIES

An encounter with villain Bomb Voyage inspires Bob to begin training the next generation of Supers, Dash and Violet. Mr. Incredible will find himself needing to pull his family back together . . . because Bomb Voyage is still at large! In another story, Bob tells the kids about a battle from his glory days that seems too amazing to be true—but they never imagined the details would include their mom and dad's super secret first date . . . Finally, in two adventures all his own, baby Jack-Jack and his powers are set to save the day.

978-1-50671-019-8 • $10.99

Disney · PIXAR

INCREDIBLES 2

SECRET IDENTITIES

It's tough being a teenager, and on top of that, a teenager with powers! Violet feels out of place at school and doesn't fit in with the kids around her . . . until she meets another girl at school—an outsider with powers, just like her! But when her new friend asks her to keep a secret, Violet is torn between keeping her word and doing what's right.

978-1-50671-392-2 • $10.99

DARK HORSE BOOKS

AVAILABLE AT YOUR LOCAL COMICS SHOP OR BOOKSTORE! TO FIND A COMICS SHOP IN YOUR AREA, VISIT COMICSHOPLOCATOR.COM

FOR MORE INFORMATION OR TO ORDER DIRECT, VISIT DARKHORSE.COM

DISNEY COMICS

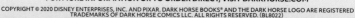